ALSO BY JEREMY ROBIN

The Jack Sigler Novels
Prime
Pulse
Instinct
Threshold
Ragnarok
Omega
Savage
Cannibal
Empire (2016)

Cerberus Group Novels
Herculean

Chess Team Guidebook
Endgame

The Chesspocalypse Novellas
Callsign: King
Callsign: Queen
Callsign: Rook
Callsign: King – Underworld
Callsign: Bishop
Callsign: Knight
Callsign: Deep Blue
Callsign: King – Blackout

The Jack Sigler Continuum
Guardian
Patriot (2015)

Secondworld Novels
SecondWorld
Nazi Hunter: Atlantis

Sta
The Didy.
Raising The Past
Beneath
Antarktos Rising
Kronos
Xom-B
Flood Rising
MirrorWorld

The Antarktos Saga
The Last Hunter – Descent
The Last Hunter – Pursuit
The Last Hunter – Ascent
The Last Hunter – Lament
The Last Hunter – Onslaught
The Last Hunter – Collected Edition

Nemesis Saga Novels
Island 731
Project Nemesis
Project Maigo
Project 731
Project Hyperion

Horror
(Writing as Jeremy Bishop)
Torment
The Sentinel
The Raven
Refuge

Post-Apocalyptic
(Writing as Jeremiah Knight)
Hunger
Viking Tomorrow (2015)

PROJECT HYPERION

A Nemesis Saga Novel

JEREMY ROBINSON

Breakneck Media

This is a work of fiction. Names, characters, places, and incidents either are the product of the author's imagination or are used fictitiously. Any resemblance to actual events or locales or persons, living or dead, is entirely coincidental.

ISBN: 978-1-941539-11-8

Printed in the United States of America.

Visit Jeremy Robinson on the World Wide Web at:
www.bewareofmonsters.com

To the fine people at Famous Monsters of Filmland
and American Gothic Press, *for taking Nemesis to new heights.*

PROJECT HYPERION

PROLOGUE I

Ancient History

Hopeless, they ran. Each had been a brave man once. Fearless and savage. Willing and capable of great feats or stunning violence. The latter paid better. Their path had been laid with glittering red—precious rubies, and blood. Drink flowed. Women were bought and sold. Children, too. They had started out stalwart, young and hopeful. Now, as they clawed up the pebble-crusted hillside, each saw inside themselves the men they had become.

And they wept.

Their voices filled the air like a pitiful crescendo, drowned out by the occasional quake, rattling the hillside. Rocks shook free and tumbled downward, not concerned with the judgment that pursued them.

"Forgive me!" Akakios screamed. He raised his hands to the heavens, beseeching the gods. "Delay your judgment!"

But Akakios's voice could not be heard, by the gods or by the four men alongside him. The only god—a *goddess* if the stories were true—paying them any heed, was the one closing in behind them.

The great Nemesis. Winged tilter of scales and lives. The immortal judge. Vengeful righter of wrongs. She was upon them.

As soon as she had risen from the ocean, just minutes ago, he knew why she was there. His life had soured. He'd reveled in debauchery. Nemesis came for the worst of men, exposing their true nature, and then destroying them—and anything in her way. She had stepped on the beachside camp where chained slaves had cheered, and then had screamed, briefly.

Akakios grasped at the hillside, looking for hand holds, but the loose and shaking rocks lifted away. So he pushed with his legs, each step sliding down almost as much as propelling him upward.

He glanced back.

And screamed.

His judge's head was above him now, ocean water still draining from the crags between her massive armor plates. Tattered, red sails bearing a symbol he didn't recognize, hung impaled on the towering spikes rising from the creature's hunched back. He stood at chest level with the behemoth, awash in the fiery glow of its glistening pectorals.

His fellow slave traders scurried past, not one of them asking why he had stopped. Not one of them called for him to carry on. They were all going to die. Each of them knew it. All they could do was live a few moments longer, perhaps long enough to receive grace. Not from Nemesis, but from those who would greet them in the next life.

Swirling orange liquid, like luminous oil inside an array of clear-skinned chambers running up the beast's torso, held him transfixed for a moment. From a distance, this creature instilled men with untold horror. She exposed them for who they were and then took their lives. But up close, it was strangely beautiful.

The creature took a step, the single movement lifting its body half way up the rise. Another step and it would be upon them.

Freed from his panic for that brief instant, Akakios saw that the goddess's course was set. Running directly away was no use. But to the side...

His legs shook as he struck out again, moving out of the creature's path. The rough surface of the hill slipped and shook, but his speed doubled.

Long, thick claws swept past overhead as the creature's arm swung forward. Its many fingers were tipped with claws the size of large ships. The swinging limb slapped a breeze against his back, shoving him down. His legs drove into the loose rocks. He felt his kneecap shift. A scream rose, but he squelched it. Nemesis's massive head, framed by glowing orange ovals, had yet to turn its gaze in his direction. He didn't want to give it a reason to.

He saw the leg rising beside him, the sun framing the armored limb in shadow. He wouldn't be out of its path in time. His death was imminent. Exhausted and defeated, Akakios fell to his knees, wheezing and coughing out prayers to any god that might look upon him with favor.

The air around him shifted, compressing him. His ears ached. He couldn't hear himself screaming, but he could feel his voice, tearing the flesh of his throat. Would he feel it? Would he experience the rupturing of his body? His insides smeared beneath the mighty foot, like an insect? Or would it pass quickly? Would it...

Akakios opened his eyes, staring down at loose stones, lit by the sun. The pressure lifted away. And then the hill shook from an impact. He turned his head up and saw the colossal foot pound into the slope, compressing it and his former compatriots, and then gripping with its massive claws as it rose higher still, to the crest.

Three appendages, whipping like cats' tails, trailed the monster, each one layered in armor. Akakios flattened himself down as the last of them passed by and slammed into the earth, carving a gully.

And then it was beyond him.

He had been spared!

By Nemesis...

The goddess did not spare anyone. He knew this as surely as he did his own guilt.

Run, he thought, but he remained still.

Nemesis crested the hill, spread her spike laden arms and bellowed. With his hands over his ears and his eyes clenched shut, Akakios could still hear the emotion in that wail. Nemesis was angry. Spiteful. Enraged.

"My god," he said, standing up on shaky legs. "She was never here for us."

He and his friends, like their campsite full of slaves, had simply been in her way.

As the monster descended the far side of the hill, moving faster now, Akakios scurried toward the top. He paused once, when his hand slipped on something wet, but he hurried past when he realized the viscous stain had been one of his friends.

He reached the top, breathing heavily, but feeling energized at being alive, and at the prospect of bearing witness to Nemesis's judgment of others.

The monster careened down the far side of the hill, which dropped into a seaside valley.

An empty valley.

What is she after? Could she really be here for one person, hiding in the valley? Someone worse than me? He realized that when her true target was dead, she might very well turn her vengeful eyes back toward him, but he stayed rooted. Fleeing would do him no good. The monster could not be outrun.

And then, Nemesis was gone. The monster slipped from view like someone stepping into a waterfall, enveloped by the air itself.

Had he hallucinated it?

Akakios spun around. The hillside behind him was decimated, the path of destruction leading back toward the ocean.

A roar turned him back toward the valley. Nemesis was still present...but unseen! A rumble rolled up the valley, the force of it striking Akakios hard, knocking the air from his lungs. But then, he could see again. An invisible veil lifted, revealing Nemesis once more, a billowing flame rising up around her.

And ahead of her...a city of ringed walls, expanding out into the ocean.

A city that hadn't been there just moments ago.

A city he had never seen, but had heard stories about. Stories he had never believed in, like Nemesis herself.

Atlantis.

PROLOGUE II

Now

The vast distance of space can be conquered, as can every small speck floating in its emptiness. The Aeros hadn't always known this. Their evolution into conquerors had taken millions of years. Hundreds of millions. And as they spread and evolved, their species branched.

Sometimes the genetic change was subtle: an adaptation to local conditions on a colony, planet or vessel. These changes led to a vast array of specializations, but always leaving the species identifiable as Aeros.

But once, just once, the genetic fracture was drastic, and the divide between species grew wider over the eons. One race—pure Aeros—became masters. The smaller, but craftier race—the Ferox—became slaves until the great rebellion set them free. The Ferox were scattered across the cosmos, pursued by their former masters, and in search of fellow lesser species they could mold and, eventually, recruit.

Across the universe, in multiple dimensions of reality, both conquered and free, the war between Aeros and Ferox continued, spanning untold years and crossing unimaginable distances. Ceaseless strategic maneuvering on both sides used species, planets and solar systems like pawns. But at the crux of the Ferox guerrilla campaign, were planets like the one most recently flagged.

Earth.

The native species was small and fragile, but they had flexible, adaptive minds. They could comprehend and adopt new technologies at a rate rivaling the Aeros themselves. But what made them dangerous was that they were a warring species with a penchant for rebellion. After being under the Ferox influence for thousands of years, humanity was primed to sympathize with the former slaves.

This could not be allowed to happen. Roughly four billion of them could fight, and scans showed that their bloodline had been fortified with Atlantide genetics. This planet and its fragile inhabitants had been discovered long ago. The small blue sphere at the fringe of a galaxy had been added to a long list of worlds to plunder. But sensors left behind remained silent for thousands of years, until the arrival of the Atlantide. The brutish race, allied with the Ferox and similar to humanity in many ways, had established colonies on hundreds of worlds throughout the unconquered universe. And each colony had been dealt with in a similar fashion: Gestorumque. The creatures, massive even by Aeros scale, cleansed the Atlantide wherever they were detected.

But on Earth, the species managed to escape eradication, despite the continued existence of the Gerstorumque they had deemed 'Nemesis.' The monster could sense Atlantide DNA, including the trace amount present in the human race, tracking down those with the highest levels of genetic similarity, which presented as a proclivity for violence, crime and foulness. These traits were desirable to the Ferox—what the humans called 'evil.' It was an interesting concept, propagated by the Ferox, but one by which the Aeros did not abide. Lesser species could not pass judgment, nor discern morality. How could a people with a perspective relative to an insect colony understand the complexities of infinite space?

They could not.

Nor could they be allowed the chance to try.

After the disappearance of the Gerstorumque, and the apparent vanquishing of the Atlantide, the squabbled-over planet received a guardian: Artuke, son of the high council. Details of his emergence and...demise... were vague at best, but he had sent a signal.

Earth belonged to the Ferox, but had not yet been assimilated into the fleet.

There was still time to reach the planet first, and eradicate its population, in all dimensions, ensuring that the species would never be a threat. And if the citadel defended by Artuke still stood, it would finally be populated. The Aeros would colonize Earth, and the arena would see the world's few surviving inhabitants battling a variety of species from around the cosmos. Earth would become another one of millions of planets used for its resources and later discarded.

But if the Ferox arrived first, supplying humanity with advanced weapons, technology and the knowledge to use them against the Aeros, it could shift the course of this unceasing war.

The recent destruction of an advance probe did not bode well, but action would come swiftly enough. As the fleet gathered, a weapon was being sent in advance. Two of them, actually. Both Gerstorumque. Both instilled with a righteous hatred for not just the Ferox and the Atlantide, but also for humanity.

The great purge would begin before the Aeros arrived, and it would not end until every human being was dead or enslaved.

Pentuke, father of Artuke and head of the war council, watched as the chrysalises containing the Gerstorumque slipped through the fabric of reality, destination: Earth, dimension 204,091.0008932. That specific plane of existence would be the first to meet the Gerstorumque, who would redirect their sister's course. That plane would also be the first to be conquered.

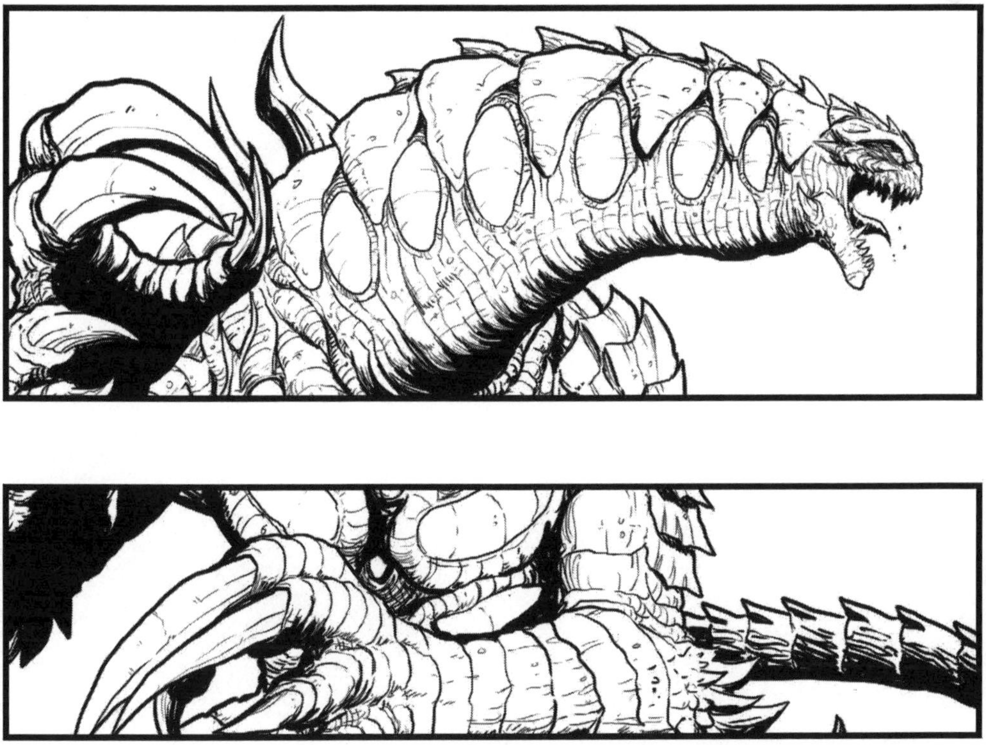

NEMESIS

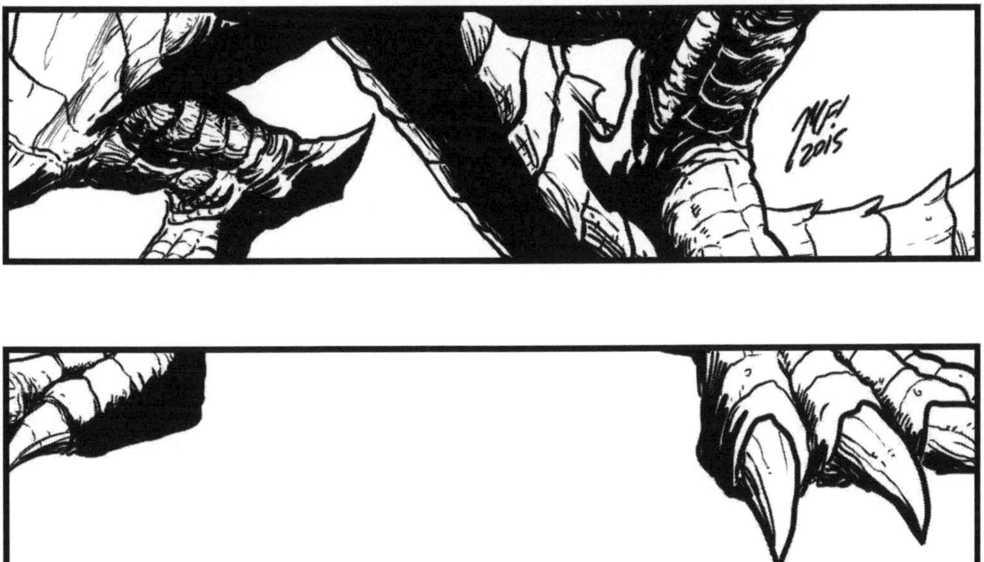

1

"I'm telling you, boss, ain't nothing out here but water and what looks like a spill of waterlogged tampons."

I laugh and sit up, the bands of my lounge chair bending beneath my shifting weight. "Woodstock, you realize this is not a phone call, right? Collins can hear you." While we're lounging about, we're all wearing comms, if only to maintain Woodstock's belief that we're hard at work while he flies about.

"So can I," Maigo says.

"Well..." Woodstock says. I smile at the approaching punch line, fueled by his insensitivity to women's issues. "Are they *your* tampons?"

There's a click, and I know that Maigo, now a full-fledged young woman embarrassed at even the very hint of such things, even with me, is likely beaming red. When it comes to ovaries and all the things that come with them, only Collins has her ear. Not Joliet. Not Lilly, who has her own set of unique issues, thanks to being a hybrid of human, panther and who knows what else—her webbed feet and gills suggest a little amphibian and fish are in the mix. She laid eggs after all, from which hatched 'the girls,' three big, black cats that now guard the FC-P's Maine property. In comparison to Lilly, Maigo has it easy. Even though her strength, her speed and her ability to feel my emotions and sometimes thoughts all make her equally unique, she's just more human than Lilly...on the outside. On the inside? Who knows. And who cares. I only think of her as my daughter now.

I have a daughter and a wife...

It was just a few years ago that I was a slacker agent at the ass end of the Department of Homeland Security: Jon Hudson, director of Jack and Shit, otherwise known as Fusion Center–Paranormal. FC-P for short. Lead investigator into the 'threats' against the United States that included everything from Sasquatch to Chupacabra.

Now, in the wake of multiple Kaiju events resulting in the destruction of several major cities inside and outside the U.S., I'm the director of the world's most cosplayed agency. I'm also filthy rich and the owner of Zoomb, Google's only real competitor in the search engine and future tech industry, thanks to the surprising generosity of my frienemy, Katsu Endo, who may or may not be alive inside the Kaiju known as Nemesis. And she hasn't been seen since returning to the Pacific Ocean.

I'm also married to Ashley Collins, the tougher-than-me ex-sheriff who kept her maiden name...which I'm *totally* okay about...not insecure *at all*... Ahem. I have an adopted kid, previously Maigo Tilley, now Maigo Hudson. She was murdered by her biological father and very dead, until her DNA was used to spawn an ancient goddess of vengeance, Nemesis, who gave 'birth' to Maigo after saving Washington, D.C. from a horde of her own genetic brethren. It's a mouthful, but that's the short version. The long version would take something like, what, three books?

That Maigo's current issues aren't much more severe than those of other teens is a relief. And says a lot about her character. So what if she's quiet most of the time? Who wouldn't be after being the conscience for a monster that destroyed cities and consumed thousands of people? She remembers every kill. What people *tasted* like. I'd get in line for a padded cell after that. She just wants to be treated like everyone else.

And no one excels at that better than Woodstock. The old pilot, grinning behind his bushy mustache, irks the girl something fierce. But while she storms away, groaning from whatever uncomfortable subject he's brought up, I always see a hint of a smile. So I don't chastise Woodstock for the tampon comment.

That's my wife's job.

"*Woodstock...*" she says, and that's all the threat that's needed.

"As long as I'm up here and you're way the hell down there..." Woodstock starts, his 'here' sounding like 'he-ah,' and his 'there' sounding like 'they-ah,' thanks to his thick Maine accent, but Collins cuts him short.

"I have a long memory," Collins says, "and I know how you old timers need your sleep."

Woodstock's only reply is indistinct grumbling.

"Finish your sweep and call it a day," I say. "Holler if you see something."

The 'something' this time around is the Great New England Sea Serpent. There are more than two hundred separate reported appearances of the creature, seen by more than two thousand people, since the first settlers arrived at the Gulf of Maine in the 1600s. On some occasions, hundreds of people lining the beach witnessed it swim past. In Gloucester, which is just North of the FC-P headquarters in Beverly, Massachusetts, two of the serpents hung out in the harbor for days on end.

While reports of strange creatures have skyrocketed in the past few years—there's even an entire DHS department tasked with weeding out illegitimate claims—creatures with mounds of historical evidence jump to the top of our growing list of cases. With two recent sightings of a sea serpent-like creature in the Gulf of Maine, we had to take a look. In part, because of the history, but also because Nemesis, and several other Kaiju, have all surfaced in this part of the world on multiple occasions.

But I'm also realistic about our odds. It's August. There are boats everywhere, buzzing, sailing and weighing anchor around the gulf while pods of whales swim all around. The odds of finding a sea serpent amidst all this activity—if it's even here—are slimmer than Mary Kate Olsen's waistline.

So I'm channeling my old self and taking a moment to bask in the sun, and in the good fortune that allowed this DHS director to buy his own yacht, *Penny*, named for my third grade sweetheart. Unlike Betty, whose name graced my old pick-up truck and now the FC-P's helicopter, not to mention our stolen future-tech X-35 aircraft, I have fond memories of Penny. She was funny. And chubby. Swam like a seal. A fitting name for a ship. I had wanted to use the name *EndoSucksBalls*, but Collins put the kibosh on that. And it's probably a good idea since if we see Nemesis again, his consciousness might be part of the mix. But how funny would that have been? I grin at the thought, imagining Endo's face as Nemesis leaned over to eat me and read the ship's name.

"What are you grinning about?" Collins asks, stepping out of the cabin. She's got that 'I'm a badass' wrinkle between her eyes, but I'm distracted by the flowing white skirt and bikini top. The smell of suntan lotion, salty sea air and the sight of Collins's red curls blowing in the wind make me forget that we're officially on the clock. "You know she hates...feminine topics."

I shrug. "Well, she's homeschooling, so someone has to tease her. Might as well be the guy closest to the grave already."

She sits down beside me and takes a deep breath. We've been so busy the last year that a day like today is a rarity. So what if it's a Monday? We worked all weekend. We work every weekend. Luckily, our team is our family and our HQ is our home, but that doesn't mean we can't get burned out.

"And besides," I say, "he thinks we're actually out here searching a grid, not working on our tans."

She opens the cooler, picks up a beer bottle and pops the cap... with her teeth. She spits the bent cap back in the cooler and takes a swig. "Your turn to drive, lazy bones." She leans back in the lounge chair and nudges me with her knee.

"Can't argue with a girl who has a jaw PSI like that. Geez."

"No. You cannot." She smiles. Fiendish. "No telling what might get bitten off."

I put my hand on her knee. "Maybe you can—"

A clearing throat snaps us out of our dirty flirtations.

I flinch and nearly fall out of the chair. "Oh, godamnit!"

Maigo stands just a few feet away, hands on her hips. She's dressed in red shorts and a black heavy metal t-shirt, her long, straight black hair tied back in a pony tail that reveals her normally hair-hidden face. She's half Caucasian, half Japanese, and one hundred percent trying not to bust out laughing.

"You and your silent ninja-like ways!" I shout, trying to mask my very own personal tampon moment. "I told you not to sneak up on me."

"I wasn't trying to," she says.

"Just...stomp your feet when you walk. But not too hard. Liable to put a hole in the deck. It's bad enough that you can get inside my head."

"Or you guys could just try to stop being pervs," she counters.

"You can take the perv out of the man, but not the man out of... Wait. You can take the man out of the... No. That doesn't work. But you get it."

"I'm not the only one who gets it," she says, snickering. "Right, mom?"

"Oh, snap," Collins says. She holds out her fist to Maigo, and the girl taps it with her own. They both raise their hands, wiggling them in the air.

"Oh, sweet baby Buddha. Did you two just blow up a fist bump?" I ask.

They're laughing now, enjoying my discomfort.

"You do realize the implications of your joke? Assuming the 'get it' about your mother relates to sexual intercourse?" And just like that, Jon Hudson turns the tables. I fist bump myself and make a 'kaboosh' sound effect. "Now who's uncomfortable?"

"I would just like to go on record," Woodstock's voice says in my earpiece, "and say two things. One, you all left your comms on. Two, you're all fuckin' bat-shit crazy."

We're all laughing now, but quickly stop when Woodstock's voice grows uncommonly serious. "Uhh, boss."

I stand from the lounge chair, trying to spot Woodstock somewhere in the distant sky. He's too far away. "Remember those, ahh, feminine products?"

"Yeah..."

"They're not tampons. They're fish. A shit ton of dead fish."

2

"Yeah, those are dead fish, all right," Maigo says, leaning over the port rail, where an oily slick of decomposing fish floats in the waves. Their tubular white bodies lack fins and scales, and on some a lot of flesh is missing, too. The scent is...unimaginable. Rotted fish and something tangy.

I throw a DHS T-shirt on, like it makes me somehow more official and back on the job, despite the fact that the only other people here are Collins and Maigo. "We should get a sample," I say, glancing at the other two.

"Yup," Collins says, looking down at the scattered dead.

"Uh-huh." Maigo looks at me and offers a phony grin. "Go for it, Director Hudson."

"Damnit," I say, thinking about how to do that. I hadn't really expected to find anything today, let alone need to collect fish sludge. "Be right back."

My journey through the yacht's air conditioned interior makes me shiver. Goose bumps rise on my arms. I blame the physical change on the temperature, and on Maigo, who likes to keep things cold. But if I'm honest, I'm feeling a little bit unnerved. Those fish haven't just been killed. They've been digested.

Whether they were a snack for a whale, a shark, a sea serpent...or some-thing larger, I have no idea. And that's what bugs me. The average depth in the Gulf of Maine, one of the most biologically productive ecosystems anywhere on Earth, is just 500 feet. That means Nemesis could be standing directly below us, and we'd have no idea. On the other hand, the Gulf is 36,000 square miles of open ocean. So the odds of that are... Who am I kidding? Nemesis has emerged from these waters twice before, both times arriving at my doorstep. If she's here, she'll find me.

And now I've scared myself. Why did I want to come out on the ocean today? Why did I even want a yacht? I should be living in a mountain fortress in the middle of nowhere with a freakin' TARDIS ready to sweep me away.

Note to self, have the Zoomb techie nerds work on a TARDIS.

I distract myself with visions of Collins dressed and speaking like Amy Pond, and I retrieve a gallon of water from the fridge. I pull the cap, drain it and use a fillet knife to carve off the top. The result is a big handled scoop, perfect for chumming, taking a piss or scooping up dead fish sludge.

Goose bumps pock my skin a second time as I step from the sixty-five degree cabin and out into the ninety degree summer heat. The stench of rot wafts over me, and I nearly gag. This time, smelling the scent anew, I recognize it. "Ugh, fish barf."

"You think this is puke?" Maigo asks.

"Sure as shit ain't shit," I say, and head for the aft dive deck. "You can smell the bile. And the fish aren't fully digested." Hanging onto the rail, I crouch on the dive deck as waves slap and gurgle against the bottom, creating a rhythmic *galoop* that would normally relax me. Right now it's reminding me of the *Jaws* chumming scene. But I'm not bothered by sharks. Not anymore. Not after what I've seen. If I see an open maw headed for the back of the yacht, it will likely be big enough to eat the whole boat.

Just scoop the fish, Jon.

I lean out over the water, reaching with the jug. Skimming the surface, I try to gather the oil slicked water without filling the plastic container. Then I lean a little further and go for a partially digested fish. The slender torpedo, ribs exposed, bounces off the edge of the jug and slides away.

"Need help?" Maigo asks, leaning on the rail, all smiles.

"You might have the strength of ten Hudson men—"

"Closer to thirty," she says.

"—but I've still got a good ten inches on you and my lovely wife, so shut it."

"We could duct tape it to a fishing pole," Collins offers, and that's not a bad idea, but I'm committed and stubborn so I just reach a little further.

The shrill whistle of DMX's *Party Up In Here* blares from my hip, but I don't really recognize it as Cooper's ringtone until DMX shouts, "Ya'll gone make me lose my mind." That also happens to be the moment I flinch free of the rail and plunge headlong into the fish-gore-slicked ocean.

I feel the film of nastiness stretch and give way to my body, or at least I imagine I do. Then I'm several feet beneath the surface, writhing and kicking and shaking my hands over my nearly bald-ish head, trying to cleanse myself, hoping that the sun block shielding my Caucasian pallor from UV rays will also prevent the stink from sticking.

My eyes open despite the sting of salt water. Bits and pieces of fish cloud around me. I glance up. The warbling shapes of Collins and Maigo hover above, leaning over the rail. I don't know if they're talking, but since they're not diving in, they must be able to see me scouring myself clean. And that's when I realize that all my efforts have been wasted.

I still need to go back up through that stuff. I'm going to smell like Moby Dick's ass for a week.

Movement spins me around, and for a moment, I forget all about how I'm going to smell, and think about how I smell right now, in the ocean, where animals that eat dead fishy smelling things live. The seven foot blue shark circling me is a perfect example. It's the fifth most dangerous shark species in the world. Sometimes called the 'wolf of the sea.' But most of that is drama played up by Discovery Channel's *Shark Week*. Only thirteen attacks on humans have been reported—ever—and only four of them fatal. Pit Bulls, which kill twenty-something people *every year*, are far more dangerous, and they can walk down the street with just a leash to keep them at bay.

The shark cuts a lazy circle around me, and I spin to match him, no longer caring about the fish flakes settling on my head and shoulders. The shark opens its mouth and scarfs down a partially digested fish.

Gross, dude.

Then he's on to the next, twisting toward me for just a moment before eating another. He moves with relaxed slowness, like he's just munched on a pot brownie. Probably been out here for hours, filling his belly. And now he's like my Uncle Tony, unbuckling his belt and pounding out a burp to make room for Thanksgiving thirds.

And then, with a flick of its tail, the blue shark proves all of my assumptions wrong. Sunlight glints off its back as it charges—and flashes straight past me, disappearing into the gloom.

What the—holy shit!

A shadow slides beneath me. It's the size of a submarine, but undulating side to side, like an eel, only with four long flippers. It slides into the depths, graceful and unconcerned.

With a kick, I rise to the surface, and this time I really do feel the filmy sludge wrap around and cling to me. Collins's hand reaches down for me, despite the stench, though she has her nose covered with her free hand, and looks like she's just sucked on a lemon. With her help, I have no trouble getting back on the dive deck, despite my shaking legs.

"Oh, God," Maigo says, backing away. "You smell like an ostrich shart."

It's a good one, worthy of the Hudson name, but I don't laugh.

"You okay?" Collins asks. "We saw the shark."

"Did you see what scared the shark?" I ask.

She shakes her head.

"Well, I think we can add the Great New England Sea Serpent to the 'shit just got real' list." I look up at Maigo. "And for the record, I smell like sea serpent shart. Why would an ostrich shart in the ocean?"

"For real?" my daughter says. "You saw it?"

"Looked more like a Kronosaurus than the sketches I've seen. And longer. Maybe a hundred fifty feet."

"Should we call it in?" Collins asks.

'Call it in' is our nice way of asking, 'Do we need the military to blow it up?' But nothing justifies that action. In fact, all of the 'monsters' we've discovered are natural occurrences. Freaks of nature maybe, but part of the ecosystem. They've all been peachy to be around. It's the ones created by humanity that have gone on rampages and treated cities like buffets.

I shake my head and motion to the fish slick. "Pretty sure we're not on the menu. And of the hundreds of sightings, not one of them involves an attack. We've been peacefully sharing the ocean with these things for a long time. No reason to change that now."

"A Kronosaurus," Maigo says, smiling, eyes glimmering with excitement. Though she was born from a monster, she is the most excited of us when we confirm the existence of another. I think it makes her feel less strange. If the world is full of monsters, she's not all that different. It's part of why she and Lilly have become so close. Like sisters. Really kick-ass, super-powered sisters. "Maybe we could call it Kro—"

A cell phone lets loose with a chipper ditty. It's Collins's.

"You really need to customize your ring tones," I say.

"Because that worked out well for you," she says with a sarcastic smile, stepping back to answer the phone. Speaking of which... I take my phone from my pocket and try to turn it on. Nothing. Good news is, I can have a new one delivered to the office before the end of the day. Bad news is it won't have all those pictures I snuck of Collins's butt.

Live and learn.

I shed my shirt and shorts before climbing back onto the deck in my mostly clean boxer-briefs. Maigo greets me with a gallon of water. She holds it out to me. "For real. You stink."

After leaning over the side and pouring the water over my head and shoulders, the smell that remains could be from me, or from the dead fish still surrounding us in the ocean. I take it as a good sign that the blue shark is back, returned to his fish binge.

The world is a weird place, and getting weirder every day.

I towel off and put it, and my clothing, in a plastic trash bag supplied by Maigo. The water and bag are small gestures, but I find them encouraging. In the past, she wouldn't have left the cabin. She might not have left the house. She would have missed all this. But now she's out here, part of the experience. As gross as it might be, it's also part of what bonds us as family.

Collins's voice slides back into range as she wanders back out of the cabin and winces at the smell. "Okay. Yeah. We're on it. Really? That soon?" She doesn't look happy, but she's listening. "Right. GOD."

For a moment, I think she's cursing, but then I realize she's using the acronym for the Genetic Offense Directive, a black ops organization within DARPA, the Defense Advanced Research Projects Agency. While the FC-P does our best to catalogue the strange and paranormal—and defend against it when necessary—GOD spends its time creating their own weaponized monstrosities. Although the creatures themselves aren't always sinister—Lilly was created in a GOD secret lab once run by World War II Japan's nefarious Unit 731—they do have a proclivity for cataclysmic destruction on an apocalyptic scale. Basically, the GOD are the bad guys. They don't just use science, they twist it. And the results are...monstrous.

But GOD's tech was also instrumental in stopping the Tsuchi—Kaiju sized spiders with a penchant for violent and unwelcome procreation. Of course, GOD also *created* that problem in the first place...so they're kind of dicks. The one good thing to come from the organization was *Future Betty*, a mirrored, wingless VTOL aircraft officially known as an X-35. One of a kind. Using 'repulse engines' it can hover just feet above the ground with little more than a hum, or zip up into orbit, which I've only done once before promptly puking. After some upgrades provided by my Zoomb techies, it's invisible to radar now, and thanks to its active camouflage, it's projecting the sky above onto its belly, and vice versa. It's also invisible to the naked eye.

"Understood," Collins says in a formal way that tells me she's 'on duty,' which means we just received a mission. "We'll be waiting." And that means we're not boating back to port, we're getting picked up. I'll need to anchor *Penny* out here in the middle of Kronosaurus land. I pat the rail.

Sorry, baby, duty calls.

When Collins hangs up, I ask, "Do I have time to take a shower?"

"Fifteen minutes," she says.

"What's the rush?"

"Cooper says we have to assume GOD is monitoring our communications and might already be en route. Our only chance of beating them there is—"

"Future Betty," I say.

"Right."

"Unless they built another."

She holds up a finger, like she's about to object, but then points at me. "Right."

"So what are we dealing with?" I ask, like I won't be rattled by any answer she gives, and like I'm a badass 80s hero in tight blue jeans. But on the inside, I'm thinking: *Please don't say Nemesis. Please don't say Nemesis.*

She taps on her phone's screen and then turns it around, revealing a photo.

I hold my breath for a moment, then ask, "Where did this come from?"

"Anonymous tip."

"Where is this?"

"Big Diomede Island, in the Bering Strait."

And just when I thought the day couldn't get worse than falling into prehistoric shart juice... I've seen the symbol carved into the stone wall in the photo only once before, in GOD's Area 51 headquarters, which is the very same place where they kept the remains of several species of alien. Well, two aliens and one over-sized alien head. The first time I saw this symbol, it was carved into a ten foot tall, blond man-thing's chest. Human or not, the giant was part of a race of humanoids from whom a certain Nazi with a small mustache believed the Germanic peoples descended.

It was the symbol for Atlantis.

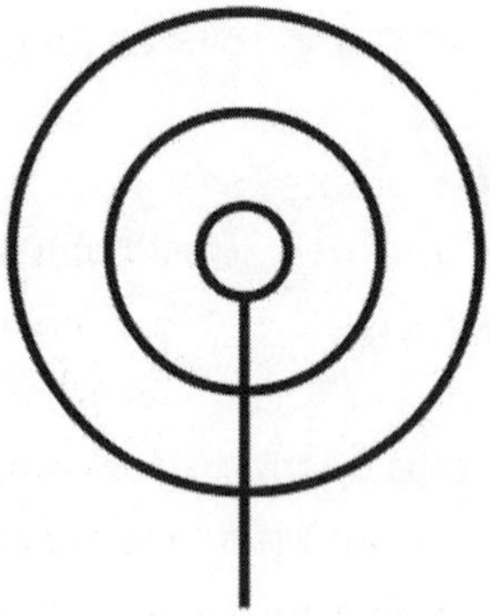

3

"Russia!" I'm seated in Future Betty's hold, which was designed to transport a team of Special Operators known as the BlackGuard. They were badass killers employed by GOD, but sometimes being the toughest kid on the block isn't enough. Sometimes you have to be smart. Or lucky.

They were neither, and now they're dead. Which is fine by me, since they tried to kill my team...my family. And now I have their transportation, which is whisking us—Woodstock, Collins, Maigo and me, northwest toward Canadian airspace at Mach 3. That's 2284 ass-puckering miles per hour. *"Russia!* You didn't say anything about starting an international incident!"

I'm sitting on one of two inward facing rows of seats lining the sides of the X-35. Collins and Maigo sit across from me, both dressed in the team's new, and stylish black combat gear. It should protect us from bullets, knives and giant spider phalluses, should the need ever arise...again. *Ugh.* When the word 'Russia' came out of my mouth, both of them paled a little bit. While most of the world is on board with the FC-P's advisement in all things Kaiju, Russia is closed off. It's not really surprising, given their competitive history with the U.S. and recent events in the Ukraine. While I agree that Russia won't know how to handle a bona fide Kaiju threat, not to mention an extraterrestrial threat, I'm not exactly comfortable with breaching their border unannounced.

"That's why you're not going to get caught," Cooper says in my ear, over comms.

"Easier said than done," I argue.

"No one can see you," Watson chimes in. They've got me on speaker phone. I hate speaker phones. "No one can hear you. You're invisible to radar. And the only people on the island are two weather station personnel and a handful of Russian Border Guard troops."

"Troops carry guns," I say. "They can also call in reinforcements."

Maigo crosses her arms and huffs. "I told you we should have brought Lilly." She's probably right, but when I decided to let the rest of our merry band chill in Maine, I didn't know we might be facing the Russian military.

I wave her away. The return trip to pick them up might only add twenty minutes to our total travel time, but we can't risk GOD getting there first. Not only are they more likely to deal with the Russians more harshly, but they'll also find a way to weaponize whatever—if anything—is hidden there. And since their last genetic experiment would have wiped out humanity if not for Nemesis, that's a very bad thing.

And I shouldn't undersell us. I've led enough of these things now to feel confident in my abilities. Collins is, well, Collins. She can handle herself. And Maigo... Okay, the Border Guards probably don't stand a chance. But if we're ID'd and word gets out, things could get messy.

Before Cooper and Watson can offer more tactical advice, I say, "Just fill me in. What are we up against?"

"It's going to be windy, cold and desolate," Cooper says. "The only indigenous life are birds."

"No people?" I ask. "Aside from the Border Guards?"

"The Inupiat Inuits were forced off the island after World War II, to make sure no one communicated with the Americans on Little Diomede, which is just two and a half miles away."

"So if things go south we can just swim to America?" I'm being sarcastic, but neither Watson nor Cooper are good at hearing sarcasm, though for different socially awkward reasons.

"I wouldn't recommend that," Cooper says. "You'll die of hypothermia long before making the swim."

"And you have—"

I cut Watson short. "Look, just send me what you have on our mysterious anonymous tip."

"There isn't much," Watson says.

I'm about to complain when my tablet chimes, declaring that I've just received an e-mail from Watson. I clamp my mouth shut, narrowly avoiding being a jerk. "Thanks. Got it. Call the others to the Beverly office. If things go south, I want Lilly and Hawkins ready."

Lilly and Mark Hawkins, her stand-in father and mentor, are often part of our field team. Sometimes they handle missions on their own. And when it comes to finding elusive creatures, they're the best. Hawkins is a former Yellowstone Park Ranger specializing in finding lost and sometimes dead people who wandered off the trail or crossed paths with a hungry bear or mountain lion. Lilly is part panther. There isn't much with a scent or a trail that they can't find. If we were looking for a person, I would have picked them up, but what we're after has likely been in the ground long enough for there to be no tracks and no scent. The third member of their team is Avril Joliet, a biologist who now spends most of her time in one of our two labs, happily analyzing blood and tissue samples from cryptozoological creatures.

I lean forward and call up to Woodstock in the pilot seat. He's chewing on a toothpick and humming a pop song. "What's our ETA?"

"Welp," he says, "Roughly 3500 miles to go, divided by bat out of hell speed... About an hour and forty, give or take five minutes."

"I'll check in when we get there," I say into the phone. "But if you find anything else—"

"We'll call," Cooper says.

I hang up the phone and turn my attention to the e-mail from Watson.

"What's with the movie style phone hang up?" Maigo asks.

"Huh?" I glance up at her from the photo of the Atlantean symbol carved in stone, apparently taken on Big Diomede Island...in freakin' Russia.

"You just hung up," she says. "No 'See ya.' Or 'Bye.' Or even a 'TTFN.'"

"Mmm," I say, eyes back on the photo.

"Dad," she says, and I don't look up. "Now you're doing it to me."

"Jon," Collins says, the singsong of her voice slipping through my distraction. "You okay?"

"What?" I glance up and see them both staring at me. I blink, playing mental catch up. "Sorry. It's just..." I look down at the photo, taken by an anonymous source. The location is identifiable as Big Diomede because far in the distance, beyond a stretch of ocean, is another island. A scattering of white buildings are clumped together at the base of a tall, rocky rise. The location has been labeled *Inalik, Little Diomede,* revealing that the Inuit weren't forced off of both islands. But in the foreground is the stone holding the Atlantean symbol. "...I was kind of hoping this would pass us by. That we wouldn't see this symbol or hear the words Atlantis, Ferox, Aeros or anything else involving the past or present invasion of Earth by aliens. Monsters I can deal with, but this... How are we supposed to defend the Earth against alien invasion?"

They're both stumped. How could they not be?

"But if anyone could..." Maigo starts. "I mean, how much worse could it be than Nemesis, or any of the other Kaiju that have come and gone?"

"That's the problem," I say. "We don't know. And even if the new Endo-infused Nemesis shows up for the fight, and isn't trying to eat *us*, it's not like she can defend the whole planet on her own."

"The way I see it..." Woodstock plucks the toothpick from his mouth and looks back. "There isn't anyone more mentally, emotionally or physically equipped to face whatever it is we find on this Russian island, whether that be ancient ruins, aliens—dead or alive—or various assorted monstrosities. We win fights with the impossible because we don't back down, and because we try shit the likes of which other people wouldn't even dream up. So quit acting like a squirrel with no nuts in his nest, or between his legs, and enjoy the flight." He taps a few buttons, and the cameras lining the outside of the strange aircraft project what they're seeing on most of the interior surfaces, allowing us views in every direction, including down. "Also, welcome to Canada, ehh. Home of hockey, maple syrup and Patti Lebeau, who broke my heart, stole my car and left me buck nekkid and fuzzy-handcuffed to a bike rack in Montreal. But in the opposite order."

I smile and say, "Thanks. For the pep talk. Not so much for the mental image."

"I do what I can, boss."

We spend the rest of the flight studying what little is known about Big Diomede (not much), the Russians stationed there (even less) and the terrain, which is barren, rocky and ice covered in the winter. It's barren, rocky and scrub-grass covered in the summer. In short, it's the most uninteresting chunk of rock west of the International Date Line, if you ignore the photo sent to us earlier.

The Canadians have no idea we came and went, which isn't much of a surprise. Not because the Canadian military is too busy curling to notice us, but because no one on the planet—except maybe alien invaders—has the technology to see us. We pass over Alaska in fifteen minutes, then we descend over the Bering Strait. I've been on flights from Boston to New York City that were more eventful.

Not that I want eventful. I would be content to be the human equivalent of the U.S.S. Enterprise, seeking out new life and new worlds, but without the new civilization bit...or the Borg, the Klingons or the Ferengi—those guys are nasty. New civilizations tend to suck. If Stephen Hawking is right—and I'm pretty sure he is—any advanced civilization that finds their way here will likely be hostile.

Future Betty touches down so gently that I don't know we're on the ground until Woodstock turns around in his seat and says, "You going to sit around all day and wait for the Ruskies to find us?"

Collins stands and gives me her hand, while Maigo heads for the rear hatch. "You seem...disturbed. Distracted."

I let her pull me up, and rub both her arms like she's the one who needs soothing. "Let's just get this done."

"Distracted people make mistakes," she says, speaking as my field partner more than my wife. "Mistakes get people killed."

"Thanks, Yoda." I force a grin, but she sees right through it, raising an eyebrow that says I better talk.

"The short version is that when I started this job—"

"It was easy."

"It *was* easy, but not in the way you're thinking. It was easy because I had no one to worry about. It was just me in the field. Now... We're married." I motion to Maigo. "We have an adopted daughter. Hawkins and Joliet might be living in sin still, but they've got Lilly. And Watson and Cooper have little Ted. The FC-P is now made up of families. Hell, even Lilly has a brood of her own."

"Babies having babies," Collins says with a mock shake of her head. She nearly gets a laugh out of me.

"It's just..."

"You want the good without the bad," she says, interrupting again in a way that would get my shoulder slugged if I did it. "But here's the thing. Without Nemesis, there would be no Maigo. We would have never met. Without GOD, there would be no Lilly. Without the hellish circumstances of the last few years, our family would have never come together in the first place."

"I'd still be flying air tours," Woodstock says. "You know how many people want air tours of Maine?"

"You could at least pretend our conversation is private," I tell him.

"That's what I'm doing," Maigo says, who could probably hear us from fifty feet away. "And she's right, Dad."

My head lolls back, mouth agape. I let out a slow groan.

"What's that you say to Hawkins when you're playing Call of Duty?" Collins asks.

"'Nut up,'" Maigo and Woodstock both say.

"Nut up, Jon," Collins says. "And instead of worrying about the worst, maybe think about what good might come from the fight."

Maigo hits the button for the rear hatch, and it lowers without making a sound. Forty degree Arctic air swirls in, stinging my cheeks and drawing my eyes to the barren landscape...where a man dressed in olive green, an AK-47 slung over his shoulder, stands with his back to us. He's taking a leak, and I think he's writing his name in Russian on a wide, flat rock.

4

The desperation of victims, guilt of perpetrators and rage of the willingly evil washed over her in waves. Every day. Every minute. Only the deepest depths of the crushing ocean gave her peace from the madness of the world. All those little creatures and their big emotions. One at a time, only the exceptional reached her thoughts, but collectively...they were enough to chase her away. People had once been little more than food, sustaining her rapid growth. But then, with the emergence of a conscience—a second voice really—she understood that they were somehow more than that.

That voice was gone now, replaced by another, less concerned with the welfare of the small creatures, but lacking rage, and more willing to let humanity be. It was a voice of contentment. Of belonging. So she and the voice hid from the world, finding a symbiosis, which both enjoyed. Conscience became intellect. Cravings, once primal and unguided, now held meaning. The world cried for justice, for vengeance, which she would soon bring, but those without guilt should be spared. The new voice believed this, just as the old voice had, but the emotion was supported by logic and confidence, lacking the chaotic emotion brought by the previous voice.

Now, Nemesis *understood.*

Now, Nemesis knew the name of her second voice: Katsu Endo.

He had been one of them. At best, food. At worst, judged. And she knew he had blood on his hands. But far less than she. And together, they had perhaps done more good than harm. What united their kindred spirits was a lack of guilt over their previous actions. They had done what needed doing.

In the stark darkness of the Puerto Rico Trench, where she was sustained by a large species of primeval shark, she turned her head up. No light reached her, but she could sense the surface five miles overhead. The ocean was empty. The faintest echoes of souls crossing above sometimes reached her, but few caught her interest. Now, something nagged.

The feeling was broad and unspecific. She wasn't tugged to any single part of the world, only up.

Toward the surface.

Toward the sky above and what lay beyond.

They're coming, Endo said.

She understood the voice, but did not communicate in the same way. While the voice known as Katsu Endo 'spoke,' the part of her that was Nemesis, felt. The words held no meaning—until he revealed it.

The memory came back in a flash, bringing a kind of burning pain with it.

Her creators.

Her tormentors.

She felt a burning hatred for a kind of being no longer wholly present in the world, but diffused in the creatures—

Humans, Endo said, and with the word came understanding that the beings she had been sent to destroy had comingled with humanity, merging species.

Her creators sent her here to destroy the non-human species. Flashes of violence played before her eyes, clear in the underwater darkness. A ringed city in flames. And then pain. Violence. A hated foe. Then nothing.

The memories weren't hers. The voice said so, and she understood. They belonged to another. The one who came before her, like the one who came before Endo. He called the old one 'Prime.' *Nemesis Prime*. The memory of that old self was ancient, but the feeling was growing stronger.

Endo focused her attention, slowing her massive heart before any men listening could hear it. Her creators were coming, but the pull on her psyche was bigger than that. One of her—of *Prime's*—targets of vengeance had returned to this planet. Not on the surface, or in the waters, but near. As were another kind of being, whose thirst for vengeance matched her own. Forces were gathering beyond the gaze of humanity, but not beyond the reach of her senses. She could feel them. Their anger. Their hatred. But not their intentions. Not yet.

She rose toward the surface, slipping from the frigid layer of water along the trench's lowest levels and into the warmer tropical temperatures above. She rose slowly, reaching out. Feeling.

Voices enveloped her, screaming for attention. For aid. For blood. Her heart swelled again. Her tail snapped in agitation, propelling her higher. But she was subdued once more by the voice of Endo.

Focus.

But she couldn't. Thousands of voices became millions.

Millions became billions.

All of them at once. A raw tidal wave that would have once propelled her to a frenzy, damning all those who stood in her path as she sought to silence the world.

Focus!

The voice directed her away from the chaos. Amidst the noise, close and distant was a rising feeling in her gut. Something was getting closer, a force that felt new, but familiar. She tuned out the humans, her ancient enemies and her creators, and she flinched in surprise.

She felt...herself. But not precisely. She felt her other selves. And two new selves. The others were already here. Quiet. Dormant. Docile. But the new selves burned with a hunger and loathing matched only by the Prime.

An ancient word returned to her mind, pronounced by the new voice: *Gerstorumque.*

The word felt like herself. Her identity. But Endo denied it. Raged against it. *You are a slave to no creature,* he said. *Prime was Gerstorumque. You are more. You...*we*...are Nemesis.*

Separation from her past returned her focus. She could sense them coming, their arrival imminent, together but separate. One would arrive at a place Endo once called home. The other would arrive on the other side of the planet, at a place the former voice had called home. She felt torn by mixed allegiances, but was surprised when Endo's thoughts agreed with her own. Their home...their family...the only people in the world either of them cared about, would soon be in grave danger.

Water swirled around the giant as she leaned forward and swept her tail back and forth. While forces gathered and weapons descended from the outer depths, Nemesis swam...for Boston.

5

I thrust my black-clad hands out toward the man scrawling his name in urine, but take no action. Instead, I turn to Collins and mouth, "What do we do about him?"

She shrugs and mouths, "You're in charge. You figure it out!"

I glance back at Woodstock, who is watching things unfold from the safe distance of the cockpit. "How did you not see him?" I mouth at him, while thrusting my hands out at the large-bladdered man.

I read the words, "I didn't think–" on his lips and turn back to Collins.

She pats the stun gun strapped to her hip. I have one, too.

"I'm not going to start an international incident," I mouth to her.

"One of us has to," she says, and though the words are conveyed in silence, I understand that she's right. The stakes are higher than a squabble between nations. Even if this guy sees us, whatever lies beneath this island might be important enough to ruffle some international feathers. And if it's dangerous, well, no one wants the Russians to have it. Except the Russians. Which means we need to get this done fast.

"Okay," I mouth. "Fine. I'll do it."

We both flinch at the sound of a thud from outside. The Russian soldier is sprawled on the rough terrain, lying beside the name Ivan, the N trailing off into a scattered dribble.

Maigo stands above him, fist clenched. She looks back at us and flashes a grin. "There's a reason mimes aren't action heroes."

"Har har," I say and step onto the island. The first thing I do is check the man's pulse. Maigo is strong enough to kill a man with one punch, and while I don't think that was her intent here, accidents happen. Especially to people still learning self-control. The man's strong pulse relieves me. Had he been dead, I would have lied about it. Maigo doesn't need another death on her conscience. But a dead Russian soldier would have made covering up this covert trip a lot harder. "Well, he'll live. So that's something."

When I stand up, Maigo looks a little concerned. "Is he really okay? I tried not to hit him too hard."

"He'll wake up with a bad headache...a really bad headache." I motion to the name sprayed on stone. "But Ivan seems like kind of a knob. He had it coming."

"A knob?" Maigo asks.

I recently started expanding my colorful language to include the best of other cultures. Not because I'm worldly, but to keep things fresh, and so the people I spend the most time around don't realize I have a potty mouth. And if no one knows the meaning, I can dilute it. "Umm, a jerk. Really, what kind of person writes their name in pee? I mean, if there had been snow, fine. I get that. But he splattered all over his boots. And he'd track that—"

"Jon," Collins says. She's stepping away from us, looking over the rocky terrain.

"Right," I say. Sometimes being a father makes me nervous, and when that happens, I lose focus. Collins is pretty good at reeling me back in. "Let's walk a grid. Twenty feet apart. We're looking for a flat-topped, jagged-edged, oval stone."

Maigo looks over the desolate plain that is Big Diomede. Tufts of hearty grass grow in patches, but the rest of the surface pretty much fits the description I just gave. We're looking for a needle in a haystack of needles. "Ugh," she says, but she starts walking.

Separated by twenty feet, Collins, Maigo and I hike across the island in silence. We cover a lot of ground, but there's no way to know for sure if we missed something. When the rocky terrain ends at a field of grass, everyone shifts ten feet to the side and heads back toward Future Betty, which is once again invisible, thanks to the closed hatch. Any Russian bored enough to be watching this forgotten island will simply see three people wandering back and forth.

We stop our second pass when Maigo reaches up and puts her hand on the invisible hull of Future Betty. Not sure how she knew it was there, but it's just another item in a long list of unexplainable abilities. Beyond the physical strength and speed, like a little Kaiju trapped in a human body, her mind is capable of fantastic things. She's got a knack for tech and is kind of a hacker savant—a humble genius mind in a powerful body—but it doesn't stop there. Her psychic connection to me, for lack of a better phrase, hints at abilities that boggle the mind. As far as I know, the only mind she can currently peek inside of is mine, a side effect of sharing a mind back when she was 300 feet tall and stomping on Washington, D.C. But she kept her physical abilities hidden for a long time. I can't rule out the possibility that she's hiding more.

I glance at the girl, twenty feet away, looking for a reaction to my thoughts. But her face is turned down to the ground, eyes flicking back and forth. She's on task. Focused. Doing a better job than I am.

"Let's keep it going," I say, rotating an index finger above my head. But the prodding isn't necessary. Collins and Maigo have a bit of a lead on me now. Maigo just sweeps her gaze back and forth, like she can see through the stones, but it's more likely that her mind can perfectly recall the photo we were sent. Collins moves a bit faster, shifting side to side, crouching and inspecting one rock after another. They're a good team, but they're even better for me.

Despite the fact that I'm in the middle of nowhere, looking through a frigid wasteland for a rock that might not be here, I feel like a very lucky man. I've survived the worst this world has to offer and come out the other side blessed. The problem with that is that I'm more vulnerable than ever, and with an otherworldly threat now looming, I'm not sure how well I can do my job while worrying about them. Hell, I can't even do a simple grid search without falling behind because I'm thinking about them!

But it's because I've fallen behind that I see Maigo stumble. Her hands go to her head like she's just been struck. Her boots scuff through the grit. A new kind of panic springs me into action, "Ashley!"

When she turns, the concern on Collins's face mirrors how I feel. It's a bitter-sweet moment. We really are a family.

Neither of us reach Maigo in time to keep her from falling, but she doesn't go far. She lands on both knees and leans forward onto her elbows, fists clenched, eyes squeezed shut. Something has shut down the strongest person on the planet. For a moment, I worry that she's undergoing some kind of transformation. She frets about it more than I do, that she'll become a monster like General Lance Gordon, the man who created her. He stole her heart, which regrew as she transformed into Nemesis. But she looks like the same girl now, only vulnerable, like when I found her encased in a fleshy pod, washed up on an island in the middle of the Potomac River.

I crouch by her side. "Maigo." I reach out for her, a father's support.

"Don't," she says, but it's too late.

My hand rests on the back of her head, and a jolt fuses me in place. Burning energy flows up my arm, through my torso and into my head. The island disappears. I hear Collins shout my name, but it fades like I've passed her in a train. An auditory glimmer. I can feel it. A force. Beneath me. I look down and see two eyes staring back.

Watching.

Waiting.

But for what?

A voice. The words aren't spoken, but I recognize the voice as Maigo's.

I turn and find myself back in my childhood home. Christmas morning. This is our meeting place. Where our inner selves—both still children—tend to meet when our minds are connected.

"What do you mean, 'a voice?'" I ask.

"It's like a pilot," she says.

I sit down by the Christmas tree, the scent of pine washing over me, the glow of rainbow colored lights reflected on my skin and the red footie pajamas that I wore until I was twelve. "You've been holding back."

She sits next to me, her hair cut in a shorter bowl, dressed in a white nightgown that looks really expensive. She plucks a gift out from the pile. The snowmen on the wrapping paper look too happy. "It's just a theory."

"Why keep it from me?"

Paper tears as she peels tape back. "You know why."

Because it scares the shit out of both of us, I think, and then I remember that when we're in this place, thinking is the same as speaking.

"So let's hear it," I say, and I lift a gift up, pretending to be more casual than I feel, which again is a wasted effort. We're sharing thoughts and feelings right now.

"I wasn't just inside Nemesis," she says. "I helped *guide* her. To her, I was an anomaly. A confusing second voice that sometimes propelled her to action, and sometimes held her back. Her allegiances shifted with mine. And on some occasions, her actions were mine."

"Nothing...you know, gross, though, right?"

She rolls her eyes and opens the gift. "Argyle socks?"

"My mother had the taste of an eighty year old man." I start peeling back layers of Santa paper from the gift I'm holding. "So you were able to control Nemesis?"

"To an extent. Like we saw Endo do in Salt Lake," she says, and I remember how Nemesis's savage fighting style became more refined and disciplined after the man allowed himself to be enveloped by her. I'd always thought it was a side effect of how Nemesis was created, like the merging of very different genetic codes. But if Maigo's theory is right, Nemesis requires a symbiotic relationship to function at her best.

"But what does that have to do with the thing beneath us?" I can still feel its eyes gazing up at us, watching, but it doesn't feel like a Kaiju. It doesn't feel alive at all.

"It sees me," she says, revealing that it's not me the thing is watching. It's her.

I tear open the gift and smile.

"This was a good one," she says, and takes the long book from my hands. She reads the title. "Scientific Progress Goes 'Boink.'" Calvin and Hobbes?"

"It's funny," I say.

She flips the book open, but the pages are blank. Our connection is slipping.

"Why is it looking at you?" I ask, worried that at least one of us will be unconscious when we separate.

"It's looking for a voice." She puts the book down, sighs and looks up at me. "It's looking for a pilot."

6

A flash of painful white light burns up the Christmas tree and erases Maigo. I'm tossed back, my body heavier and limbs longer, adult again. The cold hard ground of Big Diomede receives me with a complete lack of kindness or regard for my comfort. Jagged rocks push into my back, but I avoid serious injury thanks to the body armor, which absorbs much of the impact and prevents me from being impaled like some Neanderthal in a rock-knife fight. Consciousness returns just a moment before impact, and I manage to lean my head up just enough to avoid cracking my skull.

Despite the lack of serious injury, the physical jolt combined with the psychological effect of being propelled from Maigo's mind leaves me dazed and groaning. The conversation with Maigo filters back through my thoughts like a dream, nearly forgotten, but replaying. I hear Collins saying my name. She's concerned. I tune her out, remembering the details. The familiar setting helps. Christmas. Gifts. Our child selves.

A voice.

A pilot.

My eyes snap open to a relieved Collins.

"A pilot," I say.

"What happened?" Collins asks.

I reach up and take Collins's offered hand. She hoists me up. "I was in her head again." I look for Maigo and find her kneeling ten feet away, and realize just how far I was flung. *No wonder landing hurt so much.*

Maigo's hands are on the ground, eyes closed. She looks almost peaceful.

"Christmas?" Collins asks.

I nod. "How long—"

"Before you were turned into a human skeet?"

"I went that high?"

She points her finger in an arc and whistles as she traces the path I took, up and away from Maigo, ending at where I landed. "It looked like you were shocked. You were only in contact for a second."

"Felt like minutes." I stretch my arm as I head back to Maigo, looking her over for signs of injury. But she wasn't flung by our separation. If anything, she looks strangely at peace now. I crouch beside her, out of arm's reach. "Maigo?"

No reply.

"Earth to Maigo."

She slowly shushes me. "Shhh."

Collins looks as confused as me. Maigo doesn't seem to be in pain. And she's not unconscious. So what's she doing?

"Hey, boss?" It's Woodstock in my ear bud. I glance back to where I know Future Betty is waiting, but see only the barren, foggy island.

"Go ahead."

"Everything okay out there?" With the array of cameras surrounding the craft's hull projecting the view outside on the interior surfaces, Woodstock can watch everything that's happening outside. "That was quite the swan dive. Didn't quite stick the landing."

"Fine," I say.

"What about Maigo?"

"Not sure." I lean down to look at her face. She looks calm, but her eyes are shifting behind her eyelids, like she's in REM sleep.

"Can she move?" he asks.

I'm about to clarify the situation when I realize his asking any of these questions is abnormal. He's generally willing to kick back, listen to whatever fifty years too young pop star he's into now, and wait to be summoned. So why is he suddenly interested in Maigo's mobility?

"Woodstock...what's our situation?"

"Cloudy with a chance of Russian MiGs."

I stand and look to the western sky. "Next time, lead with that bit of information."

"They're actually north of us," he says, revealing that he is indeed watching. "Headed toward Alaska. They're probably just probing our response times. They do it a lot. And three F-22s have scrambled out of Eielson to escort the MiGs until they're headed away from U.S. airspace. But..."

"We're on Russian soil," I say. "They can't help us here."

"Bingo."

I crouch back down beside Maigo, leaning my face low to the ground, so I can look up at hers. "Maigo. I know you can feel what's down there. But we need to find a way to it. Now. Can you—"

"It's testing me," she whispers.

"Testing you? How?"

She gives a slight shake of her head. "I think...I'm not sure. But it's watching me. I can feel it." She lifts a hand and places it on her head.

"Do you know what it is?" Collins asks.

"Is it a Kaiju?" I add. "Like Nemesis?"

"I...it's big. But I don't know what it is." She grunts in pain, and I nearly reach out to hold her again. "Ugh. It... Gestorumque?"

She speaks the last word in a deeper voice, with inflections that are not her own.

"No," she says, then in the deeper voice, "Atlantide?"

"No," she answers herself.

"Vixnoctus?" the deep voice asks.

Maigo seems torn by the question, brow furrowed, fingers gripping and crushing stones to powder. Before she can answer, Woodstock's voice returns.

"MiGs just turned south! They'll be here in two minutes! Get back here now!"

"Maigo," I say, knowing she could hear Woodstock just as well as Collins and I. "We need to go."

"Can't," she says.

"We're employed by the U.S. government. My face is recognizable. Our presence here won't be looked upon kindly, and they'll have a good idea of why we're here. Whatever is buried beneath us needs to wait, or they'll–"

"It won't let them," she says.

"Jon," Collins says, her voice a warning, her eyes on the sky to the north.

"I can't move her," I say. Even if she didn't physically resist, my psychic bond with her will pull me back into her connection with the thing beneath us and send me flying again. Maybe worse.

Collins knows this as much as I do. She also knows that she doesn't have the same bond with Maigo. Before I can protest, she leans down and slides her hands under Maigo's armpits. When she's not flung away or sent into a trance, she hoists and grunts. Maigo is the same size as the average teenage girl, but far heavier thanks to the density of her muscle mass. But when it comes to the human variety of toughness and determination, Collins is hard to match.

Maigo doesn't fight the pull, and the moment she's lifted away, her body goes limp.

"One minute!" Woodstock says, and I see the Future Betty's hatch opening out of thin air, just twenty feet away. Woodstock moved closer to us without us even sensing the craft's approach or descent.

Collins isn't going to make it in time, so I run up next to her and reach out.

"Don't," she says.

"Have to risk it." Hoping that Maigo's connection with the thing below us really has been severed, I reach under her left arm and lift.

Nothing happens.

"Let's go!" I say, and together we drag Maigo across the rough surface, leaving twin trails in the loose grit and stones. She's hard to get up the ramp, but Woodstock starts raising it before we're inside, helping lift Maigo's heft. The raising ramp dumps us inside the passenger compartment. We sprawl on the floor, a tangle of limbs. "Go, go, go!" I shout.

"Hold on," Woodstock whispers and points up. Through the ceiling, which is projecting the sky above, I see two slate gray MiG-29s cut through the sky overhead. They bank hard to the left and continue in a tight circle around the island. They're looking for us. And they'll see Ivan out there, sprawled on the ground beside his piss-scrawled name.

We lift off and ascend vertically, moving slow and steady. Woodstock keeps the front end facing the two circling MiGs, keeping them in view as we rise up toward the altitude they're maintaining.

"Well, they definitely knew something was up," he says. "That's for damn sure."

"But how?" I ask, lifting Maigo into a seat and strapping her in. She's just starting to regain consciousness. She still looks a little out of it.

"Maybe waking that thing up sent some kind of detectable signal?" Collins asks, sitting across from Maigo and strapping in.

"You woke something up?" Woodstock asks. "Something small and furry this time, I hope."

I sit down beside Maigo. "No idea, but we—"

"Shit." Woodstock brings the circling Future Betty to a stop. As the two MiGs continue their loop around the island, four specks appear on the horizon. "Four more birds, incoming from the west."

I move to the cockpit, sit beside Woodstock and look through the front windshield, which isn't glass at all. Like the rest of the vehicle, it's simply projecting the outside view on the inside hull. The four craft are nearly on top of us already. "How did we miss them?"

"No radar signal," he says, pointing at the display that shows the two circling jets, but not the incoming visitors. "But they're coming from the west, and our two friends outside aren't freaking out. I think it's safe to say they're Ruskies, too, and that we should get gone."

Maigo gasps. When I look back, she's sitting up straight, eyes wide. Her head snaps toward the cockpit. "Look out!"

A cloud of black dots drop from the bellies of the four approaching aircraft and then cruise toward us at hypersonic speed.

"Strap in!" Woodstock yells at me.

The buckle clicks just as Woodstock launches us vertically, crushing me into the seat. Even if I hadn't been buckled in, I wouldn't have been able to leave the seat. We stop hard and the belt pulls on my gut. Then we're spinning and turning downward, watching the missiles pepper the island where we had just been. Fireballs erupt across the rocky surface. I see the now tiny figure of Ivan sit up. He raises his hands before being consumed in flame.

"They knew we were here," I say. "They were hoping to catch us on the island."

"Like I said, it's time to get gone." But instead of taking us up and away, Woodstock quickly descends. I realize why a moment later when four fighter jets rush past, the roar of their engines blocked by Future Betty's sound dampeners. The bi-wing design and stealth approach help me identify the craft as Russian Mikoyan LMFS. They're fifth generation multirole aircraft capable of attacking land and air targets with an array of weapons concealed in their oversized weapons bays. Until this moment, myself and everyone else in the U.S. government, at least officially, believed they were still in development.

"Up, up and away," Woodstock says, and I'm crushed into my seat again as we rocket straight up to forty thousand feet, far above the fighters, and cross into U.S. airspace just seconds later.

7

We're back over the East Coast fast enough that Russia could never claim I was anywhere near Big Diomede without looking like buffoons. Of course, for that to really be true, I have to be seen, my presence here a matter of public knowledge. So as we descend over Beverly, Massachusetts, I ask Woodstock to let Collins and me off at Lynch Park.

Maigo hasn't said much about her encounter with the mysterious thing beneath the island, and I don't think she's going to. Not until it starts making sense to her. But we've confirmed that something is buried there.

Something big. Something that requires a pilot. What it called a Vixnoctus. A voice. The same way Maigo had been for Nemesis, and Endo was now. That alone tells me that I want whatever is buried there to stay that way. I'm sure a lot of paleontologists and archeologists might disagree, but some secrets are better left buried.

"You sure you don't want me to stay with you?" I ask Maigo, while standing by the still-closed hatch with Collins. "We don't have to do this."

"I'm fine," she says, sounding drowsy. "I'm going to sleep."

"With Lilly at the house?" Collins says, sounding skeptical. Lilly is a bundle of mischievous energy. She's more level-headed than she used to be, especially when on mission, but locked up in the Crow's Nest, she can be trouble. We've negated this somewhat by purchasing every game system imaginable, but she beats and grows bored with games nearly as fast as we can buy them.

"We've got Titanfall," Maigo says. "Will take her at least a few hours to beat. That's all I need."

For Maigo, four hours is a good night's sleep. She doesn't seem to need much more, and this is really the first time I've actually seen her sleepy.

"Okay," I say. "But if she keeps you awake—"

"I'll tell Hawkins," she says.

"Tell Joliet," Collins says. "She's small, but I've seen her crack the whip."

"Nice," I say and chuckle. "Try not to use that phrase with Lilly."

Collins looks befuddled.

"Crack the whip," Maigo says. "It's an allusion to lion taming."

"Geez," Collins says. "Shit. Please don't repeat it."

"Just go," Maigo says, smiling and shooing us toward the ramp, which has started to descend. "Have fun being spotted in public."

I turn toward the exit and stop. The view ahead is leafy green. "Uhh, Woodstock..."

"You said you didn't want to be spotted," the old pilot gripes. "Too many people in the park to set down in the grass, so this is the only way. You can either make like monkeys and climb down, or we can let the world know we have an invisible stealth plane."

I look back out. We're just fifteen feet from the ground, backed up to a tree on the backside of the park, overlooking the rocky coast of Beverly Harbor. Then we're inside the tree, pushing slowly into the branches.

"Better?" Woodstock asks.

I lift a branch and see a clear path down through a maze of sturdy limbs. I motion toward the hole I've just made and turn to Collins with a grin. "After you, madam."

Collins shakes her head, but offers no complaint. She slides down onto a branch and climbs toward the ground.

Maigo takes the branch from me so I can follow Collins, but I pause for a moment. "If you think of anything—"

"I'll call you," she says.

I hold out a pinkie. "Pinkie swear?'

She raises a single eyebrow.

"They grow up so fast," I say, and I climb down onto the branch. I cling in place, watching the hatch close. Maigo maintains eye contact with me, until the hatch is closed. Then they could be gone, or they could be laughing at me while I climb down. It's impossible to tell with the X-35.

I drop down from the tree next to Collins and scan the area. I can hear people in the distance, but there's no one around. The park was destroyed three years ago. Its two beaches, open grassy area, half-shell theater and ice cream stand were reduced to char. Only the brick walls of the old rose garden survived the moment Nemesis's orange membrane was punctured by an overzealous Air Force pilot. The resulting explosion destroyed a good portion of the harbor in both Beverly and Salem, crushing homes, busi-nesses and parks alike. While many homes are still being rebuilt, the park looks like new. It became a symbol of the city's resilience. The grass grew green. The melted playground was replaced by a megalith of primary colors. And the rose garden blooms with an array of roses from around the world, including an orange variety at the center, symbolizing the containment of the blast that claimed thousands of lives. That blast nearly destroyed the Crow's Nest, which is just a mile away atop Powder Hill.

We head down the sloping grass toward the red brick walls of the rose garden. It's become one of our favorite places to get away. To think. And other things. The smell of roses reaches us before we even enter. I pause at the main entrance. Two lion statues face inward, just beyond the entrance, looking at a columned atrium on the far side of the sunken garden. There used to be a fountain inside it, but it hasn't worked in decades. I read the saying carved into the walls on either side of the entrance. "Whosoever enters here let him beware. For he shall never-more escape nor be free of my spell."

Collins steps past the entryway and into the garden. "I, for one, wouldn't mind staying here for a lifetime."

We meander along the paths for a moment, the warm sun on our faces, surrounded by the buzzing of bees and the scent of roses. Then voices. Loud ones. We walk to the open side of the park, facing the Atlantic Ocean. Just beyond the marble statue of The Falconer, standing guard between it and the garden is the seawall, which drops down to the park's beach that wasn't melted into a sheet of glass three years ago. But standing between the statue and the ocean is a group of people arranged in a circle, throwing a ball back and forth, chatting loudly. The few people outside the circle snap photos with their phones, no doubt updating Facebook or Twitter or Tumblr or whatever it is hip people use these days. I still have a MySpace account.

These are the people I need to see me, I think, and I head toward them.

They don't spot me right away, but one of them misses the ball and it rolls to a stop at my feet. I bend and pick it up, only it's not a ball. It's an orange. *The hell?* What kind of people stand in a circle and play catch with an orange? "Are you guys like a rehab support group or something?"

One of them shouts something, and I swear it's 'Argh,' like a pirate. Okay...maybe not the best group of people to approach.

"Toss the orange!" a girl with a pink streak in her hair shouts. While there's a wide range of ages represented here, she's by far the youngest.

"Throw it, ya wanker." And an Aussie? I try to come up with something funny to say, but then I spot another woman holding up two fingers in some kind of reverse peace sign. These people are a little nuts.

"You all come on the short bus?" I ask. Probably not best to instigate them, but I really can't help myself. To my surprise, they all start laughing. Then one of them, who I swear is something close to my twin, steps from the circle. "You're Jon Hudson."

Perfect. That's all I really wanted. Recognition and an alibi. The man, who I dare say is quite handsome, shakes my hand. A real fan boy. The others start snapping pictures, and I think someone else shouts, 'Argh' again. *The hell are these people smoking?*

"Thanks," the man says, "for everything you've done." And that's when I notice a lot of them are wearing Nemesis T-shirts.

Wait... I know who this is... "You're the guy who fictionalized Nemesis. Wrote the novels."

"And the comic book," he says, and then he turns to the group of people, who I now realize are just fans being goofy, visiting one of the locations featured in those books. "These guys are—"

"Holy shit!" the young girl shouts, pointing up at the sky.

A flickering beam of bright white light cuts through the atmosphere high above, filling the air with a sharp crackling. It's bright enough to make me squint, but I keep watching. Then, moving within the light, something huge strobes into the view, shooting straight down at the open ocean. The massive beam of light arcs over the horizon, carrying the object toward the water and out of view. While the group of people start backing away, Collins and I head for the ocean wall.

A sonic boom slams into the park, sparking screams and the sound of fleeing people. But Collins and I watch it pass the horizon, waiting for it to hit. While we wait, I make a quick call. "Coop. I need Woodstock in Future Betty. Lynch Park. Now."

"Got it," she says without question.

The crackling beam of light disappears, its radiance replaced by a blooming glow on the horizon. Touchdown.

"Wait..." I say, "Get everyone on board."

"Everyone?" Cooper asks.

A warm breeze tickles my cheeks.

"Just a precaution. Now! Hurry!"

I pocket the phone just before a shockwave reaches us with a cacophonous boom. Collins and I are lifted off our feet and sent sprawling to the ground while a hot wind scours our skin. Then it's past us, lashing through the still recovering city.

I'm on my feet first, hobbling back to the sea wall and looking down. "Shitty, shit, shit."

Collins arrives next to me and looks down at the receding ocean. "Shit."

"I covered that already," I say.

My phone rings and I answer it. "Hudson."

"Woodstock is on his way in Betty," Cooper says, a trace of panic in her voice. The shock wave would have just hit the Crow's Nest, too.

"Wait, what do you mean, Woodstock?" I ask. "I said you all—"

"*Helicopter* Betty," she says, and I can hear her continued disdain for the name. Before I can protest, she adds, "Future Betty is gone."

"*Gone?*"

"Along with Lilly and Maigo."

I feel about ready to explode in anger, but that's not going to save Collins and me. "Tell him to meet us in the quad!"

Collins and I sprint through the rose garden and into the large grassy field on the other side. Cars are screaming out of the parking lot, which is at the top of a tall hill, a good fifty feet higher above sea level, which is a lot better than being here. When I spot a large white van and the group of odd Nemesis fans climbing into it, I tug on Collins's arm and run for it. "Hold up!"

The author spots us and leaves the side door open. "Room for two more!" someone inside the van shouts, and I swear I think these loons are enjoying this. Collins and I dive in while the driver slams down the gas pedal and we lurch into a very slow acceleration, crawling up the hill.

"Look!" someone shouts, and I turn back. A wall of water envelops the park, slides across the parking lot and starts rising up the slope behind us.

As we crest the hilltop, a man in the back pumps his fist and shouts, "Woohoo!"

What he doesn't know is that while Lynch Park is at the bottom of a hill, several beaches in the area, some in front of us, some behind us, will do nothing to slow down the tsunami. And based on the speed of the water rushing over the park, we've got just seconds before it finds us. Happily, the driver seems to understand this as well.

"We need to get to higher ground!" the man shouts.

I lean between the front seats and point. "Straight ahead. Turn right when I tell you!"

"Argh!" someone says.

Good Lord in Heaven, don't let us die with these crazy people. I open my eyes in time to see the open, wrought-iron gate of Central Cemetery. "Turn right, now!"

8

As we roar past the gravestones marking the dead, some of them still scorched from Nemesis's passing three years ago, I wonder how many more will be dead by the end of the day. The area is still far less populated than it was pre-Nemesis, but that wave isn't just striking Beverly. It's going to smash into every seaside city in the Gulf of Maine. Millions of people are at risk. But my focus at the moment is saving the fifteen people crammed into this van.

"Left!" I shout, a moment before being mashed hard to the right, face pressed against glass. I see rushing water churning through the gravestones beside us, a swell rising up the sloped lawn.

The side of the van clips a gravestone and bounces hard, righting itself on the small, crumbling paved road. My head strikes the ceiling. Someone behind me cries out, but I can't tell if they're excited, afraid or in pain. The van shakes over the poorly maintained road.

"Seriously," a woman with an English accent shouts from the back. "Do you have to hit *every* pothole? I'm going to be sick!"

You're going to be dead if the driver worries about potholes, I think, but I keep it to myself.

"Which way now?" the driver shouts, as we approach a four way intersection.

"Straight through," the author, whose name I can't recall, yells back before I can answer. He glances back at me. "I grew up here."

I nod, seeing the pain in his eyes. He's seen his home town destroyed more than once now.

"We'll fix this," I tell him, but it feels hollow. I don't even know what this is. The best I can do is put my recently acquired wealth to work. It's not really a matter of public record, but Zoomb, the Internet giant I...inherited...paid for a lot of the rebuilding projects stretching from Portland, Maine to Boston. That includes the newly renovated, now deluged, Lynch Park. Nemesis wasn't my fault, but I also didn't figure out how to stop her rampage until the New England coast was in shambles. If today is related, I'm going to have to spend a lot more money to squelch my guilty conscience.

The gate on the far side of the cemetery is closed, the wrought iron bars padlocked with a chain. The author turns back to me again, eyes widened at the wall of water filling the view through the back windows. "Crow's Nest?"

How the hell does he know...? Doesn't matter. "Yes!"

"Go through!" the author shouts.

The driver guns the engine and ducks. "Everyone down!"

The van shudders from an impact, filling with the sound of crunching metal and shattering safety glass. I feel squares of the stuff pepper my face. The van jolts again, and the engine growls as we head uphill, out of the cemetery. The wall of water behind us careens into the fence, shoving trees, home debris and a few bodies against the metal bars before rising above it and plowing into the residential neighborhood we're tearing through.

The chop of a helicopter turns me forward. I'm surprised to see the van's windshield mostly missing, along with a portion of the roof. One of the metal gates is wedged in the van's front end, where the windshield had been, just inches above the heads of the driver and author. Brave men.

Betty flies past overhead. I don't know if Woodstock knows we're in the van or not, but he's trying to help.

The intersection ahead is generally a busy one. Anyone driving on the cross street might not know about the incoming wave and might T-bone us. But it's a risk we have to take. Powder Hill is just ahead, rising two hundred feet with the Crow's Nest at its apex.

"Don't slow down," I tell the driver.

He looks unsure.

The water rises behind us, just feet away from the van that is slowing, more because of gravity than the driver removing his foot from the gas pedal.

My phone rings.

I answer it.

"That you in the van?" Woodstock asks.

"Yes."

"Intersection is clear," he says. "But you better step on it. Second wave is bigger."

I lean between the front seats. "The road ahead is clear. Don't let up. Not until we're at the top."

The driver clutches the steering wheel and locks his eyes ahead. Moving at seventy miles per hour, we crest the rise and bounce through the intersection, hitting the much steeper climb up Powder hill. The van slows on the incline, but also keeps us from flipping around the sharp bend in the road.

"I think the water is receding," someone says.

"It's not," I tell the driver.

I feel Collins's hand on my arm, gripping as she looks back. I don't need to look. I know what's there. The second, bigger wave.

"What is that?" a man asks.

"Oh, shit. Oh, shit!" a woman says. They're seeing it now, too, and their reactions are not putting my mind at ease.

When the van shakes, I can't stop myself from looking back. A wave has crested against the hillside, white froth exploding against the rear windows, drawing screams from the group, but also giving us a little nudge forward.

The water continues to rise around us, consuming the homes at the bottom of the hill. Spray hisses from the tires and then drags us a little slower. Water rises up over the back windows, swirling with debris and dead things. A man seated behind me calmly shakes his head, mumbling, "I should have stayed in Minnesota." He meets my eyes. "This kind of thing doesn't happen in Minnesota!"

The guy is about to lose his mind, and I don't blame him. But we're not dead yet. I put the phone to my ear again. "How are we looking?"

"Clear to the Nest," Woodstock says, "but the water is rising fast. Would *not* recommend heading down the far side. Roads are congested. Water is already moving around the hill."

"Have them open the doors for us!" I shove the phone back into my pocket.

The engine surges as the road levels out atop the hill and we pull free of the water. We race past homes that survived Nemesis's first arrival here, watching the water surround them. The large stone wall of the Crow's Nest grounds is straight ahead. I point to the marble staircase leading up to the perfectly maintained grass. "Stop us in front of the stairs!"

The group of people behind stare with rapt attention, perhaps understanding that their lives depend on how they react in the next seconds. "When we stop, everyone gets out. One row at a time. Anyone who pushes ahead has to talk to her." I motion to Collins, expecting her to just look mean, but she pulls a gun from behind her back and chambers a round.

Tires squeal and the van cuts hard to the right, slamming to a stop against the curb. The author is out of the passenger's side before the van fully settles and tears open the side doors. Collins and I are out first, but neither of us leave. Nor does the author or the driver.

"Get them inside," I shout to the two men. "Go!"

The van disgorges its passengers faster than I thought possible. I suppose not drowning in an apocalyptic deluge is a great motivation. When everyone is out, Collins and I follow the group up the stairs, where a brick walkway leads across the lawn to the mansion's patio entrance. The door is already open. Watson and Cooper are waving us on. Hawkins and Joliet are in the yard helping the few stragglers move faster. Maigo and Lilly, whose help we could really use right now, are nowhere to be seen. Woodstock buzzes past overhead, shouting through a loudspeaker. "Move it! You all are slower than a pregnant three-legged moose!"

The ground shakes as a wall of water slams into the property's wall, sending spray rocketing a hundred feet in the air. The van is swept away and slammed through the front door of a neighboring home. Water surges up the walled-in stairwell and explodes over the lawn, slapping Collins and me as we bring up the rear.

"Get everyone upstairs!" I shout ahead, as the group files through the patio doors, led by Watson and Cooper.

Hawkins stays behind and greets us, eyes on the still rising tsunami. "What the hell happened?"

"No idea," I tell him, "but I think our WCS might have just landed on our doorstep."

WCS is shorthand for Worst Case Scenario. Since we discovered the existence of multiple alien species, whose machinations for the human race are uncertain at best, we've discussed our response amidst ourselves, with the U.S. government, and with any nations that would take us seriously, despite our lack of physical evidence. GOD is very good at cleaning up their messes. We haven't seen or heard from them since stealing Future Betty from Area 51, their former base turned flattened husk. Zach Cole and Alicio Brice...or his clones...are in the wind. While I still have the President's ear and trust, thanks to a little brainwashing, the world hasn't come to a consensus on the topic yet, let alone a course of action. The movies are wrong. Even when faced with doom from above, the human race probably won't come together.

The stoic Hawkins doesn't say another word. He just shakes his head and closes the patio door. After one last look at the still rising water, we charge up the stairs, past the Crow's Nest operations center, where Watson and Cooper have gathered our guests, and head for the roof.

Helicopter Betty is setting down, kicking up dust that would normally be swirling around Future Betty's invisible skin. But the X-35 is missing. Clenching my fists, I head for the eastern side of the roof and look down. Water laps against the brick-walled flower beds that surround the base of the home, and then it slides away. On all sides, the ocean, now full of battered homes, crushed vehicles and lost dreams, recedes. Some of it heads back to sea. The rest flows further into town. I can't hear anything over the roar of water and Betty's slowing rotors, but in a few minutes, all we'll be able to hear are screams.

Or will we? How many people within earshot are still living?

I feel the presence of others and turn around. Collins, Hawkins, Joliet, Woodstock, Watson and Cooper are all there.

"Our guests?" I ask.

"In the office," Cooper says. "In shock."

"Do we know anything at all?"

Watson shakes his head. "No one saw it coming."

"And the girls?"

"My fault," Woodstock says. "Taught Lilly how to fly."

While I would like to blame someone and vent my anger, it's definitely not Woodstock's fault. "They're part of the team. They're responsible."

"I just hope they're safe," Collins says, reminding me that we're more than a team.

I turn and look out at the ocean, which is partly back where it's supposed to be, but now full of submerged neighborhoods and countless dead.

"Watson, coordinate a search with the military. Find out what the hell that was."

"On it," he says, and I hear him head away.

"Cooper, let's get Devine online." While Devine might sound like a 70's pornstar, it's actually short for Digital Vanguard Intelligence Network, which allows us to coordinate with state, federal and military emergency responders. It was created in the wake of the first Nemesis attack on this stretch of coastline, but it's been upgraded recently, thanks to Zoomb. The FC-P is the only government agency capable of activating the communications network, and once we do, all information flows through us, which really irks my former superiors in the DHS. "Organize relief efforts."

When I turn around, Cooper is headed for the door.

"Coop," I say, stopping her. "Is Spunky okay?"

She looks a little paler when I ask, but nods. "The daycare is fifteen miles from the coast."

I nod and she leaves. The others wait for their orders, but I have nothing for them. "The rest of you, eat your Wheaties and get some rest. I have a feeling this day is about to go from shitty to Montezuma's Revenge. We need to be ready to react."

When I turn back to the view, I hear three sets of receding footsteps. Collins steps up next to me, looking out at the scoured-clean view, tears in her eyes. "I'm getting tired of being stepped on."

I catch sight of something when I nod. Although most homes have crumbled or been yanked back toward the ocean, a single house stands alone on the far side of the hill. It's a white home with light blue/gray shutters. After Nemesis first laid waste to the area, the family there, including three boys and two golden retrievers, had left. Thanks to Zoomb, and I suppose to me, they had returned. I'm about to head down and see if anyone is there and alive, when I see motion on the roof. The family is there, safe and dry. Even the dogs. One of the boys is waving at me. I return the wave, and turn to Collins. "Me, too."

I take out my phone and speed dial a number.

"It just came on the news," Alessi says. She's Endo's half sister, and now she's running the company I own. "What do you need?"

"Full relief package for every community hit," I say.

"On it. Anything else?"

"Put the WCS protocol on standby."

"Are you sure?" she asks.

I look Collins in the eyes and see the same determination I feel. *No more getting stepped on.* "I'm sure."

9

"Chill out. It's not like they can see us." Lilly leaned forward in Future Betty's cockpit, looking down at Big Diomede. The surface crawled with Russian military. Helicopters came and went, transporting personnel, most of whom carried assault rifles. Those who didn't, carried an array of scientific equipment that Lilly couldn't identify. Lines of men walked patterns around the center of the island, sweeping metal detectors back and forth. At the far end of the island, opposite the ramshackle Russian outpost, stood a series of domes connected by tunnels. The prefab base had been flown in and set up in just hours.

Maigo stood in the cargo bay, turning slowly to take in the three hundred sixty degree view. "No, but they can still run into us. We're not immaterial."

Four Russian MI-24 Hind attack helicopters, big, imposing and armed with enough firepower to lay waste to a city, circled the island. Further out, the Russian stealth fighters did laps, sometimes cutting through the air just over the island. They were surrounded by enemy activity on all sides, top and bottom. Despite the X-35 being the world's most advanced aircraft, capable of hiding in plain sight, Maigo had no doubt that they would eventually be discovered if they stayed too long. The island was home to a lot of very annoyed birds. How long before one of them flew into the hull?

"Bonus points for the five syllable word," Lilly said. "But we're *not* stationary. I can move if anything comes our way."

"We should at least let the others know what's going on he–"

Lilly craned her head out in slack-jawed shock. "Are you serious?" She extended a black, clawed finger. "First, they'll make us go back." Two fingers. "Second, they'll never let us leave again." Three fingers. "Third, they still treat us like kids–"

"Technically, both of us *are* under five years old," Maigo said. "They might have a point."

Lilly groans. "Seriously? They take us on field operations. Like, all the time. We helped save the West Coast from the Tsuchi. And you nearly sacrificed yourself. It's cool if we do that? But show a little initiative–bonus points–and what? We get in trouble? They can't fire us. They can't ground us. Or spank us. We're two of the most powerful people–"

"Sort of."

"*Sort of* people on the planet. If this is what we have to do to prove ourselves..." Lilly shrugs. "So be it. I can handle red faces and angry voices. But I'm tired of being second string. I love all of them. I respect all of them. But who else can jump two hundred feet out of Future Betty and into a Russian camp without getting spotted?" She turned her index finger to herself, and then to Maigo. "No one else, that's who."

"Still," Maigo said, "we should at least let them know we're okay. They're probably worried."

"Radio silence," Lilly said with a roll of her eyes. "Remember? Unless you think broadcasting our presence to the Russians will make a good impression?"

Maigo sat down and sighed. While she was good on mission and had few qualms about action, or danger, Lilly lived for this stuff. Like most cats, she didn't shirk from danger, Lilly headed straight for it. Said it was part of her feline DNA. But how much did that really influence her personality? She grew up on an island where danger and survival were a way of life. Adrenaline and tension were the norm for her. Maybe her behavior was just learned? Nurture over nature? Maigo hoped so, because her DNA wasn't just feline, or any of the other animals making up Lilly's patchwork genetic code. Maigo had the DNA of a vengeful alien killing machine polluting her humanity.

And that was why she was here. She wasn't seeking respect or thrills, like Lilly. She wanted to know she could do this without being a monster. And if the worst happened, and she went full-Kaiju, she didn't want Hudson or Collins—Mom and Dad—being anywhere nearby. Lilly could take care of herself, but the others...if things went bad and she lost herself, they wouldn't stand a chance. And she couldn't live with the idea of hurting them. So when Lilly approached her about this little side mission, she saw it as a chance to prove to herself that the monster inside her really was contained. Plus, the force beneath this island had reached something inside her, something buried and powerful. She wasn't sure what it was. She had to know.

Maigo leaned her head back. "How long until night?"

"Ten more hours." Lilly smiled and faced forward again, watching the array of moving targets with the twitchy attention of a house cat.

"Wake me up when it's time." Maigo closed her eyes. She had no intention of sleeping, but didn't want to spend the next ten hours in conversation. Lilly had become a sister to her. They weren't just the most powerful sort-of people on the planet, they were also the weirdest, and no one understood their unique issues better than each other. Hudson was a close second. He had been inside the head of a Kaiju after all, but he wasn't a girl. Just minutes after closing her eyes, her thoughts drifted to the past. To the memories of carnage she fought so hard to block out.

Go back to Christmas, she thought.

"You don't need to open that."

She opened her eyes. Christmas morning. Her dad's childhood living room. The glowing tree. Scent of pine. But it lacked the aura of childhood nostalgia that her dad's presence usually infused.

Instead, it felt heavy.

She looked for the person who had spoken and found Alexander Tilly, her biological father...her *murderer*...seated across from her in a rocking chair. He smiled at her, bobbing forward and backward. "I don't know what it is, but it cost a pretty penny. I swear your mother is trying to bankrupt me. We can return it."

Maigo looked down at the gift in her hands. The wrapping paper was thick, gold and perfect. A store job. Nothing personal about it. And it was heavy.

"That's not for you," said a deeper, angrier voice. Maigo flinched as General Lance Gordon stepped out from behind the Christmas tree. He held a steaming mug in his black hands. His face looked human, but his eyes glowed orange.

Maigo sneered at the two men. She was strong enough to deal with them both. "Leave. Now."

The men chuckled in unison.

"Leave?" Tilly said.

"We're both a part of you," Gordon said, and then he looked at Tilly. "Or is she a part of us? Doesn't matter. Either way, you're stuck with us. Forever." He pointed at the gift in her hands. "But that...we don't like it."

"Anything you two don't like has to be a good thing," Maigo said, and she tore into the gift. With each rip of paper, her apprehension grew. Gifts could be burdens. The packaging was white, red and black, but the logos and images were blurred. With just a single shred of paper still covering the plastic window behind which was some kind of toy, she paused. Her father and Gordon stared down at her, looking serious, but not really complaining, or acting mortified. Was she being manipulated? Did they want her to open the gift?

She decided to go with the standby advice of her new father: Screw it.

She tore the paper away, revealing a masked metal face with glowing red eyes.

"Hey, Sleeping Beauty," the mask said. "Wake up."

Maigo flinched away, gasping and swatting at the air.

Lilly ducked away unscathed. "Geez! Night terror much?"

"It was Christmas," Maigo said, rubbing her eyes and stretching.

"With Hudson?" Lilly asked. She knew about their occasional psychic meeting place. Everyone on the team did. It was part of her dad's policy of full disclosure. Secrets got people killed. Was sneaking out with the X-35 any different than keeping secrets? She could have told him how she felt. He might have even come with her. But Lilly hadn't given her time to process all that. She couldn't blame her though. Lilly was impulsive, and Maigo knew it. But something about this island, about what was hidden beneath it...*that* was a secret Maigo needed to uncover alone. *As alone as I can be with Lilly and a few hundred Russians.* She would tell the others everything just as soon as she and Lilly were on their way home.

Maigo pushed herself up. "Ugh, with Gordon. And my father. The one that killed me. The old me, anyway."

"Sounds fun," Lilly said, and held out a black mask. "It's time."

Maigo took the mask while Lilly put on her own. Lilly's entire body was black fur, head to toe, but she still wore body armor to protect against bullets, and a mask to conceal her feline identity. While the FC-P was now a very public agency, Lilly and Maigo were their best kept secrets.

"Have they found anything?" Maigo looked down at the floor where the action far below was projected. She could see black circles amidst the men still walking back and forth.

"They drilled a bunch of holes. Not too deep. Maybe fifteen feet. Haven't found anything. But they're just guessing." Masked and cloaked in black armor, the only part of Lilly that looked like Lilly were her yellow, feline eyes. "What about us? Are *we* guessing, too?"

Maigo pulled on her mask and motioned to the cockpit with her head. "Take us closer."

Lilly's squinting eyes hinted at a smile before she bounded for the cockpit and slid behind the controls. Maigo barely felt the shift in motion, but the view below grew larger as they descended. "Stop us ten feet from the ground."

They came to a stop just a few feet above the heads of two Russian soldiers. One of them sucked on a cigarette, its orange glow bright in the bleak night. Then he turned his face upward, looking right at Maigo, and blew smoke from his nostrils. He laughed and spoke to his partner. Then they wandered off, patrolling the island.

"Move toward the center of the island," Maigo said.

They slid through the air without making a sound, passing more soldiers, scientists and holes leading nowhere.

Then the tug returned. Maigo ground her teeth and resisted its influence. "Here. Stop."

She worried the pull on her would continue. That she would end up in another trance, but it left as fast as it came this time.

Lilly leaped into the cargo bay. "Right spot?"

Maigo looked down and saw a bore hole. They'd managed to hit the right area, but hadn't gone deep enough. "Do you have the remote?"

Lilly pulled the device from her pocket. It was small, with simple controls, but it let her operate the X-35's most basic functions, including the rear hatch. It would allow them to get back inside when they were done, hopefully with whatever was buried beneath the island.

"Let's go," Maigo said.

Lilly turned off the interior lights. The hatch lowered without a sound. Even with the hatch wide open, they would be hard to see. Just an absence, or bending, of stars. Lilly's squinted eyes revealed a smile again. "Insert witty Hollywood catchphrase here," she said, and then jumped.

Maigo leapt into the dark behind her, hoping they wouldn't start an international incident.

Lilly landed beside the pit, with catlike grace, scanning the area for danger and then using the remote to send the X-35 a thousand feet up, after Maigo leapt.

Maigo dropped right inside the pit, falling twenty-five feet before landing with the same ease other people feel when hopping off a single step. The drop didn't frighten her, but what she saw at the bottom did.

Lilly leaned over the top, her body a silhouette surrounded by a circle of Arctic stars. "Uhh, something wonky is going on. Everyone is clearing out."

"It's because these aren't test pits," Maigo said, looking at the digital display counting down from ten. "They're drilling holes. For explosives. Run!"

Maigo leapt for the opening. Lilly didn't need to help her out, but caught her arm anyway. "How much time?"

Maigo just shoved her and ran, counting down the seconds in her head. But they didn't just need to get away from the one drilling hole—they needed to clear a field of them. She headed for the domed, prefab base, which was no doubt set up in a spot free of explosives.

"Three," she whispered.

Lilly glanced at her. "What?"

"Two..."

Lilly's eyes went wide.

"One..."

Maigo grabbed hold of Lilly's back, picked her up off the ground and heaved. Lilly soared through the air, arcing over the domed base. Maigo took two more steps before she felt a burst of heat, a slap of energy and then the rush of wind against her face. Like Lilly, she'd been flung through the air. Unlike Lilly, she'd also been scorched, compressed and knocked unconscious by the explosion that covered the island's core, reducing stone, grass and countless bird nests into dust.

10

Night has arrived, cloaking untold destruction in darkness, and bringing nothing but questions. All we really know is that something big crashed—scratch that—was *propelled* into the Gulf of Maine, creating a tidal wave that wreaked havoc with coastal cities between Cape Cod, which was all but washed away, and Portland, Maine. Homes and businesses have been destroyed. Entire cities are flooded. The official death toll won't be known for weeks, maybe months, but it's probably going to eclipse three hundred thousand. For all of Nemesis's rampaging, she was never responsible for wholesale destruction like this.

I'm not even sure what to be angry at. An asteroid? Thor swan diving from Byfrost, the Rainbow Bridge? Something else? Something worse? The impact site is underwater. The military is searching where they *think* the object landed, but so far, it's just empty ocean and lots of dead fish.

A second object is believed to have touched down in the Pacific, but the waves that reached the West Coast, Japan and other island nations, were far less severe. Maybe water depth played a role. Or its distance from land. Or maybe it just slowed down. We might not *know* what it is, but I have a short list of suspects, and none of them are benign. But without an actual enemy to shoot at or run away from, my hands are tied. The New England seacoast has been declared an emergency zone, and crews from across the nation are already filing in to help, but my gut tells me they'll be forced to turn around before arriving.

I grip the balcony railing outside the Crow's Nest kitchen and look up at the stars. I've spent a lot of nights out here, sometimes alone, more often with company. Being in the heart of a city with 40,000 people, I don't get to see a whole lot of stars. But tonight...surrounded by a city without power and wiped clean of homes, the night sky is alive.

"C'mon, you bastards," I grumble. "Show yourselves."

A lone satellite sparkles as it glides past, far overhead. It could be beaming a TV signal down to Earth, receiving GPS data or helping in the search for answers. At least it's doing something other than waiting. Cooper and Watson are overseeing the rescue efforts, but we're leaving the details to the people who do it for a living. Without some kind of weirdness to focus on, we're just bystanders.

I hear the kitchen door open and close. I know it's Collins before she's standing beside me. Anyone else would have said something before joining me.

"Anything new?" I ask.

Her hands slide up on my shoulders and squeeze. "Nothing actionable."

"Big Diomede?"

"Satellite coverage in five minutes." She runs her knuckles down my back on either side of my spine, smoothing out the tension.

"Has Watson found a way to track the girls yet?" I ask.

Collins's hands stop on my back. "You heard me say, 'nothing actionable,' right?"

I turn to face her. She's dressed in black field-ops garb, minus the body armor. Ready to go. "What about our visitors?"

Collins points past me to the lawn off to the left of the property. I can barely make them out, sitting in the grass, talking lightly. One of them laughs. At least they're a resilient bunch. Weird, but resilient.

Collins leans on the rail beside me. "Cooper wants them here until the roads are clear and power restored. They didn't seem disappointed."

And why would they be? Not only are they fans of the fictionalized exploits of the FC-P and Nemesis, but the Crow's Nest, unlike most of the seacoast, has power. We have a battery backup good for forty-eight hours and then a propane generator with a full tank. If power takes weeks to restore, we'll still be shining bright.

Her hand slides down to mine, our fingers interlinking. "You worried about her?"

"Worried I won't have a chance to kick her ass. Both of their asses." I shake my head, trying to come up with a reason Lilly and Maigo would desert us. Even if they were going out for a joy ride, they would have come back the moment that white light cut through the sky. Them not being here means something bad has happened.

"Kids do this kind of thing," she says.

"You had an invisible super-sonic flying machine when you were a teenager? I didn't. And they're *not* kids. Not really."

"They're young and impulsive, regardless of whether or not they can jump off buildings or pick up cars." She lets go of my hand, takes hold of my cheek and turns my face toward her. "Have you considered the possibility that they had a good reason to leave?"

They've been part of this team for a while. They perform well on all field missions. Even Lilly. She used to be a cocky little shit, but now she's a team player. Maybe they're being teenagers, but there's also a chance they're doing what they think is best for all of us...something that only the two of them could do.

I stare at her for a moment. "Asses are getting kicked, one way or the other."

She smiles and kisses me. "Without a doubt."

The window above us bongs twice. Watson is in the window waving us up, a frantic look in his eyes. We run through the house, up the flight of stairs and stumble into the Crow's Nest operations center before Watson can step away from the window. The open concept space that takes up the entire third floor of the house is less spacious than it used to be. There are more workstations spread out around the hardwood floor, to accommodate our burgeoning staff. The brick walls are all but covered with maps, screens and white boards bearing the faded scrawl of investigations come and gone. A lot has changed in the past three years, when the office was mostly empty and boring, but it feels more like home than ever.

"Over here," Watson says, heading for his workstation. Since becoming a married man, and a father, Watson has improved his image. He's lost weight, cut his hair and improved his wardrobe. Honestly, I think Cooper dresses him. But all of that polish has been worn away. His hair is a mess. His shirt hangs open. And he looks hopped up on caffeine.

Cooper, despite being married to Captain Disheveled, and the mother of a toddler, has managed to keep her schoolmarm appearance intact: power suit unruffled, black hair pulled back tight, black-rimmed glasses in place, perfectly accentuating her olive skin, a gift from her black father and white mother. She's also on the phone, talking in rapid, hushed tones, so I head for Watson.

He sits at his new workstation, the curved screens creating a semicircle around him. He says it's the future, and the nerds at Zoomb agree, but seeing a screen in my periphery fills me with nausea. Charts, statistics and scrolling bits of code fill the expansive screen, but it's the series of photographs in the center display that catches my attention. Despite the view being in reverse black and white thermal imaging, I recognize the view from above, because I saw it in person earlier today: Big Diomede.

The island is crawling with soldiers. A small domed base has been set up. A prefab of some kind. A series of small black holes pock the surface of the island, though they only look small from far overhead. Up close they must be a few feet wide. Helicopters circle the island. How did they know? How the hell did they find us? "When was this taken?"

"Five minutes ago."

"Can we get closer?"

The image shifts to a full screen view, wrapping around us. We zoom in, seeing the Russian soldiers in sharp detail, the heat of their exposed faces blazing stark white. Watson scans across the island, pausing over each soldier and hole.

"What are the holes for?" Collins asks.

"No clue," Watson says. "But they're all in this part of the island. Nothing near the new structure."

"Hold on," I put one hand on Watson's shoulder and point past his head, to a gray speck inside one of the holes. "What is that?"

"I was getting to that," Watson says, zooming in on the small rectangle of heat. "Pretty sure it's explosives. The heat is from a timer."

"What makes you think—"

The image switches view. A white hot fireball covers a large portion of the island's core.

"Over here," Collins says, pointing to the far left area of the curved screen. "Look."

A lone person with a feminine figure, clothed in black from head to toe, most of her heat signature cloaked, stands in the face of the explosion, arms raised protectively. While the woman stands against the force of the explosion, debris and flames blow past her. There's only one woman on Earth who could stand up to that kind of force, and I've come to call her my daughter. "They went back to the island."

"I don't see Lilly," Collins says.

"Don't see Lilly where?" Joliet stands behind us. She's a petite, blonde, French Canadian, generally as intimidating as a baby duckling, but when she's angry, she's a lot more frightening than Lilly at her worst. We part, so she can see the image. She takes a deep breath, displaying admirable self-control.

"You're going to have to get in line for the ass kicking," Collins says.

"If they're alive," Joliet says, all her anger melting into concern.

"Do we have the next image?" I ask.

Watson minimizes the image and opens a folder. "Just came in." After a quick double-click, the image expands and we see what has become of the island.

"Hell," I say.

The center of the island is partially concealed by smoke and debris, though much of the stone surface has been flung away. But I can still see enough to know the island is more important than we first thought. Where there had been flat stone and patches of grass, there were now three, perfectly smooth rings, one inside of the other, all connected by a central line.

"Whatever is under there, we don't want the Russians to get it," Watson says.

"We need to get over there," Joliet says. She hasn't been on a field mission since being shot a year ago, but the look in her eyes says not even a Kaiju could stop her. Unfortunately, international borders can.

And honestly, the Atlantean *whateveritis* isn't my biggest concern at the moment. "Can you find her again?"

Watson zooms in and scrolls to the left, nearly reaching the domed structure. Maigo is sprawled on her back. All of her limbs are intact, but that doesn't mean she's okay. And the line of rifle-wielding soldiers filing toward her is a very bad thing.

"Look for signs of Lilly and Betty," I say to Watson. "And send every incoming satellite image to my—"

"We have incoming!" The volume and suddenness of Cooper's normally restrained voice makes everyone jump.

"What is it?" I ask.

"Could be Nemesis." Cooper turns on one of many view screens now positioned around the Crow's Nest. We can get video from just about any TV station, CCTV camera and military feed in the world—at least from cooperating nations, which includes all of NATO and a few that want into NATO. The feed displayed on the screen is infrared, looking down from a helicopter.

Surrounded by cold blue ocean is a body displayed in bright white, yellows and oranges. It's something close to an amorphous blob. The outline is distorted by water, but it's huge and moving. Fast.

"ETA?" I ask.

"Just over an hour."

I point at the video feed. "Where is this?"

"Above Wildcat Knoll," she says. "Forty five miles out."

"Do I want to know which direction it's heading?" I ask.

"Do you have to ask?" Cooper raises an eyebrow. And the answer to her question is, *No, I don't freaking have to ask.* Because we're a magnet for this crap. "How do you want to proceed?"

I look at the colorful infrared image again. "It's not Nemesis."

All heads turn toward me.

"The shape is wrong," I explain. "And it's swimming with its legs, not its tail. I don't even *see* a tail."

"Does its identity have any bearing on our response?" Cooper asks. And that's the million dollar question.

If this *is* Nemesis, with Endo as her 'voice,' then he/she/it/they might not be coming here to lay waste to the Massachusetts coastline. Not that there's much left to lay waste to. But that can't matter. Where Nemesis goes, destruction follows.

"No," I reply. "Hit it with everything we have in the area, from a safe distance. Nemesis or not, I want it reduced to a lifetime supply of chum before it reaches land."

As we start to disperse to our various stations, Joliet takes my arm in her hand. "What about the girls?"

That last image of Maigo laying on her back, about to be captured by Russian soldiers flashes through my mind. They're half a world away, beyond our legal reach, and without Future Betty, our physical reach. "They're on their own."

"They don't need to be," Hawkins says, arms crossed, his anger barely contained. But is he upset that the girls have screwed the pooch, or that I've declared them a second priority? Probably both. I'm not a fan of the situation, either. "Send me after them."

"How are we supposed to send—"

"Don't send Dustin Dreyling," he says, using the name we gave him. It's a cover. None of us use the name, but it's on his ID badge, and his true identity, Mark Hawkins, is now a ghost. Technically, he doesn't exist, just like Lilly. Unlike me, he has remained out of the public eye. No one would recognize him if he was caught. But there is still the question of transportation.

"You have the President's ear," he says, one step ahead of me. "We know there are options." He's referring to a ride I took on a supersonic stealth transport a few years back. It could whisk him from here to the other side of the planet nearly as fast as Future Betty. The VTOL plane could pick him up anywhere there was room, like at Hurd stadium, just down the street. But they wouldn't be able to drop him off. And he once again shows he's thought this through.

"If they can get me there, I can jump."

"Over the Bering Strait?" Joliet says, her shock finally catching up with her. "Onto a Russian island? It's a small target, Mark. If you miss—"

"They are our daughters," he says, looking from my eyes to Joliet's. "They might not have been born to us, but they're still ours. I was raised by a man who wasn't my father, too, and he would have given his life for mine. Would have risked starting a war to save me if he could. It's our job to put them first."

"I don't know," I say. It's a compelling argument, but being the Director of the FC-P means that I'm in charge of protecting millions of sons and daughters around the world.

Hawkins leans in close and says, "You know what they'll do to them if they're captured, right?"

"You should have led with that," I say, and pull out my phone. A speed-dialed call to the U.S. President later, and the gears start spinning. Hawkins will reach the far side of the country around the same time the rest of us rendezvous with the big-ass something cruising toward the coast.

11

"The Dalai Lama said that sleep is the best meditation," said a deep voice with a trace of electronic distortion. "He was speaking of dreams, of course, of how the subconscious mind can work through problems while the body and conscious mind slumber. It's not really meditation, mind you, that's a simple explanation from a simple mind with simple views of the world and the universe that surrounds it."

Maigo opened her eyes. A man stood above her. He was short and broad, with slicked back hair and a perfectly trained mustache. Dressed in an expensive looking suit coat, he reminded her of her father. But this man wasn't her father. He was Zachary Cole, director of the Genetic Offense Directive. She wasn't surprised by his presence on the island, but she was taken aback by his apparent collusion with the Russians. GOD was a black organization within DARPA. And while Hudson had tried to route the organization through his DHS and White House connections, GOD remained elusive. Now she knew why.

"Not much of a patriot, are you?" Maigo asked and tried to sit up. Restraints snapped her back against a cold metal surface. *Cold,* she thought. *They've taken off my clothes!* She leaned her head up and looked down. Several pairs of handcuffs held her hands to the sides of a bare metal stretcher. Her ankles were restrained in the same way. She had been stripped to her bra and underwear, but most of her body was covered by a long black strap that had been wound around her and winched tight.

"My loyalty doesn't belong to any one nation, but to the human race. The future." Cole leaned closer. "I wonder, what do *you* dream about?"

Maigo lay her head back down and looked at the room. She was inside one of the domed prefab structures. It looked like a medical bay of some kind, stark white and clean. She couldn't see any supplies. Wall mounted cabinets wrapped around the curved sidewall were closed. But the smell, and the stretcher she lay on, smacked of a doctor's office, for healing—not the kind she had to worry about being dissected in.

That opinion changed the moment the door slid open and a second man stepped inside. She recognized him, too. Dr. Alicio Brice. The FC-P had files on both men. Most of the information was from their own experiences, and the images of their faces were hand drawn, but she'd studied them enough to recognize both. Brice looked a good twenty years younger than the sketch.

"Which generation are you?" she asked Brice. The original Alicio Brice had been dead for more than thirty years, but had been cloned multiple times, passing down his mental capabilities and knowledge to each subsequent generation. The first Brice had worked on Island 731, and he had been partially responsible for the monster known as 'Kaiju,' not to mention the Tsuchis. But his work also resulted in Lilly, her best friend.

Brice looked confused for a moment, looking her over. "I'm sorry, have we met?"

"Pretty sure the Brice whose memories you're missing got blowed up," she said, trying to mirror her father's sarcastic confidence, which was often just a show. He'd never admit it, but when things got rough, he got funnier. It kept people off balance, not knowing if he was serious, afraid or just plain nuts.

Brice smiled and ran a hand through his thick blond hair.

"Hasn't started falling out yet," Maigo quipped.

Brice locked his eyes on hers, looked ready to say something, but grinned instead and turned to Cole. "We'll be ready in ten minutes."

"Ready for what?" she asked, showing a crack in her confident veneer.

"For you." Cole folded his hands together over his belly. "We've been studying Atlantean technology for a long time, and while little has survived the ages, what we do have can be utilized only by those with certain genetic predispositions. My intention was to try something...less conventional, but your presence here makes that a risk not worth taking."

"You think I'm going to find the door in?" Maigo asked.

"No, my little Kaiju friend—"

Maigo sneered at the man.

"—I think you're the key to *open* the door. You have a unique genetic code—human, Atlantean *and* Kaiju, that could—"

"How do you know what my genetic code is?" Maigo looked at her bound arm and saw red needle marks. She clenched her fists in anger, but maintained control, doing her own kind of wide awake meditation.

"It's what we do," Brice said, looking a little sheepish. "Your DNA could help us control—"

A look from Cole silenced him. Brice tilted his head in something like shame and took a step back.

Maigo's head swam with questions. About what they'd done to her. About what they would do with her DNA. But none of that mattered right now. "Outside...is that Atlantis?"

Cole chuckled. "Good God, no. If you were an ancient alien civilization far more advanced than the indigenous life, is this frozen hell where you would build a vast city? No, this is where you would go to hide something important. As far as we can tell, Atlantis is in ruins, and even if it was found, it would be entirely unrecognizable."

"Why?"

"Because it was destroyed. By you. Well, not you exactly. More like your grandmother."

"Prime," Maigo said, squeezing her eyes shut. She tried her best to look calm as ancient memories transported through alien DNA resurfaced. She remembered a city. The screams. Red eyes. And a face. A *metal* face.

She opened her eyes and gasped when she saw Cole leaning right over her, staring into her eyes. "You...*remember?*"

Maigo shook her head.

"You *do*, don't you?" He turned to Brice. "We've underestimated her importance. When you're done here, sedate her and bring her with you."

"But Hudson," Brice says. "You promised him—"

"Promises are for presidential candidates and middle school girls," Cole said. "The FC-P has proven itself irrelevant and woefully unprepared for what is coming." He turned his attention back to Maigo. "Aside from you, showing up here alone. You felt it, didn't you? Knew it was here? We had feared our intelligence had been intercepted, that the X-35 might be used to infiltrate Russian territory. God knows, your 'father'—" He made chubby-fingered air quotes, "—is brazen enough to try it. But the island was empty, until your poorly timed arrival."

"Sir," Brice said. "What if she's not alone?"

Cole squinted. "They would have come for her by now. They're not without the means. Nor is this one." He motioned to Maigo's arm. "Best to keep her partially sedated."

Brice gave a quick nod, opened a drawer and started preparing a syringe.

"The X-35 *is* out there, isn't it?" He turned to Brice. "Have the men look for it. If you can't find it, feel free to *persuade* her cooperation in the matter. Learning her...tolerances will be enlightening."

"Yes, sir," Brice said, and he stepped *through* Cole on his way to the stretcher. The big man shimmered for a moment and rolled his eyes at Brice. *Another hologram,* Maigo thought. Cole rarely made in-person appearances, which given his work—creating genetic monstrosities to be used as weapons—the precaution made sense. *How many Brice clones have they lost over the years?*

Maigo tensed as Brice leaned closer with the needle. Before she could pull away, he put a hand on her arm and said, "It's only a sedative. It will make you sleepy, but not knock you out." Then he winked. And it wasn't in a creepy way, like he was getting his jollies from giving her an injection. The wink was conspiratorial. Like he wanted her to trust him. She didn't, but she still wanted to see how this played out. She was gambling with her life, with her future, but that came with the job, didn't it? Her life had stopped being a cakewalk the moment General Gordon had pulled her heart from her chest and triggered her transformation into Nemesis.

The needle slid into her arm without a trace of pain. She watched the clear fluid slide into her arm. Then Brice withdrew the needle and stepped back, keeping his eyes on Maigo's. "She shouldn't be any trouble now."

He's telling me to play along. But is this a game? Are they manipulating me?

The only way to find out was to play along.

She feigned sleepiness.

Before she could test out her groggy act and try to get more information from Cole, he turned to the side like someone was speaking to him. Then he looked genuinely surprised by something. Concerned. "Yes, yes. It must be there for the triad. Let them loose." Annoyance swept over his normally calm features. "I realize that, but there is little choice. Set them loose!"

Cole steadied himself with a deep breath and waited for his face to fade to a lighter shade of red before facing Brice again. "Take care of this quickly. Things are progressing in Boston and Tokyo. We need to get inside, *now*. Understood?"

"Y-yes, sir, "Brice said.

"Do keep in mind that unlike me, you are very, very expendable."

"Yes. Sir." Brice squinted subtly at Cole's back.

Was that defiance in his eyes?

"Kozlov," Cole said, and the door opened immediately.

A brutish and scruffy looking man dressed in a parka and carrying an AK-47 stepped into the room. "Sir." His Russian accent was thick.

"Contact me the moment you gain entry," Cole said.

"Sir."

"And if you run into any trouble—"

"Any incursion by foreign agencies will be treated as an act of war, and we will respond accordingly."

Cole nodded to Maigo, looking a little annoyed. "I was talking about her. If she causes any trouble, use the Leshiy."

The big Russian paled, but managed a fervent "Yes, sir."

Cole turned to face someone none of them could see, saying, "Leave Boston be. Focus on Japan." Then he flickered and was gone.

Brice cleared his throat and turned to Kozlov. "We'll just be a minute. Then I'll need a few men to carry her out."

Kozlov sneered at Brice, who apparently wasn't normally in a position to boss the big Russian around. "The men are deployed around the island. It will take time to—"

"She's been sedated," Brice said. "We need to transport her to the doorway at the center of the rings and allow her to make physical contact. It's the only way we can get inside."

Maigo didn't feel tired at all, and felt certain Brice's words were really meant for her. But was it a trick?

Brice took her wrist in his hand, the multiple handcuffs clanging against the rail. It took all her will power to not react to his touch. "She's nearly ready," Brice said, monitoring her pulse. "Four men, please. She's heavier than she looks."

Kozlov grunted and turned toward the exit. It was as close to a 'yes, sir,' as Brice was going to get. When the door closed, Brice leaned in close to her. "Where are the rest of you? Are they on the island? In the X-35?"

"You're trying to trick me," Maigo said.

Brice shook his head, but it looked something more like a manic twitch. He looked genuinely nervous.

"The injection was saline," he said. "You got my photo? The stone. The symbol?"

"That was you? Why?"

"We're born, sort of, with the same body. The same knowledge. But not the memories. Not the experience. We're not all identical where it matters."

He rapid-fire tapped his head, and then his heart. "We're not all insane, though I will admit we are genetically predisposed to greed and ambition. But some of us are not part of all this by choice. I sent you the image because I have seen what GOD does with alien DNA. They justify it because of what's coming. Fire with fire. Monsters with monsters. But there is a point when we become the monsters, when we lose our humanity, when it becomes not worth the cost of saving it."

"So helping me is you saving your humanity?" Maigo asked.

"You can understand that," he said. "Can't you?"

She glared at him for a moment and then said, "Yes."

"I can set you free," he said. "Give you a head start. But once they know you're missing, you're on your own." He pulled a key from his pocket and reached for the first pair of handcuffs.

Maigo lifted her arms, feeling a moment of resistance before the chain links stretched and snapped. She reached down and tore through the polyester straps like they were duct tape. Once they were loose enough, she pulled her legs up, breaking the cuffs around her ankles, and then yanking them off, as well as the ones on her wrists. She swung herself around on the table and hopped onto her bare feet. "I can handle myself."

Brice staggered back and caught himself on a counter. "I-I can see that."

Maigo looked down at her black bra and underwear. "Clothes?"

"Uhh."

"Nevermind." Maigo said. The cold wouldn't bother her much, and the white lab clothes Brice wore would stand out even more than her slightly tan skin. "What's a Leshiy?"

"Russian folklore. The 'one in the woods.' The name was chosen to...intimidate our comrades, but it is somewhat appropriate, given the creature's tendencies. It—"

Maigo's attention snapped to the door. There were footsteps outside. Someone was coming. "This is for your own good," she said quickly, and then snatched Brice's throat in her hand.

The door opened and Kozlov stepped inside. "If we are to—" The big man froze for a moment when he saw Maigo, upright and clutching Brice. He reached for his weapon, but before he could reach it, Brice crashed into him and both men went down. Maigo stood over the two men, cocked a fist back and knocked the Russian unconscious with one well placed, and carefully controlled punch.

She looked down at Brice, who was cringing in fear. "Thank you." He nodded, and she started to step away, but stopped. "And if I were you, I'd let him wake up first."

"Right," Brice said. He didn't move.

Leaving the two men on the floor, Maigo entered the hallway connecting two of the domed sections and opened an outer hatch.

Frigid wind swirled inside, biting her skin. Then she stepped out into the darkness and snuck around the side of the building until she saw the three-ringed structure revealed by the explosion, now lit up by a circle of halogen lamps. She would glow like a road flare under all that light.

Just get to the center, she told herself, repeating Brice's advice. *Make physical contact with the door.* "Easy peasy, half-Japanesey," she whispered, trying to channel her adoptive father again. Then she ran into the light, and all hell broke loose.

12

"Just like old times!" Woodstock shouts over the chop of Helicopter Betty's rotors.

I climb up into the passenger seat of the red Bell 407 holding a hard black case stamped with the Zoomb logo. I've never been a fan of the Zoomb name, logo or their personal history of meddling in secret projects, but now that I'm the primary shareholder with access to those secret projects and enough money to have a Scrooge McDuck gold-coin swimming vault, I'm learning to deal with it. In general, I try to keep Zoomb projects separate from the FC-P, but on special occasions, like when a space monster is swimming toward the coast of Massachusetts, I make exceptions.

There will likely be blowback from my superiors and the military when they discover Zoomb has been developing anti-Kaiju weapons systems, but if it works, they'll get on board. And then probably place an order for themselves. I'd like to say I can trust DARPA to develop these kinds of weapons, but there's no way to know if GOD still has an influence there. I find that 'Jon's rule of thumb' from my college days applies to government organizations as much as it does to women: if she makes you burn when you pee, let her be. Solid life advice I will never say aloud now that I'm married and a father, but Hawkins has heard it.

I pat the hard case on my lap. "Not quite."

Collins climbs into the back and slams the sliding door shut. She's seated next to an FN MAG machine gun that's loaded and ready to go, but probably won't be very useful. We should have upgraded the weapon to something a little more hardhitting, but with Future Betty, I didn't think we'd need Helicopter Betty for combat again. The weapon probably won't do much damage to what's coming, but it can be a useful distraction tool, just in case we feel like incentivizing something to eat us.

"Take us up," I say, but I don't really need to. We're already lifting off the Crow's Nest rooftop. My thoughts shift to the girls for a moment, worry clouding my mind. *They can take care of themselves,* I tell myself. Physically, they're unmatched, but they've already proved themselves lacking common sense.

As we head out over the open ocean, barely visible in the half-moon light, I turn my attention back to the task ahead of us. Something Kaiju-sized—but not Nemesis—is coming our way. And before we just let something new savage this already ruined stretch of coast, we're going to, at the very least, shoot the shit out of it. At the most...I look down at the case in my hands...we're going to field test the *Swarm.*

I toggle my headset, which is patched into Devine, but currently transmitting only between us and the Crow's Nest. "Do we have eyes on the target?"

Cooper responds, calm and collected. "Forty miles out. Trajectory now has it headed toward Boston."

The city has spent the past three years rebuilding. Hundreds of years of history were lost in Nemesis's assault on the city, but the country rallied around its rebuilding, just as they had for Washington, D.C. and the West Coast cities that were destroyed a year ago. To let Boston get decimated again, just as it's picking itself back up in good ol' Yankee fashion would be a crushing blow to the country's morale. To the world's.

"What's our ETA?" I ask Woodstock.

"Between our speed and its," he says, chewing on his bottom lip. "Ten minutes, give or take."

"Get us above the action," I tell him. "Cooper, I want the Navy to torpedo the crap out of this thing in ten minutes. Drive it to the surface.

Then the Navy and Air Force can unleash hell in unison. But...tell them that in a more official sounding way."

"Always do," she says. "What if it's like Nemesis? The orange membranes?"

"We'll be far enough from the coast," I say. "Doesn't matter what it looks like, or if it will explode with nuclear force. We need to stop it before it reaches the coast."

"Should we consider nuclear options?" she asks, still calm. It's the one thing we haven't really tried, in part because it would cost human lives, but also because Nemesis survives detonations of that magnitude, sans the radiation, on a regular basis. With such a high price tag, and no evidence to support its effectiveness, that option has remained off the table. And I'm not about to be the one to put it on the table. I have no illusions going into this fight. If this creature is anything like Nemesis, we're not going to kill it now, nuke or not. We *are* going to hit it with the equivalent force of several nukes, but the best I'm hoping for is to deter the thing. Turn it around. Give us time to regroup. Because so far, the only way to kill a Kaiju, is with another Kaiju. And Nemesis hasn't been seen in a long time.

"No. I want MOABs in the air, though," I tell Cooper. "Ask them to drop a few on its head...if it has one."

"Better keep your distance," she says.

"I'll take us up to fifteen thousand," Woodstock says. "Should be plenty of wiggle room."

The minutes tick as we rise high above the Atlantic, the monotonous chop of the helicopter broken up by status reports. Two Ohio class nuclear submarines are giving chase. If we wanted the nuclear option, they'd provide it. A third Virginia class fast-attack submarine stands between the monster and Boston. The subs will kick things off by launching an array of Mark 48 torpedoes designed for sinking other subs. Once the creature hits the surface, they'll follow up the torpedoes with cruise missiles. They're joined by two Zumwalt class destroyers. The ship's stealthy build won't help it against a Kaiju, but distance will. They'll be miles away when they launch Tomahawk missiles. And all of that will be joined by the most advanced aircraft from the U.S. Navy and

Air Force: five brand new F-35s and five F-22 Raptors, not to mention a B-2 bomber carrying more than a few MOABs. While the Mother Of All Bombs didn't stop Nemesis in Boston, and very nearly killed me, it's the biggest non-nuclear option we have. It's the biggest boom we can make without the threat of fallout peppering the already battered New England coast.

This all feels like déjà vu. We've been down this conventional warfare road before, and we got nothing for it. But until the slightly less conventional Swarm arrives, we're stuck with weapons that blow up.

"Target in sight," Woodstock says, pulling me from my mental inventory.

"How'd you see it from—" Collins leans forward, between the front seats, and sees what's ahead at the same time I do. "Oh."

While the creature is definitely below the water, its position is easy to see, thanks to its gleaming white body. But is it glowing, or simply reflecting the moon's light? I glance up at the half-moon. *Glowing,* I decide. *A bioluminescent Kaiju.*

I toggle Devine so the FC-P and all military assets in the area can hear me. "To all U.S. Military in the Gulf of Maine, participating in Operation—" I switch Devine over to Cooper. "Coop, did we name the operation?"

"Blockade One," she says.

"That's a horrible name," I say and switch Devine back to the military broadcast. "—Blockade One, this is FC-P Director Jon Hudson. If you are prepared, please indicate by—"

The smart phone connecting me to Devine vibrates in my hand. The screen shows a series of green lights appearing next to the names of ships, subs and aircraft. In less than a second, all have indicated their readiness. And they're all seeing the same thing.

"On my mark," I say and switch off Devine. "Take us in a wide circle, counterclockwise. I want to see this."

Helicopter Betty banks hard to the left and then cuts a slow right-hand circle around the target area. As we come up behind the creature's backside, I marvel at its size, even from this far up.

Is it bigger than Nemesis?

Doesn't matter.

I toggle Devine back to the military channel and say, "Phase one, fire, fire, fire."

My phone vibrates. The names of the three subs are blinking. The message 'Torpedoes away,' appears beside each of the names.

It takes a few seconds to see any real world results, but then several dull white streaks slide up behind the massive shape. The bubble trails *are* reflecting the moon's light. And then there are too many to count.

"Here we go," Collins says, peering out the side window.

The first torpedo strikes with a plume of white. It's followed by more and more, until the water behind the creature churns. Water cascades into the air, propelled by the explosive force, but nothing else rises.

Streaks from the east cut into view, heading toward the creature's head, and torpedoes continue to detonate behind it. They strike with equal force, but the result is far more explosive. A mountain of white frothy water bursts hundreds of feet up into the air. For a moment, I think someone has prematurely dropped a MOAB, but then a shape resolves amidst the foam. A massive, luminous white body lifts itself free of the water, extending two ape-like arms up toward the sky, and issuing an angry roar that shakes my insides.

Bolstered by phase one's success, I shout, "Phase two, go, go—"

My third 'go' gets lost in my throat as the behemoth turns free of the exploding waters and turns its head in our direction.

"Oh my god," Collins says. "Is that..."

"Cthulhu," I say. "Fucking Cthulhu."

13

"Vy! Stoy!" The bellowed Russian words chased her into the light. Maigo didn't understand them, but was fairly certain someone was telling her to stop. The path ahead lay mostly open. The three rings of the Atlantean struc-ture were separated by three-foot-deep, six-foot-wide circuits, cut through by a single raised line, which could act like a walkway toward the center, but was far to the right. Rocky debris covered everything, most of it dust, but some the size of desks, which would make good cover.

But I won't be taking cover, she decided. If she stopped, she'd get pinned, and if that happened, she would be dead. Russian soldiers weren't just chasing her. They were everywhere. She could see them on all sides of the Atlantean structure, raising their weapons toward the mostly naked woman bolting through the night.

"Rasstrelyat'!" came the voice again, this time quickly drowned out by the sounds of automatic gunfire.

Maigo dove forward and rolled. Bullets pinged off a rock as she passed. She planned to follow through back to her feet and keep running, but halfway through the roll, she reached the first ring. She fell inside the ring, dropping three feet, flat onto her back. The solid metal surface drove the air from her lungs, and rough stone scraped her skin.

She hissed in frustration more than from pain and got her feet back under her. Bullets ricocheted off the ring wall, just missing her head and forcing her back down. Pinned after all.

She tried to crawl along the ring's curve, but men were closing in on all sides.

Nowhere to go.

She glanced up past the halogen lamps' glare, to the faint image of the stars above.

Almost nowhere.

"Don't shoot!" she shouted, hoping the Russians would understand more English than she did Russian. She raised her hands up, but stayed down in a crouch, getting her bare feet beneath her, ignoring the sting of cold metal. "Don't shoot!"

"Vstavat'," a man said behind her.

She turned her eyebrows up and stuck out a quivering lip before looking over her shoulder at the man. "W-where am I?" she sobbed, looking frail and lost.

The man's AK-47 turned slightly. If she attacked, he might be able to bring it to bear, but she had no intention of attacking. Just as the man opened his mouth to issue some sort of order, and before his comrades arrived, Maigo heaved herself up. She left the ground behind and sailed up into the darkness above the halogen lamps.

The men below turned their weapons up and fired at the night sky, but had nothing to aim at. Bullets buzzed around her, but none struck home as she arced over the ancient site and descended toward its core.

She landed without a sound, employing the techniques taught to her by the naturally lithe Lilly, whose fate was still unknown. She'd thrown her clear of the explosion, and probably the base, but had Lilly been injured? Maigo doubted it. Like all good cats, Lilly always landed on her feet and could handle drops that seemed impossible to master, even for the stronger Maigo.

As soundless as Maigo was, her body still glowed like a beacon in the harsh light.

"Tam!" someone shouted. She turned and saw a man on the far side of the rings lift his AK-47 toward her. She saw the perfectly round barrel and knew it was aimed at her head. Right between the eyes.

The soldier pulled the trigger, but his shot cut through the empty sky instead of her head. He'd been jerked back and thrown out of the light. A shadow pounced on him and then slid through the darkness, bounding with ridiculous agility and a complete lack of fear. "Go, girl, go!" Lilly's shout was followed by the scream of a man caught off guard, and then an "oof!"

Lilly was providing a counteroffensive.

Maigo leapt for the center of the structure and was pursued by bullets. Before she was struck, a second weapon joined in, this one targeting the lamps. With a spray of sparks, the halogens burst in rapid succession, plunging the site into darkness.

Maigo fell atop the center of the structure, a broad slab of cold metal. She squeaked to a stop as her skin rubbed against the surface. Before she could stand, a loud clunk reverberated beneath her. *Physical contact,* Maigo thought, recalling Brice's words. *It's the only way inside.* The clunk was followed by nine more, and then the floor fell away, taking her down with it.

Maigo coughed as the floor came to an abrupt halt. Had she been... human, the impact would have broken bones. She glanced up and saw the circular entrance a hundred feet up. *More than broken bones*, she thought. *Another security measure to keep out the unworthy?*

A wave of nausea roared through her body and kept her pinned for a moment. She saw red eyes in her mind again, but they came and went without any additional fanfare. *Preapproved*, she thought, and the sound of gunfire, now far overhead, encouraged her back to her feet.

Find what's down here, she thought, formulating a plan. *Get back to the surface. Find Lilly. Retreat to the X-35. And get the hell out of Mother Russia.*

But when she stood up and looked around, that plan didn't seem quite as simple. She stood on a round platform, twenty feet across, surrounded by black. The ceiling above her was a smooth, stone dome. The Atlanteans had carved out the inside of Big Diomede, creating an enormous space. But how big was it?

"Hello," Maigo shouted, and her voice echoed loud and far, sliding down around her for what must have been hundreds of feet.

Maigo stepped up to the side and looked down. She had better-than-human night vision—not as good as Lilly's, but even Lilly might have had trouble in this soup. She could see just twenty feet down, where a staircase descended, wrapping around what she could now see was a tall spire. The stairs were six feet wide and two feet tall. Not designed for people.

How tall is this thing?

She considered leaping, but there were heights even she couldn't safely land from. There was no choice but to take the stairs. She leapt down the twenty feet and then followed the stairs around. Her bare feet slapped over the smooth metal stairs, and she was forced to slow down as she nearly slipped over the railing-less side. With every revolution downward, the temperature increased. After thirty trips around, she was glad to be dressed for the beach.

How much further? she wondered, and then she had her answer, as the stairs stopped and a walkway led out over the darkness. She crept onto the walkway, testing her weight on the ancient surface and wondering why there were no railings. The Atlanteans seemed to have had little regard for personal safety. Then again, all of this was designed by an alien species that resembled human beings, but stood ten feet tall.

When the floor didn't even wiggle, she stepped out more confidently. She saw a round platform ahead. At its center was a metal sphere standing atop a cone. The top of the sphere rose above her head, out of reach. She stepped onto the platform, looking at the sphere. Aside from its highly reflective surface that bent Maigo's face into something horrible, it was featureless.

She raised her hand toward its surface, ready to test Brice's physical contact theory again, when a voice stopped her.

It came from above, echoing and distorted, but Maigo recognized it as Lilly. "Maigo! It's coming!"

She sounded uncharacteristically worried. Almost like she was in pain. Had she been injured? And what was coming?

It's coming.

A laugh, closer and louder than Lilly's voice ripped through the air. The sound of talons scrabbling against a hard surface filled the air like static.

It.

Leshiy, the Russian monster. But what was it?

She would soon find out, of that there was no doubt. The only way out of here was back out the way she had come, past Leshiy, and past the Russians. But she wasn't worried. She was a monster, too. And while most of the time she hated that truth, there were occasions where she embraced it.

She stood on her tip-toes and placed her hand against the sphere.

She felt a tingle of energy and tried to pull her hand away, but found herself locked in place.

There was a loud thud behind her.

She tried to turn around, but her locked arm restricted her movement. She craned her head around and saw it. A large creature with gray skin, wild tufts of hair and black claws lay motionless at the far side of the walkway. Its back was toward her, but she could see rolls of muscle, bony protrusions along its back and a long, still tail, dangling over the side, into the abyss.

The thing had slipped and fallen.

Leshiy looked like a powerful foe, but clumsy footwork and tall heights don't make good friends. She turned her back on the creature and tried to pull her hand free again. She stopped pulling when the sound of grinding gears and snapping locks roared out all around her. The floor vibrated. Loud clacks issued from far below, repeating every second and bringing orange light to the gloom. The glow rose up beneath her as ancient lights came to life.

And then something giggled.

She looked back over her shoulder. The Leshiy still lay motionless. But then, movement. The long tail dangling over the side twitched. The creature's head lifted off the floor, revealing a purple stain. She saw a face turn toward her, partly human, partly something else. Its snout curled in a sneer, and it let out another laugh. Then the creature sprang into motion, righting itself onto all fours, its forelimbs splayed wide for balance. Its hind legs were curled and ready to pounce. The creature's two human eyes were framed by four more solid red eyes, all squinted, all looking straight at her.

The human parts were easy to recognize, and after a moment of looking, Maigo recognized the rest of it, or at least some of it. GOD was creating chimeras again, as they had done on Island 731, but instead of merging various animal species into something more deadly, they had thrown alien DNA into the mix. In this case, Ferox DNA.

Leshiy hissed and took a step forward.

Orange light blazed around them as the sequence of igniting lamps reached their level with a clack. Leshiy skittered back in surprise. At first, Maigo thought it was strange that the clearly savage creature would react so strongly to light, but then, as it slowly craned its head upward, she realized it was reacting to what the light revealed.

Maigo's hand sprang free from the orb. Then she twisted around and looked into a pair of massive, blazing red eyes.

14

I look down at the bulbous, white head and see eyes as black as night and the size of commuter buses staring back at me.

Not at us, I think, *past us.* Of all the things in the sky right now, Helicopter Betty is the least dangerous.

Pulses of blue-green color ripple through the Kaiju's bulbous, bald head as the tentacles hanging where its mouth should be snap open in an obvious threat display. The shifting colors remind me of a cuttlefish. Unlike the tentacles of squid or octopus, these are not covered in round suckers, but long, sharp spikes. They remind me of pale, white, starfish limbs, and even more like the alien head GOD had floating in a giant tube beneath the sands of Area 51. Its name was Artuke. One of the Aeros.

But while the Kaiju below bears some resemblance to the Aeros, I think this is something different. Created by them, maybe, but not one of them. For starters, it's too big. The thing is standing chest deep in water that descends three hundred feet. And that's with a slight hunch. If it stood up straight, it would be taller than Nemesis. But it also lacks a certain intelligence. There's no way to know how smart this thing is, but I get the impression that this thing is more primal rage than brains. I don't see it flying around the galaxy subjecting planets. No, this isn't the enemy, this is their weapon.

As the ten tentacles spread wide, a circular mouth is revealed. Layers of long, pointed teeth surround the mouth. Layer by layer, the teeth bloom into a kind of death flower, ready to stab and shove food into a mouth big enough to swallow Betty whole. If that wasn't bad enough, a tongue of twitching red tendrils warbles just inside the maw.

The creature is one nasty sonuvabitch. But part of me knows that while this monster, and the alien species that spawned it, are the inspiration for Cthulhu, this isn't the actual monster. Cthulhu was fiction. This...this is real, and deserves its own name. *Lovecraft,* I decide.

Lovecraft's threat comes to an abrupt end as a hellfire missile screams in below us and detonates against the open tentacles. There's a body-shaking roar, first from the explosion, and then from the Kaiju. When the ball of fire fades, I see Lovecraft staggering back, but there's no obvious sign of injury. All tentacles are present and accounted for.

Then it's hit again, this time from the back. The Kaiju spins around in the ocean, lashing out with its massive, ape-like arm. The creature's swinging at something that's already gone, but it manages to swipe a third missile from the sky before it explodes. And then, chaos erupts. Missiles cut through the air from every direction. Torpedoes slide through the water. Enough firepower to sink Atlantis a dozen times over converges on the creature.

And Lovecraft sees it all coming.

Knows what it means. I can see understanding in its black eyes. And then, defiance.

In the face of the U.S. military's Earth-shattering power, the monster doesn't cringe or raise its arms. It stands still, and waits.

Not a good sign.

"Fuck me sideways," Woodstock mumbles. "Thing is either fearless or a tough sumbitch."

"I think it's both," Collins says.

The fusillade of missiles, rockets and torpedoes strike in unison. The Kaiju is lost in the world's most expensive fireworks display, costing untold millions of dollars. Helicopter Betty shakes as a pressure wave slides past like an incoming tide. Smoke billows around the monster, hiding its luminous form even better than the water could.

Far below, three Apache attack helicopters swing low and fly circles around the expanding cloud.

On Devine, the helicopters are displayed as War Party Zero. War Parties One–Three are deployed between us and Boston. I tap the icon and connect to the pilots directly. "War Party Zero, this is Hudson, do you have eyes on the target?" I nearly say, 'Over,' but since Devine works through an encrypted satellite network, there's no need for the standard radio jargon.

"Negative, sir," one of the pilots says. "Target is concealed."

Maybe the thing is pulverized. There's no way to know. But in a situation like this, better safe than sorry. At $14.6 million a pop, MOABs, officially known as GBU-43/B Massive Ordnance Air Blast bombs, are a pricey option, but in this case, I think the expense is justified. The 30,000-pound bunker busters are designed to punch through 200 feet of concrete before detonating. If it can punch through this thing's skin, it should turn the rest of it into a smear. *Should* being the operative word. We *are* dealing with a creature from another planet, most likely created by an advanced civilization, for the express purpose of destroying and/or subjugating entire worlds.

"Get out of there," I tell the pilots. "We're going to—"

"Hold on," a pilot says. "I see something."

Outside the window and far below, I see a flicker of light from within the rising smoke. Did a missile hit late? A few taps on Devine's interface confirms that's not the case.

The light flickers again, this time with clear hues of green and blue.

Shit.

"War Party Zero, get the hell out of—"

An explosion cuts my voice short. One of the helicopters has exploded. The other two are peeling away.

A large, white hand with two fingers and a thumb reaches through the smoke. Pulses of light ripple through the skin, forearm to fingertips. I catch a glimpse of what looks like short wriggling tendrils coating the fingers, and then they're wrapped around the chopper. The Apache explodes, but most of the force is contained within the massive fist.

The lone surviving member of War Party Zero dives to the deck and cruises low over the frothing waters. But the Kaiju somehow sees, or senses the fleeing vehicle. And instead of reaching out and plucking it from the sky, Lovecraft swipes a massive hand through the water, kicking up a wave that wraps around the chopper and pulls it into the sea. No longer mobile and slowly sinking, the Apache is defenseless.

Smoke parts as Lovecraft steps through it, raises a hand and slams it down on the helicopter.

Each Apache held a two-man crew. Our first encounter with this thing has cost six lives, but that's really just the beginning. If this creature reaches the coast...if it moves past the coast and heads inland, like the Tsuchi did a year ago...then a *lot* more people are going to die.

The Kaiju bears the scars of our assault, but they're little more than blackened star bursts from where missiles struck and detonated. There's no blood. No charred skin. Like Nemesis, this thing can handle conventional explosives, but if the MOAB can pierce its skin, there might still be a chance of stopping this thing, or at the very least, turning it around.

With a quick tap on Devine, I give the B-2 bomber the green light to drop not just one MOAB, but three. Their combined might outpowers everything that has hit the creature so far.

"Give us a little more wiggle room," I say to Woodstock, and I feel myself pushed back into my seat as we ascend to 18,000 feet.

There will be no whistle as the first of the three bombs approaches and passes. There'll be no spotting it. No anticipating it. MOABs just arrive. Devine posts a message. The first bomb is away. The B-2 is swinging around for another pass. Unlike many bombs, MOABs aren't dropped in a cluster. They're precision ordnance, guided to the target by GPS, and deployed one at a time. In fact, this is the first time in military history that the bombs will be used in rapid succession. Why? Because usually, one is all you need. It will take just seconds to—

Betty shakes. "What's happening?"

"Gust of wind," Woodstock says, fighting the controls. "Came out of freaking nowhere."

For a moment I worry that we're too close to the target area, that the first MOAB has just missed us, but we're miles away. That's when I see the smoke around the Kaiju. It's swirling as though caught in a cyclone.

"The hell is that?" I ask.

I'm not expecting an answer, but Collins pipes up. "Look above it."

"I don't see anything."

"I saw a red pinpoint of light just before—"

The ocean erupts. The first MOAB has struck, piercing several hundred feet of ocean and detonating. The upheaval of water is massive. Catastrophic. It's also a quarter mile off target, cast aside by what must be category five hurricane winds.

My phone vibrates. The second MOAB has been released.

"There!" Collins says, pointing. And I see it. It's barely visible, but I see the small red light, and then some kind of black sphere, lit up from below by Lovecraft's ambient glow. It's floating a few hundred feet above the Kaiju's head, and it's at the center of the storm.

"Take us closer!" I shout.

"You're nuts," Woodstock says, but he banks Betty hard and flies into the target zone. "Good thing we're both nuts, or this relationship would be in trouble."

"Lower," Collins says, at home in the nut house.

We carve a circle lower, descending thousands of feet fast enough to make my stomach lurch.

The second MOAB strikes, hitting the ocean on the far side of the Kaiju. Betty is jolted by a pressure wave, but the monster has absorbed most of it, without slowing down. Lovecraft takes one long stride out of the smoke, its body in the clear once more, twitching with colorful irritation.

"Down!" I shout. "Go! Go! Go!"

Betty turns in a dive, dropping us toward the black sphere, which I can now easily see. It's silhouetted against the luminous creature below.

"Collins!" I shout. "Do it!"

Fighting gravity, Collins yanks the side door open with a grunt. The cabin fills with a roaring wind. Woodstock has to adjust for it, but has no trouble. We're in the eye of the storm, just above the sphere and about to pass it. Collins shoves the FN MAG machine gun into position and it locks in place. She chambers the first round and leans out into the cutting wind, just as Woodstock arrests our descent and puts us into a tight turn around the sphere. Once we pull alongside it, the wind slams into us, drawing a shout of concern from Woodstock, now fighting for control.

Collins pulls the trigger and holds it down. Over the pounding chopper blades and rushing wind, the staccato boom of the machine gun is deafening. I watch tracer rounds, blazing bright orange, cut through the sky, their trajectories twisted by the wind. Collins compensates for it by aiming to the side of the sphere and letting the wind pull the bullets back on target.

Sparks erupt from the smooth black sphere as high caliber rounds strike its surface. The first five seem to have no effect, but the sixth brings its smooth surface into clear focus. It had been spinning and is now perfectly still.

Devine vibrates my phone.

The third bomb has been released.

With the sphere sitting still, Collins focuses her attack and pours on the lead until the small red light on its surface blinks and goes dark. The sphere falls from the sky and the cyclone fades.

"Get us out of here!" I shout, just a second before the third and final MOAB drops from the sky and strikes its target.

15

Maigo stumbled back from the giant eyes, caught off guard by their serious gaze and proximity. But she hadn't forgotten the creature behind her, and the competing threats twisted her up. She tripped over herself and fell to the floor, her bare skin slapping against the perfectly smooth surface.

The thing called Leshiy burst out laughing, sounding something like a hyena, the cry part humor, part threat, and absolutely grating.

Maigo pounded her fists in the floor and pushed herself back up.

The creature facing her swayed back and forth, each movement fluid, its long mohawk of hair wavering over the top of its head, down its long neck and along part of its spine. Drool dangled from between its teeth, which were a random mix of human and canine. It couldn't even close its mouth all the way.

"The hell are you?" Maigo asked.

Leshiy let out a whoop and stood up on its hind legs. Its belly was crisscrossed with twitching muscles. The sounds of breaking bones made Maigo wince. The creature's body contorted, and then shifted into some-thing new. It stood tall now, almost human with a face that...

Oh my god, Maigo thought, *it has Brice's face.*

She took a step back, fists clenched, but she stopped when she remembered the burning eyes behind her. She wanted to turn and look, to really see what was there, if it was alive, but Leshiy was a predator no matter what shape it took. She couldn't turn her back to it.

Leshiy giggled and shifted its body again, the crack of bones emanating mostly from its face. As the facial structure changed, muscles contracted and loosened. The eyes clouded and black pupils emerged.

Maigo gasped, sparking a tidal wave of laughter from the creature.

It took all of Maigo's willpower to hold her temper in check. The creature hadn't just stolen her face, it had given life to the nightmare that plagued her. The memory of her transition from human girl to full grown Nemesis was hazy. She'd done her best to forget it. But she remembered a moment, staring into the reflective surface of a morgue cooler door, where she saw her human face snarling from the body of a monster.

She had looked a lot like this.

It's not me, she told herself. *It never will be.*

Leshiy dropped back to all fours with a crackling of bones, its body reverting back to its original predatory form. But it kept her face, frozen in an ugly smile, eyes wide and unblinking.

The air grew warmer around her. She could feel the thing behind her. Was it alive? Was it *breathing* on her?

She started to turn and saw Leshiy move in the corner of her eye. She turned back and found the creature already halfway to her, reaching out with both clawed hands.

Maigo dived to the side, landing on the floor. Her bare skin squeaked on the smooth surface, stopping her before she reached the platform's edge.

The creature with her face flew past. With a squeal of nails on chalkboard, Leshiy scraped its talons across the floor as it slid toward the edge. When it stopped, white lines traced the path of each nail. A thin spiral of metal curled from the floor at the tip of each claw.

Maigo stared at the lines dug by the impossibly sharp claws.

If it hits me with those, even once...

Giggling the whole way, Leshiy moved around the outer edge of the platform. It stayed low to the floor, ready to pounce.

Maigo moved around the outer edge, keeping the metal sphere positioned between them. She could feel the red eyes staring at her, beckoning for her to look, but she kept her gaze leveled at Leshiy, and it did the same to her.

It peeked around the column supporting the metal sphere, using her own face to mock her. The thing turned its head ninety degrees and let out a laugh.

She laughed back at it, mocking and annoyed.

The creature's head snapped back as though slapped. The frozen humor faltered.

The absolute shock from the creature drew an actual laugh from Maigo.

It flinched again. All traces of twisted humor faded. It hissed through misaligned snarling teeth.

Then it attacked.

Leshiy lunged in one direction, then scrambled over the floor, rushing in the other direction. Maigo was thrown off balance by the change in direction, but it was the sudden change in tactics from savage beast to skilled fighter that really threw her. Leshiy caught the orb's spire and swung around it. Both its feet hit Maigo in the chest, kicking her hard and throwing her back.

She crashed down atop the long walkway and tumbled head over heels, stopping against the massive spire wall, the staircase rising up above her. She pushed herself up with a grunt and pressed her fingers against her ribs, testing for breaks. But her bones seemed just as solid as ever. Leshiy might be able to slice her open, but it wasn't strong enough to break her bones.

Good to know.

With a heckling laugh, Leshiy charged.

Maigo raced to meet it.

The beast dove forward, swiping for Maigo's gut with both hands. But she was no longer there. Maigo leapt over the creature and kicked the back of its head. By the time she'd landed on her feet, it had crashed into the spire wall. When it turned to face her again, curling its lip back into a sick grin, several of the teeth were broken, tendrils of drool dangling from the new gaps.

Maigo wanted to laugh at it, to taunt it into taking action before it was ready, to use its own tactic against it, but she couldn't. The sight before her was as pitiful as it was horrifying.

Like her and Lilly, this creature hadn't been born this way. Nature hadn't designed it. The corrupt minds of modern men were responsible for its existence, and for sending it down here after her. It wasn't her enemy. Not really. In some ways, it was similar to Nemesis Prime, the monster created and tortured, then set loose upon the world. The ancient Prime had been no more a creature of free will than this hideous creation. She couldn't hold it responsible for its actions.

But she *could* put it out of its misery.

Leshiy charged again, swiping with one hand and then the next. Maigo leapt back from each blow, the talons narrowly missing the flesh of her belly. When the creature's second missed strike left it overextended, Maigo drilled her fist into the thing's face.

She felt bones buckle and break.

Its face wrapped around her fist.

And then it fell back, still and unmoving.

Maigo looked down at the creature, its face folded inward where her fist had struck.

Ugh, she thought, disgusted that she had just done that to a living creature.

Then a bone cracked.

And another.

The face puffed out, bones sliding back into place. The reconstructing face no longer held her image, but it frightened her even more. If it could survive having its face inverted...

Maigo's thoughts were interrupted by a pressure around her ankle. She glanced down and saw Leshiy's tail wrapping around her leg. Before she could react, the tail snapped up and pulled her off her feet.

The creature sprang to its feet, cackling.

Cast in the red light of those big, red eyes, the monster raised its hands, claws extended, ready to eviscerate Maigo.

It stopped at the sound of a hiss, growing louder, coming from above.

The creature turned its head up just in time to see Lilly drop from a hundred feet up and land hard upon its shoulders. Leshiy crumpled as bones snapped and gave way to feline weight.

Lilly stood above the motionless creature and clapped her hands together. "What would you do without—"

Before Maigo could offer a warning, Leshiy's tail wrapped around the girl's waist, lifted her off the floor and tossed her over the edge. Lilly reached out with her claws, but she was too far. Maigo watched her fall over the side, and for the first time, she saw real fear in Lilly's eyes.

"No!" Maigo said, and kicked out.

Leshiy slammed into the spire wall, and quickly started pulling itself back together. But Maigo was there, full of rage, punching and kicking and breaking bones faster than they could reform. With a gargled laugh, Leshiy struck out and caught Maigo's shoulder, opening up four red stripes. Maigo responded by slamming her head into the creature's face, three times, until it was nearly flattened. She stepped back, breathing heavily, and watched as the body and head started pulling itself back together.

She lifted Leshiy off the ground by its hair, and dragged it to the edge. Then she tossed it over and watched it fall. The whole way down, at least four hundred feet, was lit in orange light. Leshiy fell the distance, landed with a thud and lay unmoving. She suspected the creature might survive her assault, and the fall, but she didn't see any stairs up. It wouldn't be getting out any time soon.

"Ey!" shouted a muffled voice. "Et ee uh!"

Lilly?

Maigo rushed to the ramp and dove to her stomach. She leaned her head over the side and saw Lilly dangling from a long pink appendage jutting from her mouth.

"Urry!"

The pink glob of flesh at the end of the long tongue was peeling away from the walkway's bottom. Maigo thrust her arm out and caught Lilly's hand, just as the tongue slipped free. The pink appendage snapped back into the girl's mouth. "Yeah," she said, "I have a chameleon tongue. Tell anyone and you're dead."

Maigo pulled her up onto the walkway. "I think it's pretty cool."

"You think *what* is pretty cool?" Lilly said, looking on the verge of anger.

"Nothing," Maigo said. "I don't know what you're talking about."

"Good." Lilly looked over the edge at the still motionless form far below. "Now what the hell was that thing?"

Maigo watched for any hint of movement and saw nothing. "A little of this, a little of that."

Lilly frowned. "Not all of us can turn out goo— Holy shit sticks!" Her yellow eyes grew wide as she looked beyond Maigo.

The eyes, Maigo thought. Part of her didn't want to see them again, but she had to know what was there. Had to see the real monster for herself.

She turned and saw the eyes.

And then the rest of it.

Maigo staggered back and raised a hand to her mouth. "I remember... I remember it all."

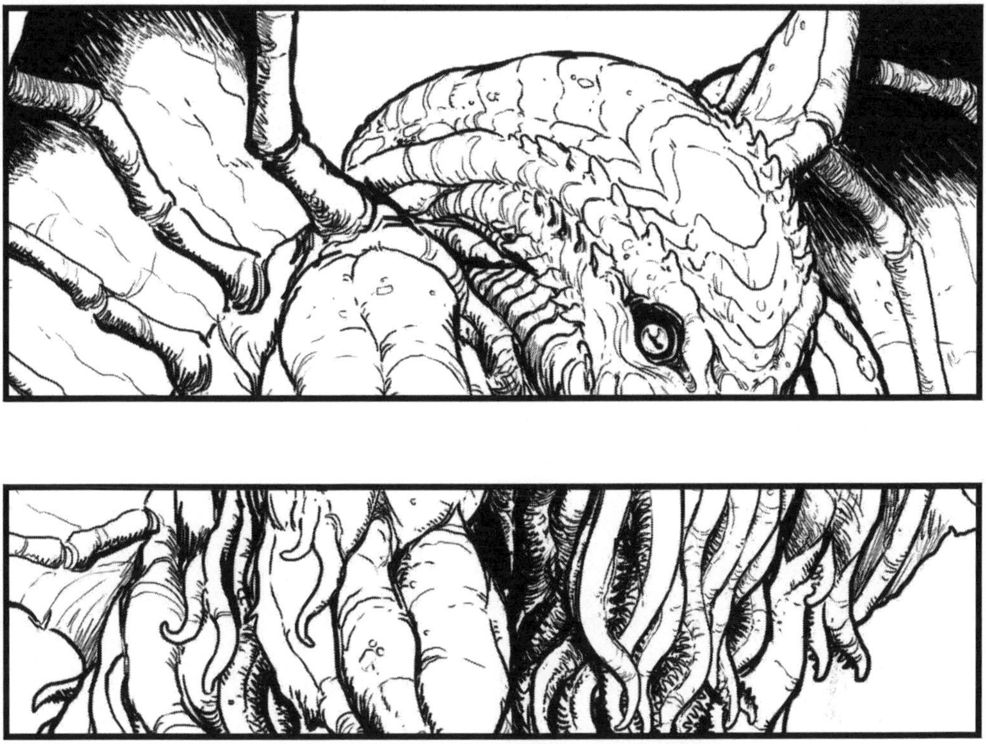

LOVECRAFT

INTERLUDE

Ancient History

Akakios's limbs shook and gave way, partially because of the rumbling ground, partially because of the horrific scene playing out in the city below. He fell back to one hand and then sat. The uncomfortable rocky slope beneath him went unnoticed. The pain in his knee was forgotten. He was a spectator for an event few people could imagine and even less ever saw. His memory of this day would be told for generations! He watched the spectacle with a keen attention to detail.

Nemesis, the beast, the goddess, had gone mad. Surely, she had not come to the ringed city to judge an individual or a small group. She had laid her gaze on the entire legendary city and found it lacking. But it was worse than that.

She found it...offensive.

Stone shattered and exploded into the air as she swiped her massive, spike laden arms back and forth through the immense structures that grew taller toward the city's center. Amidst the stone flew people, their features surprisingly large despite the distance.

They're giants, he thought, *no doubt standing twice the height of many men.* Their heads were topped in golden strands, far whiter than any hair he had ever seen. Their women would probably fetch a fortune in the slave trade, assuming women of such stature could be subdued. But he doubted there would be any of them left to trade, beyond the scattered bits and pieces being flung across the city.

Walls crumbled. The ocean, once held at bay by the ringed walls, flooded in. The giant people wailed in fires. They drowned in the water. They were crushed underfoot. Had there ever been such a slaughter? Every minute ended thousands of lives.

And then, the city was abandoned. The yellow haired giants fled in all directions, flowing from the few remaining gates.

Nemesis spun around, her three tails smashing through the tallest structures at the city's core. The buildings toppled and imploded. Horrified screams echoed off the valley walls. Nemesis drowned them out with a war cry of her own. The bellowing baritone rumbled up the valley and made Akakios's insides quiver. He could only imagine the raw force experienced by those surrounding it, their bodies crushed by the sound, the air driven from their lungs, along with all hope.

Akakios smiled. Nemesis's wrath, so feared mere minutes ago, had become a thing of poetry. A rare beauty. Like watching a lightning storm as a child, aware of its potential for primal destruction, but still captivated by it. Still awed by the vast power on display.

After slamming its mighty arms down on what remained of the city, Nemesis stepped through the ruined wall, back into the valley, where it was followed by the ocean that had been held at bay.

The monster had set its sights on the thousands who had managed to flee. The giants ran in an ever widening circle. Some of them would eventually pass him by. The sight of them might normally make him run the other way, but he didn't think any of them would pause long enough to do him harm and risk being caught.

But the beast seemed staggered by indecision. It turned its massive head in one direction, slowly surveying the widening circle of giants. It swiveled around, and after a false start, turned back the other way. Then it stopped, roared again and lifted its clawed hands in front of its glowing chest. The claws turned inward.

It's going to impale itself, he thought.

Had the goddess seen the yellow haired giants' flight as a failure? Did it intend to take its own life?

The claws stabbed forward, but stopped quickly, a loud clang filling the valley.

Akakios blinked. The image before him had changed drastically enough for him to doubt what he was seeing, despite the surreal nature of everything he'd witnessed up to that point.

But it was real.

A second monster, equal in height, but smaller in stature to Nemesis, and built more like a man, had appeared and caught the giant claws before they could impale the orange chambers on her chest. The two titans stood face to face, each pulling on the other's limbs, neither gaining any ground.

Nemesis looked beyond the newcomer, who Akakios could now see was like a metal man, and roared at the still fleeing giants.

The metal man is protecting the giants, Akakios thought. *He is helping them escape.*

Akakios had no real opinion on whether he would prefer to see the giant men killed or freed. They no longer held his interest. This new struggle, which would be more of a fight than a mass execution, was far more compelling. And the giants were faster than they looked. Many of them had cleared the valley and were no doubt headed for lands far away.

Nemesis saw this, too. The beast raised her head to the sky and let out a roar. Then with a swiftness her size made look impossible, she drove her head down and forward, striking the metal man's chest.

The colossal man fell back, crashing to the ground and providing Akakios with his first view of the newcomer's front side. He saw the face first, concealed by an armor mask, but revealing glowing red eyes. Something about that gaze made him think this thing was noble. Worth cheering for. A defender of men, or at least of giants. Its body was armored from top to bottom, but not in the way Nemesis was armored. Her thick plates were organic. This metal man looked like he'd been cast in a forge of gods, shielded in hues of silver, black and glowing red. At the center of the broad chest was a symbol that matched the layout of the now destroyed city, three rings united by a single vertical line, rising from below. The center line and outer ring currently glowed with the same red blaze as the eyes.

Nemesis lifted one of her huge hands and slammed it down atop the giant man, pushing him into the valley wall. She drew back and struck again, but this time, the man raised his fists. Three blades, as large as Nemesis's claws snapped out of the metal man's forearm, evenly spaced around the limb and extending far out past the fists on both hands. Metal pierced flesh as Nemesis's hand landed atop all six blades.

The divine judge reeled back, roaring, but not blindly. She spun around bringing all three long tails around like whips. The spines at the end gouged three divots across the metal body, but did no serious damage that Akakios could see.

The man, who was perhaps also one of the gods, staggered away from the strike, the two titans regrouping.

Nemesis hunched and roared, arms splayed wide, ready to attack again.

The blades on the metal man's right arm snapped back inside. With a flick of the giant's wrist, three metal prongs shot out of the forearm from hidden compartments beside those that housed the blades.

It keeps its weapons hidden inside its body, Akakios thought. While Nemesis was pure rage and passion, the metal man was a thinking fighter.

The goddess charged.

The metal man stabbed with the left hand, plunging the three blades through the armor of Nemesis's shoulder. But he was caught. Nemesis lifted him up, leapt in the air and drove him toward the ground. They landed together. The valley shook. The walls collapsed inward. Rocks rolled past Akakios on all sides, some thumping against his back, but he remained fixated.

And then, just as it had arrived, the metal man disappeared in a flash of blue light. But as quick as he left, the man returned, winking back into existence above Nemesis. He fell on her back, narrowly avoiding the bevy of spikes large enough to cleave his waist in two. While the goddess pushed herself up, despite his weight atop her, he drove the left hand, with those three blades, into her back. Held in place, he lifted the right hand, and those long prongs into the air.

What is it doing? Akakios wondered. The metal spears atop the raised fist didn't look sharp enough to pierce the monster's hide. But then, with a crackle of power, the prongs unleashed the very power of the storm that had once impressed Akakios as a child. Lightning arced between the metal spears, which were then thrust against Nemesis's back.

The goddess writhed and wailed, her booming voice once conveying deep rumbling rage, now shrieking in high-pitched pain.

The three tails rose again, wrapping up and over the metal man, grasping his shoulders. There was a moment of resistance before the man was lifted off his feet and tossed, head over heels, into the ocean.

Blood poured from Nemesis as the monster climbed back to its feet and staggered around. Flesh and armor seemed to be peeling free, revealing patches of white flesh beneath. The sun struck Nemesis from behind and those white spots glowed brightly enough to make Akakios squint. The goddess was changing.

The ocean heaved and then burst as the metal man stood. Water poured from the great body, now gleaming in the sun. Aside from the three scratches across its chest, the man-god still looked unharmed. The first and second rings on his chest now glowed bright red. He stood at the ready, weapons hidden inside the arms. The two titans both seemed to be waiting, but for what?

Flesh dropped away from Nemesis's body, revealing blinding white diamonds. But whatever the goddess was doing, it wasn't fast enough.

The innermost ring on the metal man's body blinked bright red.

A flurry of movement sprang from the arms, forming things Akakios couldn't make sense of. And then the same happened to the giant man's head.

Sound like thunder.

Blinding light.

Roiling heat.

It struck him all at once, burning his clothes, raising boils on the outer layers of his skin.

And then it faded.

He opened his eyes and saw the impossible. Nemesis stood before him, her back to him, but he could still see the metal man on the other side, staring at him through a hole in the giant creature's chest. The metal man tilted his head as though they had actually made eye contact.

Akakios held out his hand in a wave.

The metal man transformed back into his original form and held out a hand, acknowledging Akakios. Nemesis dropped to her knees, and without another sign of life, toppled forward.

The goddess of vengeance had been slain.

As Akakios shivered from the burns covering his body, the metal man lifted Nemesis's tails, pulled them tight and then dragged the monster into the ocean. Akakios watched them go, mind running rampant with thoughts of how to tell this story. But before he could finish his mental ramblings, or even attempt to stand, a shadow fell over him.

He looked up into the upside down face of a giant, yellow-haired Atlantean—one of thousands who had fled and no longer needed to fear the wrath of Nemesis. Aside from his size and the three-ringed symbol carved into his chest, the man looked human, but in Akakios's heart, he knew it wasn't true.

"The goddess is slain!" Akakios said, hoping his enthusiasm might endear him to the large man.

"These things were not meant for your eyes," the Atlantean said.

Akakios stammered, unsure of how to proceed. Then he managed to say, "I—I won't tell anyone what I saw, if that is what you want."

"No," a second voice said. "You won't."

Akakios turned and found a very ordinary man standing beside the giant. He was dressed like a traveler. A fellow witness perhaps. Then the man shed his clothes and fell to his hands and knees, his body bending and contorting, changing into something else. When he—*it*—looked up again, many more eyes looked upon Akakios, framed by bony horns and a sharp-toothed grin.

Akakios tried to shove himself away, but his body revolted. His skin cracked and made moving nearly impossible. "What are you?" he shouted as the transformed man stalked closer.

"I...am hungry."

16

The wave of pressure that strikes Helicopter Betty pitches the vehicle forward and carries it for a moment, before releasing it into a free fall. Before we can recover from the blow, the thunderous sound of a MOAB detonating chases the pressure wave and tears through us. If the others are shouting, I have no idea. Even with headphones on, designed to protect the wearer from the constant beat of the rotor blades, the roar has set my ears buzzing. My body feels like it's been liquefied, and I find myself puckering my asshole, just in case.

Warning lights flash across the dash. Betty's insides have been shaken loose. The chopper levels out, but shudders violently. Woodstock is shouting, pulling on the controls. I've seen him go through a lot. I know what his surprised face looks like. This is different. This is worse. I can see it in his eyes. Betty's fate is sealed.

Woodstock's voice crackles to life in my ear, pushing its way past the buzz. "Satan's taint!" He's fighting the controls, somehow keeping us in the air despite the warning lights and the shaking.

"Can we make it back to shore?" I ask.

He glances at me, his mustache bending up with a lopsided smile. "Can a moose lick its asshole?"

"Umm, no?"

"God damn right, no." The other side of his mustache lifts, completing the smile. "But I can get us close. Probably."

"Before you do," I say, and he grunts. Knows what I'm going to ask.

"Hold on," he says, and he puts the chopper into a slow counter-clockwise spin while keeping us heading toward shore. After turning ninety degrees, he stops, letting Collins and me look out the side window.

"I don't see it," Collins says. Lovecraft is once again cloaked in rising smoke and steam.

"It's there," I say, "watching, waiting."

But is it in one piece?

Collins leans closer to the window, her forehead against the glass. "I see it."

And then I do, too. A breeze thins out the smoke for a moment, revealing what looks like a ribbed cocoon. Shimmering greens and blues ripple through the broad sheets of flesh, revealing sinews and veins large enough to drive a car through. Despite its opacity and apparent thinness, the surface looks undamaged.

The cocoon separates.

Pushed from the inside out, the column of smoke bulges, rises and billows away, propelled by the opening cocoon.

Wings, I think, *they're wings.*

I've been calling this thing Lovecraft because the tentacled face bears a striking resemblance to the fictional monster Cthulhu, created by weird fiction author, H.P. Lovecraft, and because Alicio Brice theorized that Lovecraft had been influenced by a Ferox, whose goal was to condition the human race to fear beings with similar appearances. But I still believed it was more coincidence than conditioning. This Kaiju's obvious similarities to Lovecraft's creature solidifies Brice's theory. For me at least.

The monster stands up tall, revealing a bulky torso covered in random spines and tufts of undulating tentacles. Despite the wings, this thing seems inspired by sea life. Some of it is clearly Aeros, but they've merged that ugly mug with who-knows-what, from who-knows-where. The end result is this abomination, and I'm pretty sure every person on the planet will be scared shitless when they see it, whether or not they've been exposed to Lovecraft's story "The Call of Cthulhu."

The Kaiju stretches its wings wide, curls its long arms and fists to the sky and then lets out an angry bellow, tentacles warbling, its ring of teeth splayed wide. It's in one piece, but that doesn't mean the bomb didn't hurt it.

Energy flickers over the creature's body and then it goes dark. The wings fold in tight. The tentacles pull down into smooth ribs. And then the beast lowers itself into the water, slipping into the depths, this time invisible from above.

A clang and momentary grinding sound reminds me of our plight. We're headed back to shore, but losing altitude. Starting at 18,000 feet might be what saves us. That, and Woodstock's skill as a pilot.

"How we doing?" I ask.

"Let me put it this way," he says. "Ain't no way I'm putting her down in the drink with that fugly SOB swimming around out there. If I have to sprout wings and fly us there myself, I will."

Betty jolts and coughs, but the rotor keeps spinning, just fast enough to keep us from plummeting out of the sky.

Bouncing and shaking our way back toward the coast, I contact Cooper and put things in motion. Lovecraft is gone. It's not even showing up on sonar, which means it either has a way to avoid detection, or it's hugging the sea floor. But we're going to assume it's headed toward the coast.

For now, the military is standing by just outside Boston, ready to deliver a second round of entirely ineffective ordnance. But if we can make it back to dry land, that might not be necessary. I look down at the hard Zoomb case, now sitting between my feet. After hanging up with Cooper, I call Alessi.

"ETA?" I ask as soon as she picks up.

"Ten minutes. Are you okay?"

"Been a bumpy flight, and there aren't any peanuts. Any trouble getting our assets in place?"

"None, and no questions asked. They even gave us a fighter jet escort." Her delivery of this small bit of good news is followed up by a more glum, "It's on the news, you know."

I didn't know, but how could it not be? "Let me guess: Lots of speculation, no real facts, and a lot of scared people."

"A news chopper caught the last explosion from a *very* long distance. The image was pixelated, but clear enough to see something big still moving around after the blast. And everyone still alive on the coastline heard it."

"Evacuations underway?"

"Slow, but yeah. It's hard to evacuate people who need to be in hospitals. We're doing what we can, though."

In this case, her 'we're' is Zoomb, not the FC-P, and I'm glad my inherited multibillion-dollar global corporation is doing something more than adding zeros to the bottom line.

"I'll let you know when we're on the ground." I move my thumb to disconnect the call, but pause. "Thanks for being on top of this. If Endo were around, he'd—"

"Probably be pissing you off," she says.

"Good point. Never mind then."

"Thanks, though," she says, and then hangs up.

The next thirty minutes are a slow motion, yet white-knuckled descent toward the ocean, where a real life sea monster lurks. It's a big ocean, but I have a bad history of attracting trouble's ugly attention. After several lurching falls and kick starts, the coastline emerges from the darkness. Normally, it would be easier to see, but most of the coastal cities have no power after the tsunami, and the sun isn't up yet. The only lights I can see now in the pre-dawn gloom are the blue and red flashing of emergency vehicles.

"We're going to make it," I say, and I see Woodstock wince. "What?"

"Hate to break it to you, but seeing land and making it there are two different things. We're just a thousand feet up and still dropping."

Looks like we'll be swimming after all, if we survive the crash at sea. "Cooper is tracking our GPS. I can have her send—"

"I said we weren't going to make it to the mainland," he says, "I didn't say I was going to put the old girl down in the water." He points out the windshield to the left. I have to lean forward, but then I see it. The bright beam of a lighthouse twitches past.

"I don't see the island," I say.

"Best I can do," he says. "An' if we get wet, the swim'll be a short one."

I give him a nod, and he says, "Buckle up!"

Collins and I glance at each other. We've been buckled and grasping various 'oh shit' handles for the last thirty minutes. Then we twist to the side and dive down. For a moment, I think we're actually crashing, but we level out with a grind of gears that shakes the seat beneath me. The lighthouse is straight ahead, beaming its light into the cockpit every few seconds. The moonlit island comes into view, and my eyes widen. It's less of an island and more of a collection of jagged rocks emerging from the ocean. The base of the lighthouse is actually submerged in the ocean, partially surrounded by the stony islet.

"Geezum crow," Woodstock says, pulling hard on the control stick. "Going to be a rough one."

The engine coughs.

The rancid scent of fuel smoke fills the cabin.

Woodstock puts the chopper into a slow spin, descending toward a ragged chunk of stone that looks just large enough to catch the chopper's skids. We slow a bit, but then something clangs. The rotor snaps to a stop, and the chopper spins on its axis.

The list of things I hate seems to grow every year, but one of the very first things on the mental tally is the Tilt-A-Whirl. I puked a centrifugal-fueled ring all over my classmates in seventh grade. It even got in Jenny Stillwater's mouth. The incident scarred me for life, the bright side being that no one saw from where the spew originated. But *I* knew. And if I had a repeated episode now, Collins and Woodstock would definitely know.

So I tighten my core, swallow hard and then scream when I see the ground rushing up. The skids hit hard, catching on the stone and slamming my head into the side door. I recover from the blow fast enough to realize we're tilted at a pretty severe angle, but no longer in the sky. I glance out the side window and see a rotor blade wedged into the ocean below, holding us in place.

Then, with a groan, the blade rotates and the chopper topples off the rock. My seatbelt tugs hard against my body, and nearly Heimlich maneuvers the puke out of me, but I survive our second fall with little harm done. As water rushes into the cab, the plastic case between my feet jostles loose and falls. I reach for it, but it's Collins who catches it, just above the water. She's already unbuckled and righted herself. She's bleeding from a gash on her forehead, but she seems alright otherwise.

"We sinkin'?" Woodstock asks. He digs into his pocket, plucks out a toothpick and inserts it in his upside down mouth.

"Just a few feet of water," Collins says. "Probably dry land when the tide is out."

"Well, that's sumthin' I s'pose. Now, help an old man down."

After a few minutes of falling and cursing and crawling and splashing, we clamber onto the rocky shore.

Woodstock pauses to give Betty a salute. "You done good, girl."

Then we hoist ourselves onto a metal platform built several feet above the high tide line and head for the granite lighthouse's door.

"Graves Light," I say, reading the sign beside the door. I grin at Woodstock. "Well, you managed to crash us on the most foreboding island in Boston Harbor, so that's great."

"Better than the ocean," he says.

"Touché."

Collins tries the door and upon finding it locked, kicks it in. The door moves in just a little bit, and then bursts outward, nearly knocking us off the platform. Water pours out from the inside, washing past our already wet legs. After the water clears, I step inside. Glass crunches beneath my feet. The windows, top to bottom, are blown out, evidence of the tsunami's passing. Five flights of spiral stairs later, I'm winded and looking out the watchroom window. Boston is barely visible in the glow of an early rising summer sun still over the horizon. Inside an hour, we'll be able to see without a problem, but do we have an hour?

I climb the last flight from the watchroom to the lantern room. The harsh light forces my eyes closed until it passes, then I find the door and step out onto the catwalk, leaving the musty lighthouse interior and entering the humid, sea-scented outdoors once more. I put my hands on the railing, and look down. An array of solar panels are mounted to the tower, just below my feet. That's how it still has power. I turn from the view of a darkened, partially rebuilt Boston and look north up the lightless coast. *This has to end sometime,* I think. Then I spot motion off to my right as something is caught in the lighthouse's beam. My mind replays the image frozen into the back of my eyelids, and I see it for what it was.

A wave.

A big ass wave.

Taking some small comfort in the fact that the granite lighthouse is still standing after the last wave that struck the coast, I dive back inside, crashing into Collins and Woodstock, and tumbling the three of us down the spiral staircase, just as the structure rumbles from an impact.

17

"What the heck is wrong with you?" Lilly asked as Maigo backed away from the massive, stoic head with glowing red eyes. The masked face, armored and ancient, was clearly not alive, but the thing radiated power. "I mean, yeah, it's freaky and intimidating, but it doesn't look like it's going anywhere."

Maigo didn't stop backing away until her back was against the tall spire rising up through the island's core. Maigo could be all kinds of weird, Lilly knew, but after what she'd lived through, she was rarely afraid. Aside from the fear of becoming a monster, which she didn't mention much around Lilly on account of her catlike appearance, Lilly found it hard to believe any kind of external force could affect Maigo so profoundly. She looked mesmerized. She looked...lost.

"Maigo." Lilly stood between the girl and the giant head. The masked, metal face looked like all robotic visages, in that it lacked any emotion other than the stern gaze with which it had been constructed. But she hoped blocking Maigo's view would snap the girl out of the trance. "Hey!"

Unblinking eyes stared right through Lilly. "It killed me."

Lilly leaned in close. "Hate to break it to you, but you're still alive." She gave Maigo's face a pat. "Snap out of it."

"It *killed* me."

Lilly nearly lost her patience, but then realized there might be some context for the statement that she hadn't fully realized. Maigo had been murdered, after all. It might not have been this Maigo, but she still had some of the first Maigo's memories, transferred by DNA, much of it not human. But her murderer had been a man. Her father. Not a giant robot.

"It didn't kill you, Maigo. You're alive. You're with me." Lilly leaned in closer, her piercing yellow eyes impossible to ignore. But Maigo pulled it off, staring straight ahead.

Lilly lifted her black gloved hand, and with a quick flex, pushed her long black claws out through the fingertips of her thumb and index finger. "Have it your way."

Using her claws, Lilly pinched the skin on Maigo's arm. No reaction. "I know you're tough, but *come on.*" She looked down at the skin pinched between her claws and winced. "You asked for it." She pushed hard, harder than she thought she'd have to, and punched two small holes in Maigo's arms.

The reaction was powerful and unexpected. Maigo kicked out hard, sending Lilly sprawling away. Then she clawed at the air and fell to her butt, trying to push away from something unseen. *She's lost in a memory,* Lilly realized. *But not her own.*

Maigo's body seized for a moment and then went slack.

Lilly dove to her side and caught the girl before she slumped over. "Hey." She checked Maigo for a pulse and after finding one, tapped the girl's cheek. "Hey. Wake up."

Maigo's eyes fluttered and then opened. For a moment, Lilly thought her friend was still out of her head, but then Maigo looked up at her. "It killed me." Her eyes welled with tears.

"Who killed you?"

Maigo leaned over and looked past Lilly at the robot. Its face hadn't changed. The glow of its serious red eyes remained constant.

"Uh huh," Lilly said. "Whoever it killed, it wasn't you."

Maigo crushed her eyes shut and rubbed her head. "It wasn't me." She pushed herself up into a sitting position. "It was Nemesis. The first one."

"Prime."

Maigo nodded. "It was a long time ago, but I think I just relived it. Some of it anyway. I remember that face. And pain. And anger. I haven't felt like that since...ugh. We don't need to talk about it."

Lilly pulled Maigo to her feet, glad to have her friend back. "So, what now? We came here to find and take what was hidden here, but..."

"The plan hasn't changed," Maigo said.

"You want to take *that?*" Lilly thrust her hands out at the robot head, and then waved them up and down to indicate its entire, massive body. She moved to the edge of the platform and looked down at the armored body. The broad chest bore the three-ringed Atlantean symbol that had brought them to this island. The silver body, almost like brushed metal, gleamed like new. It looked built for power, its limbs thick, and yet somehow it appeared ready for action, as though it could spring to life at any moment. In some places it bore the marks of ancient battle, including claw marks. In many ways, it reminded her of some kind of ancient warrior, like a Spartan, or Samurai, but it lacked any real resemblance to any single human culture.

Because whoever made this wasn't human, Lilly thought. "How the hell are we supposed to get that out of here and past the Russians, never mind to the other side of the planet?"

"I'm going to talk to it," Maigo said.

"You're going to what now?" Lilly looked at the large face, searching for hints that it was anything more than a giant robot. Badass? Yes. Dangerous? Absolutely. Alien? Without a freaking doubt. But *alive?* "You're not saying this thing is—"

"Artificially intelligent," Maigo said, putting some of Lilly's concerns to rest. "But it can't function without a Voice."

"So it what...needs a speaker system?"

"Voice with a capital V," Maigo said, stepping closer to the head. "A pilot."

"And what makes you think you can—"

"I have experience," Maigo said.

Lilly squinted at her friend. "You mean Nemesis."

Maigo gave a faint nod and raised her hand back to the metal orb at the center of the platform. She twitched as though shocked, but then turned to Lilly. "Last time, it was communicating. Now, it's waiting. It's listening."

"For what?"

"For orders."

Lilly smiled. She couldn't help herself. This was mind-blowingly awesome.

Maigo returned the smile, reaffirming their conspiratorial relationship. "Open sesame."

A loud clunk made both girls leap back.

Maigo withdrew her hand from the orb, but the noise continued. After several clunks and a whirring of gears, the massive face split open at the center, and segment by segment, it slid apart.

"It's like that lady's face in Total Recall," Lilly said. "You know, when it splits open and Arnold is underneath looking all like, 'shit, my covah is blown.'"

"Haven't seen it," Maigo whispered, and she stepped to the edge of the platform. The open head was ten feet away, the gap between them hundreds of feet deep.

Lilly followed her to the edge and cringed when she saw what was inside the head.

At first she saw a rough approximation of what she expected. Metal parts. Cables. Lights. But at the core of it all, was what looked like an oval shaped bed mounted at an angle and covered with a shiny black sheet. Then it began to warble. "It looks like a funky-ass water bed from some kind of 70s porno."

"You know far too many pop culture references for someone who has only lived in this country for two years," Maigo said.

Lilly bristled at the comment. "You try spending all your days in hiding."

"I do," Maigo said. "We just hide for different reasons...and only one of us watches 70s porn."

Lilly chuckled and shrugged. "People were hairier back then."

Then the water bed sprang to life, as the black separated into tendrils and reached out.

"Nemesis did the same thing," Maigo said. "When Endo..." She closed her eyes, sounding a bit more afraid than she had a moment ago.

"You don't have to do this," Lilly said. "We don't know anything about it. We don't even know if you'll be able to get out."

"This thing is selective about who it lets inside."

Lilly rolled her eyes, took off her glove and put her hand on the orb. It was probably a stupid thing to do, especially if there was a result, but nothing happened. She felt absolutely nothing.

"It has less to do with your physical or mental abilities and more to do with biology. Neither of us is fully human, but you're at least made from creatures that evolved on this planet. Part of me is human. But the rest of me...it's not even terrestrial."

"So it's biologically locked?" Lilly asked.

"In part," Maigo said. "But it also got a good look at what I was, what I did and who I became. It knows that I was part of Nemesis, but it also knows I was revolted by it. I think that qualified me. Look, the real point is this, there is a chance that anyone...or any*thing* else that passes the same test could be very bad for the human race. It needs to be guided by the right person, or we could all be screwed." She turned to Lilly. "No one else can do this."

Lilly took a step back and flashed a feline grin. "Then do it."

Maigo didn't hesitate. She jumped out over the gap and easily cleared the ten feet to the open head. She climbed up toward the black tendrils, which seemed to relax as she got closer. Standing before the oval, the thin limbs opened to receive her. She turned back toward Lilly, gave a wave and fell back into the black surface. The tendrils caught her, wrapped around her body and then enveloped her, pulling her down.

Seeing Maigo slide away filled Lilly with a sudden panic. Her muscles tightened as she prepared to jump the distance and tear her friend out. But the head slammed shut, one section at a time, until it looked like it had, just minutes ago.

Lilly stood, dumbfounded.

Nothing changed.

Then a booming voice filled the chamber. "Can you hear me?" The voice was deep and masculine, digitally enhanced to sound foreboding, but it was still Maigo.

Cringing from the volume of the voice, Lilly cupped her hands over her ears and shouted, "Too loud!"

The deep, commanding voice whispered, "Oh my god, I'm sorry," and drew a cackling laugh from Lilly.

"You did it," Lilly said. "Are you in control?"

"I don't know," the mighty whisper said. "I'll try, but I think you should get out of here first."

"Makes sense to me," Lilly said. "Just don't waste time coming up. There's still a bunch of salty Russians topside." Then she sprang up onto the staircase and instead of taking the long, tedious way up and around, she leapt from level to level, climbing hundreds of feet in under a minute. She reached the top of the spire, expecting to be greeted by bullets, but instead she found a complete lack of welcoming committee.

Either the Russian military is slacking, or they're just waiting us out.

The spire shook beneath her. Maigo was moving.

No choice, Lilly decided. She sprang up through the hole high above, teeth bared, claws extended and ready to fight.

18

Water sprays through the lighthouse's broken windows with the frenetic energy of a psychotic waterpark fun house. The torrent surges against us, pushing us down the spiral stairs. The only thing that keeps Collins, Woodstock and me from spiraling down to the bottom is the fact that we're all twisted up with each other and the metal balusters. Saltwater forces its way into my mouth, gagging me. I turn my head, coughing hard, as more water cascades over my head.

I blink away the stinging saltwater and see Collin's face beneath mine. At the bottom of our human pile, she's being doused again and again, but she never flinches. She's got her eyes clenched shut and her teeth grinding. *Why isn't she moving?* I wonder, and then I see the truth. We're not tangled in the balusters, Collins is *holding on to them,* supporting our weight and fighting the rushing water. Her Herculean effort is keeping us alive. Could there be a better woman than this?

The spray of water stops as quickly as it arrived. The wave is beyond us. Collins sucks in a deep breath and coughs. Her arms start to shake. "Get...off."

Muttering curses to the sea, the Kaiju and a bunch of people I've never heard of, Woodstock pries himself off of me and takes hold of one of Collins's arms, easing her burden. I push myself up next and take her other arm. Working together, we pull her up.

There's no congratulations, praise or thanks between us. That will come later. Right now we're still in survival mode, and that means pleasantries can wait until after we're sure a 400-foot-tall, violent death machine isn't about to squash us.

Leaving Collins to catch her breath and Woodstock to work the kinks out of his old joints, I scramble back up to the lantern room and out onto the catwalk. The wave rolls toward Boston Harbor, but I don't see anything else. *Where the hell are you?*

I take out my phone, but when I try to wake it up, the screen blinks funny shapes at me and then goes blank. It's soaked. Two in one day. I grip the railing, fighting a growing sense of hopelessness. I can't communicate with the Crow's Nest. I can't coordinate with the military. I can't even summon a boat to come pick us up. Even if I can figure out how to beam lighthouse Morse code back to the coast, there won't be many people paying attention. Granted, the military might see it. Might even understand an old fashioned S.O.S., but they won't know it's me, and odds are, they'll be facing down Lovecraft.

Then I remember the Zoomb case, and I nearly leap for joy. There is one person I can contact, *and* I'm not actually out of the fight. Far from it. I'm about to head inside to find the case and make sure its contents are still in one piece, when something about the fading wave catches my attention.

It's not straight.

The further away it gets, the clearer it becomes. The wave that nearly drowned us is shaped like a V. It's not really a wave at all.

It's a wake.

Lovecraft is *here.*

Chased by the first hint of sunlight on the horizon, the monster slides through the lingering gloom, rising from the depths. I'm sure the monster has been sighted by now, but no one is taking action. Are they waiting for me? Are they sparing the city from an assault they know will be futile? After all, we don't really know what this creature intends to do once it rises from the ocean, but if recent history has taught us anything, it's that when a Kaiju steps onto dry land, cities are destroyed and people are killed. Maybe it's just looking for a good spot to bask in the sun, and tan that pale skin. But even a benign Kaiju will still lay waste to anything it touches.

I hurry back into the lantern room and nearly knock Woodstock over. "The case. Where is it?"

Collins rises from the watchroom hatch, holding the case up to me. "Lovecraft is here?" When I take the case and place it on the floor, she answers her own question. "Of course it's here. You know, I was kind of hoping our dates would improve after we got hitched."

"Well, you know what they say about relationships forged in stressful circumstances," Woodstock says, but he stops short when Collins gives him what he calls, 'that look.' The old pilot raises his hands. "Won't be a problem for you two, of course. Stressful circumstances are what we handle."

"Nice save," I say, and I open the case. The waterproof seal has done its job. The devices inside, encased in foam, are dry and held perfectly in place. Two black remotes, comparable in design and function to Wii remotes, lay on either side of a virtual reality headset. I pry the black headset out of the foam and slide it onto my head. The black design with a red band across the front makes me look like the X-Men's Cyclops, and ultimately, the effect of this helmet isn't too dissimilar from the eye-laser-blasting mutant. The lasers just won't come from my head, and they won't be bright red. They'll be invisible to everyone, but me.

With the device in place, I tap the power button on the side and get an OS display projected in front of me. I lower a microphone from the side of the helmet and wait for the system to connect to the satellite. Once the connection is made, I hold my hands out. "Remotes?"

Collins places the two remotes in my hands. I can tell it's her by the way her fingers linger over mine. Collins is a tough woman. Far tougher than me. We've both had our fair share of monstrous battles, but she managed to free herself from an abusive relationship and rebuild her life, not to mention her body, to become who she is today. Not many people could pull that off. It's a horrible past I wouldn't wish on anyone, but it's part of why I love her, and a big part of why we're still alive. No matter what the circumstances, I know she'll never give up, and I'm able to borrow that strength when necessary. And sometimes, I get to add crazy, cool, killer technology to that strength.

Remotes in my hands, I connect to the Zoomb Swarm system, which instigates a connection to Alessi.

The control room at the secret Zoomb operations center, located in New Hampshire, where no one would ever think to look, is projected into the VR headset. I turn my head and see Alessi standing next to me, despite being a hundred miles away.

On her end, she's looking at a screen that can show an icon of me... riding a Velociraptor, holding a machine gun and wearing a monocle...or footage captured by the camera mounted in the front of my headset. I figure out it's the latter when she asks, "Are you in a lighthouse?"

I turn my head left and right so she can see the lighthouse, and that Collins and Woodstock are with me. "Graves Light. Off of Boston. Going to need a ride at some point. Now, fill me in."

"Well, you're alive," she says, sounding relieved. "Devine shows you went offline after touching down."

"Landed upside down, in water, and then got hit by a tidal wave. Nearly drowned. No biggie. Are we still in place?"

"In a holding pattern three miles out from Boston. Whenever you're ready."

This contingency plan would normally have me on a plane, or in a bunker many miles away from the battle, to ensure I'm not taken out of the action prematurely. But we're not going anywhere soon, so the granite lighthouse will do. The Kaiju has already passed us by, so we should be good. *Should* isn't always a good friend, though. Sometimes *should* kicks you square in the nuts.

"I'm ready," I say and then, despite the horrid circumstances, I smile. Since taking over Zoomb and being made aware of this black project—one of many—I've been itching to say my next words. "Release the Swarm."

"Feed loop to Alpha One—"

"Whoever came up with that name better be wearing a T-shirt that says 'Captain Redundant' by tomorrow. From now on, Alpha group is Hydra."

To my surprise, Alessi actually smiles. "Appropriate. Feed loop to Hydra One in three...two..."

I brace myself for the transition. I've done this several times, first in a VR simulation and then with the real thing. But this will be my first time with the entire Swarm.

"One."

The Zoomb operations center disappears, and I'm suddenly falling out of the back of a plane. The view, high above Boston, is dizzying. I flinch, but I'm steadied by Collins's hands. My vision might be telling me that I'm miles above, but I'm still standing in the lighthouse, seeing the world through the eyes of a drone, of which I am now in control.

Gripping the two remotes, I pilot the drone in a wide circle. A mostly dark Boston slips past below. A slice of sun peeks up over the horizon. And then I see them. The Swarm. One hundred gray drones—more stealthy looking than those used by the U.S. military, and capable of Vertical Take Off and Landing—spilling out of the back of a C-130 Hercules transport plane. And one by one, they fall in line, behind Hydra One.

While I pilot the control drone, an AI guides the rest, enabling them to follow my lead, stay out of each other's way and intelligently avoid collisions with each other, buildings, planes or Kaiju. If the group is separated, they'll come back together. Individually, they're eight feet across and powerful enough to carry a person, but they're not especially intimidating. When they fly together, like a shoal of fish or a swarm of bees, well, they're pretty impressive. And if Hydra One is destroyed, my control will leap to Hydra Two, and then Three, and on down the line until there are no more drones left. Essentially, I'm the immortal head of Hydra that keeps coming back.

"Swarm released," Alessi says. I can hear her through the headset, though Collins and Woodstock can't. I can hear them, though.

"It's past the outer islands, boss," Woodstock says. "Headed for Pleasure Bay. Other side of that is South Boston."

South Boston, unlike the North End, Waterfront, Financial District and the Back Bay, survived Nemesis nearly unscathed. People are still living there while the rest of the city has been rebuilding. I'm sure the tsunami did some damage already, but it's still the worst possible place in Boston, in terms of lives at risk, for Lovecraft to make land.

I bank hard and descend toward the city, which looks more like it's built of scaffolding than actual buildings. A display in the upper right shows the Swarm following my turn and then spreading out around me like aerial soldiers charging into battle.

I spot the broad wake nearing the city, but Lovecraft is still hidden by the dark water, and until it rises, the Swarm's weapons won't be effective. Each drone is equipped with a high power direct-energy weapon system, which is a fancy way of saying *motherfuckin' lasers.* Individually, they could kill a person or destroy a small target, like a vehicle's tire. And in its own way, that's great. The practical applications for the military and law enforcement, who can turn the power down and make the laser a non-lethal stun gun, are immense. But that's not how I'm going to use them. The lasers, mounted in the nose of each drone, have a 180 degree range of motion, and each one will aim where Hydra One aims, the AI adjusting for the slight difference in position and perspective. A hundred small lasers quickly become one large laser with enough force to carve a sky-scraper in half.

They're limited by line of sight and inclement weather, but there isn't a cloud in the dawn sky and the harbor is empty. On the bright side, while each of those useless missiles cost millions of dollars, each laser blast with the equivalent force costs fifty-nine cents, times the number of drones, in this case, fifty-nine bucks. That's math even I can do.

The harbor churns.

White froth explodes.

Lovecraft rises at the center of the explosion. Its wings, long arms and many tentacles stretch out in the morning sun. While I can't hear its roar through the Swarm, I can hear it just fine from the lighthouse.

"Better hurry," Collins says. Her voice is lost in a breeze, and I realize she's standing outside, watching the Kaiju.

"A little closer," I say, piloting Hydra One straight toward the giant. I want to hit this thing with a full power blast out of the gate. And Lovecraft makes it easy for me. The monster has risen, but it's not moving. It's standing still.

"The hell is it waiting for?" Woodstock asks.

"Hudson," Alessi says, "I've patched in Watson. I think he has an answer."

Watson's voice comes through a little too loud. He's shouting and excited. "Second target incoming. Still two hundred miles out to the east, but moving *fast*. This time we have visual confirmation. Jon, it's her. It's Nemesis."

I'm thrown by the news, but not entirely surprised. Nemesis has gone from the wrathful judge of mankind to our abusive protector. Maybe that has something to do with Endo's new role in her life, but I think it's mostly because the vengeance goddess with an overzealous moral compass has realized there are much worse things in the world than humans. This changes things, and might explain what Lovecraft is waiting for, but I'd rather the Kaiju didn't turn Boston into a WWF 'squared circle,' and I'm not about to waste the opportunity to hit a stationary target. I engage the weapons system and use the controls beneath my right thumb to target Lovecraft's head. A quick button tap locks the laser on target and the Swarm follows suit.

Then I pull the trigger.

19

Two minds working as one.

That was the simplest way Maigo had expressed her connection to Nemesis. Her body had been torn asunder as the monster grew, but then it reformed inside the beast as a separate, but connected being. While they didn't share thoughts, their egos pushed and shoved for supremacy. But ultimately, it was Nemesis who was in control, and during those chaotic days of rapid growth, Maigo's 'voice' was limited to its most primal state, which cried out for vengeance—a mission the ancient beast gladly accepted.

But now, connected to a much different kind of monster, Maigo felt some comforting changes, the first of which was that her voice was dominant. The second voice was different. She could feel its intelligence, but there was a complete lack of emotion. It didn't burn with uncontrollable rage the way Nemesis did. The artificial intelligence that guided the robot reached out to the world, detecting planes, helicopters and people above. Beyond that, it felt radio, satellite and cell signals, patching into the world and taking in untold bytes of data, encrypted or not. But these actions were automatic, like breathing or a heartbeat, not extensions of a will.

Another drastic difference was that with Nemesis, she could feel, see, smell and taste everything that Nemesis experienced. It had left her with nightmares that plagued her mind, whether or not she was sleeping. But her connection to this non-organic robot didn't experience the world in the same way. She didn't feel what the robot felt, she simply knew it. In some ways, it felt like a video game. Knowing rather than experiencing. The giant machine could lose an arm, and she'd know it. Maybe even be shocked by it. But she wouldn't feel pain the way she had with Nemesis, who was hit by scores of missiles, subjected herself to self-immolation and shed her own skin.

Maigo looked up and saw the spire rising up, the ceiling hundreds of feet above. *Four hundred thirty two feet, six and a half inches,* she thought, the AI transferring the information to her mind. The system also identified Lilly, rising quickly toward the top, where a bunch of Russians waited to greet her.

She's going to need backup, and faster than she could think, she knew how to climb out.

"What is this thing?" she thought.

Ikthius Umbridle. The alien words entered her mind as a deep voice.

"I don't know what that means."

She sensed the AI unraveling all of Earth's languages at once, understanding which she spoke and then adjusting its internal dialogue to suit her.

Translation: I am the Watcher of this planet. Of Earth. Mission parameters: One. Atlantide defense. Two. Gestorumque eradication. Three. Defense of local population. Four. Early detection of Aeros oppressors. Mission parameter one: failure. Mission parameter two: success. Mission parameters three and four: ongoing.

"The Watcher," she thought. "That's not nearly catchy enough for Dad."

Jon Hudson, the deep voice replied, and Maigo felt some of her memories of her adoptive father slide into the Watcher's memory.

"Hyperion," she thought to the Watcher. Over the past year, she'd studied history in detail, searching for clues about the Atlanteans, Nemesis Prime and other hints that Earth really had been visited and influenced by a race of aliens known as the Ferox. Hyperion was a Titan, the god of light, and translated to 'watcher from above.' Seeing as how this Watcher had come from very, very far above, the name fit. "Your name is Hyperion now."

Confirmed. Watcher designation is now Hyperion. Jon Hudson will approve, the voice said.

"Yes, yes he will."

She felt another wave of memories transfer to Hyperion. Once again, it was an involuntary part of the Watcher-Voice connection, but these memories, of Nemesis, prompted a response.

Gestorumque detected.

"Nemesis," she corrected.

Gestorumque designated 'Nemesis,' detected.

"It's a memory," she thought. "It's just—" And then she knew she was wrong. Hyperion had accessed her memories of Nemesis, but it was detecting the actual Nemesis through its connections to the outside world. Nemesis was in the Atlantic, headed toward Boston.

Father...Dad, the voice said. *Jon Hudson is in Boston. Mother...mom, designation Ashley Collins, is in Boston. Dickhead...old man, designation Woodstock, is in Boston.*

Gestorumque detected, Hyperion said. *Designation unknown.* Maigo saw what looked like highly zoomed-in news footage of a massive explosion. *Designation unknown.*

Before she could react to this news, the voice repeated, *Gestorumque detected.* The view this time was from a weather station camera pointed at the ocean. She didn't recognize the view, but the information gathered from the signal source identified the location as Tokyo. The ocean rose up as something large surged toward the coast. *Designation unknown.*

"Nemesis and two unknown Kaiju?" A lot had happened since she and Lilly had left for Big Diomede, and she quickly realized that the FC-P now had to face Nemesis and an unknown Kaiju in Boston without the speed and protection provided by the X-35.

She watched Lilly leap through the hole above, planning to give her a minute to get clear, but Hyperion detected gunfire. Prompted by Maigo's burst of concern for her family, both for Lilly and for the others back in Boston, Hyperion reached out and dug its massive hand into the stone wall, rising toward a world the robot hadn't seen in thousands of years.

20

Mark Hawkins sat alone in the rear cargo area of the massive VTOL stealth transport. He'd been surprised by its crescent shape when it slid out of the night sky and landed in the middle of Hurd Stadium's football field. It was essentially a long, curved wing, shaped to avoid radar detection. In that way, it was similar to Future Betty, but this aircraft was big and loud in comparison. During the day, its black surface would also be visible to the naked eye.

Hawkins sat still, elbows on his knees, head lowered like a man in prayer, which wasn't far from the truth, if you ignored the black body armor, sinister looking helmet and visor and the oxygen mask over his face. He couldn't decide if he looked more like a Star Wars character or Daft Punk. The body armor and helmet were there to protect him from the elements—outside the plane was 25 degrees below zero—and from the enemy. The oxygen mask was there to protect him from the bends. He'd been wearing it for forty minutes, pre-breathing pure oxygen to purge the nitrogen from his system.

Looking at the cargo bay's floor revealed nothing more than grated metal and his boots. But the digital display in his facemask revealed outlines of the world below. He'd watched the coastline of Alaska come and go, and was now over the open ocean of the Bering Strait, headed for Russian airspace.

Hawkins had seen and done a lot in his life, but three years ago, he believed his life and death struggle with a grizzly bear at Yellowstone park where he was a ranger, would always be the hardest experience of his life. The bright red scars running across his chest were a constant reminder of that near-death experience. But in the years since then, he had endured a trial by fire that revealed dangers far worse than a bear, and his ability to help overcome those dangers. He'd faced the twisted chimeras of Island 731 and the deranged and powerful General Gordon in Washington, D.C., and he had helped defeat the Tsuchi, both large and small varieties, just a year ago. On top of all that, he'd been a father to a cat-girl turned cat-woman, whose unique physiology and needs made her the biggest of all his life's challenges. And yet he loved her like she was his own.

So as he bowed his head and stared at the floor, he said a prayer for Lilly. That she would be safe, and that the Russians hadn't taken her or harmed her, so help them God. His next prayer was for Maigo, knowing that Hudson was feeling similarly right now, even if he was focused on a different task.

"Ranger." The pilot's voice was crystal clear in his headset.

"Amen," Hawkins whispered, and then louder, "I'm here."

"We're two minutes out. Time to get ready."

Hawkins stood and headed for the back of the plane. He carried an unmarked Israeli X95 submachine gun, armed with rubber bullets and a Zed-5 stun gun developed by Zoomb. The weapon used electromagnets to silently propel two pronged darts with enough power to jolt a human being into unconsciousness. He also carried several flashbang grenades. All of it was non-lethal. If Russians were killed, the finger-pointing that would take place after his escape could turn deadly.

"One minute," the pilot said.

Hawkins's felt the plane begin to bank and slow. "Why are we turning?"

"Once we open the back, we'll be visible on radar, so we're not actually going to fly into Russian airspace," the pilot said. "That's your job."

"Right," Hawkins said.

He was going to free fall from 30,000 feet, for a full two minutes, long enough to cross over the imaginary line drawn between Big and Little Diomede islands. There was a time in his life when he and Hudson had pursued adrenaline for fun. They'd jumped out of planes, dived to the ocean's depths and jumped off a number of tall bridges with little more than a glorified elastic band to keep them from violent deaths. But a HALO (High Altitude Low Opening) was one of the most extreme things Hawkins had ever done, and this would be his second. The first was in FC-P training, six months previous. They'd had a BBQ after landing. This time, he was dropping onto a remote island populated by Russian soldiers and patrolled by a swarm of helicopters and jets. His only advantages were that no one would expect a lone person to drop in from 30,000 feet, his plummeting body wouldn't be picked up on radar, it was still dark out and he was dressed in black. Once the sun came up, he would lose all of them.

"Ten seconds," the pilot said. "Once the hatch is down, you'll get three seconds before it comes back up." The lights inside the cabin went black and the helmet's night vision quickly compensated, shading everything in hues of green. The cargo hatch lowered, and a gust of wind filled the open space.

"Go, go, go," the pilot said.

Hawkins didn't hesitate. He threw himself out of the plane, into the night sky, where he was struck by a frigid, roaring wind. He spun around as he fell, looking back to where he'd just leapt, and he saw nothing. The transport was already gone. He twisted back and saw the green outlines of two islands far below him. He angled himself toward the larger of the two and pulled his hands back, accelerating to his terminal velocity.

He could see tiny red lights of jets making broad circles around the island. And then, the lights of helicopters, much closer and lower, shining spotlights back and forth over the island's surface, like they were looking for something.

Not a good sign.

But most of the island itself was dark. He knew that lights had been erected, along with the prefab base, but something had happened to them, which suited him just fine.

One minute into his descent, he passed the elevation at which the fighter jets were patrolling without being carved in half by gunfire. The island loomed large below him now, its form digitally outlined in green. He angled himself toward a portion of it still cloaked in darkness and waited for the altitude-triggered parachute to deploy.

He heard the chop of helicopter blades a moment before the chopper passed beneath him, the vortex of air pulling him toward the rotor. He flared his arms and legs, and grunted as the wind buffeting them stretched his muscles to the breaking point. But the subtle shift in speed saved his life. The chopper charged past below him and swept around the island's outer edge. He turned his head back toward the ground and nearly screamed. He was seconds from impact. He could clearly see the silhouette of the rocky surface partially cloaked by thin fog.

And then, just a thousand feet from the ground, deployment. The expanding parachute felt like a giant reaching out and plucking him from the sky, but that jolt wasn't the worst of it. The parachute would stop him from being smeared on the ground, but he would still hit hard. Broken bones from HALO jumps weren't uncommon, and his first and only experience had dropped them into a lush, grassy field. Hawkins tucked and rolled over the uneven, hard ground, thankful for the body armor that absorbed much of the impact and spared his skin from being torn apart.

The roll carried him back to his feet as a breeze caught and yanked the parachute. He caught the lines and dragged the chute in, detaching it and crumpling it into a tight ball before putting a rock on top of it.

But the snap of the chute opening hadn't gone unnoticed.

He heard voices approaching, slow and cautious. The beams of two flashlights mounted to the barrels of AK-47s, cut through the fog, mostly failing, but the men were already on top of him, their Kevlar-armored bodies and pale skin coming into view. He drew the Zed, took aim and pulled the trigger. It struck the first man's forehead and delivered a shock that sent him into a momentary seizure before dropping him to the ground. Hawkins took aim at the second man, who was bringing the barrel of his AK-47 around. Even if the man fired and missed, Hawkins would be screwed.

He pulled the trigger twice. The first round struck the man's body armor protecting his shoulder; the second found his neck. The man dropped beside his partner, both of them unconscious. *For now,* Hawkins thought. He had about ten minutes before they woke up, and he wasn't about to kill either man. He did take their ammunition and the antennas from their radios. It would buy him a few extra minutes as the men stumbled their way through the thickening fog.

Viewing the island through his visor, Hawkins headed for the core, which had been radically changed by the Russian demolitions. The closer he got, the more voices he heard, all angry, all Russian. Something had them irked, and few people could irk a gaggle of grown men like a pair of teenage girls, especially when those girls had the strength, speed and will to make fools of the men.

Hawkins switched out the Zed's magazine while he slid through the night. He was a good shot, but the Zed carried only eight rounds, and it sounded like there were at least double that number of men up ahead. When he reached the outer ring of the exposed Atlantean symbol, he slid down into the recess and crept to the other side. He could see the backs of several men standing at the core, looking at a black hole descending into the island. He couldn't see the men on the far side, but he could hear them, and if he got close enough to see them, they would see him.

He took aim at the closest man, working out his course of action—in which order he would shoot the men before leaping forward and unleashing a torrent of rubber bullets, all aimed at chest level.

Hopefully there weren't any short Russians on the receiving end. A rubber bullet to the head—or worse, to the eye—could still kill a man.

Then the island shook.

He braced himself and wondered if the Russians had set off more explosives underground. But they sounded just as surprised as he was. Several of them backed away from the hole.

The ground shook again, this time more violently, and as the men shouted and stumbled, a black blur exploded up out of the hole. When the blur reached the apex of its jump and unfurled clawed hands, Hawkins knew who it was.

Lilly!

The cat-woman descended toward the men with a hiss, triggering a fusillade of chaotic gunfire. Hawkins rose from his hiding spot and pulled the trigger, firing eight shots in rapid succession and dropping five men. He could hear Lilly working her way through the men on the far side of the hole. Gunshots, hissing and grunts rose from the fog like a punk band had kicked off a concert. He switched out the magazine and dropped two more men, turning toward a black shape emerging through the fog like a specter.

His finger froze over the trigger, aimed at his target's head, just as his target pulled up short, sparing his face from a hard punch.

Lilly's yellow, feline eyes went wide in time with a smile. "Dad?"

"Are you okay?" he asked. "Where's Maigo?"

Lilly's already wide eyes broadened.

The ground shook again, even more violently than before.

"Grab some of these guys," she shouted. "Pull them back!"

Hawkins didn't question her. He took two of the men by their uniforms and dragged them out of the circle. By the time he returned for more, Lilly had moved most of the rest. She threw two of the remaining three over her shoulders as Hawkins picked up the final man.

"What's happening?" he asked as the ground trembled.

"She's coming!"

"Who is coming?"

"Maigo!" Lilly shouted, and then she leapt away.

Hawkins carried a man through the large rings, fighting to stay upright against the quavering ground. Lilly greeted him at the edge and took the man from him, quickly depositing the soldier another hundred feet back.

What the hell are we running from? he wondered. As strong as Maigo was, she couldn't move an entire island. The ground beneath his feet rose up and cracked. Then it fell away.

Hawkins dangled over the open space for a moment before Lilly yanked him up by his arm. She carried him back away from the widening pit. Soil poured into the hole, and then something massive rose from it. At first, it was just an immense shape pushing through the fog, but then it rose up, climbing out of the Earth, a hundred feet at a time.

When it finally cleared the massive hole, the thing—the *robot*—stood over three hundred feet tall, its armor gleaming in the first rays of the morning's sun.

Lilly tugged on Hawkins's arm, pulling his attention away from the mechanical behemoth that somehow looked both futuristic and ancient.

"The hell is that?" Hawkins asked, looking back at her to find Future Betty descending toward them, the rear hatch lowering. Lilly held the craft's remote in her hand.

Lilly climbed inside the X-35 and turned around, glancing up at the colossal machine. "That...is Maigo." Lilly toggled her headset. "You hear me, Maig?"

"I'm here," said an electronic-sounding version of Maigo's voice. "Hyperion is transmitting my thoughts on our frequency."

"Hyperion?" Lilly asked. "You named it already?"

"Like father, like daughter," Hawkins said.

Hyperion raised its massive hands up and clutched its head.

"You okay?" Lilly asked.

"Just a lot of information at once," Maigo said, her projected voice sounding strained. "Dad's in trouble. In Boston. Tokyo has problems, too."

A loud hum rumbled from the giant robot.

"What's happening?" Hawkins asked.

"I don't—" Maigo let out a grunt. "Get back! Quick!"

As quick to act as ever, Hawkins charged into the X-35, dragging Lilly behind him. "Get us out of here!"

Lilly dove behind the controls and sent them hurtling skyward, rising up past Hyperion's stoic face and going hundreds of feet higher. Warning chimes started sounding, but they had nothing to do with Hyperion and everything to do with the incoming missiles. The Russians had launched an attack on the robot.

Watching the scene through the projection on the floor, Hawkins saw Hyperion bend its knees and flex its arms like it was preparing to fight the missiles off.

Then, in a blink, Hyperion was gone, as though it had never existed.

Russian missiles and rockets rained down on the island, laying waste to the surface, and to a large number of Russian soldiers. That all those men had died was tragic, but it also meant the Russian government would never talk about what happened here today. If anything, they'd quickly cover it up.

Hawkins slid into the cockpit passenger's seat beside Lilly.

"Sorry," she said. "For—"

"Later." Hawkins looked at his daughter, feeling a mixture of anger, relief and pride. She had broken some serious rules and put people they cared about in danger, but they had also managed to recover a massive robot, which would have been dangerous under Russian control. He didn't know what happened to the robot when it disappeared, but he was pretty sure it was out of the Russians' reach. He pointed to the south and said, "Get us to Tokyo."

Lilly leaned forward, looking through the windshield. Hawkins looked out and saw a lone man, running toward the island's coastline.

"Hold on...is that?" Her eyes widened with recognition.

Hawkins saw the man, but without Lilly's superior vision, he couldn't make out anything identifiable about him. Lilly on the other hand...

They swooped down toward the man, still invisible to the surrounding Russian forces, as Lilly said, "Just a quick stop first."

21

To anyone viewing the swarm from the outside, they'll see the drones spreading out around Hydra One, heading straight for Lovecraft in Boston Harbor, but nothing else. I'll be viewing the scene through the VR headset. It detects the fired lasers' heat signatures and highlights them in red. It's like watching Star Wars, without the sound effects. In that way, the invisible and silent lasers are kind of anticlimactic. The effect is anything but.

A hundred lasers, fired in unison and moving at the speed of light, strike the left side of Lovecraft's broad white forehead a fraction of a second after I pull the trigger. Each laser strikes with 30 kilowatts of destructive force capable of slicing through a steel girder. Multiply that by 100 and I've just drilled the monster with 3000 kilowatts.

To my delight, the Kaiju reels back, its head snapping around as it turns skyward and lets out a shriek that hurts my ears back in the lighthouse where I'm hiding.

"Gawdamn," I hear Woodstock say in the real world. "Nearly pissed myself. Think you hurt it, boss."

I hear the door open and feel an ocean-scented breeze flow past. Collins has gone outside, and her voice sounds distant. "It's definitely injured."

I see the damage as the Kaiju recovers. There's a small hole in the left side of the forehead surrounded by a starburst scorch mark. I have no idea how far down the attack penetrated, but I'm encouraged by the small amount of purple blood leaking from the wound. The one drawback of fighting an organic enemy with lasers is that any wounds created are also cauterized. So Lovecraft won't be bleeding to death from anything I do to it. But if I can punch a hole through its skull and turn its brain to Swiss cheese, the Swarm might be worth its exorbitant price tag. That's assuming this thing has a brain large enough to target, and that it's in the creature's head. I am dealing with an alien, after all.

A green battery symbol blinks in my heads-up display, revealing that the lasers have all recharged and are ready to fire. I pull the trigger again, and I'm pleased to see the same effect duplicated and another hole drilled into the monster, this time in its cheek.

The monster's second shriek is even louder than the first. The painful effect on my body confuses me and ruins the illusion that I'm flying above Boston.

"Mother," Woodstock grumbles. "I think I actually pissed myself."

Focusing back on the VR projection, I watch Lovecraft spin around, arms splayed wide, tentacles flared open. A guttural growl rolls over the harbor.

Am I hurting it, or just making it angry?

As the lasers' batteries fill up again, I bank left, taking the Swarm with me. When the battery symbol flashes green, I turn back toward Lovecraft and find the behemoth staring up at me, its black-eyed gaze haunting.

Back in the lighthouse, goose bumps cover my arms and legs.

"It's seen you," Collins says.

I target the center of the thing's head, hoping the brain is where it should be, and that it's not the size of a baseball. The Swarm flares out around me, the AIs matching my target. With all hundred directed energy weapons focused on the same spot, I pull the trigger.

But even as my finger pulls against the remote control's trigger, the Kaiju is in motion, anticipating the attack. It leans to the side, but the lasers' guidance systems respond, tracking the monstrous forehead.

And then the target is gone, covered by a white cloak.

With the target lost, I pull the trigger and fire one hundred 30-kilowatt lasers. Lovecraft's raised wing is peppered with laser blasts, which spark against the skin, scoring it, but not punching through. Those wings are strong enough to fend off a MOAB attack. Without the focused targeting, the lasers are all but useless.

Ripples of blue and green light surge through the beast, building to a crescendo, and I realize what's about to happen just a moment too late. The massive wing sweeps open with enough force to send a cyclone of air spiraling toward the Swarm. Hydra One hits it head on, and I lose control. Spinning toward the ocean, I catch glimpses of several other drones, falling toward the water. I try to regain control, but fail. I flinch when Hydra One plunges into the ocean.

Sensing that the drone is out of commission, the AI toggles my control to the next still functioning drone in the sequence, Hydra Seven. On the far right side of my heads-up display, there are two vertical lines of fifty dots, each one representing a drone. A moment ago, all one hundred were green. Now more than a quarter of them are red.

The bad news doesn't hold my attention for long. The sudden shift in view staggers me again, but there's no time to acclimate. The Swarm is still on a collision course with Lovecraft's head. I bank hard to the right while targeting the monster, locking onto its black eye. Just before I lose sight of it, I pull the trigger. I have no idea how many of the Swarm have locked on target, but as I peel away, I'm chased by an angry wail.

Careening around the Kaiju, I see a large number of the Swarm rounding the far side, the AI's collision avoidance system taking an alternate route around the monster, which means only a small number of drones could have fired on the monster. I doubt I did any serious damage, but the creature sounds pretty upset.

"That do anything?" I ask.

"Made it angry," Collins said. "Clutched its eye for a moment, but it looks fine now. It's tracking the Swarm. Maybe it will follow you back out to sea?"

"Good idea," I say.

If I can't kill it, I can at least draw it away from the coast. While I can't predict what Nemesis will do when she arrives, I doubt it will be anything Boston could survive. Better if the fight takes place out at sea.

"Coming around for another strike, then I'll head for deeper water." Boston sweeps past below me as I direct the Swarm around in a wide arc, keeping a careful distance from Lovecraft. When I turn to face the beast again, its wings rise up in front of it, cloaking its body and partially covering its face. It peers over the wings with a glowering hatred that reminds me of my third grade teacher. Sister Mary Phelps was a tank of a woman who ate salads in a trough-sized bowl, which wasn't enough food to keep her from occasionally passing out. She compensated by writing all of the class notes on the chalk board before class started. She generally had the energy level of a beached whale, but if you crossed her, and she raised her head from the desk and you saw those eyes glaring at you over her arms, a ruler would soon be rapping your knuckles. The look in Lovecraft's black eyes tells me it might have a similar punishment in mind, but instead of a ruler, it might use a Navy Destroyer.

I target the forehead between its eyes again, hoping it won't anticipate the shot. As quick as it is, it can't move at light speed.

When the targeting system locks on, I notice the side of its head and the two holes I drilled into it. The purple stain of blood and the black starburst are still present, but I don't see any other damage. The wounds have healed.

Nothing short of incinerating this thing's brain is going to put it down. And maybe even that won't work. Who's to say the alien brain would cease to function with a hole in it? For all I know, this thing shits out of its mouth and has a brain in its ass, which is still submerged in the water.

"Fingers crossed this thing shits out of its ass," I say.

When Woodstock says, "What now?" I pull the trigger.

As hoped, Lovecraft doesn't see the attack coming. Sparks and gore fly away from the target area. The head snaps back, the wings spring open, and its arms splay wide, fists clenched. But it doesn't roar in anger. Doesn't shriek in pain.

For a moment, I think I've done it.

Fall over, I think. *Fall over, damn you.*

The only reason this thing would remain silent is if the blast destroyed its brain, right?

The massive head comes forward again.

The wings and arms draw in.

The eyes return their gaze straight at me.

Wrong.

The alien Kaiju *let* me take the shot. It absorbed the pain, showing a massive force of will to not react to it. And now, locked in its gaze again, I can feel what it's thinking: *You're fucked.*

"Oh, we're fucked," Woodstock says, seeing the same message I am.

"Heading out to sea," I say, banking the Swarm toward the harbor's exit and slowing so I don't pull too far ahead. "Is it following?"

"Hold on," Collins says. "It's—yeah, it's coming. But it's—you might want to slow down some more so it—"

Lovecraft roars, this time with a guttural rage that dwarfs all of its previous vocalizations. I clutch the headset, pushing it harder against my ears, and scream. I can't hear Collins or Woodstock screaming until the roar suddenly stops. Our screams die down a moment later, but not fast enough.

"It heard us," Collins says. "It's looking right at—oh, shit, it's coming this way!"

I set Hydra Seven on autopilot and peel the VR headset off. The shift back to the real world is disorienting.

I stagger out onto the catwalk and see the giant white body, lit in the warm orange hue of a clear sunrise. Blue and green shimmer through its tentacle-laden body as it wades through the harbor, heading straight for the lighthouse.

I slide the headset back on and say, "Get me downstairs."

"What? How—"

"Carry me!" I shout, taking back control of Hydra Seven and banking around toward the lighthouse and Lovecraft beyond it. I feel myself being lifted up by Collins, whose arms are under my armpits, and by Woodstock, who's holding my legs. I can feel myself being carried. Can hear Woodstock grumbling and Collins breathing heavily. But I keep my attention solely on what I can see.

I target the beast, and it takes no defensive measures. Doesn't need to. I know that now. The best I can do is stagger it. Buy us some time. My first shot strikes its chest, where if it were human, its heart would be located. The Kaiju grunts and flinches, but continues forward.

These quick bursts aren't getting it done, I think, and I disengage the lasers' safety limits. If I can keep a sustained blast focused on one area, I should be able to punch a hole clean through it. If that doesn't kill it, it will damn well hurt it, and maybe distract it long enough for us to make an unconventional getaway.

After switching off the AI's collision avoidance protocol for all but three of the drones, I target the creature's head again. With all seventy-three drones locked on, I fire. The invisible beam of energy glows red in my VR view, striking the Kaiju's forehead and then sustaining as the fleet of aircraft close the distance.

Lovecraft presses forward, roaring in anger, and then in pain as the directed energy weapon burrows into its skull. The creature turns its head to avoid the shot, but the targeting system moves with it. Steam erupts from the wound, spraying purple. *It's working,* I think.

Then the wings come up, shielding the head and throwing off the targeting system. The lasers hammer against the wings, but separately. Then all at once, the overwhelmed batteries are fried. The barrage ceases with a blinking Christmas display of warnings clouding my view.

Screw it, I think, and I direct the Swarm to collide with the monster. Maybe the force of seventy drones slamming into it will knock it back.

The drones explode upon contact, striking the monster nearly as one. And to my delight, the already stunned Lovecraft is knocked back. The monster stumbles and falls into the ocean, sending up a wave that will hammer the coast.

Still in the VR headset, I feel the air change around me and know that Collins and Woodstock have managed to carry me down the spiral staircase and out the door.

I swing the remaining drones around toward the island and select a small stretch of stone just barely large enough to accommodate the three small aircraft. I direct the AI to perform a vertical landing. When I feel the AI take over, I reach up and yank the helmet from my head.

We're at the end of the platform leading to the lighthouse door. Collins has just leaped down and turned around to catch me. Woodstock is behind me, ready to lower me down. "I'm good," I say, and I jump down beside Collins. "Our ride will be here in a minute."

"Ride?" Woodstock asks and slides over the edge on his stomach.

I point up to the three drones lowering toward us.

"Uh, boss, those things don't have cockpits." Woodstock says.

I leap over the craggy rocks, heading for the designated landing zone. "Nope. But they have handles."

"For fuck's sake," Woodstock says, but he follows with Collins.

The ground shakes, stumbling us.

"I think it's up," Collins says, picking herself up.

A quick glance over my shoulder confirms it. Lovecraft steps up to the small island, rising high above us, wings outstretched, fists raised. I have no doubt this thing has the power to erase the island from existence. We just need to be gone when that happens.

As the giant arms descend, I know that's not going to happen. We need another minute. We have a second. I catch hold of Collins's hand and squeeze. Our eyes meet, saying a lot in a fraction of the time we would by speaking.

This is the end.

I love you.

See you on the other side.

And then, something like a force of nature appears between us and the Kaiju. *A giant man? A suit of armor?* My mind struggles to recover from the fact that we're still alive, and it races to identify the thing that has just appeared and caught both of Lovecraft's arms in its big, metal hands.

Metal hands.

It's a robot.

A Kaiju-sized robot. And for some reason, it arrived just in time to save us.

Still clutching Lovecraft's wrists, holding the Kaiju at bay, the robot's head, with its glowing red eyes, turns down, looks right freaking at me and shouts, "Dad! Get out of here!"

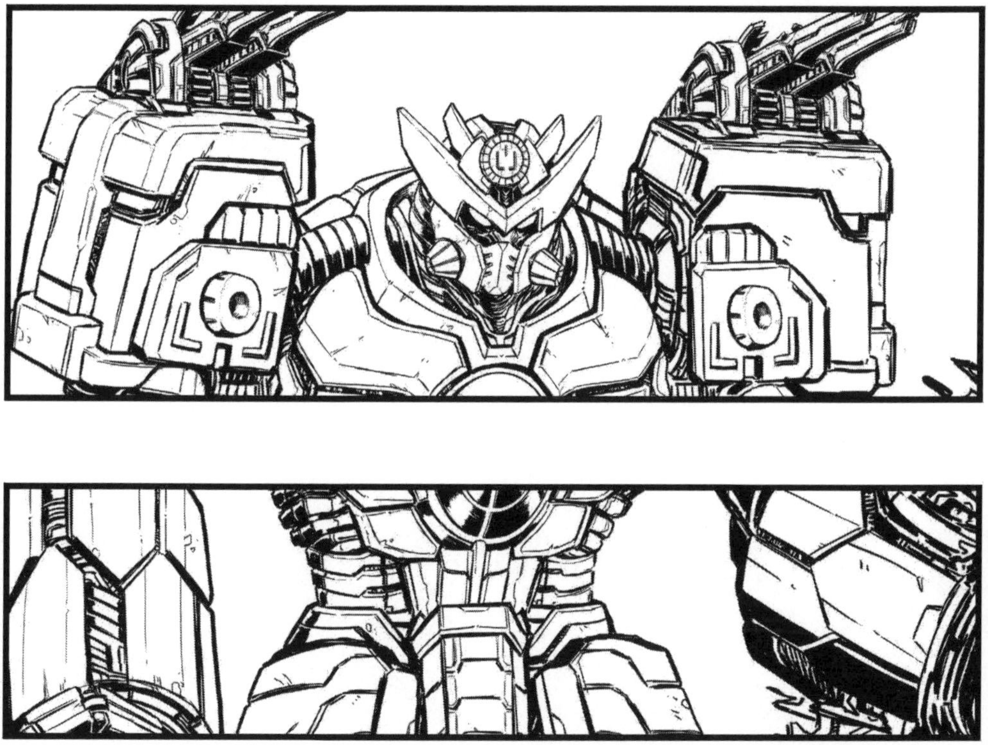

HYPERION

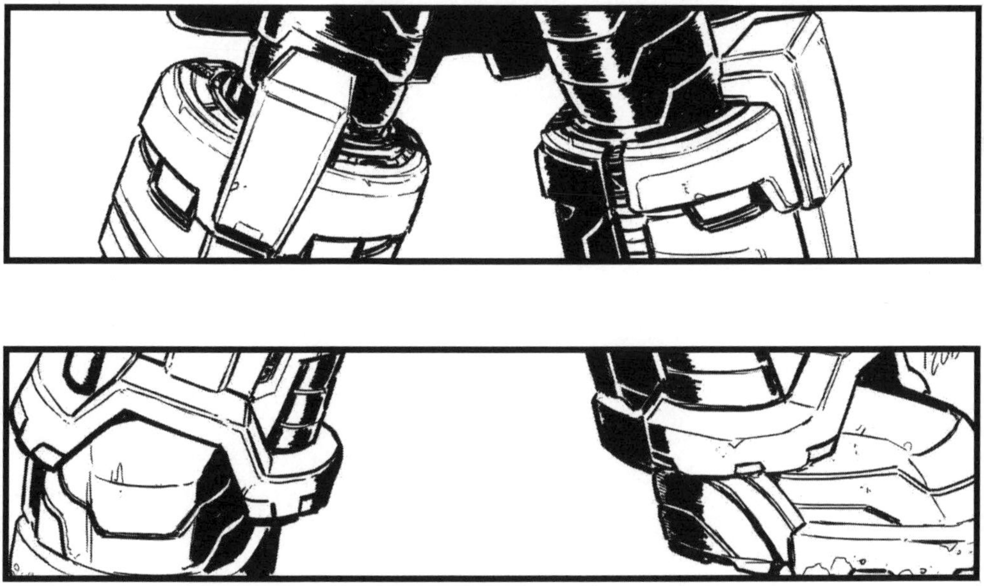

22

Nothing about the massive machine standing above me looks familiar, other than a hint of 1980s Saturday Morning Cartoon style. In all our sifting through history and the files pilfered from GOD, there has never been even a hint that something like this existed. I'm taken totally off guard by its appear-ance, and I'm nearly unhinged by its use of the word, "Dad."

I stagger back as the robot's arms shake under the weight of Lovecraft's limbs, pushing down. The masked face that reminds me of a Spartan warrior's helmet with dashes of Samurai, a smackerel of *Wolverine* and clearly non-human influences turns back to its Kaiju adversary and pushes back. The robot is a little smaller, but their strength seems equally matched.

My heel catches on an outcrop of rock, and I fall to my ass, looking up at the robot's back. It's armored, clearly designed for battle, maybe even battle with a Kaiju. Ancient and/or alien symbols are carved into the armor, forming decorative patterns, or maybe just warning messages that say, 'Stay the hell back,' in Klingon. I see the thing's face in my mind's eye again. I see the glaring eyes of a solemn judge, but it doesn't have the vengeful hatred of Nemesis.

How could it? I wonder. *It's a robot.* Then the single word repeats in my mind.

'Dad.'

The deep baritone voice projected from the robot sounded foreign, but the inflections beneath the rumbling exhortation...and the word.

Dad!

Collins grabs my shoulder, yanking me back to my feet. "Jon!"

I stumble back, staying aloft only because Collins didn't let go of me. "Maigo..."

"Jon!" Collins shouts. "We have to go! Now!"

I turn toward her, eyes wide, no doubt looking manic. "It's Maigo."

Collins's next shout catches in her throat. "What?"

I point up at the robot struggling with Lovecraft. "*That's* Maigo!"

She stands in shock for a moment, and I see her mouth the word, 'Dad,' as the color drains from her face. Then she's back to reality, pulling me back. "If we don't leave now, we might never. Move your ass!" She slugs my shoulder. The pain pulls me from my shock.

The three remaining Swarm drones have landed on an outcrop of rock, their engines still running, ready to lift off again. Woodstock has already climbed up and is standing behind one of the drones. "Handles, my ass. How the hell are we supposed to hold on to these things? They're smoother than my ex-wife's—"

I leap up behind one of the drones, lean over the top of it and push down on a horizontal line near the nose. A metal bar pops up six inches. They're used for transporting the drones, but will work as a handle bar. "Lay on top," I say, and I demonstrate, centering myself over the drone's back. "Just don't let go."

While Collins and Woodstock climb aboard their own drones, I place the VR helmet back on and see just a subtle shift in my view, moving slightly forward and a little lower. The only real difference is that I can no longer see my arms in front of me. Feeling my way, I slide my arms under the handlebar and flex them up, holding the bar in the crook of my elbows so I can still operate the two remotes clutched in my hands.

"We're on," Collins shouts. "Get us out of here."

With the island shaking beneath us, I take control of Hydra Seven and lift off, rising straight up. When the HUD shows that Collins and Woodstock have lifted off the ground, too, I start heading away from the island, taking it slow as I start to see warning messages about balance and weight.

A grinding noise pulls my thoughts away from flying, and I hear Collins shouting over the din. "They're falling! Go, go, go!"

I punch Hydra Seven forward and clutch the metal bar with my arms, slowing only when it feels like I might let go. The warning messages being sent from the other two drones let me know that Collins and Woodstock haven't been flung free. Yet. Not wanting to pull a 'Prometheus,' fleeing in a straight line from an object falling toward me, I veer hard to the left.

I can't see what's happening behind me, but when I hear an impact, and feel a pressure wave slap my back, I know I've made the right call. I check the warning messages, confirming we're all still present. Then I take us in a wide loop, distancing us from the action, while turning around for a better view. Collins and Woodstock can turn their heads, but I'm limited by the drone's field of view, and looking back while flying forward just isn't possible.

When we come around arcing past the coastline, I see the giant robot that is either being controlled by Maigo remotely—I hope—or has her trapped inside it, pinned beneath Lovecraft. The Kaiju's wings are folded back tight against its body, which is writhing with tentacles and shimmering with color. The giant arms and three-digit hands are pushing down, reaching for the robot's head, but they're still held back.

Proving it has much more than a primal mind, Lovecraft moves its arms to the side, opening up a clear path to the robot's face. It leans in, face-tentacles spreading wide, twitching with anticipation. The layers of teeth spread wide enough to envelope its enemy's head. And once it does, I have no doubt those strange jaws are powerful enough to send those teeth spearing through the head, and whatever is inside, like toothpicks through a deep fried clam.

I target the back of Lovecraft's head, hoping three lasers will be enough to distract it. I pull the trigger and see three red beams blaze between the drones and the large white orb. There's a puff of smoke, hardly any effect compared to the scalding holes drilled into its face, but the reaction is comparable.

Wings flare wide, and the two big arms come up and over the head, shielding it behind the thick fingers. A roar rips through the air, but rather than cringe from it, I smile and make a mental note: the back of its head is sensitive. Maybe even a weakness.

I prepare to take another shot, trying to aim between the fingers, but the robot takes full advantage of the opening.

The big metal fist, which I note has just two big fingers and a thumb drives a punch into Lovecraft's side. The Kaiju's body bends with the blow. I don't think it's done much damage. But there's time for more.

Hit it, I think, *hit it again!*

But the giant robot fist stays lodged just below the Kaiju's ribs–if it has ribs.

What the hell is it doing?

C'mon, Maigo.

That's when I notice long channels along its forearm sliding open. It takes just a second, and it's quickly followed by three L shaped blades that spring out. The blades unfold and lock into place as they snap up and then forward, plunging into the Kaiju's side.

Lovecraft's anguished cry reaches a high pitch that I think will rupture my ears. But then the beast is tossed to the side. Or did it dive? Either way, its cry becomes a wet, bubbling gargle as it splashes down in the ocean.

To my surprise, the massive beast that I could so easily picture destroying entire worlds, leaps for deeper ocean and dives down when the water is deep enough to accommodate it. Then with a splurge of black goo that blackens the ocean for miles, Lovecraft opens its wings and shoves them back, propelling its girth into deep water, where it dives and disappears.

I circle the island as the robot pulls itself up from the crushed lighthouse and stands like some heroic beacon in the morning sun. The giant head turns, sees me and then follows my progress around the island. The face is a stoic mask, lacking any kind of expression other than serious determination. But then its massive arm rises, its two fingered hand opens and it waves, friendly and casual.

The arm lowers again and the head moves, still following me, but splitting at its core and then sliding apart in segments until the face is open and exposed. Inside it is a shiny black oval that looks like oil. The black surface stretches and contorts as something moves within it. A human shape emerges, arms, hands and fingers stretching against the fabric, and then sliding through. A body follows next, and despite the slimy look of the oily substance, comes out clean.

Maigo!

She waves in the same way the robot had just a moment ago, confirming that she's the one controlling it.

But how? And where the hell did this thing come from?

My eyes wander down the front of the robot, and I see a massive symbol carved into the chest, three circles connected by a single vertical line. Right now, the outer circle glows red, while the two inner circles are dark. *This thing is Atlantean,* I realize. *Holy... This is what was buried beneath Big Diomede!*

Maigo holds out her hand and raises her index finger in the same way Collins does when she's on the phone with someone and I want to talk to her. Then she lies back down, and she's greeted by black tendrils that remind me of Nemesis's back and how she pulled Endo inside of her. Maigo slides inside the black, which reverts back to a smooth, oily surface.

"Can you hear me?" Maigo says, her voice clear in my ear, though distorted somehow, like it's a digital version of her actual voice.

"Maigo," I say, relieved that she's safe. "What the hell is going on? How did you—"

"Long story," she says. "But I'm sorry I did it. I put you all in danger."

She's right about that, but I'm not sure having Future Betty would have changed the outcome of this battle the way this robot did. "Just tell me what it is."

"Hyperion," she says, and I wonder if she's expecting me to know what that is. But then she fills me in. "This is what killed Nemesis Prime."

As the massive head closes around Maigo, I take stock of the colossal machine again. From what I know, Nemesis Prime was bigger and badder than our modern day Nemesis, and if this thing took *her* out, there is more to this robot than we just saw.

The moment the head closes, Hyperion flinches and turns around, looking back out at the ocean.

"You guys better get out of here," Maigo says.

"What's going on?" I ask.

"I can feel her coming."

"Lovecraft?"

"Good name," she says, "but no. Nemesis. She's almost here."

I bank higher and look into the distance, using the camera to zoom in. A mound of water carved in half by two rows of forty foot tall spines charges toward us.

That's Nemesis all right, and she seems pissed.

That's when it hits me. Nemesis is a new creation, like Maigo herself, and like Maigo, this ancient goddess of vengeance remembers its first life, and death—at the robotic hands of Hyperion.

23

The world was becoming a strange place. Rising up to the surface brought the voices of humanity, like a thick haze, calling for her attention. For her vengeance. She felt the wrongs of the world as strongly as ever, but amidst the chaos was a beacon of interest.

The creature felt familiar. Like family. But wrong.

She could feel its power, but was it a threat?

Not to her, she thought, but the Voice wasn't so sure. Endo was suspicious. The Gestorumque was aware of Nemesis's approach, but wasn't projecting any rage toward her. Instead, she felt kinship from the creature. Welcome. And this confused her.

But not Endo.

For even more profound than the sense of belonging with this Gestorumque, they could feel its contempt and rage for the people they cared for. People who were in danger. And despite the impressive speed at which she could swim, Nemesis knew she would not arrive in time to intervene.

She was no stranger to extreme emotions. They'd been tortured into her Prime self and passed down to her. But failure and shame, those were new, and they came from Endo's voice. At first, she sneered at the emotions. They felt weak, which wasn't how she thought of Endo. But discomfort quickly changed to a new kind of rage, and she found her broad tail pounding through the water even faster. And then a new sense reached her mind: exhilaration. From the speed. From the anticipation of battle. From the hope that this new burst of energy might help them arrive in time.

As they neared the scene, Endo focused their thoughts on what they could detect. The people. The locations. The Gestorumque. While they couldn't see what was happening, a lot could be inferred by what they felt from those involved. The humans were frightened, desperate, and yet, they were determined and defiant. She and Endo admired these humans for similar reasons despite having very different kinds of interactions with them.

The Gestorumque was more confusing. It was angry and full of vengeance that mirrored the memories of Prime, but all of that emotion was expertly directed, combining primal power with intelligent focus. It was the kind of symbiosis that Nemesis was only starting to find with Endo. And right now, all that rage and intelligent guidance was directed at humanity, who were simply defending a landscape that had been forever altered by Nemesis.

The Kaiju felt no remorse for her previous actions, for the destruction of the city ahead or for the coastline she swam along. It felt righteous then, and her memory of the events remained the same. There had been no other option. Not with that wounded voice.

A sudden shift in emotion revealed a change in the battle's direction. The humans, their friends, spiked with fear strong enough for Nemesis to feel it from hundreds of miles, and at this proximity, it felt like a slap. They were in danger, direct and immediate.

We're not going to make it, Endo thought, urging they move faster despite knowing it was no use. They still had miles to cover, and the doom roiling from their friends was growing all the more powerful, rising to a peak.

Nemesis roared. The bubbling vocalization would betray their position to the human military forces seeking them out, but it couldn't be helped. Feeling helpless was not something the Kaiju was familiar with, and it revealed itself as emotions that mirrored those of the people for whom she felt concern.

And then, in a flash, everything changed.

They felt relief and surprise from the humans. They had been saved, by something else. Something that filled their hearts with hope.

But Nemesis felt nothing.

It was like the newcomer wasn't really there, detectable only through the emotions of others.

The Gestorumque's reaction was equal to that of the humans, but vastly different. After a moment of confusion, the creature emoted waves of anger, fear and doubt. Whatever it had encountered, it was unexpected, but recognized. Nemesis sensed a struggle, reading the Gestorumque's emotions like a painting, but the image was one sided and incomplete.

And then there was pain.

The Gestorumque had been wounded.

Logic with a twinge of shame-filled fear propelled the creature away from the humans, who were now elated. The danger for them had passed.

Nemesis's charge slowed as she reached shallow waters and let her head rise up. For the first time, she saw the scene with her eyes, and for the first time, she felt complete and abject shock. She flinched in the water, slowing nearly to a stop as a memory slammed into her mind.

Her death.

She felt it again.

Saw this ancient enemy.

Experienced the pain it had wrought.

Endo felt it too, but warned against her building emotions. *That wasn't you. Wasn't us. This is not our enemy. It saved our friends.*

But as he experienced the death himself, his voice lost power, and all that was left in the void of Nemesis's primal mind, was what she had been designed for: vengeance.

She would destroy her ancient enemy, without mercy, compassion or hesitation. With a thrust of her tail, Nemesis pounded through the water, surging toward a battle once lost, but soon avenged.

24

"Kiku," Seika Ayugai whispered. "Never leave me."

Kiku stared back, unblinking, her smile warming his heart. She was always there for him. Always present. Always smiling. Always pretty. Seika considered himself blessed and lucky to have found her at a comic book convention. He didn't get out much–hardly ever–but some of his virtual gaming friends had been having an annual meet up and he had known that getting out of his small Tokyo apartment would make his parents happy.

He'd first seen her through a display of Manga, and he'd instantly been smitten by her wide green eyes and lithe figure. He had approached cautiously, with the nervousness of a thirty year old man who had never had a female friend, let alone been with a woman. Her docile demeanor put him at ease and he'd felt no judgment about his size, his balding hair or the nasal pitch of his voice.

He squeezed her soft body, pulling her against him and leaning his cheek against hers. Light filtering through the blinds made him squint.

Another morning.

Another day. From his small room, he could telecommute, do his programming, play Final Fantasy 10 with his friends and have food deliver-ed. With the attached single person bathroom, he could go entire days–weeks even–without ever having to leave this safe space. And Kiku, the ever faithful, stayed with him every second.

He sat up and looked down at her body, still as perfectly formed and creamy skinned as when he'd first seen her. "Love you, Ki–" The bed shook beneath him. "–ku?"

He looked around the perfectly organized room. A pen rolled across his desk and fell to the floor.

"Was that you?" he asked, and something about the question made him queasy. He knew it wasn't her.

The bed shook again, and this time, the room with it. The glowing screen of his laptop, wallpapered with a photo of Kiku, flickered.

Seika stood slowly, his flaccid legs straining with the effort. Hands on hips, he stretched to either side and then stepped toward the window. He didn't want to open it. Didn't want to see the city, or feel the warmth of the sun. It irritated his skin, and something about the city—and all the people in it—revolted him. But if there was an earthquake, he and Kiku might have to flee the city.

When was the last time I used the moped? he wondered, considering whether or not he'd remember how to use it, if it still had gasoline, if the gasoline had gone bad and how he would carry Kiku on the bike.

Seika's chest tightened. He leaned forward, holding himself up against the window sill, breathing deeply. *I need to exercise,* he thought. *Or I'm going to die in this room.* His eyes widened a touch. *I don't want to die in this room.* He looked back at Kiku. Her gaze filled him with relief, and his fears about spending the rest of his life in this small space didn't feel so wrong. "If you won't leave me, I will stay here forever."

He reached out for the tilt wand on the blinds. He braced himself for the warm glow of the sun and then twisted the wand.

He squinted in the light, groaning and nearly closing the blinds again. But then he saw Tokyo outside, gleaming and clean from the previous night's rain. It was still early, and the streets had yet to congest with commuters. It even seemed quiet.

Then everything shook again, more violently this time. The distant sound of shattering glass was followed by an ear-splitting warning klaxon. Were they under attack? Was it the Chinese, finally seeking retribution for World War II? He looked out the window, peering past the neighboring sky-rise buildings to Tokyo Harbor.

A wave slid into view, crashing against the docks and tossing boats like toys. He felt a twitch in his mind, as it tried to tell him he was watching a movie. He stepped back and confirmed that he was looking out a window. That this wasn't a hoax.

An earthquake at sea, he thought, and he began tallying how many nuclear power plants were in the area. The closest he knew about was Hamaoka in Omaezaki, a three hour drive to the south. They should be safe from a meltdown like the one suffered by the Fukushima Daiichi power plant, but he couldn't recall if his building was earthquake-proof. He glanced at Kiku and felt safer. As long as she was here, he was safe.

"I won't leave you," he said. "I will—"

Another quake drew his eyes back to the harbor, and what he saw drew a high-pitched scream from his lips. It slowly reached a crescendo that matched the urgency of the warning klaxons rousing the city from its slumber.

Stepping from the ocean and onto the docks was a monster...a Kaiju.

"Like Nemesis," he said. But not.

The creature before him looked about the same size as Nemesis, who had yet to make landfall in Tokyo, denying her fans the giant monster stereotype. But now...*this* monster had arrived. It rose from the water, standing hundreds of feet tall, and it spread its four arms wide. The arms were long and thin, ending in slender three-fingered hands tipped with hooked talons that were longer than the hands themselves.

Its body was covered in a kind of exoskeleton that looked like it wore the bones of another creature over its own bones, but they were still wrapped in its own rough looking, mottled maroon and gray skin. The bony framework made it look emaciated, but its size...the thing exuded power and ferocity. A line of thick, pointed hairs, each the size of a telephone pole, lined the creature's back, like the dorsal spines of a fish without the fin flesh stretched between them. The worst of it was the face, which reminded Seika of the smooth-domed heads of the xenomorphs from *Aliens*, but with three red eyes on either side of the head and surrounded by a variety of gray, bony protrusions that could act as offensive weapons or defensive armor. It turned its head, making a slow survey of the city, its lips sneering up, revealing chaotic rows of sharp teeth.

It turned around, moving too fast, like a spider, twitching quickly, moving from one place to another in a blink. The sudden movement sent a fresh wave rolling down the city streets. A bony-looking, whip-like tail sailed out of the water and struck a building, slicing clean through it at an angle. Gravity tugged on the top half of the building, sliding it toward the ground. Though it crumbled as it moved, the building remained in two distinct slices until the top half spilled over the side and crashed into the ground, pulverizing the building across the street and sending up a plume of dust that partially obscured the monster.

Seika took in a deep, wheezing breath and staggered back. When his legs struck the bed, he fell back, sitting atop Kiku's legs. She didn't complain. She never complained. He reached out for her and grasped a handful of her leg, squeezing hard. "We need to leave," he said, looking around the small room.

When his eyes settled on Kiku again and he saw her unconcerned smile, a rush of dopamine put him at ease. It was a big city. The Japanese Defense Force and the American military would respond soon enough. The Kaiju looked dangerous. Ferocious. But it didn't have the glowing membranes that Nemesis did. It couldn't level entire cities with the force of a nuclear blast. To reach him, it would have to move through a wall of buildings.

He pushed off the bed and watched the creature twitch around in the harbor, like a dog sniffing out a trail. It didn't seem particularly interested in the city. *It's here for something else,* he thought and then he turned to Kiku. "We're safe here."

A crash spun him back around and made him gasp. A second building was falling.

His thoughts turned back to the moped. If it still ran, he could be out of the city quickly, even if the roads were congested with fleeing cars, the moped would find a path through.

It's my best chance, he thought, and he turned to leave.

Kiku's smiling face locked him in place. He said he wouldn't leave her. She'd been with him, without fail, for years. Never complaining. Never asking anything of him.

He stood still, clenching his fists. "You've made me a prisoner."

I was already a prisoner, he thought.

"You made me a content prisoner."

She didn't blink. Didn't move. Said nothing.

Tension crept up the back of Seika's neck, propelled by the klaxons, the sound of destruction and a warbled, haunting cry that made tears well in his eyes.

Then he snapped, thrusting an accusatory finger at Kiku. "You're just a pillow!"

A wave of true relief rushed through him.

The truth freed him.

And then, with a groan of airborne metal, and a quickly muffled scream, the tossed hull of a fifty foot fishing trawler crushed him.

25

The closer they got to Tokyo, the more reports of carnage began to filter through over the radio and the emergency channels. Something big—a Kaiju—had surfaced in Tokyo Bay. It hadn't moved inland yet, but it was making a mess of the coastline. Several buildings had been destroyed, and in a city like Tokyo, that probably meant thousands of lives lost. But most major coastal cities around the world had developed emergency evacuation plans after what had happened in Boston, Washington, D.C. and Los Angeles. The populations of landlocked cities had more time to get clear, but when a Kaiju rose from the depths, the time between life and death was reduced from days or hours, to just minutes.

Neither Hawkins nor Lilly could speak Japanese, but from what they got from the U.S. Military in the area, it sounded like the mass exodus of Tokyo had already begun. A counteroffensive from the U.S. Navy and Air Force—jointly operating with the Japanese Defense Force—would begin in the next ten minutes.

Hawkins glanced back at their passenger and noticed the man's attention fully on Lilly. *"Hey."*

The man blinked and turned to Hawkins. "Sorry. She fascinates me."

"She," Lilly said from the cockpit, glancing back, "is sitting right here." She raised and flexed her hand, extending her retractable claws. "And she isn't above skewering your nuts."

Alicio Brice leaned back in his seat, grimacing, and he kept his eyes turned toward Hawkins. "Did you need something?"

"You speak Japanese?" Hawkins asked.

Brice shook his head. "Some of my predecessors did."

Hawkins knew Brice was talking about earlier clones, men who had lived and worked on Island 731. They had performed human experimentation on countless people since World War II. Their creations had killed many of his friends and nearly killed him and Joliet, not to mention decimating Los Angeles, Salt Lake City and a line of cities between and around them. Everything he knew about the man sitting in the cargo bay, hands and ankles bound, said that he was a monster.

The *father* of monsters.

And he didn't deny it. But he also claimed to be different from those who had come before him. He had the same interests and mental agility—his words—but he lacked their ruthless ambition. He also claimed that he was the one who had set Maigo free. Lilly couldn't confirm it, but she had seen Maigo captured, and soon after, seen her walk out of the Russian prefab base with the ease of someone set free. But that didn't mean Brice was telling the truth. He was still an employee of GOD, and that made him dangerous.

"Do you know what's happening in Tokyo?" Hawkins asked.

"Only what you know," Brice said. "As one of the younger versions of me, I have yet to earn my seat at the inner table."

"Yet?" Hawkins said.

Brice frowned. "It's not a table I have any desire to sit at. But the alternative is death, and despite the seeming immortality of my...selves, I have no desire to die."

"They would kill you?" Lilly asked.

"I'm as expendable as a Dixie cup." Brice leaned his head back against the now opaque wall of the X-35.

Hawkins thought the man seemed genuinely disheartened, but he wasn't about to set him free or trust him.

"What are the reports saying?" Brice asked. "Are there any descriptions? Anything familiar?"

"You mean like Nemesis?" Lilly asked.

"Nemesis." He shrugged. "Like Nemesis. Either. Both."

"It's not Nemesis," Hawkins said, feeling certain Brice knew more about what was happening, or at least what might be happening, than he was saying. "Now is not a good time to hold back information."

Brice met Hawkins's eyes. "If I talk to you, they'll find out."

"And he's a Dixie cup," Lilly said.

Brice laughed, but then looked saddened.

"And if you don't go back?" Hawkins asked.

"If I don't... There isn't a reality where Cole lets me leave. Not alive, anyway."

"Unless you're already dead," Hawkins said. "A lot of men died on Big Diomede. Who's to say you weren't one of them. No one saw us pick you up. No one saw you leave. If you can help us, *really* help us, the FC-P can hide you."

Brice sat up, looking eager, but cautious. "You're lying."

"I don't lie," Hawkins said.

"He doesn't even cheat at Monopoly," Lilly said. "*Everyone* cheats at Monopoly."

Brice sat still for a moment, eyes on the floor. Then he took a deep breath and started talking. "If the creature in Tokyo isn't Nemesis and bears no resemblance to her, then the event we have long feared has already begun."

"The Aeros," Hawkins said.

Brice nodded.

"But there are only two Kaiju," Hawkins said. "One in Boston, one in Tokyo. They can't possibly plan to destroy—"

"Harbingers," Brice said. "Advance troops. Scouts. A first strike. To test our defensive capabilities. There is any number of reasons they would send just two Kaiju first—they call them Gestorumque, by the way. The first of their kind sent here—"

"Nemesis Prime," Hawkins said.

"I heard that's what you called her, yes. She was sent here for the Atlantide. Atlanteans to you. At first, the people she killed were simply in her way, but when the Atlanteans started interbreeding... Well, that all stopped when she was killed, and I think we all now know what killed her."

"Hyperion," Lilly said.

"An adequate name," Brice said.

Lilly glanced back. "You can take that up with Maigo."

"Was she..."

"Inside," Lilly said, but before she could offer more, Hawkins put his hand on her shoulder. She understood the message and clamped her mouth shut. At the moment, the flow of information needed to go in one direction.

Lilly pointed through the windshield. "Tokyo Bay is just ah—Holy shit."

The Bay was still miles ahead, but they could easily see the massive creature darting back and forth, raking its tail across buildings and snapping its fearsome jaws at the air. The water around it frothed white and swirled with the remains of countless ships. The creature's four arms scratched at the air like a cat in a fight, but there was nothing there.

"It's going nuts," Lilly said.

Brice hopped his way toward the cockpit and clung to the back of Hawkins's seat with his bound hands. "Fascinating."

Lilly raised a single eyebrow at the man. "Really? You're going to put me and that thing under the same verbal umbrella?"

"Different kinds of fascinating," he said, and then he offered the uncomfortable grin of a man who passed gas in an elevator. "There can be no doubt. This creature is not terrestrial. The Aeros are here."

"Their harbingers, anyway," Hawkins said.

Brice nodded.

Lilly took them in for a closer look, but kept a safe distance. The creature didn't seem to notice them, but was looking for something.

"Why is it here?" Hawkins asked. "Why Tokyo?"

"Are there any foreign nations offering assistance?" Brice asked.

Hawkins eyed him for a moment, but then put on a headset and listened to the nearly chaotic communication between military forces. After a moment, he heard a distinctly Russian accent. "The Russians."

"It will be an aircraft carrier," Brice said. "No support vessels."

"But why would the Russians—"

"It's not the Russians," Lilly said. "Not really, right?"

"GOD," Hawkins grumbled.

"They have research centers in many countries," Brice said, "but have also learned that mobility has its advantages."

"The aircraft carrier is a laboratory?" Hawkins felt sick to his stomach. It was bad enough that GOD had taken over an island and filled it with monsters, but an aircraft carrier could take those monsters anywhere in the world. "What's on it?"

"Among other things," Brice said. "The Prime."

"And in Tokyo?"

Brice motioned to the windshield with his head. At first, Hawkins couldn't see what the man was motioning toward. The writhing, twitching Kaiju held his attention. But then he saw the ocean parting, and a head emerging. For a moment, he thought it was Nemesis, but they had already confirmed that Nemesis was outside of Boston. So what was this?

The answer rose out of the water, looking just as massive and callous as he remembered. The glowing orange eyes were followed by a deeply frowning mouth that Hawkins knew could spring open like a bobbit worm. As it rose higher out of the water, the luminous orange membranes came into view, leaving no doubt about the monster's identity: Typhon.

"What did you people do?" Hawkins asked, the horror he felt reducing his normally powerful voice to a whisper. When two more heads rose from the ocean behind Typhon, Hawkins just watched in silence.

The first head was broad, like a hammerhead shark, the wide-set eyes glowing bright orange, the mouth hung open, revealing lines of long, curved, needle-like teeth.

"There's Scylla," Lilly said, pointing. Then her finger moved to the right, where a third creature was rising, effectively blocking the mouth of the bay and the alien Kaiju's watery escape route. Two massive spines rose from the water first, followed by a powerful body with large glowing membranes and a face that looked like a cross between Nemesis and a dragon. A tail whipped out of the water behind it, thrashing and agitated. "And Karkinos."

Hawkins had no idea what was about to play out, but he thought there was at least one guaranteed outcome: Tokyo was screwed.

26

Maigo couldn't see Nemesis coming, but she could feel the monster, surging closer with each passing second. She lacked the direct mental connection that existed with Hudson, but the Kaiju's emotions reached out to her, the familiar violence of them making her stomach knot.

You're angry, she thought, trying to reach out to the monster with her mind. With her father, it was easy, but with Nemesis...that was a connection she had worked hard to sever. *You remember Hyperion. But it's just a shell. I am its Voice now.*

She felt nothing in return other than her own growing apprehension. Hyperion had defeated Nemesis Prime, but under the guidance of an experienced Voice, who knew what he was up against. He had trained for the battle, and was a ten-foot-tall Atlantean named Kaa Tunis. After vanquishing Prime and burying her carcass in the remote wilderness of Alaska, he had stored Hyperion on Big Diomede, where he lived out his days keeping watch over the planet, spending long stretches of time in suspended animation. He had died alone, of old age in the 1500s, believing that the Aeros had lost interest in the planet, and that his brethren, scattered to the wind, would survive either alongside humanity, or as a part of it.

Hyperion's AI was preprogrammed with a variety of combat strategies and maneuvers, but it relied on the Voice for instinctual responses that the system couldn't replicate. On one hand, Maigo's experience with Nemesis gave them an advantage, and she had some hand-to-hand combat training, including lessons from Lilly on fighting dirty. But Nemesis's Voice was Endo, who Hudson frequently called a sociopathic ninja. He meant it in the nicest way possible, of course. They had a complicated relationship that ranged from sarcastic bromance to outright hatred. But what really irked her father was that he now owed the man for taking Maigo's place as Nemesis's Voice.

None of them believed it was a true sacrifice. The man was obsessed with Kaiju, and even Alessi believed Endo was exactly where he wanted to be. But still, his actions had kept Maigo from reliving her nightmares, and kept her new family together. She owed him. They all did. And in a very real way, despite the death and destruction wrought by Nemesis, they owed her, too.

No one would ever forget the number of people she'd killed during her growth spurt, or those she'd killed while fighting other Kaiju, but how many lives had she saved by defeating the five Prime offspring, and the Tsuchi? Probably more than she'd killed herself. A lot more.

Given all of that, Maigo had no desire to fight Nemesis. But she also didn't want to die.

I have to reach her, she thought. *Get through to her. Or to Endo.*

But how could she do that while contained in a giant robot whose face was etched in her and Nemesis's memories as their killer? The rage Nemesis felt toward the ancient robot was akin to what it felt toward her biological father and murderer, Alexander Tilly, while Maigo had been the Kaiju's Voice.

What chance did she stand in the face of such rage?

Hudson had no real way to help her.

The U.S. military, currently ordered to stand down, wouldn't be any help, even if they tried.

Right now, she was the only thing that stood between Nemesis and Boston, which historically was a bad combination, and something no one else wanted to see again.

So I'll fight.

And probably die.

But she wasn't convinced she had the nerve to kill Nemesis, and Endo, even if she found she had the ability.

Thinking about Endo again triggered a chain of thought that slowly unraveled a revelation. *Hyperion has a Voice. As does Nemesis, but only because we shared our DNA.* The Prime offspring—Typhon, Karkinos, Drakon, Scylla and Scrion hadn't had Voices. That could have been part of why Nemesis was able to defeat them all, though she had had a little help from the FC-P. That meant the two new Kaiju probably had pilots, too. *But what about Nemesis Prime?*

Before she could think about it any further, the ocean rose up and parted. A black shadow rose up. Nemesis burst from the water and un-leashed a roar that Hyperion's AI quickly muffled, sparing Maigo from the discomfort its volume should have created.

Nemesis looked a little larger than her previous three-hundred-fifty-foot height, but she moved with a new swiftness and coordination. Her eyes, once brown like Maigo's, blazed orange like the membranes on her neck, chest and torso. Her armor was as thick and dark as ever, gleaming as the morning sun reflected off the water coating her body. Nemesis charged, seamlessly switched from swimming to running, rising higher as the ground beneath her feet rose toward the ruins of Graves Light.

Maigo's gut twisted in fear. She had seen Nemesis's rage before. She had felt it. She had partaken of it, and fueled it. But she had never been on the receiving end of it. She took up a defensive position, ready to grapple Nemesis, but the monster, like Lilly, didn't fight fair.

Lost in bloodlust, Nemesis plunged the long claws on the ends of her massive hands into the orange membrane of her chest. Hudson called the technique Self-Immolation. Nemesis had used the attack in the past, some-times involuntarily, sometimes inflicting the damage on herself. But the result and every self-immolation event was the same—a very big boom.

Nemesis withdrew her claws, sending gouts of luminous liquid spraying out in twin arcs, filling the space between her and Hyperion.

Maigo drew Hyperion's thick forearms up as a shield and braced herself for a violent death.

The AI responded to her fears. *Hyperion is designed to—*

Bright orange light filled Maigo's vision, searing for a moment before dulling.

Maigo screamed, but the sound was just in her mind. Her body was encased inside Hyperion, unable to move or speak.

When the orange light faded, Maigo saw a flash of blue sky, which was quickly distorted by roiling water. She was alive, and she knew, unharmed. Despite the vast amount of energy unleashed upon Hyperion, and the fact that the robot had been flung back into the ocean, she had felt nothing. No pain. Her body had been spared from the heat, and the violent impact. And Hyperion had survived almost completely unscathed, having an epidermis even stronger than Nemesis herself.

Sensing her shift in confidence, Hyperion said, *Energy systems at Level Two*. Maigo knew, suddenly, what this meant. Level One weapons were essentially melee, and all the robot was capable of after teleporting. How it did that, she still didn't know. There hadn't been time to question it. But she did know it sucked most of the robot's power away. Hyperion had been nearly drained when they had arrived, and it had had just enough energy to momentarily repel Lovecraft and extend the wrist blades. Level Two allowed her to use a voltage amplifier weapon, which was basically a massive taser capable of stunning an enemy—or frying its brain—depending on the charge and placement. It was the closest thing the robot had to a non-lethal weapon. Then there was Level Three, which Hudson would appreciate, but Hyperion took things to a level her father could never imagine.

Maigo willed Hyperion to get back to its feet, and the AI did it in the fastest, most efficient way possible. Back on her feet, Maigo looked down at her robotic body, which was surreal in part because it was a robot, but also because it had a masculine build. The surface was charred, but still in one piece. She also noticed that the ancient claw marks across the chest were gone.

Hyperion is capable of nano-cell regeneration, the AI informed her. *We have been 'healing' since you were established as our new Voice.*

"But why was the damage still there? After thousands of years?"

Kaa Tunis desired it remain as a reminder. Of what he faced, and of his near defeat. But a damaged chassis serves no purpose in battle.

"Works for me," she thought, and she turned her attention to an explosion of water a half mile away. Off balance when she'd self-immolated, Nemesis had been tossed back by the blast, which had incinerated The Graves along with the rest of the islands in the Harbor. It looked like Boston had been spared a repeat performance, but the coast was hard to see past all of the steam generated by the heat.

Nemesis thrashed in the ocean and got her feet under her. When she stood and saw Hyperion already standing and waiting, she leaned forward, splayed her arms wide and let out a spittle flinging roar. The Kaiju, who looked no more damaged than Hyperion, charged again, feinting one direction and then the other in a very human attempt to throw Hyperion off balance. But the AI compensated for Nemesis's speed with its own. When the Kaiju lunged forward, jaws open wide, angled to bite down on the robot's neck, Maigo reached out and caught her by the shoulders. The powerful robotic arms kept Nemesis at bay, but couldn't stop the Kaiju from reaching up with her massive claws and punching them into Hyperion's sides.

Maigo didn't feel pain, but she knew the damage was severe. *Survivable,* the AI assured her, but not if they slid much deeper, or were plunged in again, higher, where they risked striking the mech's power source—what it called a *Suun Czuar,* which translated to Rift Engine.

It's me! Maigo thought at Nemesis, but she detected no response, mental or physical. The monster's rage-fueled strength was starting to overpower Hyperion.

With little recourse, Maigo triggered the voltage amplifier. Three prongs sprang out of each of Hyperion's forearms, each to the side of where the blades had come out earlier. The blades were now back inside the arms. And as she saw this, Maigo knew that the Level Three weapons system would emerge just to the side of the voltage amplifier's pointed, metal electrodes. The rods punched into the thick flesh of Nemesis's shoulders without puncturing any membranes. As soon as two rods made contact, a massive burst of electricity flowed into Nemesis's body.

The Kaiju roared in pain, but then leveled her gaze at Hyperion and leaned into it, shoving her claws a little deeper.

With the AI warning of imminent and permanent damage, Maigo turned the juice up to full. Nemesis flinched from the electricity, twitching and roaring in pain, but she didn't withdraw.

We're going to kill each other!

Level Three weapons systems are now charged, the AI informed her. Feeling desperate, Maigo triggered just one of the Level Three weapons. Hyperion's back opened and a massive cannon pulled out and rose up over the robot's head. It didn't change Maigo's view, but she knew that wherever she looked, the cannon would be able to fire. The laser cannon dwarfed the power of the Swarm, and with a sustained blast at close range, it could remove Nemesis's head. The weapon locked into place and hummed with a full charge, just feet away from Nemesis's face.

Maigo just had to will it to happen, and Nemesis would cease to exist.

Damnit! Maigo thought, and the weapon snapped back off the head and retreated back inside the robot's back.

Action recommended, the AI said, but Maigo's command was not what was expected, or even predicted by the system that could calculate variables and probabilities better than C3PO. That was the point of the Voice, so the system complied.

Maigo's view shifted from the one projected into her mind by Hyperion to her own eyes, sliding up out of the black goo holding her in place. Hyperion's head opened around her, exposing her to mortal danger, and Nemesis's eyes.

For a moment, the Kaiju showed no reaction, and when it roared, Maigo took the blast head on. Then she stood up, raised a hand and shouted, "Nemesis!"

27

What the hell is she doing, I think, when the massive robot's head splits open. Then she's standing, raising her hand toward the Kaiju and shouting something. My zoomed in view through the VR headset is shaky, but I don't need to be a world class lip reader to know what she's saying, and to figure out what she's doing. She's reaching out. Trying to communicate with a monster. I tried the same tactic standing on the rooftop of a Boston skyscraper. Like a 350-foot-tall dog, Nemesis actually responds to her name, though back when I tried it, I had to call her by her human name: Maigo.

While my communication with Nemesis worked out and ended her wrath-filled destruction of Boston, I had sacrificed a man's life to do it. Right now, the only thing Maigo has to offer is her own life.

I'm five hundred feet up, doing slow circles around the scene, taking Collins and Woodstock along for the ride as their drones follow Hydra Seven's lead. They're probably getting tired—well, Woodstock at least—but I can't abandon my daughter. Not now.

There isn't much I can do if anything goes wrong. I have no illusions about the effectiveness of the three lasers now under my command. But I'd never be able to forgive myself if things went badly while I was hightailing it back to the coast.

Nemesis faces down the small Maigo, leaning in close, her lips curled up, her teeth bared. She could snap Maigo up before I realized it had happened.

But she doesn't.

Instead, the destroyer of Boston leans closer, lowering her snout toward Maigo's outstretched hand.

The shock I feel at the moment of contact is replaced by a tingling in my toes that quickly slides up my body. When it reaches the base of my skull and my vision starts to fade, I realize what's about to happen and attempt to put the drones on autopilot.

A charred and steaming Boston harbor fades. Nemesis, Maigo and Hyperion, slip from my vision. The smell of salt water becomes pine and cinnamon. My downward view flips over. I'm staring up at pine needles and branches laden with gaudy Christmas ornaments and a rainbow of lights.

"Why are we here?" I ask in the voice of my child self, knowing that Maigo is in the room. At the moment of connection with Nemesis, she reached out and connected with me. I really wish I had some kind of control over this, or at least could accept or decline the mental call, but here we are once again, celebrating our childhood Christmases in my living room.

"I didn't do it," she replies. "Not on purpose, at least."

A third voice joins us, making sound effects. "Meeroooow. Pew, pew, pew. Kaboosh!"

I sit up fast, dragging my face through the pine branches, scratching my skin and sending a few ornaments tumbling to the hardwood floor. I don't worry about the scratches, or the ornament that shatters. None of this is real. It will all be back to normal the next time we end up here. But the addition of a third person is new, foreign and disturbing. As surreal as this place is, it's always been a private place for Maigo and me to talk honestly, stripping away all the awkwardness and baggage that comes with growing up.

An Asian kid who could be Maigo's half-brother if she had one, sits cross-legged beside her. He's dressed in lime green pajamas with a yellow striped belly, like a lizard. A hood is pulled up over his head. It has round black eyes, a cute black nose, a little smile and round green fins running down the back. He's a poster child for cute, Japanese kids everywhere. He doesn't notice my attention, or he doesn't care. He's enraptured with two toys in his hands—Nemesis and Hyperion. He's making them fight.

"Eaarrgh!" The kid says, and then he laughs as Nemesis swipes Hyperion down with her tail.

"Having fun?" I ask, my voice laced with sarcasm and annoyance.

The kid pauses and looks up at me. When we make eye contact, I know, but his next words confirm it.

"You should lighten up, Hudson. It's not every day you get to play as your inner child."

Katsu Friggin' Endo.

"Happens more than you'd think," Maigo says, seemingly nonplussed by the man's arrival, which I see as a desecration, in this private place.

I get to my small feet and clench my fists. "What are you doing here, Endo?"

He lowers the toys and smiles up at me. Even as a kid, that cocky smile just begs to be slapped off. "Violence against me will serve you as well here as it does in the real world."

"Says the man who happily became a monster," I say.

"The question is, why are *you* here. This meeting of minds is for Voices."

I hear the capital V, but don't understand the significance.

"It's like a pilot," Maigo explains, "but it's closer to a relationship. Like two voices, separate but joined. For a time, Nemesis and I were one and the same as she formed from my body, but then I formed within *her*. When death seemed likely, I was expelled from her body."

"And now Endo is her Voice," I say.

"And I am Hyperion's."

"Which brings us back to the question of your presence," Endo says.

"This is *my* living room," I say. "*My* childhood you're invading."

"This is where we have met since Washington," Maigo says. She seems to have no problem divulging information that I would consider private, if not confidential. "And while Dad hasn't been a true Voice, he has had some experience–"

"Scylla," Endo says, naming the Kaiju whose mind I controlled, albeit in a much more direct way than as a Voice seems to. If Scylla had opinions about that relationship, I never heard them. "I remember.

"I suppose he's to be tolerated then," Endo says, and when he cracks a smile, I know he's just trying to egg me on. He might be merged with a monstrous alien Kaiju, but some things never change.

I cross my arms and don't take the bait.

Endo's smile fades and he turns to Maigo. "Why is our killer here?"

He's referring to Hyperion, but his use of 'our,' which I take to mean himself, Nemesis, Nemesis Prime and Maigo, doesn't make me happy. She's been trying to separate herself from the monster for years. She doesn't need Endo making her feel like part of the Kaiju family again.

"Hyperion never left," she says. "Though his Voice died long ago."

"Hyperion," Endo says, trying the name on for size. He motions toward me with his head, but talks like I'm not here. "Did he name it?"

"*I* did," Maigo says, looking the young Endo in the eyes. "You should know, I remember it. *Our* death. At the hands of this robot. As well as you do now. As well as Nemesis. But without the original Voice, Hyperion is mine to control. The AI sees Nemesis as a threat, but will not take action without my say, which I might add, is why she still has a head, and you're here at all."

They stare at each other in silence.

"Don't forget that I have been the Voice for both," Maigo says, her voice deadly serious. "Gestorumque are powerful rage machines designed for mass destruction, and the slaughter and consumption of smaller beings. Hyperion was created for a more singular purpose."

She doesn't say what that purpose is. Doesn't need to. The giant robot was clearly created to kill Gestorumque.

God, that's a mouthful, I think. *I'll stick with Kaiju.*

"And right now," Maigo says. "There are two Gestorumque to deal with."

Endo turns his head up like he can see through the ceiling above, like there is an actual sky over us. "And more on the way." Then he flinches. A shiver runs through his body.

"What's wrong?" I ask, ashamed by the concern in my voice.

"C-can't you feel them?" Endo asks.

Maigo shivers next and through her, I feel them, too. Kaiju. Three of them, one of whom feels very familiar. "Scylla."

"Karkinos and Typhon, too." Endo adds. "Our brother and sister. But they lack Voices. They're...in Japan. Tokyo. My home..."

"There's nothing we can do," Maigo says, "but hope they are successful."

I put a hand on my forehead. "Wait, now we're rooting for the monsters that wiped out our nation's capitol?"

"There are things far worse than Voiceless Gestorumque," Endo says.

Gestorumque with Voices, I think. Like the one Maigo chased away.

"Nemesis will always hate Hyperion," Endo says to Maigo.

"And Hyperion will always see her as a threat," Maigo counters.

Endo leans forward and smiles. "She will never forget you. Or the strength you gave her. As long as you are Hyperion's Voice, you have nothing to fear from Nemesis." Endo looks at me. "Nor do you, or the rest of humanity."

"You really think you can control her?" I ask.

But before Endo can answer, his eyes go wide with a strange kind of earnest fear. "Pull up," he says, and then he shouts, "Jon, pull up!"

I snap out of the dreamlike state, bewildered and confused by the view ahead of me. The blue gray surface warbles. A voice fills my ears. Alessi. "Pull up, Jon! You're going to crash in the water!"

The ocean! That's what's beneath me.

I pull up hard and am pressed against the drone's back as it angles upward and its VTOL engines kick in. I feel the tug of water against my toes, but then we're airborne again.

After running through a collection of rarely thought, and even more rarely spoken cusswords, I confirm that Collins and Woodstock are both still clinging to their drones. I set a more leisurely pace toward the shore. "Maigo, you copy?"

"I'm here, Dad," she says. "You okay?"

"Fine. You and Endo can meet us at the Crow's Nest."

"Endo is gone," she says.

Figures.

"Endo?" Alessi says. "You saw him?"

"Sort of," I say. "But he's alive and still annoying. I can tell you later. Right now, I need you to catch me up on what's going on in Japan."

"Nothing good," Alessi says. "Hawkins and Lilly are there."

I'm relieved to hear that Hawkins successfully reconnected with Lilly and that both are safe, but I'm more interested in what's happening with the second Kaiju. "Patch me in to Hawkins."

"We're connected," Alessi says.

I hear a click and don't wait for a verbal confirmation that we're connected. "Hawkins, what's the situation there?"

"You wouldn't believe me if I told you," Hawkins says, sounding a little like he's just woken from a dream where he was naked and late for a test.

"Pretty sure I would," Hudson replied, feeling close to the same. "What happened?"

28

The very human-like Typhon stood knee-deep in the sea, arms slack by its sides, eyes on the alien Kaiju, who had stopped twitching in the bay and focused on the newcomers. Scylla strode up beside Typhon. The hammerhead Kaiju was shorter than her brother, but her more monstrous appearance more than made up for it. Arriving on Typhon's other side was the far larger Karkinos, whose girth was unrivaled, even by the newcomer. In some ways, he was more like Nemesis than the other two, with large spikes running down his back, and a long, blade-tipped tail, but he looked more like Nemesis on alien steroids. His power also made him slower than Typhon and Scylla, and far slower than the thing they were facing down.

"We should name that thing," Lilly said from the X-35's cockpit.

Future Betty hovered a mile over the bay, invisible to Kaiju and military alike. Hawkins was in the back, sitting across from the still bound Alicio Brice, watching the action through the floor, which was projecting the scene below—the same view that was being projected onto the vehicle's smooth roof so that anyone above would effectively see right through them. Hawkins lowered his hands to the floor and moved them apart, zooming in on the action.

"That usually falls within Jon's purview," Hawkins said.

"Purview?" Lilly said. "Geez, you're old. Maigo named the robot, so I'm claiming this one."

Hawkins had no desire to argue about something like the monster's name, and he knew that Jon might usurp her choice anyway. The official report containing Kaiju names was his to write.

"Giger," she said.

"Giger?" Hawkins had no idea what the name meant.

"Oh, yes," Brice said. "I see it. Excellent choice."

"Brownie points for the mad scientist," Lilly said to Brice, and then to Hawkins, "H.R. Giger designed Ridley Scott's alien." She pointed at the floor, toward the creature facing off with Prime's brood. "That looks like something he would have come up with."

"It's moving," Hawkins said, watching the creature move toward the others, stepping further into Tokyo Bay and a little further from the city. Lilly cleared her throat and Hawkins said, "*Giger* is moving."

The twitching creature stepped toward the other Kaiju, moving with careful steps, legs coiled, ready to leap back.

"How is this possible?" Hawkins asked Brice.

"The Aeros sent Giger to—"

"Not Giger. The other three. Nemesis killed them.. I was there."

Lilly leaned her head back. "*We* were there."

"I saw them die," Hawkins said.

"Just as you saw Nemesis die. But that monster still roams the Earth as well." Brice waved his bound hands in the air, like he smelled something foul. "I apologize for my combative language. It's a personality flaw I have been simultaneously trying to rid myself of, and do more often, so Cole doesn't notice my proclivities differ from those of my brothers. And you are correct. The Kaiju who perished in Washington, D.C. are still dead, and on ice, literally. Their corpses are in Antarctica."

Hawkins glared at him. "Then these things are like—?"

"Me," Brice said. "Yes. They're clones, with control mechanisms implanted into their minds at birth. Unlike Nemesis, these Kaiju were grown without human DNA. What you see down there are shells, controlled by human operators safe on GOD's aircraft carrier."

As if to prove this point, Scylla and Typhon broke in different directions, moving fast through the bay. With the city behind it, Giger twisted back and forth, watching the three Kaiju, but not attacking. When the alien Giger was flanked on both sides, the standoff continued. The opponents sized up the others.

Hawkins wasn't sure how smart Giger was, but it clearly didn't see the three monsters as potential friends. But it had yet to attack. Was it afraid?

He didn't think so.

"Why play with fire?" Hawkins asked. "These things are powerful enough to lay waste to entire cities in an afternoon."

"Keep in mind that I'm speaking for GOD, not myself," Brice said, and then he continued. "In the face of overwhelming odds from the outer reaches of space, Cole decided that fighting fire with fire was our best chance of survival."

Hawkins shook his head. "He who fights monsters should see to it that he himself does not become a monster."

"An oft used trope," Brice said, "Except in this case, becoming a monster might be the only way the human race survives."

"Hey, Dad," Lilly said from the front, "Before you argue the point, keep in mind that some of us are *already* monsters."

"You're *not* a monster," he said.

"She threatened to skewer my testicles," Brice said. "With her talons. Even if you shared her sentiment, you lack the talons." He held up his bound hands before Hawkins could reply. "The point is, it might be time to reassess what defines a monster, seeing past what's on the outside and evaluating what is on the inside."

"I'd give you more brownie points," Lilly said, "if I didn't think you were actually referring to dissecting me."

Brice sighed. "Cole is misguided, ruthless and terrifying, but there is a chance he might be our best hope of surviving what comes next."

"If we survive the day," Hawkins said, and he motioned to the scene below them.

Typhon and Scylla moved in from both sides, their postures shifting from neutral to outwardly aggressive. But their snarls and teeth gnashing looked unnatural and repetitive, like they'd been preprogrammed to look fierce.

Giger twitched one direction and then the other, spinning its body around with a suddenness that seemed impossible, and sending seawater spraying in every direction. The Kaiju was cornered, but would it retreat or attack? And could one Kaiju really hope to defeat these three behemoths?

Hawkins knew it was possible, of course. Nemesis had done the same, though she'd had help.

Then all the twitching stopped, and Giger froze, its attention on Scylla. Typhon approached from behind, moving in calm, measured steps, its actions clearly those of a human being. Typhon reached up under Giger's topmost arms and wrapped its mighty hands around the back of its adversary's neck, folding over a group of the hair-like spines.

Giger was lifted up, held in place, its feet lifting up out of the water.

Why did it do that? Hawkins wondered. The alien Kaiju had given the Kaiju-clone the perfect opening. *Maybe it was expecting a more savage attack? The kind that these Kaiju might have delivered before they were under the control of human minds?*

The truth of the situation was revealed in the blink of an eye, as Giger's bony tail snapped up out of the water, and the end pierced up through Scylla's chin. The sharp tip drove through the skull and burst from the top with a spray of gore. Before anyone, or anything, could even think to react, the tail pulled out of Scylla's head and cracked down, like a whip. The blade slid through Scylla's armored skin, deftly avoiding all the orange membranes. The wound bulged and then split, disgorging a mass of entrails that splashed into the bay and sent a wave sliding toward the shore.

Scylla fell backwards, trailing its insides, and landed in the water. The cloned Kaiju sank down so that just its frozen face rose partially from the water.

Giger pitched forward, planting its feet on the ocean floor and lifting Typhon up. The man-shaped Kaiju flipped through the air, landing atop his dead sister. Before the Kaiju could right himself, Giger was upon him. Typhon's face flexed and snapped open, revealing ferocious mandibles that would make the average creature think twice about tangling with him, but Giger was far from average.

Two of the alien Kaiju's hands snapped out and grasped the mandibles. The other two wrapped around Typhon's throat. Then Giger was airborne, driving its feet into Typhon's gut, punching through flesh with black claws. They fell together, and while Typhon twitched, Giger peeled open his face, yanking the mandibles apart. The neck went next, compressing inward with enough strength to force blood from the monster's eyes.

With two Kaiju killed in seconds, Hawkins held out little hope that Karkinos would fare much better, but the monster was at least double the size of Giger. He just needed to get in one good strike.

Karkinos never got the chance.

Giger spun around as the larger Kaiju stepped up behind it and raised its massive claws up. The lightning fast tail snapped up again, puncturing Karkinos's chest, but instead of eviscerating the Kaiju, it acted more like a grappling hook. With a quick yank of its tail, the lithe Giger launched up over Karkinos, grasped his head and flipped around to Karkinos's back. Again, Hawkins noticed that while Giger could have mortally wounded the larger Kaiju, it didn't.

What's it doing?

Clutching to Karkinos's back with all six limbs, Giger's tail rose up behind it. While the massive Kaiju bucked and thrashed, the tail hovered over the back of its head. And then, with the precise aim of a surgeon and the speed of a lightning bolt, the tail shot into the base of Karkinos's skull.

The massive monster shuddered, went still and crumpled into the bay. Giger leapt free, landing a safe distance away. Then it moved closer, inspecting Karkinos's body.

"Is it going to eat him?" Lilly asked.

Hawkins was wondering the same thing, but Brice saw what they had missed. "It's still alive. Karkinos is alive. My god, it severed the connection!"

Giger clung to Karkinos and dragged the larger Kaiju toward deeper water. When it got deep enough, Giger dipped beneath the waves and pulled the massive creature with it. The alien Kaiju had killed two of the cloned offspring of Prime, but had taken Karkinos. *But why? Food? A trophy?* Hawkins couldn't guess.

But Tokyo had been spared. And that was at least something.

There was a click, and then Hudson's voice filled the X-35. "Hawkins, what's the situation there?"

"You wouldn't believe me if I told you," Hawkins said, looking down at the corpses leaking gore into Tokyo Bay.

"Pretty sure I would," Hudson replied, and Hawkins realized there were events happening on the far side of the world that he hadn't witnessed. "What happened?"

Hawkins tried to think of the best way to summarize what they had seen, but it was Lilly who spoke. "Giger just kicked the shit out of Typhon, Scylla and Karkinos."

Hudson was silent for a moment, no doubt absorbing the news that their old enemies were alive again.

"Typhon and Scylla are shark chum," Lilly continued, "Karkinos is MIA, and when I say MIA, I mean it. GOD was controlling them. Oh, and we took Alicio Brice captive. Well, one of him. This one seems pretty docile."

"Hawkins..." Hudson said. "Is she yanking my chain?"

"Actually, that was a pretty accurate description of the situation."

"Fantastic," Hudson said. "I'm currently clinging to the back of a drone over Boston Harbor, but I'll get back to you both for a full debrief once I'm on the ground."

"Should we head back?" Hawkins asked.

"Not until we know where things are going to go down next," Hudson said. "In the meantime, get what you can out of the Brice."

Hawkins forced a grin at Brice. "Will do."

"Who came up with 'Giger'?" Hudson asked.

"I did," Lilly said. "But before you—"

"H.R. Giger?" Hudson asked.

"Yeah."

"First, you watch too much TV, kid. Seriously, your pop culture knowledge is out of control. Second, I like it."

Lilly smiled.

"But it doesn't make up for stealing Future Betty. You and Maigo will be making that stunt up to the rest of us later. For now, keep on kicking ass."

"Will do," Lilly said, impersonating Hawkins.

Hudson chuckled and disconnected.

Hawkins turned his attention to Brice. "Tell me about the aircraft carrier."

29

Seeing Maigo separate from the machine fills me with more relief than I'm emotionally prepared for. Since I'm the first to jump from *Penny*, who was recovered by the Coast Guard, to Hyperion's shoulder, where Maigo awaits, no one sees my glassy eyes. Well, Maigo does, but she's kind enough to not point it out. Instead, she wraps her arms around me and returns my hug.

The mammoth mech is lying down in the ocean, just off West Beach in Beverly Farms. From above, it looks like it's taking a leisurely bath. Waves lap against the top of its torso, which rises a few feet above the surface. I have Alessi and Zoomb working on a place to keep the giant robot, but for now, there's no hiding it. While most of the coastline is currently uninhabited, several news choppers are circling outside the military-enforced no-fly zone we had declared around Hyperion. It's not that we want to keep it a secret. There's no putting that cat back in the bag. It's that I have trust issues with anything taller than André the Giant. This ancient tech is a massive liability. Until I can guarantee that Hyperion won't spring to life and lay waste to humanity, I'm going to try to keep humanity far enough away that they have a good lead when they start running for their lives.

"I'm okay," she says as I squeeze her. "Really."

"You stole an aircraft, flew across the country into Russian territory, recovered an ancient Atlantean Kaiju-killing robot, fought Lovecraft *and* Nemesis, and I'm not supposed to be concerned for your well-being?"

"All good points," she said.

"Can I ask why you're only wearing underwear?"

"I think you just did," she says, and she smiles in a way that says she thinks I'm going to let the subject go with a joke.

I take her arm. "Seriously, I need to know if there's anyone I need to murder. Where are your clothes?"

"Nothing like that happened," she says. "I...I was captured."

I already knew that. Hawkins filled me in on Lilly's side of the story. But I need Maigo to tell me. "By the Russians?"

"I think they were working for GOD. Or at least with GOD. But Brice set me free."

"And your clothes?" I ask.

She smiles. "There's no one you need to kick in the junk."

"Get out of my head, kid," I say, unable to hide my own smile.

"Doesn't take a mental connection to know that's what you were thinking."

Collins joins us on the broad flat surface of Hyperion's shoulder. She greets Maigo with a hug, kissing the flat black hair atop the girl's head. Then she helps Watson make the jump from the bobbing yacht to Hyperion's shoulder.

When Watson gets his feet beneath him, he studies the broad surface of Hyperion's body, his facial expression torn between horror and fascination. "Are we sure this is safe? Couldn't it stand up or something?"

"Hyperion and I..." Maigo looks at me, like what she's about to say will disappoint me, "...are tethered. Mentally."

I can't say I'm surprised. That's how this Voice thing seems to work, and Nemesis's response to Maigo's presence confirms that the connection isn't forgotten, though it can be replaced. I cross my arms. "How long will that last?"

She shrugs. "Until I die. I think." She turns to Watson. "He knows I'm here. Knows that people are supposed to be protected. He wouldn't do anything to hurt us."

"Like Asimov's laws of robotics?" Watson asks.

"More like Maigo's rules for good behavior," she says.

"And if Nemesis shows up?" Collins asks. "Or Lovecraft?"

"Then Hyperion will be the least of your concerns," Maigo says, revealing a twinge of annoyance. She is the most powerful woman on the planet, now in control of the most powerful technology we've ever seen. But she still has parents, and like all parents, we're doubting her, second-guessing her and worrying about her. It's not that we don't trust her, we just don't want her to make any mistakes.

But maybe that's the mistake? People don't learn much when everything is peachy and life presents no challenges. And the last thing we want to do is push her away. The most powerful woman in the world, with the most powerful robot, would make a horrible rebellious teen.

"Nemesis was last seen headed north, toward the Arctic," I say, trying to put everyone at ease. "And the reports of giant waves making landfall an hour ahead of her seem to indicate that Lovecraft is headed in that direction as well."

I turn to Maigo with an exaggerated grin that says it's time for everyone to be nice. "Now, what can you tell us about Hyperion?"

She gives us a basic run down of what we already knew or suspected. Hyperion was built by the Ferox for use by the Atlantide, for the express purpose of killing Gestorumque and defending Atlantis. While it failed to protect the fabled city, it did kill Nemesis Prime, and that ain't nothing. Its size and physical strength is equal to most, but not all, Kaiju. It's also faster than the average Kaiju. Like Nemesis, it's a good balance of strength and speed. And what it lacks in ferocity, it makes up for with firepower—including face-melting laser cannons. They make my recently defeated Swarm seem like bees rather than the most advanced, unmanned aerial-combat vehicles ever developed.

"Where does all this power come from?" Watson asks. His eyes are wide and squirrely, darting back and forth as he takes in every inch of the impressive metal physique. And I'm using the word 'metal' loosely. It will probably be a while before we fully understand how this thing was built. From a distance, its surface looks like solid sheets of armor, but an up close inspection reveals countless octagonal cells that can actually heal in time, which is what Hyperion is doing right now. Maigo says the puncture wounds inflicted by Nemesis were nearly catastrophic, but since they damaged only armor, it would be just a few hours before the big robot was battle-ready again.

"It's called a Rift Engine," Maigo says, leading us from the shoulder to the broad chest.

I feel like a kid, scrabbling over the ridges of armor like rocks at the beach. Maigo leaps up onto the chest with ease, but I have to give Collins and Watson a ten finger boost and rely on Maigo to yank me up.

"Rift Engine," Watson says once he's back on his feet. "That implies some kind of splitting is taking place. It's not nuclear, is it?"

Maigo shakes her head. "I don't know the science behind it, and even if Hyperion could give me that information, I doubt I'd understand it. But I'm pretty sure no atoms are being split. I think the 'rift' is closer to a description of what it can do, rather than how it works.

"Teleportation," Watson says in the way a preteen might whisper the name of the latest prefab heartthrob's name. And I'm right there with him. As a fan of Star Trek, there are two things that have always been on my future bucket list: 1. Getting beamed up, and 2. Thirty minutes in a holodeck preprogrammed with Seven of Nine and T'Pol.

"How long did it take to get from Big Diomede to Boston?" Watson asks her.

"It was instantaneous." Maigo snapped her fingers. "I was there, and then I was here. It wasn't really something I meant to do. It was more like Hyperion inferred it, and took action. I wasn't exactly prepared for what came next."

"You weren't the only one," Collins says. "Lovecraft seemed caught off guard."

Maigo stops short of the large three-ringed Atlantean symbol on Hyperion's chest. Each ring is embedded a little lower than the first, fifteen feet down from the edge to the core.

"We can fill it with water," I say. "Go for a swim."

Collins and Maigo both give me the one eyebrow-raised stink eye. Watson just smiles and nods. The over-stimulated fan boy in him would be willing to try anything associated with the giant robot.

"So," I say, "can we see the Rift Engine, or is that a secret?"

Maigo rolls her eyes at me. "I don't keep secrets from you."

"You just steal aircraft," Collins said, and the two women direct their stink eyes at each other.

I clear my throat, "Ahem," and sweep my hand over the broad chest. "Mighty Hyperion. Reveal the source of thy power!"

Nothing happens.

I glance at Maigo when nothing happens. "Spoilsport."

She crouches and places her bare hand on the octagonal pattern covering the chest. She blinks twice and one of her cheeks twitch. She might be connected to Hyperion in some kind of loose way, but she still needs to make physical contact to command the thing. I'm not sure if that's a good thing or a bad thing.

There's a clunk as the center ring moves inward and slides to the side. The second ring splits down the middle and pulls apart. The outer ring breaks into three triangular segments and twists apart. When everything is done moving, there's a massive hole revealing Hyperion's inner workings. Most of what's inside is covered in a second layer of armor, including a large bronze ball at the core. The sphere lifts up, and its octagonal plates flip back and scroll away, revealing a device that must be the Rift Engine.

It doesn't look like much, and I have a hard time imagining that this thing could power a giant robot, let alone transport anything from one side of the country to the other.

"Looks like a bell," Collins says.

As she speaks the word 'bell,' Watson flinches like he's been slapped. "Oh my god. I've *seen* this before."

That gets my full and immediate attention. "Excuse me?"

"The bell. Die Glocke," Watson says. "It was a secret weapon, a Wunderwaffe—a wonder weapon—developed by the Nazis during World War II. There have been reports that the device could fly, that it melted people and that it opened a portal...a rift...between dimensions."

"Why would technology developed by Nazis power an Atlante—nevermind." The pieces fall into place just a moment before I make myself look like a doofus. "They didn't build it. They *found* it."

"Possibly at the ruins of Atlantis," Watson says. "Heinrich Himmler led an SS unit called the *Ahnenerbe* for a decade. Part of their mission was to search for the location of Atlantis, which they believed was populated by an Aryan master race."

"An *alien* master race," I say. "I wonder how they would have felt if they'd known the genes they cherished so much weren't even human."

"I think they would have been pleased," Watson says. "But by that time, the Atlantide had likely polluted most of humanity with their genetics."

"While the Ferox polluted us with their warlike ways," Collins says, arms crossed, frowning deeply. She doesn't like the idea of being ruled over or controlled, but that's exactly the kind of personality the Ferox built into us, along with a healthy dose of, 'That thing with tentacles! Kill it!'

I keep that to myself, though. While I'm not a fan of being manipulated, there's a possibility that the Ferox influence that kept the human race warring and refining ways to kill each other, gave us the tools to fend off the Aeros, who would enslave us all...they say. According to Zachary Cole—and the files stolen from GOD—the few survivors of an encounter with an Aeros named Artuke confirmed the squid-faced alien race's nefarious intentions. That didn't make the Ferox our friends. From what I under-stand about them, their human equivalent would be a terrorist organization...if terrorist organizations had just causes. But does any cause justify the killing, manipulation and endangerment of entire civilizations over thousands of years?

Where is Jean Luc when I need him?

"What happened to Die Glocke?" I ask.

Watson shakes his head. "Disappeared at the end of the war. Could have been hidden, destroyed or lost in the shuffle. For all we know, it could be collecting dust in a warehouse."

I grasp Watson's arm, smiling. "Are you saying..."

It takes him a moment, but he sees where I'm going and says, "Yes. We have top men working on it right now."

"Who?" I ask.

"Top...men."

"Ugh," Collins grunts and then says, "We're going to need a bigger boat." Followed by a thick Aussie accented, "That's not a knife, this is a knife." And she finishes with, "Get to the choppah!" She looks back and forth between us. "Will that hold you over for a little while?"

I raise an index finger and say, "They mostly come out at night–" but she slugs my shoulder before I can finish. "Yow!"

"Jon," she says. "Seriously, a lot of people are dead. There are at least three Kaiju on the loose, and no one knows where they're going to show up next. We–"

"Portland," I say.

"*Maine?*" Watson asks.

"Oregon."

"What makes you think that?" Maigo asks, adding her skeptical eyebrows to the others already conspiring against me.

The long answer is that I've had a team of trusted and well paid Zoomb techs–my very own 'top men'–going through the GOD files, searching for patterns, clues and details. They're looking for anything actionable or pertinent to our safety, with a focus on Aeros and Ferox activity. Up until now, aside from the events ten years ago in the Arctic, it's been clear that the Aeros haven't been hanging around. But in those same ten years there has been an influx of new residents in Portland. People who have suddenly changed career paths and moved. People who have left families and friends to start new lives. It's the kind of thing normal people sometimes do, but the sheer amount of these people moving to Portland has been vastly disproportionate. "If you were a shape-shifting savage alien and wanted to hide in plain sight, there's nowhere better to go then the land of happy-tappy hipster-lovin' Portland." When all I get are looks of doubt, I add, "Seriously, who would suspect a lumbersexual riding a banana seat bike?"

Watson is the first to admit defeat. "No one."

Maigo raises her hand. "I would."

Collins raises her hand. "I have a standing policy to coldcock the first lumbersexual I come across."

"Well," I say, looking out over Hyperion's massive body. "If I'm right, you might get a chance sooner than later. Just try not to get your hand bitten off in the process."

30

Lilly felt like she had dodged a bullet. So far, the ramifications of stealing the X-35 had been fairly tame. Hardly a stern talking to. She knew that taking the craft had been reckless and impulsive. But she was a teenager, right? That's what real teens did. Stole the car. Got drunk. Stupid stuff that wasn't nearly as forgivable once you were an adult—a line she and Maigo were going to cross in record time, thanks to their unique physiologies.

In fact, she could probably argue that stealing the X-35 had saved Boston. Sure, the futuristic aircraft would have helped keep the team safe, but Hudson's best shot—some kind of aerial swarm—had failed. Thanks to Lilly and Maigo, Hyperion had arrived in Boston just in time to turn the tide and save the others. And they'd managed to keep the robot out of the reach of the Russians and GOD. Granted, neither of them had known there was a giant, Kaiju-fighting, alien mech hidden beneath Big Diomede, but results were results. They couldn't be argued against.

She glanced at her father, seated beside her in the cockpit. He had interrogated Brice, but he hadn't even needed to resort to a raised voice. The man was a free-flowing fountain of information that lent credit to his claim of wanting to defect from GOD. But they still didn't trust him. There was a chance that every truth he told was laced with lies and misinfor-mation.

"We'll believe it when we see it," Hawkins had said at the end of the conversation that had set them on their current course over the Pacific Ocean.

The Genetic Offense Directive had redefined its core values and operational parameters in recent years. Though they had been created, in secret, as a black operation with DARPA, they now claimed no allegiance with any single nation, and were willing to work with any country that didn't require oversight—meaning they could continue their inhuman brand of experimentation, unhindered by laws or morality. Brice had defended the move to a point, noting that the enemy GOD was preparing for didn't see humanity in terms of nations, but he had backed down on the experimentation, which continued at locations around the world, including aboard a Russian aircraft carrier.

The Kuznetsov class aircraft carrier, named the *Sidorenko* after Ivan Mihailovich Sidorenko, the deadliest World War II sniper in the Red Army with 500 confirmed kills, wasn't as large as its American rivals. But what it lacked in size, it made up for in speed—despite being propelled by oil-fired boilers, rather than a nuclear reactor. And they had overcome the size issue for the more modern aircraft it held: Mig-29s, Russian Mikoyan LMFS and MI-24 Hind attack helicopters. But the ship was equal parts war machine and advanced genetics laboratory, operating in international waters, where laws did not apply.

It was also, Brice claimed, a prison for monsters, created...and captured. As a younger variant of Alicio Brice, he hadn't been privy to exactly what was there, but there was one prized possession that had been recovered from the ruins of GOD's destroyed West Coast facility: *some* of Nemesis Prime's remains, including its massive head and neck, which were the most pristinely preserved parts of the monster's ancient body.

"Target in sight," Lilly said, looking toward the horizon, where a large vessel steamed due east.

"They're really moving," Hawkins said.

"Twenty-nine knots," Lilly said, looking at the advanced targeting screen, which displayed the ship's name, speed, size and known armaments. There were also several buttons that would lead to more detailed information about the crew and schematics, but in the case of GOD's aircraft carrier, Lilly doubted the information would be accurate.

"Top speed," Brice said.

Hawkins placed his hands on the windshield and spread them apart, zooming in on the large ship. "The question is, are they charging toward a fight, or running away from one?"

"Running," Brice says.

Lilly and Hawkins both turned around to see Brice looking at the floor, which still projected a view of the ocean, four miles below. A long, thin shadow moved beneath the waves, sliding through the ocean and slowly gaining on the *Sidorenko*. A massive shape dragged through the water behind the first. Giger was still hauling Karkinos's body along for the ride, and was probably the only reason the Kaiju hadn't overcome the vessel already.

"Well," Lilly said, "they're screwed."

Brice didn't argue with her assessment, but surprised them both when he said, "You have to help them."

Lilly laughed. GOD was responsible for creating her, and in that weird sort of way, she owed them her very existence, but they also wanted her back. In their eyes, she was a success story among years and years of monstrous failures. She was fast, strong and deadly with the mind of a human—a soldier for the coming cosmic war, who they'd like to study and duplicate, like feline Brices. "Are you *serious?* I'm going to cheer when that thing sinks."

Hawkins frowned at her, no doubt thinking about the humanitarian side of things. The soldiers and scientists on that ship were human beings, some of whom might not be aware of what was happening on board. That was the way his well-rounded mind worked. But then he said, "There isn't much we can do. You saw what Giger did to Typhon and Scylla."

Brice looked torn. He held out his hands, preemptively beseeching mercy for what he was about to say. "Zachary Cole is on board the *Sidorenko.*"

Lilly snarled at the name. "Even better."

"You need to save him," Brice said.

Lilly and Hawkins stared at him for a moment, looked at each other and then turned back to Brice. Even the noble Hawkins looked dubious.

"Why...would we do that...exactly?" Lilly asked.

"He's a monster," Brice said. "I agree with that. He wasn't born with a moral compass. A true sociopath. But he is loyal to the human race as a whole. He might have no regard for the rights or sanctity of individual people, but when it comes to defending the human race, no one is better equipped or knowledgeable. I don't want to see him again, anymore than you do, but if Giger and Lovecraft really are just the beginning of something larger, we're all going to need what's in his head.

"Try to think of him as just another monster, like Nemesis. She has killed thousands upon thousands—far more than Cole. She has consumed people and destroyed cities, but some would argue that in doing so, she has also saved us from worse fates. I believe that is Jon Hudson's stance. He might not have publicly declared such a thing; it would be career suicide. But his actions—and yours—speak loud enough."

"Monsters with monsters," Hawkins said.

"Human and otherwise," Brice said. "As repulsive as Cole and Nemesis are, they aren't that different in the end, and we need them both."

Lilly growled, but she was distracted by the suddenly chaotic view of the *Sidorenko.* "They're launching aircraft."

Three Hind attack helicopters peeled away from the deck, heading south, as MiG-29s took off and tore into the sky. The deck cleared in what must have been record time as three Mikoyan LMFS fighters took off and followed the MiGs up and away towards the east.

"What the hell are they doing?" Hawkins said.

Lilly watched the planes fade into the distance. "Looks like they're abandoning ship."

"How far is Giger from the Sidorenko?" Brice asked.

"Fifteen miles," Hawkins said. "Closing at about a mile a minute."

"They're taking precautions," Brice said, "getting as many assets away from the ship before..."

"Before what?" Hawkins asked.

"GOD might be in charge of the research done on that ship, but it's still a Russian vessel, making this the first time the Russian military has had a direct conflict with a Kaiju." Brice looked Hawkins in the eyes. "Ask yourself, if you were Russian, and had already seen the ineffectiveness of America's military response, how would you react, in the middle of the Pacific Ocean."

Hawkins's eyes widened. "Lilly, get us out of here."

"What? Why would—"

"There," Brice said, pointing at the windshield. "One of them has turned back."

Hawkins centered their view on the single aircraft and zoomed in. It was flying high, too high to see clearly, but its distinct shape made it easy to identify.

"It's a Mikoyan," Hawkins said. "They're multirole combat aircraft."

"And?" Lilly asked.

"They have nuclear capabilities," Brice said.

Lilly believed in the official FC-P and U.S. government's position that nuclear weapons wouldn't work against Nemesis. The creature shirked off MOABs and was capable of unleashing the force of a nuclear blast on her own. But this wasn't Nemesis, or the U.S. military. This was the Russian military under the influence of GOD, in the middle of the Pacific, with no civilians to worry about.

"Buckle up," she said.

Brice held up his bound hands. "I can't!"

"Too bad for you," Lilly said with a grin, and then sent the X-35 into a steep climb that took them above the *Sidorenko*, which was still at a safe distance. Not wanting to find out if the EMP generated by a nuclear blast was strong enough to knock Future Betty out of the sky, she took them far beyond the ship, and climbed to forty thousand feet. The maneuver took less than a minute and left Brice sprawled against the rear hatch, bleeding from a head wound, but still conscious.

The lone Mikoyan shot past beneath them and quickly covered the now thirteen miles between the aircraft carrier and its target. Something small fell from the plane's bottom, and then the plane continued forward while climbing higher.

"Will the cameras filter out the light?" Brice asked, rubbing his head and climbing back onto the cargo bench.

Lilly and Hawkins looked at each other. Neither of them knew. Lilly quickly turned off the X-35's displays, and the entire interior of the craft became a series of flat gray surfaces.

After ten seconds, an already impatient Lilly asked, "How will we know when–"

A wave of pressure slapped into the X-35, shaking it for just a moment before passing.

After a few more seconds, Hawkins gave a nod. "Should be okay now."

Lilly activated the view screens again, and the outside world was projected around them. A brilliant, orange mushroom cloud rose up before them. Within seconds it matched their height and continued to rise into the stratosphere, while a massive ring spread out toward them, raging with the might of mankind's most powerful weapon.

31

"Take us down," Hawkins said, as the nuclear ring widened toward them. His stomach lurched as the X-35 dropped straight down. He heard Brice thump against something in the back and was positive the girl was trying her hardest to make the man's flight as uncomfortable as possible. He didn't blame her. Alicio Brice was connected to her tortured past. But this wasn't the same man, and Hawkins suspected that the man's defection from GOD might be genuine. If it was, keeping him alive was important. With his knowledge of GOD and genetics, he could be useful.

The *Sidorenko* came into view below them, cruising away from the nuclear blast at its back, still functioning, still in one piece.

Still shit out of luck.

The massive ruddy-black shape of Giger, hauling the still body of Karkinos, had not only survived the nuclear blast, it had closed the distance. If anything, all the Russians had managed to do was make it angry and turn a cautious approach into a mad rush.

"It's getting smaller," Brice observed, as the looming shadow surging up behind the *Sidorenko* shrank.

"It's diving," Hawkins said, his muscles tensing. He'd dealt with enough predators to know when one was about to strike. "Keep us at a safe distance."

They hovered at five thousand feet, which still felt close, because of the carrier's thousand foot length. A dark shape rose up below the port side, growing suddenly larger, and just before breaking the water, it resolved as the hideous, snarling face of Giger. With a burst of white water, the Kaiju lunged from the water and grasped onto the broad, flat deck with its four arms. The massive ship tilted from the sudden weight, but didn't flip. Then the emaciated looking tail rose up from the ocean behind Giger and speared the control tower, before thrashing back and forth, removing the flight control, bridge and flag bridge, along with everyone in it. Some of the debris fell into the ocean, the rest scattered across the deck.

The spines along the creature's bony exoskeletal back sprang up, like a wolf's hackles. It scoured the deck, looking back and forth with its six red eyes. With a snarl, it climbed a little higher and plunged its tail into the deck. But it didn't punch all the way through the ship. *It's controlling the power of its strike,* Hawkins thought, as the creature lifted its tail free and stabbed it back into the deck again, sending debris flying and opening a second hole.

"What's beneath there?" Hawkins asked.

Brice studied the scene for a moment. "Main hanger deck. It's normally where they'd keep aircraft but—"

"It's big enough to house Prime's remains," Lilly said. Hawkins didn't need Brice to confirm it to know she was right.

"What use would it have for a petrified Gestorumque?" Brice asked.

"They've found soft tissue in the fossil remains of a T-Rex, right?" Lilly asked. "Prime is what, a few thousand years old? Five thousand? Maybe it's not quite beef jerky all the way through?"

"The Aeros have access to Gestorumque DNA." Brice shook his head. "There's no reason... It doesn't matter. You still need to get Cole off of that ship."

"There're a few thousand men on board," Hawkins said, watching as sailors started climbing out of various staircases, and leaping into the sea. Something about their urgency didn't seem quite right. The ship was under attack by something horrifying, but the ship wasn't about to go down, and Giger was showing no interest in anything beyond carving open the flight deck. The way the men were running over each other and flinging themselves into the ocean...

Something got loose, he thought.

GOD was once again reaping what they had sown. And there was nothing he could do to save the men below. Not from Giger, and not from whatever monsters they'd created.

But could he save Zachary Cole?

Should he?

The man would be a treasure trove of information, if they could capture him and make him talk. The files stolen from GOD had given them a lot of information, but much of it was still encrypted. If there really was a war coming, Cole might be their only chance to fully understand the enemy before they arrived.

Giger punched another hole in the deck and reached two of its four hands inside, tearing the deck back. The tail punched more holes, growing more twitchy and frantic with each movement, but it was still solely focused on the middle of the main deck, and what was hidden beneath it. If Cole was on the bridge, he was already a lost cause. But if he was still alive...

"Put us down on the aft deck," Hawkins said. "Keep us hidden."

"What?" Lilly said. "Are you nuts?"

"Cole could—"

"He deserves whatever he gets."

Hawkins put his hand on her arm, "No one knows that better than me. But we've been running and hiding from that man for too long. Better to have the Devil in the cage than on the loose. It's not impossible that he might survive and get away. I'd rather know exactly where he is, wouldn't you?"

Lilly just stared at him.

"And if he can tell us anything—"

"In a cage," she said. "We'll put him in a cage."

Hawkins had meant the cage metaphorically, but understood Lilly was being very literal. He gave a nod. "In a cage."

Lilly piloted the X-35 toward the rear deck, coming in from behind the aircraft carrier to avoid the swinging tail. The deck was canted at a sharp angle and shifting back and forth under Giger's weight, so landing wasn't possible. But it also wasn't necessary.

Hawkins slipped into the back, took an FN SCAR assault rifle and several spare magazines from the small armory and bound Brice to an arm rest. Then he walked to the lowering cargo bay hatch and turned back to Lilly, who was leaving the cockpit. "Ready?"

"I was *made* ready," she said, guffawed, scooped him off his feet and leapt from the invisible craft. They dropped fifty feet to the tilted deck, where Lilly landed gracefully, despite the two-hundred-pound man in her arms. Hawkins slid out of her arms and swept the assault rifle back and forth, looking for targets. All he found were terrified men, running in all directions. Many of them noticed him and Lilly, but they didn't stop to question or combat them.

Three hundred feet away, Giger stabbed and tore at the deck, roaring a high-pitched warble, as it leaned back and pried off a large swath of deck.

And that's when it happened.

Like a pricked spider egg, the hull gave birth to a scurrying horde of eight-legged creatures with which both Hawkins and Lilly were intimately familiar. The creatures, once called 'BFSs'—Big Fucking Spiders—and later deemed Tsuchi, hadn't been eradicated. Given the number of them, GOD hadn't just continued studying them; they had been manufacturing the creatures.

The turtle-shelled spiders exploded in all directions, hopping and attacking. Men screamed as they were tackled and stabbed in the gut, three times, quick and surgical. Hawkins knew that three new Tsuchis would explode from inside each man. Soon, the ship, holding at least two thousand men, would be overrun by *six thousand* Tsuchis.

And if the creatures managed to implant their fast growing DNA into Giger... Hawkins looked up at the giant monster. Two of its arms still clung to the deck, while the other two reached into the gaping hole. Tsuchis scurried over its bony digits, stabbing at it with their tails, but failing to puncture the taut skin.

"There!" Lilly said, pointing to the far side of the deck. A large man with a mustache was accompanied by a squad of ten men dressed in black body armor. Unlike the Russian sailors, these men weren't running, they were waiting. Holding their ground. Protecting Cole. But they wouldn't last long.

"Let's go!" Hawkins said, and he opened fire on a Tsuchi scurrying toward them. The thing burst and slid to a stop. Hawkins took the lead, his accurate aim and steady pace guiding them through the chaos. There were enough screaming men below and streaming out over the deck that they weren't the Tsuchis' only target, which was good. But it wouldn't be long before the rabid spiders' numbers increased exponentially. He and Lilly had just minutes to get clear of the doomed vessel.

"Look out!" Lilly shouted.

Hawkins spun toward movement in his periphery, but he couldn't get the rifle up in time. Eight spiny legs clutched his face.

Hawkins knew what would happen next. Three sharp puncture wounds followed by a minute of agony, as the Tsuchi's progeny ate him from the inside. Then a horrible death as they tore free and continued the savage cycle.

But none of those things happened.

The Tsuchi sprang back off of his face—or rather, it had been yanked back. Lilly spun the creature by its tail and slammed it to the deck. The Tsuchi survived the impact and tried to lunge at Hawkins again, but Lilly pinned it to the deck with her foot and tore the thing's tail clean off. Red and white gore spilled from the body and tail, and the twitching legs fell still.

"Slow and steady might win the race," Lilly said, "but this isn't a race." She took the lead and glanced back with a feline grin. "Try to keep up." Then she was off and running, diving atop Tsuchis and dismembering them with the same ease with which the killer spiders dispatched men. Hawkins fired his weapon just twice as they ran past Giger, who had yet to pay attention to a single man or Tsuchi.

Hawkins nearly stumbled when he saw an enormous head rise up out of the deck. His first thought was that Nemesis or Karkinos had somehow surfaced through the great ship, but then he saw the empty eyes and the dried skin and armor. It was Nemesis Prime, head and neck, lifted free.

Gunfire from ahead pulled his attention back to their destination. Cole's men had engaged a wave of Tsuchis. The men were professionals, carefully picking targets and firing in controlled, three-round bursts, but they were outnumbered.

As Lilly and Hawkins neared the men, Lilly fell back. "You go first."

He didn't ask why. He knew why. In a battle of men versus monsters, it was possible one of the soldiers might mistake her for the enemy. Lilly ducked down behind Hawkins as they approached, but two men swiveled their weapons toward them anyway.

Hawkins raised his hands. "Cole!"

Behind the line of men, Zachary Cole, who had been scanning the sky, no doubt waiting for a pick-up, shifted in their direction.

When the men didn't open fire, Hawkins trained his weapon on a fresh wave of approaching Tsuchis and drained a magazine. He hoped that the men would see him as an ally. While eight of the men continued firing on the spiders, the other two kept their aim squarely on his head.

"Cole!" Hawkins shouted again. "Ma-uh, Dustin Dreyling, FC-P."

The two soldiers guarding Cole separated when he put his hand on their shoulders. "I know who you are, *Mr. Hawkins*. The question is, what are you doing h–"

Cole's eyes widened as he peeked around Hawkins and made eye contact with Lilly. A lopsided grin turned his mustache up. "Lilly."

Hawkins held an open palm out to Lilly, and he was relieved that she obeyed the silent command to not attack the man. "We're here to save you."

Cole's eyebrows rose up. He adjusted his suit coat. "I sense a lack of conviction. I will await my ride."

"You don't have time for that," Hawkins said, spotting the approaching helicopter, still miles off. "You don't need to hear conviction, or even kind intent. You didn't see us arrive, which means you know how we're leaving."

A man screamed, and one of the soldiers in black went down. A Tsuchi clung to his waist, plunging its tail into his gut. The man next to him shot the Tsuchi and killed his comrade, but the three creatures inside were already growing. Already eating.

"Lilly," Hawkins said. "It's time."

She took out the remote and summoned the X-35.

A second man went down. The gunfire intensified.

And then, Giger let out an ear splitting shriek that sounded almost like joy. All eyes turned to the massive creature as its tail finished cutting through the back of Nemesis Prime's neck. Two of the four arms peeled the flesh apart and the other two reached inside. When the spindly hands pulled back, they clutched a white creature, curled up in a ball and covered in viscous goo. The white flesh, bulbous head and collection of tentacles where there should have been a mouth, made the creature easy to identify: an Aeros.

"We're good!" Lilly said, motioning up with her head.

Hawkins glanced up and saw the inside of the X-35 slowly revealed as the hatch descended, twenty feet above. He gave Lilly a nod and she sprang into action, kicking the closest guard in the gut, and snagging the second with her tail. Cole tried to shout for help, but Hawkins punched him in the face, staggering the man back into

Lilly's arms as she flung the second soldier away. She hefted Cole up in her arms, said, "Holy go on a diet," and then tossed him up into the open hatch. Hawkins lifted a foot into Lilly's lowered hands and she tossed him up next.

Hawkins landed hard with a cough, and rolled to a stop next to Cole.

"I'll have you hung by your—"

Hawkins punched him again, silencing the threat.

Lilly sprang up into the hatch and slapped the button to shut it. Then she dove for the controls and pulled Future Betty up and away from the overrun aircraft carrier.

Cole groaned and looked at the scene through the floor. Giger was sliding back into the ocean, the Aeros clutched in its hands. "My respect for you people is becoming a deep-seated loathing." Then he reached into his pocket, pulled out a small device and pushed a button three times. Explosions swept across the ship, from one side to the other, tearing the vessel apart and plunging it into the ocean. Giger fell away and disappeared beneath the waves along with countless Tsuchis, which Hawkins knew couldn't swim. Sinking the ship was the perfect countermeasure against the creatures, but there was no excuse for spawning more of the monsters that had killed many of his friends, and wiped out entire cities.

He got to his feet, snatched the remote detonator away from Cole, and stood over him. "Well, we've always loathed you." And then he punched the man a third time, knocking him out cold.

32

The Crow's Nest stands solitary atop the hill, save for the lone white home down the street, a sentinel over a wasteland that had endured the fires of hell and now the floods of God's wrath. If you count Lovecraft and an alien race as gods. I'm sure some fruitcake is already putting together a Lovecraftian bible that they'll discover in a cave, or just post on Reddit.

But I wouldn't know. Right now we're on a media fast. Speculation is so rampant that 99% of what's being reported is misinformation. The DHS is monitoring emergency responders and military sources linked to Devine, but only information deemed urgent is being sent through to the FC-P. It's not that we don't care, or that I've devolved back into a slacker. It's that my team is human...well, most of them...and we're spent.

The shit is still hitting the fan, but right now, it's stuck to the blades, and until it's flung free, rest and recovery are our top priorities. Lovecraft and Nemesis have both fallen off the radar, and sonar, but they were last seen headed north at ridiculous speeds. Giger has disappeared with the recovered Aeros and Karkinos's body. Given what we now know about the Gestorumque/Voice relationship, it seems likely that the recovered Aeros Voice will find a new home in Karkinos, where it should feel right at home. That means we've got three Kaiju on our hands, each with Voices to help guide them.

It's a little disconcerting to think that when we faced five Kaiju two years ago, they weren't at full strength. If they'd had Voices, would we have stood any chance of success? Nemesis would have been outmatched, and my control of Scylla might not have been possible. Granted, we've got a giant Atlantean robot, and Nemesis—if Endo is to be trusted—but I'm not sure that will be enough. From what I've seen of these new Kaiju, they're heavy hitters, and Karkinos, under the control of a Voice, will be equally dangerous. I'm not too keen on the idea of Maigo jumping in a mech and facing off against them, but when the survival of the human race is at stake, it's our job to risk everything, even the people we love.

Hawkins and Lilly are on their way back, and when they arrive, my personal R&R will come to an end. The arrival of Zachary Cole is the equivalent of Lucifer being dragged back through the pearly gates. Would Jesus put on a pair of Holy Brass Knuckles, or just kick him straight into the lake of fire? My own personal thoughts of violence were put to rest when I heard that Hawkins had clocked the guy—three times. No one has more of a reason to put the hurt on Cole than Hawkins, and Lilly. That they actually *saved* him shows a staggering amount of self-control and clearheaded thinking. It would have been easy to watch the man go down with the hell ship he created.

Collins leans out the kitchen's sliding door. Her tactical gear has been replaced by shorts and a T-shirt. Her curly red hair has been pulled back in a pony tail, still wet from a recent shower. She holds up a small cup and spoon. "Pudding? It's chocolate. I know how you like it when you're licking your wounds."

I wave my hand like I've got my monocle in my eye. I often wear it when visiting Zoomb facilities. "Chocolate pudding is hospital food. Do we have tapioca?"

She rolls her eyes and disappears back into the kitchen.

I turn back to the view. The Crow's Nest grounds look largely unchanged despite the deluge they survived. A large number of trees still stand between here and the ocean, but most of the neighborhoods are just gone. If not for the vast destruction, the day would be picturesque. The clouds overhead are pink from the setting sun in the west. The air is warm, but a cool breeze is rolling in off the ocean, which sparkles, its beauty unfazed by the passing of monsters.

And despite the atmosphere, and the fact that my gorgeous wife returns with not one, but two cups of tapioca, my wan smile is forced. If all the warning signs are to be believed, the destruction of the past few years is just a small taste of what's coming. Even if we somehow manage to defeat the three Aeros Kaiju, what chance do we stand against an army of them? All the tapioca in the world can't put a dent in my worry. The woman now sitting next to me...she can at least share the burden.

She pops open one of the puddings, stabs a plastic spoon in it, and hands it to me. She prepares the second in the same way, and to my surprise, she takes a bite. "I thought you didn't like pudding."

"This is tapioca," she says, taking a second bite.

"Tapioca *is* a kind of pudding."

"I like the little balls."

Our eyes meet. Slow smiles spread. We speak in unison, her saying, "That's what she said," and me saying, "That's not what you said last night."

We share a good laugh, and I find myself relaxing a little. I lean back in my seat and kick my feet up on the deck banister. "Yep. The fate of the world rests on our shoulders."

"It's not the first time," she says.

"I can't help feeling we've been lucky up until now."

She takes another bite, pondering, and then says, "Maybe. But not all of the time. The reason we're still here, and the world isn't a wasteland, is that when it comes time to make the hard calls—like sacrificing a man's life to save a city—you don't back down. None of us do."

"Sounds like the world's worst Hallmark card."

She polishes off her pudding. "I write poetry and shit, too." Before I can stop her, she takes my untouched tapioca and helps herself. "Thanks for holding that for me." She takes a bite and points at my head with the spoon. "You haven't been wearing the hat."

"I'm the director of the world's most notorious government agency. Trying to look the part, I guess. Don't worry, I won't grow a mustache."

"I like the hat," she says, and I'm a little surprised by the confession. She's never once mentioned it before. "It's kind of iconic Jon Hudson."

"You mean it hides the fact that my hair is receding?"

"Reced*ing*?"

I groan. "Receded."

"Nah," she says with a smile. "It just fits your personality. Screw the DHS. Everything we do is unconventional. Keep the hat." And with that, she pulls my red beanie from her back pocket and hands it over.

Hello old friend, I think and put it on. Strange that something like a hat can make me feel better, but it does. Everyone has their security blankets, I suppose.

"Are you two being gross?" Maigo asks from above. I look up. She's halfway out the Crow's Nest office window, looking down at us.

"Oh my god," I say, laying on the sarcasm, "are you *not* reading my mind?"

She smiles. "I try not to. Makes me feel dirty."

Despite our joking, she really has made an effort to control her connection to my mind. Not only are there privacy issues, but we have enough nightmares between the two of us that when we share them, neither of us sleep. She's made controlling our connection a discipline, limiting it to Christmas morning conversations, which generally happen when her fear of becoming a monster gets the best of her and she doesn't want anyone else to know.

"What's up?" I ask.

"Watson is connected to Hyperion."

I sit up. Watson came up with the idea to interface with Hyperion, who, according to Maigo was able to monitor, decrypt, translate and filter communications worldwide. Military, television, radio, Internet, satellite. Hyperion has access to it all. But it wasn't looking for State secrets or trying to uncover terror plots, it was scouring the world for signs of Gestorumque. Maigo maintained her connection to the robot, despite it being miles away, but that connection was more of a feeling than a direct flow of information. If Watson connects to the robot, we might have something close to a Kaiju early warning system. "Already? Doesn't seem very secure for alien tech. How'd he pull it off?"

"I asked for him," she says. "Come see."

She slides back inside.

I turn to Collins, who's finishing her second pudding—my second pudding. "You ready, Pudding Monster?"

She makes a pouty face at me. "Aww. Did I make you sad?"

Before I can reply, she pulls out a third pudding cup from behind her leg and puts it down between us with a wink. "I wouldn't do that to you, hubby. I know how much you like little balls, too."

Still smiling, we head upstairs to the Crow's Nest operations center. The large space is more crowded than ever, but it's neat and organized thanks to Cooper, who's seated at her desk, scrolling through computer documents.

"Cooper," I whisper. "Go home. Doesn't Spunky need to suckle or something?"

"Ted's with his grandparents," she says. "And I'm pumping. There's enough in the freezer to last a few days."

"Gross. You should try adopting. You get to skip the chapped nipples, and sometimes they come with super powers."

"Ha, ha," Maigo says. She's standing behind Watson with Joliet, looking at the information displayed on his large, curved screen.

"We'll see this through until it's done," Cooper says. "Chapped nipples or not."

"It might not *get* done this time," I say, earnestly wanting her to consider being with her son.

She turns to me, looking over her glasses. "Pretty sure the first priority of a mother is to make sure the world exists for her child."

"Good point," I say. "Morbid, but good point."

Collins and I join Maigo and Joliet behind Watson, who's working his keyboard like a flock of manic woodpeckers. Information scrolls over the screen. None of it means anything to me, but Watson's eyes bounce back and forth, and he's making quick grunts like he's having a conversation.

He leans back, pulling his hands away from the keyboard and rubbing his face. After taking a deep breath and letting it out slowly, he says, "It's too much to follow. We're just going to have to trust that Hyperion's systems work."

"They do," Maigo said, speaking from personal experience.

"And if he detects something?" I ask. "What then? He's ten miles away, taking a catnap in the ocean."

"He'll come and get me," she says.

"And then...poof, the Rift Engine whisks you away to engage a Kaiju in mortal combat. Are you ready for that? Have you even eaten anything yet?"

She takes the pudding from my hand and takes a bite.

Joliet pats my arm. "Look at you. Dad of the year."

"God damn, did you all conspire to tease me and eat my pudding?"

"It's tapioca," Maigo says, talking with her mouth full.

"Hudson," Watson says, and I miss the serious tone.

"Et tu, Watson?"

"Huh?" he says. "What? No. Look." He points at the center of the curved screen where a transcript is scrolling.

This is oil rig Polar Explorer, operating in the Beaufort Sea. We've spotted the Kaiju known as Lovecraft heading due west.

"When did this happen?" I ask.

"This is a real time feed," Watson says.

It is accompanied by the Kaiju known as Nemesis, also heading—hold on, oh shit!

Watson looks up at me. "This is happening right now."

33

Jeff Lane lived a life on the fringe of the world, surrounded by roughnecks, roustabouts, engineers and the occasional scientist or company man. He didn't interact with the outside world that much. Had no family. Preferred books to television. And any news he heard was filtered through his crew. Most often that news had to do with weather, which was generally the only outside force that had any kind of impact on his day-to-day life. Despite the sometimes odd length of the days and nights, he enjoyed the cold and the occasional storm. For an oil rig boss who spent most of his time on the ocean, rough seas were the spice of life. On a floating rig the size of *Polar Explorer*, there wasn't much he had to worry about aside from finding oil, which he was very good at.

The day had been uneventful and the weather as boring as an after-school special, so he was surprised when the Rig Medic, John Calvin Scott, who went by Calvin, said, "Oh my god." Not only was he not the kind of man to take the Lord's name in vain, he was also hard to get worked up. He dealt with broken bones and blood on a fairly regular basis, and weathered the worst storms Mother Nature threw at the rig without raising an eyebrow. He'd come to the control room with coffee and a deck of cards. While most men were hitting the mess at the end of a long day drilling a test pit, the Captain, Chief Engineer, Rig Medic and Safety Man lost and made money over games of poker.

Calvin put his coffee down, nearly dropping it from his shaking hand.

"The hell has him so spooked?" Brandon Kent, the Chief Engineer, asked. He was a big man, with the build of a roughneck, but a mind made for structural engineering. He was also bluffing. Lane was sure of it.

"Cards face down," Kent said.

Both men lay down their cards and Jim Tzeng, the Safety Man, complied as well, laying down his cards.

"What is it?" Lane asked before standing and grunting.

"I—I'm not sure," Calvin said. "It's pretty far off. Could be a rogue wave."

Rogue waves didn't happen frequently, but they also weren't unheard of. Lane moved to the wide window and picked up a pair of binoculars. He raised them to his eyes and peered out over the ocean. He scanned up from the main deck and all the way to the horizon without seeing anything.

"I'm not seeing anything, Calvin." Lane glanced back at Kent and Tzeng, positive he was being played, but neither man was looking at his cards. He turned back to the window feeling less apprehensive. A rogue wave would have been large enough to see. "Where is it?"

When Calvin pointed to the right and Lane saw movement, he raised the binoculars again. It took a moment, but he found the aberration. It looked like a hill moving through the water. "That's not a rogue wave."

"What else could it be?" Calvin asked.

"Rogue waves don't come in lumps. No waves come in lumps. They're long."

Kent and Tzeng joined them at the window. The four men watched the strange wave rolling toward the rig. It looked harmless. Hardly big enough to shift the big rig. But it was an oddity.

Then Tzeng gasped, the sound coming out almost high-pitched. "It's one of them."

"One of what?" Kent asked.

Tzeng leaned forward, hands on the glass. He was clearly afraid, but not about to run away; there was nowhere to run. "Kaiju."

"Nemesis?" Calvin said.

"Which one of the sonsabitches on board you think wronged someone?" Kent asked.

"Doesn't matter much, does it?" Lane said, knowing that it could very well have been him. He hadn't always been a good man. He wasn't really a good man now.

"S'pose not," Kent said.

"I don't think that's Nemesis," Tzeng said.

Unlike the rest of them, Tzeng followed the news, especially in regard to the past Kaiju appearances and the government agency responsible for dealing with them: the FPC, or something. Lane had no time for monsters, and living in fear of them wasn't his style. Up until this moment, they'd been a fantastical element of the world that had as little influence over his life as the monsters in movies.

"It's the new one," Tzeng said.

"The one that attacked Tokyo yesterday?" Kent asked.

Lane was surprised the big man knew about current events, but this one sounded significant enough that it would reach his ears. This was the first time Lane had heard of it. "What happened in Tokyo?"

"Kaiju," Tzeng said. "The three from Washington, D.C. and a fourth."

"Thought they died," Lane said, referring to the creatures named Typhon, Scylla and Karkinos.

"They did," Tzeng said. "But I don't think it's them, or the monster from Tokyo. It's coming from the east." He looked out at the wave, which had grown larger and a lighter blue color. In fact, the water appeared almost turquoise, like the ocean over a tropical white sand. "It's *white*. This is the thing from Boston!"

"Lovecraft," Kent said. "I saw a picture of it."

Now they're screwing with me, Lane thought. "Lovecraft was a weird fiction author..."

Water lifted up and ruptured as a monstrous white head surged out of the three-hundred-foot deep water. Waves of shimmering blue and green slid through the skin, dramatically revealing black eyes and a mass of writhing tentacles.

"It's real," Lane whispered. "Holy hell, it's real." He looked back and forth for some imaginary means of retreat, but he knew there was no escape. The life rafts wouldn't do them much good if the monster decided to start snacking, and no one was going to get a helicopter out to them in time.

"Look!" Tzeng shouted. "A second one!"

A pair of tall spikes carved through the water like massive dorsal fins. Then the water split and a monster Lane did recognize rose up.

Nemesis.

Lane sat down, feeling a bit stunned. He picked up the radio mic, set it to transmit on all frequencies and said, "This is oil rig Polar Explorer, operating in the Beaufort Sea. We've spotted the Kaiju known as Lovecraft heading due west. It is accompanied by the Kaiju known as Nemesis, also heading—hold on, oh shit!"

Lane dropped the mic, as he got back to his feet. Lovecraft had risen higher out of the water, lifting two massive arms tipped with two-fingered hands. Its back split open, and two bat-like wings spread out, the trans-lucent membranes shimmering with colors. With its arms and wings unfurled, the creature absolutely dwarfed the rising Nemesis. It leaned forward and roared, tentacles warbling.

"I don't think these boys are traveling buddies," Kent said.

Nemesis plowed forward, undaunted by the threat display, shoving through the water, rising higher. The monster started gagging, lurching forward like a dog about to vomit. A luminous orange blob launched from the Kaiju's mouth and sailed toward Lovecraft.

Lane knew what it was. He avoided the news, but everyone on the planet had seen footage from the destruction of Washington, D.C. Like the membranes on her body, if the orange globule ruptured, it would explode, taking out the rig and everyone on it.

Lovecraft lurched back in momentary surprise. But then a gland in its throat swelled up. A spray as black and viscous as the oil Lane spent his life seeking out burst forth. The geyser of liquid struck the orange bomb, coating it on all sides. But what could that do? Just as the black-coated blob reached Lovecraft, the monster knocked it from the air.

"It turned it solid," Calvin said. "Thank God."

But Nemesis was far from done. Moving fast for her size, she dived down into the waves, and disappeared. The ocean settled. Lovecraft, arms open, ready for action, turned in slow circles.

The ocean behind the white Kaiju flickered orange and then gave birth to an unholy spawn. Nemesis sprang onto Lovecraft's back, landing between the wings. But the larger Kaiju had prepared. *Not pre-pared,* Lane thought, *trained.* The monster was fighting like a man. For that matter, so was Nemesis. Lovecraft leaned forward, pitching Nemesis over its shoulders.

As Nemesis flipped, head over heels, Lane grasped the intercom mic and shouted to the entire crew, who might not have been watching the epic battle. "Brace for impact! Brace for impact!"

Nemesis struck the water hard, sending up a massive wave that was still growing when it rolled through the *Polar Explorer.* Metal groaned. Warning lights blazed. The drill was torn free from the bottom, which wasn't as bad as it could have been, since they had yet to strike oil. As the rig settled back down, Lane quickly confirmed they were still in one piece and not sinking, and then he turned his attention back to the action.

Instead of getting back to her feet, Nemesis remained underwater, until her tail rose out like a spear, piercing the large Kaiju's gut. Lovecraft shrieked in pain, but caught the tail, preventing the trident tip from puncturing any deeper. And the tail was no match for the two massive arms, which pulled the blade free, unleashing a gout of purple blood that stained the white skin.

Nemesis pulled back, and burst from the ocean again, mouth open, teeth bared, going for the neck. But Lovecraft coughed a fresh spray of black into Nemesis's face, which froze in place. The black goo had solidified and locked her jaws open. Nemesis sprawled backward, clawing at her face, chipping the black away with some of her skin.

Lovecraft took one step after Nemesis, but stopped short and looked down at its still bleeding wound. The Kaiju roared in anger, clearly wanting to continue the fight, but thinking better of it. With a final spray of black that went rigid on Nemesis's body, Lovecraft stepped back, crouched down and with a deep, resounding roar, vacated into the ocean. An oily swirl of black, purple and white fluid plumed out around the creature, draining away its girth and leaving a much more slender monster behind. After the fluid came bulbous globs of what looked like fat, which bobbed and rolled in the soiled water. While most of the monster had grown thin, its barrel chest looked as large as ever, its pectoral muscles twitching beneath the luminous skin.

The wings spread wide again and then beat down. A hurricane wind slammed into the rig, shaking the structure and rattling the windows. But no one paid them any attention. With a second beat of its wings, Lovecraft lifted out of the ocean. The third beat pulled it free, and up it rose, free of the water and Nemesis. Wings spread wide, the Kaiju turned south and glided into the distance.

Four sets of eyes in the control room turned back to Nemesis, just in time to see the hard black coating covering her face shatter and fall away. Nemesis bellowed after the fleeing Kaiju, but it paid her no heed, gliding toward the coast.

Nemesis slammed her arms into the ocean with a very human display of frustration and then dived back into the water, destination unknown.

Lane reached for the radio mic, fumbling with the coiled wire. He put it to his mouth with a shaking hand, and spoke.

34

Uhh, this is Polar Explorer... Um, they...they fought, but both Kaiju are gone now. One by sea, the other by, uhh, air.

I stare at the scrolling text captured from north of the Arctic Circle and transcribed on Watson's computer screen by an alien robot. I know it wasn't Nemesis who flew. She has wings hidden beneath all that thick, black skin and armor, but they're not used for flying. I have a hard time imagining how something as large as Lovecraft could get off the ground, too, despite the size of its wings.

"Any sign of either of them?" I ask.

Watson uses a combination of military networks, Devine and his connection to Hyperion, scouring for both monsters. "Nothing."

I clench my fists, tired of being outfoxed by creatures the size of sky-scrapers. "How is that possible? I get that they can hide in the ocean, but in the air?"

"The terrain in that part of the world is rough. Radar is line of sight. If it's low enough..."

"You're telling me a Kaiju is flying under the radar?"

"The mountains are—"

"They're big, I get it." I sigh and put my hand on Watson's shoulder. "Sorry. Not upset with you."

"It will turn up," Watson says. "Between the military and Hyperion, if anyone sees it, we'll hear about it."

"I've scrambled fighters across Alaska," Cooper says, walking up behind Watson and rubbing his shoulders. "Night is falling soon, but if it's still luminous, someone might get eyeballs on it."

"And then what?" I grumble.

The building shakes, making us all stumble around like we're simulating a battle on the bridge of the Enterprise. I turn to the window, expecting to see a Kaiju charging us. Wouldn't be the first time. Instead, I see a massive metal face leaning down, its glowing red eyes blazing. Hyperion has appeared just beyond the grounds, crouching down on what would have been a home before the tsunami. It leans forward, plants its big two-fingered hands on the lawn and leans further forward, waiting.

I turn to Maigo. "Real subtle."

She looks as stunned as the rest of us. "I didn't... It just..."

That Maigo didn't somehow communicate her desire for Hyperion to beam himself over is disconcerting. Would it have chosen the same location had there still been families living in the neighborhood? Just because it was designed to kill Kaiju, doesn't mean it respects the sanctity of human life. But it's connected to Maigo, who managed to infuse the goddess of vengeance with a conscience, so I'll give it, and her, the benefit of the doubt. I'll also pray it doesn't squash anyone. It's a risk, but there's no denying the fact that we need Hyperion. And people are going to die. There's no avoiding it.

"Hey," Watson says, motioning to an alert that just popped up on the far right hand side of his curved screen. "They're here. Hawkins and Lilly..."

He doesn't say it, but we're all thinking it: and Brice and Cole. The few seconds we all stand there, holding our collective breath, feels like an hour. "Okay," I say, raising my hands. "Everyone at least pretend to be doing something important. I don't want Cole to think he can get under our skin. Let's just be calm."

"Cool heads prevail," Cooper says.

I snap my fingers and point at her. "Cool heads prevai–"

"Mr. Hudson." The voice is deep and familiar. I turn toward it and find Hawkins and Lilly entering from the roof. Hawkins has a handcuffed Zach Cole in front of him. Lilly has Brice, who is definitely a younger version of the man I met. But there is also something different about him. It's his eyes. He lacks the cold ruthless nature of his other selves, or he's very good at hiding it.

I turn my attention to the well dressed Zachary Cole. His suit is wrinkled, but he's still the best dressed man in the room. "You look upset. Do you need a cheeseburger? Maybe ten?"

Lilly raises her hand slightly. "I could–"

"I'm trying to mock him, Lilly," I say, stopping in front of Cole.

"Still," she says. "I'm hungry."

I turn my eyes to Hawkins. "You sure he's not a hologram?"

"Jon," Collins says. She knows me well enough to see where this is going.

"It's alright," Cole says. "Let him punch me. It's how more primitive minds deal with emotions."

Son of a motherless Cyclops. I turn away so he can't see my red face. It takes all of my self-control to not sucker punch the man in his bulbous gut.

Woodstock walks into the room, looking a bit weary. "You all know there's a giant–" He sees my face. Then sees Cole. A fire lights in his eyes. The old man moves with surprising speed and power, slugging Cole in the stomach. But the big man doesn't even flinch.

"Feel better?" Cole asks.

"Not remotely," Woodstock says, and then turns his back to Cole, rubbing his hand. He leans up close to my ear and whispers, "If you have a go at him, his belly is like punching a bag full of wrenches." He gives me a wink, and then points at Cole. "You sir, bring shame to mustached men everywhere."

Cole ignores the jab and leans his head to the side, looking out the wide window and at Hyperion beyond it. "What's it like?" he asks, and turns to Maigo. "To be the Voice for a Gestorumque and a Mashintorum? I'm not sure that's been done before."

Something about the way Cole is talking doesn't jibe. He knows a lot about the Aeros and Ferox, but he's speaking with the kind of intimacy that says he's not just knowledgeable—he's experienced.

He's just trying to get you worked up, I tell myself.

I step in front of him, blocking his view of Hyperion and Maigo.

"Tell me about the new Gestorumque."

"You can't defeat them," he says.

"I'm not the one with a sunken aircraft carrier," I say. "Or two dead-again Kaiju. And I'm certainly not the one who gave them a Kaiju for the Voice that's been hibernating inside Prime for millennia."

"An unfortunate oversight of the Mashintorum's first Voice."

"And yours," I say.

He gives just a hint of a nod. "Perhaps."

"You have a track record of miserable failures," I say. "Island 731, the lab in Lompoc, Area 51, and now the *Sidorenko*. You have lost thousands of men, multiple facilities and I can only guess at how much money. And for all of the death and destruction you have wrought, you still have nothing to show for it, aside from *strengthening* the enemy."

"There have been other failures," Brice says, sounding eager. "And there is still the citadel in—"

"There is no place in the coming war for turncoats, cowards or uncertain allegiances," Cole says, and he cranes his head around to face Brice.

"You can't control me anymore," Brice says with enough fire to convince me he really intends to jump ship from GOD and join the good guys.

Cole glowers at the man, locking eyes with him. Brice does his best to return the glare, but lacks the intimidation factor. I'm about to step in when Cole growls a single word. "Petunia."

There is a moment of stunned silence as everyone, including Brice, tries to understand the significance of the word. Then blood pours from Brice's nostrils. He raises a hand up, touches it to the blood and looks at the bright red now coating his digits. "Oh, no." Then his eyes roll back and he collapses to the floor.

Joliet dives to the man's side, checking for a pulse, but I'm already certain about what she'll find.

"He's dead," Joliet says, looking ready to put Cole in a hurt locker. And she's impulsive enough to try. But she won't have any more luck than Woodstock.

I hold out a hand, signaling her to calm down. That doesn't stop Hawkins from wrapping one of his arms around Cole's neck. He isn't squeezing hard enough to knock Cole out, but it won't take much more pressure to send the bulbous asshole to sleepy time.

"Petunia?" I say. "*Petunia?* It's not that uncommon of a word, you know."

He grins. "I speak it quite rarely, I assure you. Very few of them—" He motions to Brice with his head, despite the limited movement. "—rebel against GOD. If they survive their own experiments, many of them live long lives. If it makes you feel better, you can add his death to your list of my failures. Or yours. Boston. Washington, D.C. Los Angeles. Salt Lake. Has the Mormon church forgiven you yet? No proxy baptisms for you, I'd guess."

Lilly steps closer to the man, and I notice her claws are extended.

I glance at Maigo. She's glaring at Cole from behind her hair. Fists clenched.

Collins has a hand on her sidearm, a big ass revolver.

Even Watson looks ready to throw down.

Cooper is the only one of us who looks unruffled by Cole's comments and the fact that he's just murdered a man inside the Crow's Nest.

A low growl fills the room, and I'm surprised to see Buddy, the FC-P's mascot Australian Shepherd, snarling at Cole. I've never heard the gentle dog growl. Lilly looks down at the dog and grins, the pair coming to some kind of silent truce in the face of a mutual adversary.

"In case you haven't noticed," I say to Cole, pinching my index finger and thumb together. "You are this close to being lynched. So, I suggest you answer my questions now and—"

"You have yet to hear of my successes," Cole says. "Everything you have said is true, but in failure, there is refinement. The hardships of life strengthen." He looks at Collins. "Don't you think?"

She pops the button from the revolver's holster, but stops short of drawing the weapon.

"The Island gave us you," he says to Lilly. "And your adoptive parents." He turns back to me. "Boston gave us you." To Collins. "And you. The fires of that city turned the FC-P from a joke, into this planet's best defense against Kaiju." To Maigo. "Washington freed you from Nemesis, a girl with unmatched strength and DNA that allows her to pilot that." He leans to the side, looking out at Hyperion. "And Salt Lake gave Nemesis a new Voice, whose influence has only increased her lethality.

"You all have become a fine sword." He smiles. "GOD has simply provided the fire to refine your edge."

I laugh and realize it sounds a little crazy. "Are you actually taking credit...for us?"

He lowers a sinister gaze in my direction. "You don't really think a religious senator snuck the creation of the FC-P into a bill to defend the United States from paranormal and demonic threats, do you?" He laughs. "Not as sharp as I'd hoped. The FC-P exists because I willed it to. Your trials and tribulations have been manipulated from the beginning. Even General Gordon was a pawn, his greed for life made him malleable. Like you, Jon. Like all of you. Clay in the hands of GOD."

My mind reels from this revelation, part of me screaming that it can't be true, and the rest of me seeing the puzzle pieces fall into place. We're just another one of GOD's creations, perhaps the best of its creations. What really solidifies this for me is that we have become what GOD has been working on all along: the best defense for Earth against an Aeros invasion. We're definitely not ready for the fight, but we're still the best chance this planet has.

I glance at the level-headed Cooper, raise my eyebrows and motion to Cole's face with my hands. She gives a nod. "I'm not going to stop you."

I cock my fist back and refrain from delivering an 80s style one-liner before driving my knuckles into his mouth.

The punch stings my hand, but seems to have no effect on Cole.

Then he grins, and I see that he's bleeding...

Purple.

35

"Aww shit," I say. "Are you *serious?*"

Cole chuckles through his purple stained teeth. "You've been right about a lot, Jon. You have good instincts. About Gestorumque. About Portland. And you should trust them."

How the hell does he know about Portland? I think, and then I realize that if we've been manipulated from the beginning, by GOD, then it's likely that we've been monitored all this time. They practically gave us Future Betty. They allowed us to take GOD's files, and probably just the files they wanted us to have. They've invaded our lives? How much have they seen? I feel violated, but not just for myself. For my wife. My daughter. For everyone in this room. But at the same time, I realize how inconsequential all of that is in relation to the fact that the bead of blood dangling toward the floor is purple.

It's alien.

He's one of them.

A Ferox.

A shape shifter.

And he's not just hiding in plain sight, he's covertly directing the actions of nations.

"If you think complimenting my instincts is going to lead to a My Little Pony Brony hug fest, you're mistaken." I step closer, ready to knock his alien teeth out. "I'm going to—"

"Let me go," he says.

"I was going to say something about your ass and a unicorn horn, but—"

"It wasn't a suggestion," he says, lifting up his handcuffed hands. He slowly spreads his arms apart, and it's like the cuffs aren't even there. The metal stretches and pops apart without a hint of resistance from the links or any struggle from Cole. Hands free, he takes hold of Hawkins's python-like arm and calmly pries it away with the same effortless exertion. Hawkins shakes as he resists, his face turning red, but there's no stopping Cole.

With his neck free, Cole leans forward and whips Hawkins across the room. Lilly dives in front of her father, catching him and easing him to the ground.

I'm about to suggest a calm resolution, as I'm not sure this is a fight we can win, but hotter heads react faster than I can talk.

Joliet dives forward with surprising speed, landing three punches before Cole calmly swats her aside while staring at me as if to say, 'Really? *Really?* This is the best you can do?'

Collins is next, drawing her revolver with typical lightning speed, but in that fraction of a second it takes her to lift the weapon and slide her finger around the trigger, Cole closes the distance and slips his meaty digit behind the hammer. With a twist of his hand, Cole elicits a shout of pain from my wife and frees the weapon from her grasp. The revolver hits the floor around the same time I think, *Screw it,* to the idea of a peaceful solution. I drive my fist into the side of Cole's head.

It's a solid punch to the temple. The kind that crumples a man's legs under him. But Cole barely flinches. Hawkins mentioned that he'd knocked Cole unconscious before their trip back, but it now seems likely that the big man-alien was faking it.

"This is not helping solve your problems," he tells me.

I swing again, but he leans back and avoids the blow. Does that mean he's toying with me, or did the first punch hurt him?

"We are on the same side of this war," he says.

Another swing and a miss. "This is your war. You brought it here."

"We brought your simple people out of the caves. We strengthened you with Atlantide blood. We gave you technology. Taught you how to defend yourselves. Your planet."

"You taught us how to kill each other," I say. "En masse. You gave us nuclear weapons, chemical weapons, biological warfare and genetic nightmares. You gave us genocide."

"A sword can't be–"

"You're the forge that refined humanity," I say in my most obnoxious, sarcastic voice that sounds a little bit like Yoda. "Blah, blah, fucking blah."

He settles into a more relaxed posture, his grin returning. "I have always found you amusing, Jon."

I flip him off with both hands and step closer, obscuring his line of sight.

"Whether you agree with the...manipulations used to influence your species into a warlike people is of no consequence. You would not exist without it. None of you would. The people you love. The cities you protect with such devotion. All of it exists because you have been infused with a desire to expand, to explore and to fight for those things. You revolt against the idea of being controlled because that is exactly how you were conditioned. It's an ideal that the founding fathers of the United States fully understood, and not one of them was Ferox.

"Freedom is everything. It is the *right* that unites us. You speak of genocide, but you have yet to comprehend it. The worst genocide in human history was the holocaust of World War II. Between five and eleven million people were killed, seventy-eight percent of them Jewish. The slaughter was confined to Nazi occupied Europe. A single continent."

"Which the Ferox no doubt organized," I point out.

"A final lesson, to help the world understand the stakes."

I feel another swing coming on, but I resist. The girls are almost ready.

"Imagine an even more efficient holocaust not confined to a single continent, or planet. Imagine the slaughter of hundreds of billions, spread across the cosmos, over millennia. Imagine fighting against this unstoppable purge, to the point of extinction, only to rally back, again and again. Finally, upon discovering a species sympathetic to your plight, a victory. You mewl over a few thousand years of manipulated evolution, while we have endured millions of years of evolution and conditioning to the point that we no longer physically resemble the race we started out as."

He's actually managed to bait the hook and interest me in his story of cosmic woe. I don't say anything, but he sees the question in my eyes.

"The Ferox were once Aeros," he says. "We are now genetically different enough to be considered a different species, but we were once the same, separated only by a subtle shift in skin color, white and gray. What would you do under similar circumstances? Would you roll over and let your species be eradicated, or would you do anything to save them—" He glances at the others congregated behind me. "For the people you love. Freedom, love and loyalty, are emotions *taught* to humanity. Your once primal drives to reproduce have also been refined."

"Bullshit," I say.

"An individual with no concept of love will not risk himself for another. Empathy lacking love is nothing more than the curiosity of a sociopath."

"Says the sociopath," I say.

"There is no greater love than to lay down one's life for one's friends."

I flinch back, verbally slapped. "Did...did you just quote the *Bible?*"

"The words of the Anomaly," he says. "You don't need to love the Ferox, Jon, but when the war comes to your planet, you will fight, and you will join the Ferox, or perish. And that is something your love, and the love of billions, won't allow. Not without a fight."

"Well, you're right about that," I say. "We're not going down without a fight. Against the Aeros, or you."

I step to the side and see a glimmer of surprise on the chubby man's face, as Lilly flings Maigo past me. She strikes with the force of a wrecking ball, driving her heels into Cole's chest. There's no defense against a hit like that, and Cole flies back through the room, into the broad stairwell where he topples down the stairs and out of view. The house shakes when he stops against the brick wall.

We're about to chase after him, expecting to see a twisted, broken body, but we stop short when we hear his bones breaking. The slick crack of bones, popping of joints and slurp of flesh is impossible to mistake.

Neither is the growl that follows it.

A flowing mane of black hair rises first, followed by a smooth, gray snout framed on either side by three red eyes, six total, and a sharp-toothed snarl. Bony spikes jut from the flesh of his face. A muscular body rises up, followed by a twitching tail tipped with a tuft of black hair. All of Cole's fat was simply misdirection, hiding powerful mass that looks like a cross between The Rock and a lion. As it steps back onto the hardwood floor, its long claws tap out an irritating rhythm that reveals frenetic energy hidden just beneath the surface of this monstrosity.

The Ferox that used to be Zachary Cole, twists its neck from one side to the other, popping vertebrae into place. It takes a deep breath, filling its powerful chest, and lets it out with a sigh. For a moment, I think the monster might start monologuing again, but he dives to the side, heading for Woodstock.

Despite not standing a chance against the monster, Woodstock balls his fists, and shouts, "Bring it on, Nancy!"

But the attack is a feint. While the Ferox bounds for Woodstock, its tail lashes out around Maigo's leg and yanks. She falls hard, hitting the floor, and she's then flung down the staircase. The move is well thought out, and clearly vengeance for Maigo's attack, but also it's far from lethal.

Never one to shirk from a fight, Lilly dives into action, raking her claws across the Ferox's shoulder. The attack draws purple blood and proves that the creature isn't impervious. But it also makes the alien angry. With a roar that hurts my ears, the Ferox dive-tackles Lilly. Hawkins launches himself at the Ferox's back, but he's caught around the waist and tossed across the room, crashing into a work station.

Lilly is pinned.

Collins is bending to pick up her gun, but won't be fast enough.

"Cole!" I shout. "Don't!"

The Ferox turns its horrible, alien head toward me and lets out a bark. Then it leaps away from Lilly, bounds across the office, charging through workstations.

Collins and Cooper both track the creature with guns, but they're vastly different. Collins's fires lethal rounds. Cooper's fires tracking darts—the same kind we use to observe the movements of the cryptids we've discovered. I grasp Collins's arms and shove them up just as she fires. The bullet punches into the ceiling. A moment later, Cooper pulls her weapon's trigger and the small projected device finds its mark in the Ferox's thick hide.

Monster-Cole jumps Hawkins as he tries to get back up and then flings itself at the broad window stretching across the Crow's Nest's east-facing wall. The usual view of the ocean is currently occupied by Hyperion's face. Glass gives way to the Ferox's solid mass, shattering and exploding outward.

I run to the broken window in time to see the alien throw itself off the deck below and land in the yard with less effort than it takes me to lift the toilet seat at night. Then it's gone, bolting around the house.

At the sound of people taking action, I shout, "Everyone stop!"

I turn to find Lilly and Maigo in the stairway leading to the roof. The girls could easily throw themselves from the roof, and could probably catch Cole. But what good would come from that? Would they kill him? Would he kill them? Neither possibility does us any good. I point at Cooper, who holds up the dart gun with a grin. "Let's see where he goes."

No one looks happy about it, but we've all trained with Hawkins enough to hear his voice urging us to use our brains before our brawn. When the big man gets to his feet and looks at me, I hitch my thumb at the window. "I don't know about you, but I'm getting *really* tired of replacing this window."

36

In the moments after Cole's escape, an adrenaline-fueled FC-P tried to spring into action, but then we got the collective shakes, followed by exhaustion. Cole, no doubt in human form once again, had made his way inland and was now headed toward the West Coast, probably on one of GOD's private jets. Or maybe he discovered the tracker and put it on a plane. Who knows? Reality feels broken. He's manipulated us on a level that has left me questioning what's real. My life for the past few years has been arranged and guided in a way that only God is supposed to do, and even then, most people hate the idea of a higher power influencing their lives. But even that is a manipulation. It's exactly how the Ferox want us to feel.

Does that make valuing freedom wrong?

Or did they simply teach us a lesson? A long, cruel, sadistic lesson.

Are we even free at all? Or just pawns?

I stare at the bedroom ceiling thinking all of this and more, searching the nooks and crannies of the room for any sign of cameras and listening devices. Do advanced alien species even need to bug a room? They might be able to see and hear us from orbit, for all I know.

Despite all this, I did sleep fairly well. Collins and I all but passed out beside each other. We're both still fully dressed, lying on top of our blanket.

"Find any?" Collins asks. It's the first thing she's said since we hit the mattress.

"Nope," I say, "But we'll have the DHS and a team from Zoomb scour the Crow's Nest from top to bottom for bugs and cameras before I feel comfortable here again."

"There's nothing they're going to see that they haven't seen already." Her fingers crawl down my arm and interlace with mine.

Memories of heated nights and...compromising positions flow through my mind. I cringe at the idea that someone, or thing, was watching.

"Try to not let it bother you," she says.

"You're not bothered by the idea of some alien watching a video feed of us, jerking off and getting his jollies while you change, or we..."

"Might not be *me* they're getting off on," she says.

I turn my head toward her. She's just a few inches away, her face framed by crazy, red, morning bedhead. She's adorable, and maybe, somewhere in the world, someone else could be sharing this moment with us.

She pats my cheek. "I know you like Star Trek, where Kirk works his way through a rainbow of alien floozies, but it's more likely that an alien species finds us as attractive as we do a sheep."

"Says the person who was a sheriff in the backwoods of Maine. You could yell 'hey, goat-humper' and get half the population to turn arou—ouch!"

Collins pulls her fist back, ready to slug my shoulder again.

"Uncle," I say, rubbing my arm. "But you can't tell me you never once got called out to a farm for...inappropriate relationship with a farm animal."

She purses her lips, trying to squelch a smile. She manages to hold on for three seconds before laughing. "Just once. Once!"

"Uh-huh," I roll onto my back and stare at the ceiling again. There's a crack that looks a little like a Kaiju. I've been trying to find something more pleasant in the crisscrossing lines—a pony or field mouse or something—but my life is full of monsters now. There's no escaping them. But with Collins, I can at least forget them for a bit. "Thanks for marrying me."

Her arm slides over my chest. "Sorry I almost didn't."

She's referring to a chunk of months between the destruction of Washington, D.C. and the Tsuchi attacks where she got cold feet. She called off our engagement, and given her previous marriage, I never held it against her. I was just happy she didn't want to leave me. Married or not, I wanted to be with her. But we've been married for a year now, and her past is now officially behind her.

Cole's words slip back into my mind. Collins is the strongest fully human woman I know, but would she be without her hard past? If she had never married an abusive husband, she would have never sought to make herself powerful, would have never pursued law enforcement or become a sheriff. Would have never met me. Would have never helped save multiple cities, and wouldn't be on the cusp of fighting for our entire planet. And I'm pretty sure I couldn't have done all of that without her strength supporting me. So can I really say I wish those horrible things had never happened to her? When the Aeros arrive and humanity puts up a fight, can I really say what the Ferox did was wrong? They brought this fight to us, but the Aeros would have eventually come on their own. And without the Ferox influence, the Aeros would have found a docile human race, perfect for enslaving, or consuming.

"Earth to Jon," Collins says, "Come in, Jon."

I sit up and put my legs over the side of the bed. Nothing wakes me up faster than thoughts of an alien invasion. I squint at the sun cutting through the sides of the shades. It's morning. Late morning by the looks of it. I glance at my watch. "Holy shit, it's eleven."

Collins climbs out of bed, and after sharing a quick kiss, during which we both hold our breath, because morning breath—*Yuck!*—we leave the room. We're greeted with the smell of coffee. The kitchen is empty, but two mugs wait beside a full Mr. Coffee. After sipping the hot brew—Collins's black, mine loaded with sugar, no cream—we head upstairs to the operations center.

The broad room is silent aside from the hum of computer fans. But it's not empty. Cooper and Watson are at their desks, eyes on their computer screens. Woodstock is seated in one of a few lounge chairs scattered around the room. He raises a cup of coffee to us in greeting, but says nothing. Hawkins is sitting at his station with Joliet. She gives a wave, but looks exasperated. Hawkins directs a nod in our direction, but he doesn't look happy either, probably because of the brace on his right arm. The sprained wrist means he's off of field duty, and stuck here, vexing Joliet. There is no one more discontent than a man of action being forced to watch from the sidelines. When things get nuts, and they will, he's going to be here, chewing his lips and being grumpy.

At the far end of the room, standing before the shattered window, which has been cleared of its jagged shards, are Lilly and Maigo. They're both fully dressed in black battle armor, ready and waiting for the fight to begin. Both girls turn their heads slightly, revealing that they've detected my silent approach. Their conversation comes to a quick end.

"You don't have to stop talking about Justin Bieber because of me," I say. "We're all beliebers here."

When Maigo's face turns red, I realize my jab might have been a little too close to home. They *are* teenage girls, after all. Talking about boys is what they do, end of the world or not.

I flinch when Hyperion's big face comes into view. The big robot's expressionless stare is unnerving. But at least the big guy is on our side. For the first time, we have an actual weapon that can stand up to a Kaiju. But can it stand up to three of them? I doubt it, and that means if I give Maigo the green light, I might be sending her to her death. I console myself with the knowledge that there is literally nothing I could do to stop her.

I stand between the girls, silently taking in the view.

I sip my coffee. Turn to Lilly. "Calm before the storm. Am I right?"

She smiles and leans around me to look at Maigo. "Your dad is a dork."

"Life would be boring without me," I say.

She points a furry finger out the window, where Hyperion continues his creepy gaze. "Pretty sure that's not true."

"Good point." Another sip. I turn to Maigo and motion back to Watson and Cooper with my head. "Have they been up all night? Again?"

She nods. "They haven't found anything. No sign of Lovecraft, Giger, Karkinos or Nemesis."

"And Portland?" The city, its surrounding suburbs and everyone living in the sixty miles between the city and the Pacific, has been under an evacuation order since ten minutes after Cole left. Part of me wanted to head for the city, but I don't know if Cole was playing me or not. I can't trust anything he tells me until I see it for myself. And we can always get there quick enough if things go down.

"People are still leaving, but most are outside the target area..." her pause reveals there's more.

"But..."

"There are a large number of people refusing to leave."

"How many?"

"Two hundred thousand, give or take."

"Geez," I say. That's a lot of people willing to put their lives in serious jeopardy. Holdouts are to be expected. Paranoia can make people fear the wrong thing. But two hundred thousand people... "They're not people."

I head for Watson.

"Can you isolate the locations of the people still in Portland?"

Ever the pro, Watson doesn't comment on the fact that I haven't said good morning, or even hello. His fingers simply spring into action. "I can't track them all, but I can use Hyperion to access cameras in the city. Security cameras. Phones. Laptops. We can check activity on cell phone towers. Buildings with security logs. Internet activity."

I glance out at Hyperion, the robot's gaze as steady as ever, even while it reaches out around the world, pillaging information in a way that would give the NSA a serious case of nocturnal emissions.

"Looks like there are three main groups." Watson points at a satellite map of the city, displaying thousands of red dots representing the stragglers. There's a clear pattern, like three walls of defense. "One on the west side of the city, then a second group spread out across the middle and the largest group here." He points to the city's core.

There are a few tall buildings that qualify as skyscrapers, but other than a few five-hundred footers, most of the buildings are smaller than the average Kaiju. I scan the buildings for a moment, imagining how easy it will be for the Gestorumque to charge through them. Then I spot an aberration. I point to a building that's still under construction. It looks a bit like the Arc de Triomphe in Paris, but hundreds of feet tall, and built from shiny metal instead of stone. "What's that?"

He taps on the building and a scroll of information opens. He reads it faster than I ever could and condenses the information. "The Luminox. It's a monument designed by a local architect, Becki Tapia Laurent, and it's being built on what used to be Chapman Park. They lost the park, but the city saw it as a tourist attraction, so they approved construction, which is supposed to be complete next year. When it's done, the outer surface will display a real time view of the stars, sent from a telescope in orbit. The building will hold a natural history museum, 'chronicling mankind's rise from the primordial ooze.'"

"Sounds like Ferox propaganda," Collins says.

She's right about that, and I'm sure the museum is just another way to continue conditioning humanity. I'm also sure it's a cover for something else. I point at the three bands of stragglers still in the city. "They're setting up a defense. That building is more than a museum."

"What?" Lilly asks.

I shake my head. "No idea, but we're going to find out." I turn to Collins. "Get ready. I'll be right behind you." To Woodstock, "Time to fly, old man."

"Ayuh," he says, and he pries himself from the chair.

To Lilly, "No funny business. No solo missions. I need to know I can count on you."

She nods, and I don't detect a trace of annoyance.

"Go."

As the group disperses, I'm left with Maigo. I put my hands on her shoulders. "No one will think less of you if you decide to–"

"I can handle it," she says. "And so can you. We have to, right? It's what we do."

I grin. She hasn't been my daughter for long, and she looks nothing like me, but there's no doubt about it. She's my kid. "Just give us a head start. Let us recon the situation before jumping into a city with that thing."

"And if the Kaiju show up?" she asks.

"Then the Hudsons will kick some ass," I say. "It's what we do."

GIGER

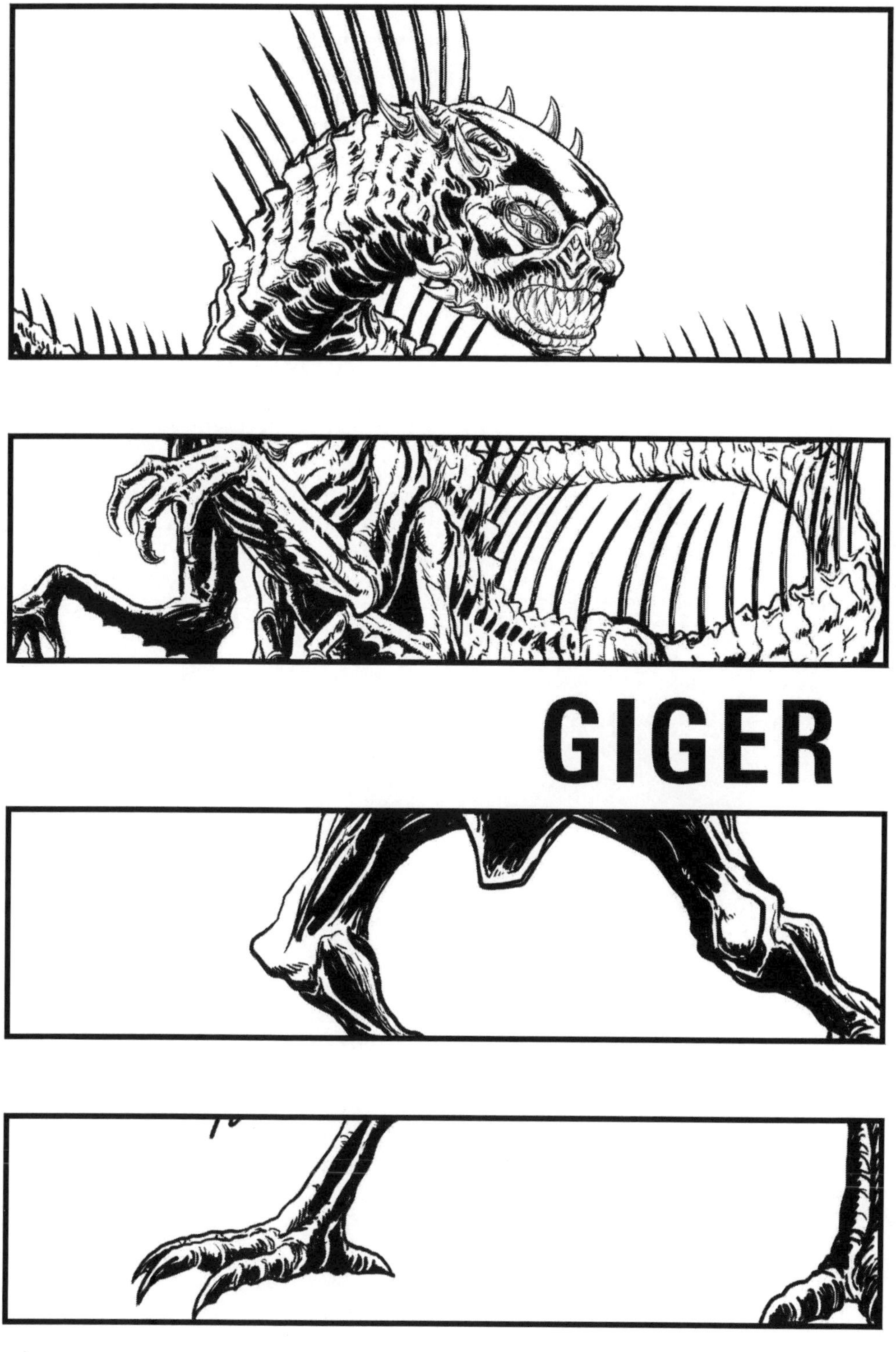

37

"Where is he now?" I ask, speaking to Watson through the throat mic and ear bud system we're using. We'll be able to communicate directly with the team, including Maigo, while Watson and Cooper relay information and/or orders to the military through Devine. Right now, as is usual these days, we've asked the military to hang back. All they can really do is cause collateral damage. But when we need a distraction, a few hellfire missiles should do the trick.

"Portland," Watson says, "like you guessed."

The moment Future Betty left the Crow's Nest rooftop, Cole's tracker made a super speed bolt toward the northwest, reminding me that while we're tracking him, he's still watching us. I flip the bird to the wall and then work it around so that anyone watching us gets a clear view. "Woodstock. ETA?"

"Ten minutes," he says.

I look down. The terrain below us, projected onto the floor, is just a blur. At Mach 3, the flight from Beverly to Portland takes just over an hour.

"Send Cole's coordinates to Woodstock," I say, and then lean toward the cockpit. "Put us down on his head."

Woodstock rolls his toothpick to the side of his mouth. "You got—"

"Hudson." Cooper's voice brings the conversation to a screeching halt. She doesn't interrupt unless it's important. "Reports of deceased whales are coming in from the Gulf of Alaska to Cape Blanco. Most have been partially consumed."

My first thought is Nemesis, but the only time she ate on that scale was when she was growing. She probably still eats whales, among other large ocean creatures, but she wouldn't have any reason to start a buffet. But Lovecraft... If reports from the oil rig are accurate, the monster dropped a large portion of its girth into the ocean, lightening the load so it could fly. If it's replenishing that mass, the dead whales make sense. It also explains why no one has spotted the massive creature in the air. It must have dropped back into the ocean after clearing Alaskan airspace during the night.

"Incoming," Watson says, sudden and loud, his voice cracking. "At the coast. Tillamook Bay."

"Get us there," I say to Woodstock. "Now."

There's a subtle shift in our speed, but not much. Woodstock's had the speed pegged since we left Beverly.

"It's Karkinos," Watson says. "Heading east."

Portland comes and goes in a flash. The city looks mostly empty. I get a brief glimpse of the Luminox. It's a lot bigger than I thought. *Big enough to fly a spaceship through,* I think, and when my stomach clenches, I think, *Holy shit, it's big enough to fly a spaceship through!*

A theoretical problem for another time. The remaining sixty miles pass in moments. When we reach the coast, Karkinos has moved beyond the bay and into the evacuated Bay City, which is smaller than it sounds. But that doesn't change the path of destruction it's carving through people's homes, or its obvious destination.

We need to stop it, here and now.

"Maigo, are you ready?"

"Good to go," she says, and even though the voice is a digitized projection of her actual voice, I can still hear how nervous she is.

"Second target incoming," Watson blurts, and I turn toward the ocean in time to see it. I've seen photos of the bony exoskeleton covering Giger's body, but it's far more frightening in the flesh. The creature's otherworldliness is exaggerated by the twitchy way in which it moves. And where Karkinos is big and lumbering, this Kaiju is fast. It's through the bay in seconds, charging through Bay City and past Karkinos, heading toward Portland with the eagerness of a golden retriever chasing a ball. Between Bay City and Portland is a good thirty miles of rough terrain and rain forest.

"Get after that thing," I say to Woodstock. We spin around and give chase.

"We need to stop them now. Before they reach the city. Maigo, is Hyperion tracking Future Betty's—"

"Coming," she says.

"Third target," Watson says. I look back at the now shrinking coast. Lovecraft explodes from the ocean, as large as ever and fueled by gorging upon whales. His wings splay wide, sending cascades of water in all directions. The morning sun refracts through the beads, forming a rainbow around the beast. Then the monster steps through the bands of color, surging west behind his brother, or sister, or whatever the hell they are. Kaiju don't have sex organs—at least, not obvious Michael Bay Constructicon balls. If they did, we'd know where to target.

Before I can warn Maigo about the odds, Hyperion appears ahead of us, and ahead of Giger. The fast Kaiju flinches and tries to sidestep around the robot, but there's no avoiding the collision, which Maigo was prepared for. Giger is lifted WWF style, flipped up over Hyperion and then slammed into a hillside. The terrain collapses under the monster's mass, its arms and legs scrambling through the air like an overturned bug. Three blades, the only weapons available after teleporting across the country, pop out of Hyperion's forearms. Maigo's going to skewer the monster with all six blades, and if she can hit the right spot, maybe it will be enough.

But Giger's speed is unmatched. The long, bony tail snaps up like a whip and wraps around Hyperion's head. With a tug, Hyperion is lifted off the ground and flung. The robot rights itself in midair, compensating for the move like only an AI-controlled robot could, landing on its feet. But not fast enough.

Giger takes off at a sprint, headed east like a running back who's just outwitted the defensive line.

"I can't catch it," Maigo says.

"Don't bother," I tell her.

"But Portland—"

"I don't think the city is as defenseless as it looks."

When a shadow falls over Hyperion, her choice is removed. Karkinos has arrived, and Lovecraft isn't far behind. In fact, it seems to be giving Hyperion a wide berth, heading to Portland with no intention of stopping to fight. I miss the days of primitive-minded Kaiju, unable to turn down a good scrap.

Karkinos spins around, swinging its massive tail toward Hyperion's waist. If the blade at the end struck, it might very well sever the robot in two. But as powerful as Karkinos is, it's not fast enough to catch the alien mech. Hyperion leaps back, waits for the blade tip to sail past and then attacks.

"Dad!" Maigo shouts, and for a moment I worry she's already been hurt somehow. But then she shouts, "Get out of here!"

Hyperion grabs the spikes on the big Kaiju's back and pulls. The already off-balance monster stumbles around, facing Lovecraft. The bulbous squid face turns toward the action, regarding it with curiosity, but nothing more. Its goal is the city, no matter what.

Karkinos is on his own.

But Maigo isn't abiding by those unspoken rules. She's taking them both on, whether they want to or not. She lunges up onto Karkinos's back and points those big blades at the two massive membranes on the sides of the Kaiju's lower neck. She's also fighting dirty.

"Up!" I shout to Woodstock. "Up!"

The world beneath us shrinks as we rocket straight up. There's a spark of orange and then a flash of light. The explosion bursts out from Karkinos and sweeps over Lovecraft. The big white Kaiju's wings wrap around it, shielding it from the heat, but the force is still powerful enough to knock it off its feet.

"Pressure wave incoming," Woodstock says. "Hold on."

We're hit a moment later, the wave slamming into Future Betty and then moving past us. The moment we're in the clear, Woodstock drops us back toward the action.

A charred and stunned Lovecraft is down, but already getting up. Karkinos has two drained membranes and is smoldering a bit, but he isn't hurt. Like Nemesis, he's built to sustain blasts like that. Hyperion is still on his back though, driving those six blades deeper into the neck.

Karkinos flings its mass back, clearly intending to pin Hyperion beneath its weight, but the robot bounds away. Karkinos lands on its massive spines, but rolls back to its feet in a way the monster couldn't have pulled off when we first saw it. *It's got a pilot now,* I think, remembering the Aeros pulled out of Prime's head. *A pilot with a bone to pick with Hyperion.*

Hyperion squares off with the big Kaiju again, and Maigo's voice fills my ears. "I can handle this, Dad. You're not doing any good, just watching." The second ring on Hyperion's chest flashes red. The blades are replaced by six long prongs, electricity arcing between them.

"Say it," Lilly says, speaking up for the first time since we reached Portland. "Say it."

"It doesn't even make sense," Maigo complains.

"You're in a robot, facing a monster!"

"There's no *'her,'*" Maigo says.

"Are you two seriously arguing right now?" I ask.

"'Get away from her, you bitch,'" Maigo says, completely deadpan, and her poor delivery deflates Lilly's excitement.

"Barf," Lilly says. "Let's go."

As we pull away toward Portland, Hyperion charges Karkinos. They collide on the horizon and then fade from view. We pass Lovecraft, who's continuing forward undaunted, and catch up to Giger a minute later, already on the outskirts of Portland's suburbs.

"Take us to the Luminox," I say to Woodstock and then say, "Alessi, you there?"

"Here," she says.

"ETA on my delivery?"

"Ten minutes," she says. "But are you sure?"

I share her apprehension, but drastic times and all that. "I'd rather have it and not need it."

"Incoming," Watson says again. "It's Nemesis...but she doesn't look so good."

"What do you mean?" I ask, confused about how the Kaiju could look anything other than horrifying.

"She looks...tired."

That shouldn't be a surprise. The creature just swam thousands of miles at a pace that's hard to comprehend. She's a killing machine from another world, but she has limits. And if she's already reaching them, that doesn't bode well for this battle's outcome. All the more reason for us to get creative.

I look at Lilly and ask, "You wanna get nuts?"

She smiles, recognizing the quote. If there's anyone who can match her pop culture references, it's me. "Let's get nuts."

38

Exhaustion from physical exertion was a new experience for Nemesis. She had felt the sting of battle, and the need to rest as a result, spending motionless months on the ocean floor. But this was different. Her encounters with the ancient enemy, and the Gestorumque, hadn't left her with any significant wounds. Her legs felt weak beneath her as she swept out of the ocean and onto the shore, which compacted beneath her weight. Her instinct told her she was under attack. She growled and snapped her jaws, but there were no enemies present. Nothing to attack.

The voice of Endo rose up through the chaos. He understood the feeling. Identified it. Revealed how to overcome it.

Slow down, he urged. *Rushing into battle will not serve us well.*

The Kaiju slowed her pace, and stopped. Leaning forward, she took a long, slow breath.

Another, he said. *Breathe.*

She acquiesced, but her patience wore thin. Limitations of the flesh enraged her. The idea that she bore similarities to humans revolted her. She was not small, or fragile or weak.

She stepped forward again, and again, her pulse beat faster and harder, fueled by rage that did more for her than breathing deeply.

But Endo had known that all along. He wasn't urging her to rest, he was lighting a fire and fanning the flames of a goddess.

When Nemesis broke into a run, Endo spurred her forward, neither of them paying attention to the destruction being wrought on the world around them. The enemy lay ahead, their congregated presence like a twisting coil of loathing that dwarfed what she felt from humanity.

These were the destroyers of worlds.

Endo's world.

Nemesis's world.

And the people they cared for.

A bright blue flash of light lit up the horizon. It was followed by an angry and familiar roar.

Karkinos, Endo thought. *But how?*

There were times his voice felt frustration at the limitations of their knowledge. He craved information. This was often offset by the constant stream of emotional information she received, and what could be inferred from it. But not knowing *how* something like Karkinos's resurrection was possible angered him. Nemesis did not care about the how. She simply felt. She knew Karkinos was her enemy, even more so now that she sensed its Voice.

She had no name for it, but she understood it had once been a part of her ancient self. And before that, her torturer. Here was the being responsible for breaking her, for molding her into a goddess of vengeance, and for controlling her former self straight to its violent end at the hands of Hyperion, who was now airborne and tumbling toward Nemesis.

Nemesis stopped among a hilly throng of trees, digging her claws into the earth, while bracing with her tail. Moving in fluid and practiced ways provided by Endo, Nemesis reached out and caught the falling robot. The force of the impact sent the big Kaiju sliding backward, her claws digging troughs into the ground, but they came to a stop, still upright. She placed the machine back on its feet. She could feel its Voice, familiar and friendly. Maigo. The first human she felt a kinship with, but strangely not the last. The man, whose name she now knew was Jon Hudson, was the second. She sensed him nearby, as well.

Probably about to do something stupid, Endo thought, but she felt his confused affection for the man as well. They would help him if they could. But first...

Hyperion stepped away and turned toward Nemesis. There was no threat in the action, but a question. *Are you ready?*

For the first time, Nemesis performed a human gesture. It felt odd, and wrong, but the slight nod conveyed everything that it needed to. That they were allies. That she was ready to fight. And that they would fight together.

They charged ahead, side by side, and Nemesis felt something new. Exhilaration. She had felt the passion of battle, and the angry glory it provided, but this was different. Fighting alongside an ally felt...good.

Karkinos was on the horizon, moving fast despite its absolutely massive size. The Kaiju was nearing the city limits, following the path of destruction wrought by the others. They weren't here to destroy the city, or eat its occupants, of whom there were few. Nemesis felt small numbers of occupants in the city ahead, but they didn't feel right...didn't feel human.

With a burst of speed, Hyperion took the lead, its mechanical limbs unable to feel tired. Nemesis felt the burn of competition, another new emotion, and part of her wanted to turn on her new ally, but Endo cautioned against it. Maigo was their friend. And she was smart. This was confirmed when just a half mile from Karkinos, Hyperion came to a stop, turned around and reached out its large hands.

Nemesis saw an attack, but Endo understood and showed Nemesis what to do. If the large goddess of vengeance was capable of smiling, she would have.

Upon reaching Hyperion, Nemesis jumped, surging forward and up into Hyperion's powerful arms. And then, flung forward by the robot, she was airborne.

39

During Maigo's life—her second life anyway—she had known Nemesis as a monster she was a part of, and a monster viewed from the outside, like everyone else. But in all that time, Nemesis had never been her enemy. Since being separated from the Kaiju, and becoming her own person again, she had never dreamed that she would once again wield the power she'd felt as Nemesis, nor considered the idea of fighting alongside her. But here she was, charging toward Karkinos with Nemesis by her side.

The monster's integration with Endo was clear. She moved differently, fought differently and that subtle nod she'd given had sent chills through Maigo's body. But how much control did Endo really have? Would Nemesis recognize and respond to human tactics or improvised fighting techniques on the fly? *Better to find out now,* she thought, and she instructed Hyperion to turn on the speed. The extra effort kept the robot from reaching a Level Three charge, but they wouldn't reach that stage in time to help against Karkinos anyway.

When the massive Kaiju showed signs of hearing her approach, she skidded to a halt, carving a deep divot into the soft land, and turned to face Nemesis. Maigo raised Hyperion's arms out to perform a move that she and Lilly had practiced, and implemented against Cole's Ferox form, but it was also fairly self-explanatory. For a moment, she thought Nemesis, lost in bloodlust, might just plow through her to get at Karkinos, but the Kaiju leapt into her hands and allowed all of Hyperion's power to launch her skyward at Karkinos's back.

Maigo let out a mental laugh that only Hyperion's AI could hear. Nemesis rose through the air, her arms open wide, her legs coiled up and her tail poised to strike. It looked like a practiced move, like something Endo would do.

This is a humorous situation? Hyperion asked.

"You don't find ninja Nemesis funny?" Maigo replied.

I do not find anything funny, but I am capable of determining the lethality of an adversary and Nemesis is—

"Not an adversary," Maigo said. She felt Hyperion in her memories, replaying her death, rebirth, growth and transition from Nemesis to human again.

She is us, Hyperion said, attempting to logically explain the complex relationship. *We are her.*

"Part of her, part of us," Maigo replied. "Like sisters."

My appearance is masculine, Hyperion noted. *As is Nemesis's Voice.*

"Family, then," Maigo said.

An acceptable term.

"Glad you approve," Maigo said, and watched as Nemesis fell toward Karkinos.

The bigger Kaiju swept its tail out hard enough to send Nemesis sprawling, but she was falling from above, not approaching from behind. Karkinos twisted around in time to catch Nemesis. But it was not a friendly embrace. Karkinos wrapped its massive arms around Nemesis's back and squeezed. Nemesis roared in pain, but quickly recovered, leaned into the embrace and buried her teeth into the flesh of Karkinos's neck.

The big Kaiju strained away from Nemesis's bite, which was burying into the neck, freeing gouts of blood. After a few gnarly moments, Karkinos released Nemesis and threw her to the side. Nemesis rolled back to her feet and struck out with a tail strike, but Karkinos seemed prepared for the attack, catching the trident-tipped tail between his gargantuan claws and yanking Nemesis off her feet. With a spin and a thrust of arms, Nemesis was thrown further into the suburbs surrounding Portland. She rolled through three neighborhood blocks, flattening countless homes before coming to a stop in the ruins of a middle school.

Karkinos then turned to face Hyperion, and Maigo had a thought. *Karkinos is just a distraction, meant to keep us from reaching Lovecraft and Giger in time to stop them...from what?*

"Scan the city ahead," Maigo said, although the interaction was closer to the AI sharing her thoughts. She felt Hyperion reaching out with its sensors while she focused her attention on Karkinos.

Maigo tried to run around the monster, but it moved to intercept her, confirming her suspicions. "Karkinos is just here to run interference."

Agreed, the AI said. *Energy signatures within the city of Portland suggest the presence of not yet functional, but advanced Ferox technology, currently surrounded by a non-human force.*

"That's what they're after," Maigo said.

As Nemesis got back to her feet behind Karkinos, Hyperion raised a hand and waved the monster onward. *C'mon, Endo,* Maigo thought. *You know what it means.*

Nemesis took one step toward Karkinos and stopped. She appeared torn for a moment, but then looked back toward Portland, where the Aeros Gestorumque were heading, if they hadn't yet already reached the city. Then she turned and ran, unleashing her impressive speed. For the first time in her existence, she ran away from a fight.

Maigo saw a flicker of indecision in Karkinos, as Nemesis made a break for it. The monster, and its Voice, were no doubt wondering if it should chase the more fleet-footed Nemesis. Not letting the opportunity go to waste, Maigo drove Hyperion inside Karkinos's reach, and extended the three blades from the left arm and the voltage amplifier electrodes from the right.

Before the large Kaiju could react, she plunged the blades into its side, where there were no orange membranes. The AI reported a momentary resistance and then a temperature increase indicating the oozing warmth of Kaiju blood. With Hyperion's left hand, Maigo punched the metal prongs at Karkinos's head. But instead of stabbing the metal into the monster's face and frying its brain—or its Voice—powerful jaws snapped down on the prongs. The jolt of electricity only tightened Karkinos's grip, and the electrodes quickly snapped, becoming useless.

The voltage amplifier system snapped back inside the forearm, where it would heal over time, but not soon enough.

Karkinos grabbed hold of Hyperion's shoulders, gouging them, but the attack came from behind. The Kaiju's barbed tail pierced Hyperion's side, and as it pulled away, it caught hold and lifted the robot away before thrashing it on the ground.

Hyperion warned of severe damage to multiple systems, but nothing irreparable—yet. The AI recommended retreat, but Maigo was defiant and angry.

She is still part of you, the AI observed, and Maigo knew it was referring to Nemesis. It was an observation she had long suspected, that she was still a monster. The idea of turning into Nemesis again, or even something like General Gordon had become, was the stuff of her nightmares.

"You think I'm a monster," Maigo said.

It was not meant to be an insult.

Hyperion, lying on his back, shuffled away from Karkinos. The Kaiju closed the distance, looming huge over the fallen robot.

"How could it *not* be an insult?"

It means you are powerful, the AI said. *It means you are resilient. Defiant. An unceasing force. Like her. Like Nemesis. Whose...soul resides in you, the way yours once did in her. I believe, given current circumstances, that your potential for...violence, is a beneficial trait.*

"So," Maigo said, "you're saying I should embrace my inner monster?"

With haste.

Maigo saw Karkinos above her, looking down with keenly intelligent eyes, now guided by a voice and lacking the pure, unadulterated rage granted to the goddess of vengeance.

As Maigo's emotions boiled to the surface, Hyperion's eyes blazed brighter, casting Karkinos in a red glow, which bloomed even brighter as the third and final ring on the robot's chest lit up.

Level Three weapons now available.

Hyperion leaned up suddenly, plunging all six blades extending from its forearms into Karkinos's gut, piercing several of the orange membranes, while simultaneously plugging the gaps.

Maigo glared up at the face of Karkinos, which showed a measure of pain, but also a look of smug assurance. *He thinks I'm beat,* Maigo thought, and then she issued her order to Hyperion with a single word: "Pull!"

Hyperion's forearms spun with a sudden mad frenzy, tearing through the monster's flesh like oversized blenders. Then the blades retracted and Hyperion winked from existence.

40

"Put us down right on top of them," I say, looking down at the people atop the unfinished Luminox building. While there is scaffolding around the bottom of the building, which still looks unfinished, the roof looks solid, and changing. Two futuristic cannons have risen from the roof and are turning toward the twitching Giger, still making its way to us. "But be ready for a quick pickup."

As we descend, I say, "Let them see us." The last thing we need is to squash someone while we're landing.

A moment later, everyone bustling about on the roof can see the X-35's mirrored surface. And yet, not one person gives it a second look. *Because they're not human,* I tell myself. For all we know there's a whole fleet of Future Bettys in the city.

The familiar figure of a bulbous, well dressed man steps from a stairwell door and onto the roof. He gives a casual wave at the landing X-35, knowing we're watching him. I have a tendency to want to punch things that annoy me, and often try with mixed results. As the hatch opens, though, I head for Cole, and I remind myself that decking the man will do no good, and will likely break my hand.

"Glad you could make it," Cole says, and I can't tell if he's being honest or facetious.

Since I can't slug him, I decide to be a dick instead. I hold a hand up to silence him, and toggle my throat mic. "Alessi. ETA on—"

"The delivery has already been made, Jon," Alessi says, but it takes a moment for me to realize her voice didn't come from my ear bud. It came from behind me. I spin around, but find only Cole, smiling at me like I'm adorable.

I glance at Collins. There's a look of horror on her face. She saw something I missed. When Lilly hisses at Cole, the puzzle pieces fall into place.

Alessi's voice came *from Cole.*

The big man steps to the side and sweeps his hand out at three coffin-like containers being rolled toward us by a group of people who look like random citizens gathered from the streets. The storage units are, in fact, what I was waiting for.

"We've made some modifications," Cole says in Alessi's voice, souring my stomach. "And some improvements."

"What have you done with Alessi?" I ask, hand on my sidearm. I'm not going to punch him, but I might very well shoot him.

"Absolutely nothing," he says.

I toggle my throat mic again. "Alessi, are you there? Answer me!"

Cole reaches up to his own neck and toggles a mic. "I'm right here, Jon." Cole's Alessi impersonation reaches my left ear normally and right ear through the bud. "Right where I've always been."

"*You* are Maggie?" Collins says, using Alessi's first name.

Cole motions to the men bustling around behind him, prepping the two cannons and arming themselves with an array of weapons I don't recognize. "Sometimes me. Sometimes one of them." He sets his eyes on me. "For all you know, your new wife is one of us, too."

I clench my fists, but show impressive restraint.

"The real Maggie Alessi died seven years ago, in a car accident. When Katsu Endo became involved with General Gordon, we resurrected the half-sister he didn't know existed, built a life for her and reached out."

My anger shifts to a strange kind of sadness, like mourning the death of a friend. Since inheriting control of Zoomb, I've become...close to Alessi. Despite the rocky start to our relationship, I came to trust her. We had personal conversations. She gave me advice, often good advice. And all that time, she—*was him? Or one of them?*

"Did Endo know?" I ask.

Cole shakes his head. "And I suggest you keep it from him, given his volatile position.

"You might not see it now," Cole says, "but we *are* friends, Jon. We are allies. And I know you better than most. How you feel. How you think. What you're capable of. I know you're about to punch me, but—"

"You're a hologram, right?" I say.

He reaches out a finger and pokes my chest. "We don't have time for theatrics. I showed you one of my true selves because I need you to know you can trust me. We have worked together for years, Jon. And you need to believe me when I tell you, the fate of your planet depends on our success today. You want to kill me, I know. We helped make you that way. But right now, we have a common enemy."

He glances across the city. Giger is coming for us, crushing buildings beneath its rigid mass.

"The Luminox is a gateway," Cole says. "The first of many. And when it is complete, our forces from around the universe, in all dimensions, will be able to join the fight, here, just as we will be able to join the fight there. We are uniting the resistance, but if we lose the Luminox, Earth will face ruin."

Some of what he's said is mind-boggling. The Luminox will be some kind of wormhole connecting Earth to other worlds, and other dimensions? This is nuts, but then, what about the past few years isn't nuts? I loathe this man, and what he's done to us, but if Lovecraft and Giger are just the beginning, I won't deny that Earth is going to need help. "Okay, Paul Revere of the Cosmos, I'll bite. What's the plan?"

He nods at the men behind us, and they open the three containers, revealing the battlesuits within. They're black, and kind of horrifying, with armored plates, face masks and red eyes that contain reverse-engineered sensors taken from GOD's night-vision goggles, which colorize night vision and provide battlefield data. The suits contain synthetic muscle fibers triggered by the wearer's actual muscle movements. With the suit on, I'll be as strong and fast as Lilly, with enhanced vision and situational awareness. And Lilly...I suppose she'll be more like Maigo.

The synthetic fibers also go rigid when impacted from the outside, protecting against falls, bullets, knives or claws. Added to all of that is an array of small repulse discs that allow for some serious jump distance, and with the wingsuit function enabled, flight...in theory. Collins and I have practiced with most of the functions, but we haven't attempted flying yet. How different can it be from piloting a drone while clinging to its back?

"You said you made changes," I say.

"To the weapons system," he says. The suits were designed with one thing in mind, responding to a Kaiju threat. The weapon we developed was essentially a laser bomb. Once launched, it would attach to the target and fire a high-powered laser into the target for an extended period of time. The four circular devices attached to the suit around the waist, have been replaced by something else...something I recognize. The four simple-looking black discs appear innocuous enough, but they're deadly as hell.

"Are you *shitting* me?" I ask. "Bacteria bombs?"

These things were the inspiration for the laser bombs, but are far more volatile. While the laser's power is finite, lasting only long enough to do significant damage, the bacteria consumes and multiplies exponentially, eating through anything it touches, including Kaiju flesh. Once released, it can be neutralized only by incineration or by salt water.

"Your use of the Swarm in Boston revealed the ineffectiveness of directed energy weapons against the Gestorumque. They're useful for causing temporary damage, and as a distraction, but we already have that covered." He motions to the two cannons tracking Giger. With a vibrating hum, one of them fires, sending a bright yellow beam of light through the side of the thirty-story PacWest building and into Giger's charging form. The Kaiju is knocked sideways, and a black line is carved into its exoskeletal body, but the damage to the monster is minimal. The building, on the other hand, is now on fire. The second cannon fires with similar results, knocking Giger onto its back, its limbs rapid-fire scurrying in the air. The blasts are really just annoying it.

"We're at *war*, Hudson," Cole says with a snarl. "Half measures and hopeful thinking aren't going to win. This time there is no one to sacrifice to the Gestorumque. The only lives we have to offer, are our own. Now will you fight with us, or not?"

Before I can answer, a massive explosion rises in the distance. The light plumes high as a shockwave rolls through the city, flattening buildings and tossing cars. It races toward us, shattering the windows of the skyscrapers around us before slapping into the Luminox with a concussive roar.

Then, out of the still rising ball of brilliant flame, a smoking projectile rises into the sky. Cloaked in smoke, I don't recognize it until Collins does.

"That's Karkinos," she says.

I nearly laugh. The Kaiju has been launched miles into the sky, and its smoldering core reveals a massive wound. But then I remember it was Maigo and Hyperion who were facing the giant.

Karkinos arcs toward the city and drops like a bomb, landing a mile away, but with enough force to knock out the rest of the windows in the city and shake the Luminox beneath us. The sound of shattering glass resounds from the shaken city, and millions of tiny dancing lights bounce off the still standing buildings, sunlight glinting off the falling shards. The sound and light display is drowned out when a twenty-story building topples on top of the smoking and unmoving Kaiju.

"Maigo," I say, speaking into my comm. "Are you there?"

When there's no reply, and I clench my eyes shut, Cole puts his hand on my shoulder. "This. Is. War. People die."

I glare up at the inhuman man, who has defiled my life and the lives of everyone I love. "Give me a damn suit."

41

Dressed in battlesuits, Collins, Lilly and I stand on the Luminox's edge. Cole and six of his men stand with us. They appear ready for battle, too, but they're unarmed and not wearing suits.

"Lead the way," Cole says.

"Umm, okay?" I say, and I prepare to launch myself off the edge. There's a grinding of bones and a slurp of flesh from behind me. I turn around slowly and find seven transformed Ferox gnashing their teeth, twitching their tails and looking absolutely ferocious.

I leap from the side of the building, but instead of falling, I launch upward. The repulse discs built into the suit turn my jump into a thirty-story vault. I catch myself on the side of the forty-one-story Wells Fargo Center building and have no trouble holding on, thanks to the strength granted to me by the suit, and the fact that every single window in the building has been blown out.

Collins lands beside me. Lilly touches down three stories above us. Dressed in the battlesuits, with their faces covered by masks, the only way I can tell them apart is by their body shapes, Collins being the taller and the more curvaceous of the two. I look back for the horde of Ferox, but they're not in the air, they're below us, charging up the side of the building, relying on their natural abilities.

I push off hard with my feet and engage the repulse discs, shooting to the top of the building and landing on the roof. From my new 546-foot-tall point of view, I can now look down on the scene. Giger is below us, assaulting the smaller PacWest building, which is now riddled with fiery holes, as the laser continues to shoot through it. The freakish Kaiju drops down low, splaying its legs wide, and scrambles at the building , avoiding the next barrage. It then spins in a tight circle, whipping its tail around and slicing clean through the already ravaged PacWest building. The structure falls in on itself and collapses, revealing the Luminox to Giger.

"Now or never, people!" I shout. Then I jump off the edge without looking to see who's with me.

The Kaiju starts through the ruined building as I fall toward it, and I have to engage the flight suit to adjust my course. The wings pop out between my extended arms and waist, as well as between my legs. My fall transforms into a glide, and when I engage the repulse discs, powered flight.

"Whoohoo!" Lilly shouts, and I know that she's still with me.

As I arc around behind Giger, and angle in toward its massive upper back, which is divided by those long, swaying spines, Hyperion winks into existence between the Kaiju and its target. The giant robot is charred, but functional.

"I'm here!" Maigo says.

"Keep Giger there!" I shout. "We're coming in behind it."

"What?" she says, and then she must see us, because she follows up with, "Are you guys insane?"

"You all should know, I'm seeing movement from Karkinos," Woodstock chimes in over the comms. "Nothing major. Just some twitching in its neck. But I wouldn't count it out yet."

"We'll check it out," Cole says, his voice deeper and more gravelly. By 'we'll,' I assume he's talking about himself and the fugly brigade at his command. They're agile and strong, but since they can't fly, they're probably having a hard time keeping up. And if they can take out Karkinos on the ground, that's a win-win.

A roar rolls up over my back, and as I close in on Giger, I glance back. Lovecraft surges toward us, using its massive wings to lift itself over the ground. It can't fly, but it's moving quickly. And I see why a moment later. Nemesis is barreling forward like a bat out of hell, gaining on the big Gestorumque, which seems to have no interest in fighting.

They really are just here for the Luminox.

"Jon!" Collins shouts, and I turn forward in time to see some of the thick black spines on Giger's back whip in my direction, as the monster rises up and grapples with Hyperion. The robot's weapons systems have been reset to Level One. I roll hard to the side, getting under and inside the swaying Kaiju spines, but I'm still on a collision course with the solid plates covering Giger's back. I retract the wings, flip myself forward and give the repulse discs everything they have, which isn't enough to stop me completely. The battlesuit absorbs a lot of the impact, but I tumble down the spine-covered back until I'm caught by my wrist and pulled back up.

The strength behind the grasp fools me into thinking it's Lilly who caught me, but when I look up, it's Collins who is pulling me up. "Always slacking off," she says. "Can we get this done now?"

"Are you with us, Lilly?" I ask.

"Up here," she says, waving at us from forty feet higher up, closer to the Kaiju's neck.

Giger roars and thrusts forward, nearly dislodging me again.

"Hurry up!" Maigo urges. "I can't hold it much–gah!"

Giger's tail has just whipped around and struck Hyperion someplace sensitive enough for Maigo to feel it.

"Two bombs each," I say, holding onto a spine with one hand, and plucking one of the smaller discs off my belt. I slap the device to the shell and am surprised when it vacuums itself down tight. Cole upgraded the bacteria bombs, too.

"These things have a one minute–" I start to say, but then I hear a hiss from the bomb I've just planted. "Scratch that. They trigger on contact. Plant what you have and get away!"

I slap down a second bacteria bomb and am about to jump away when a panel of Giger's bony armor pops open between me and Lilly. A black sphere shoots out, headed for the sky overhead. The last time I saw one of those was over Boston Harbor, where it created a cyclone.

"Cole," I say. "There's a black sphere headed into the sky."

"Weather generator," he says. "We've used them in the past. Things are going to get uncomfortable. Approaching Karkinos now."

"I'll see what I can do about the weather doohicky," Woodstock says.

When I see Collins and Lilly jump away, propelled by their repulse discs, I leap out, extend my wings and I'm struck in the side by something like a falling tree. I topple through the air and fall several stories before landing inside the blown out Wells Fargo building and tumbling through office desks, chairs and computer stations. When I finally come to a stop, forty feet from the window, I'm covered in office detritus and twisting power cables. Happily, the battlesuit has done its job. Other than some soreness–that will probably hurt like hell tomorrow–I'm in one piece.

I'm brushing debris off me, grumbling and cursing, when Maigo shouts, "Dad! Look out!"

Hyperion's face slams into the side of the building and crashes in, its blazing red eyes rushing toward me.

I try to get up and run, but slip on a stack of paper and go down. Hyperion's face stops moving just a few feet away.

"Dad," Maigo says, sounding worried. "I can't–"

Giger's tail punches through the side of the building, wraps around Hyperion's face like a constrictor and pulls the giant robot back out. I watch them fall away together, leaving a massive hole in the side of the building. I barely notice the roof crumbling in as Hyperion falls back and Giger lunges atop the robot, scratching and clawing its metal surface. Then Maigo gets in a good swing with a blade attack, severing one of the four arms completely. The result is a frenzied attack. Giger flails all about, while stabbing down with its tail, plunging the end into Hyperion, over and over.

"No!" I scream, as dust falls past my face.

Giger lifts its tail again, and stops, frozen in place as though it heard my scream. But then it arches its back and wails in pain. For a moment, it reaches for its back, like the creature's trying to dislodge something that's not there.

But it is there, I realize. The bacteria bombs are eating through its exoskeleton.

The Gestorumque flails to the side, striking the Wells Fargo building and toppling over into the street, where it thrashes about.

Hyperion lies amidst the rubble of the PacWest Center. Its red eyes are dull. All three rings on its chest are extinguished, and surrounded by an array of puncture wounds. "Hyperion is out of the fight," I say, and then I notice for the first time that the building above me is leaning at a sickening angle.

Holy shi—

Something gives way and the building snaps, collapsing downward. I leap through the ruined wall, falling for fifty feet before engaging the wingsuit and the repulse discs. Pursued by fifteen stories of building, I soar toward Hyperion's still form and pull up at the last moment. Debris crashes down behind me, sending a plume of smoke out to chase me. A thunderous crash shakes my body and knocks me to the ground, just beyond Hyperion. My landing isn't graceful, but I end up on my feet. I turn in time to see the building land on Hyperion's lower half, burying the robot in debris.

"Hey, boss," Woodstock says. "You have incoming!"

I leap to the roof of a fifteen story building and then bound off its roof, rising quickly from street level to the top of Congress Center, a three-hundred-twenty-foot-tall building. The new vantage point puts me roughly at neck level for both Lovecraft and Nemesis...who happen to be tumbling in my direction, limbs, wings and tentacles thrashing about in frenzied combat. They land atop a domed building, taking down the nearly three-hundred-foot-tall building under their coiling bodies. Smoke billows around them, swirling from the Kaijus' breath as they roar at each other. And then, they're both rising from the smoke, facing off.

I'm unsure about what to do. With the battlesuit and the bacteria bombs, I might be able to help Nemesis, but in situations like this, it wouldn't be uncommon for Nemesis to self-immolate and level several blocks of the city, which would currently include me. I either need to take action, or get the hell back, but for the moment, I'm rooted in place.

"Collins," I say. "Where are you?"

"Street level," Collins says. "North side of town."

"I'm here, too," Lilly chimes in. "Thanks for asking."

"We're beyond Karkinos," Collins adds.

I look north and see the Kaiju's massive body, still buried, still motion-less. "Jon, I don't think we're alone."

"Cole's down there," I say.

"I don't think he is now," she says, "though it's hard to tell. The bodies are a mess."

"Bodies?"

"Ferox. They've been slaughtered."

"By what?" I ask.

"By that," Lilly says, but she's not talking to me.

"Oh my God," Collins says, and then I lose her in a burst of static. "Collins. Collins! Cole, are you there? Maigo?"

"I'm here, boss," Woodstock says, "but I'm not having much luck catching this dang thing. It's as fast as Betty, and now it's spinning around like a drunk squirrel."

I glance up at the sky where storm clouds begin to swirl, condensing into a thick, gray mass, billowing with energy.

With one last look at Nemesis, I think, *You're on your own girl,* and then I remember that Endo is in there somewhere, helping direct the monster's actions. Perhaps sensing my departure, Nemesis charges, tackling Lovecraft into the building I'm standing on. Then I'm off the side, flying away from the now teetering skyscraper and flying down to street level, where I see something hideous attacking my wife.

42

Manhandled. That was the word the Voice of Endo used to describe Nemesis's current encounter with the larger Gestorumque. It had a size advantage, a far longer reach and wings that also worked like shields. Using those advantages, the creature kept Nemesis at a distance, patiently counter-attacking. The calm counter to her rapid attacks enraged Nemesis, whipping her into a frenzy that carried over into her thoughts.

Katsu Endo fought the chaos as best he could, trying to impose his will on the mind of a force of nature. He had faced adversaries like this monster, and he knew the only way to defeat them was with equal patience, measured strikes and careful probing of the enemy's defenses. The Gestorumque had a weakness. They just had to find it.

But Nemesis was lost in rage, unable to think, so Endo had to make his observations as best he could while Nemesis fought like a beast. At the very least, he'd convinced her to not attack using her explosive membranes. They already knew the creature could survive the blast, if not neutralize it entirely. And if it didn't, there were people in the city that they cared about, including one he had not expected to sense: his sister, Maggie Alessi.

What is she doing here? he wondered, and as he focused on her, he sensed something odd. She felt like the woman he had met a few years ago and quickly become close with, but this was the first time he'd been this close to her as Nemesis's Voice. There was something strange about her. Her personality... The number of voices emanating from her... There was more than one. And not all of them were human.

During this brief distraction, the tentacle-faced Kaiju swung out with a backhand, catching the side of Nemesis's head. She sprawled to the side, and caught herself on a building, which began to crumble. She turned back toward the Gestorumque, and while Endo couldn't see her from the outside, he felt the Kaiju have her very own *Enter the Dragon* moment. Nemesis slowly extended her tongue, licking the side of her face, where a small wound was bleeding red. The color separated her from her purple-blooded Gestorumque brethren. Part of Maigo's DNA had been left behind. Her gaze returned to her adversary, and then all control was lost.

Nemesis charged with such passion and speed that the Gestorumque had no time to defend against it. They toppled back together. Nemesis clawed, jabbed and bit, as did her enemy. Pain wracked her body, but mania masked it.

Endo sensed Hudson nearby, watching the chaotic brawl, no doubt wondering where Endo's influence of the Kaiju had gone. Knowing Hudson was there, no doubt judging Endo's performance and finding it lacking, gave Endo the desire to double his efforts and become an equal partner once more.

As buildings crumbled and monsters pummeled each other, Endo let himself feel the world around them. He felt a large number of foreign voices, some of which reminded him of his sister's. He felt Collins and Woodstock, and then the voice he was searching for, Maigo.

He reached out, using Nemesis's connection to the girl. *Are you there? Can you hear me?* The word 'hear' didn't really apply, since he was trying to connect directly to her mind, but it felt the most natural way to approach the situation.

Maigo! Are you—

Nemesis? The girl's reply sounded weak and confused, and she was obviously hearing his voice projected through Nemesis, which would have been confusing, since the Kaiju primarily communicated via emotion, rather than dialogue.

Katsu, he said. *The battle is not going well.*

I know, came the reply. *Hyperion...is damaged. I cannot move.*

This was unwelcome news, but perhaps there was still a way to keep her in the fight. *Do you have any functionality left?*

Power is online, she said. *Weapons systems charging. But until our legs are repaired, I'm stuck here, half buried.* Then she made an observation. *What's wrong with the sky?*

Endo slipped back into Nemesis's conscious mind and glanced up. Storm clouds were forming overhead, swirling to life with unnatural quickness. A flash of stabbing pain gripped him, as the tentacled

Gestorumque got its short limbs up under Nemesis's core, dug in and heaved. Nemesis flew backward, tumbling without a hint of the grace normally provided by Endo's experience.

Nemesis swiped her massive claws through a building and sent it toppling towards the Gestorumque, but its raised wings blocked the impact. With a quick thrust of its long arms and wings, the creature bounded back to its feet. It took up a defensive posture and surveyed the battlefield, looking toward Karkinos's still form and then the writhing Giger on the far side of the city, caught in the grip of some kind of attack, while yellow beams of light from a nearby rooftop pummeled the Kaiju. The Gestorumque then turned skyward, observing the clouds. This last gesture ended with, what looked to Endo like a smug smile. In the mind of this Kaiju, or at least its Voice, the battle had already been won. *But why? Because of some storm clouds?*

Maigo's faint voice tickled his mind. *Are you there?*

As Nemesis lunged again, Endo retreated back into the connection with Maigo. *I'm here.*

I'm going to trust you with something, she said, *but I need to know you will not use it against me, or Hyperion.*

We are not your enemy, Endo said. *Nemesis would never harm you.*

And with that, Endo felt a dump of raw information fill his thoughts. He knew everything about Hyperion, its functions and its weapons.

What do we do? Maigo asked.

I have an idea, Endo said, and he projected it to her.

I—I think that could work, she said, and she set about getting it done on her end.

Knowing he had several steps to achieve before the plan could work, Endo left the conversation and slammed back into Nemesis's mind. He wrestled with her powerful emotions, while she wrestled with their enemy. But while all of Nemesis's frenzied strikes and tail slashes were deflected by the broad wings and countered with painful effect, Endo broke through the creature's defenses and showed her what to do.

For a moment, he wasn't sure he'd reach her, but while she was a being of primal emotion, Nemesis was far from stupid. She understood the attack, and her physiology began to change as a result. A layer of mucus began to seep between the smooth flesh of her sheltered white skin, and the thick armor of her black outer flesh. It grew thicker, weakening her defenses, while freeing her to execute her highest purpose: divine retribution.

Then the first swath of flesh was knocked away by her opponent, revealing gleaming white skin that matched the large Kaiju's. The molting had begun.

43

My rushed and panicked landing would be embarrassing if anyone was actually watching me. I stumble for a few steps, trip over my own foot and fall flat on my masked face. But the bumbling move worthy of Clark Kent also keeps me from getting hammered by a flung Ferox. The alien soars over my head, broken and bloodied, its midsection open and trailing a rainbow of entrails. I don't need to ask what could have done that to one of the powerful and savage Ferox. I've already seen it. And it's bearing down on Collins.

The thirty-foot-tall Aeros, which from what I understand is fairly short for their race, reaches down for her, its two broad fingers nearly at her waist.

"Get out of there, Ashley!" I shout. But she doesn't leap away. Instead, she ducks. A black blur descends behind the creature, slamming into the back of its feet first. The big alien topples forward, its head and torso crashing into the second floor of a brick building. Collins dives out between its legs, and rolls to her feet. The maneuver was planned. While I seem to have lost my comms, they're still communicating.

When Collins turns to me and starts making hand gestures, I can see that she's talking, but can't hear her. I point to the side of my helmet, shake my head and shrug.

She yanks off her helmet and shouts, "The Ferox charged right in, all savage and no plan."

No doubt they saw the lone pilot as an easy target. Seven on one, even thirty-feet-tall, should have been easy. But they clearly underestimated the Aeros, who has been alive for thousands of years, and who's accustomed to battle and reigning in a Gestorumque.

I pull off my mask, and I'm struck by how much smoke is in the air. The mask's vision system has been compensating for the fading light, as smoke and clouds cover up the sun. And it's been removing the smog from my vision. "Is Cole dead?"

"Last I saw, he'd been tossed over there." She points to a three story building with a restaurant on the first floor and apartments above. There's a hole in the third floor wall. "Two of his team went after him. The rest are dead."

Lilly lands between us and pulls her mask off. "What's the plan?"

"We can't let this thing leave," Collins shouts, as the Aeros pulls itself free and stands up.

"We can't let it live," Lilly says.

While I don't disagree, I'm having a hard time seeing how we're going to kill it at all.

Lilly sees my apprehension, raises her hands and extends her claws. Then she pats the suit she's wearing. "They made us better than we were, Jon." When she smiles, I know she's quoting again. "Better, stronger, faster."

"For the record, these suits cost less than six million dollars," I say. I twist and face down the Aeros as it turns to look at us. It's built like Lovecraft, but without the wings, longer legs that end in tree trunk-like feet, and far fewer tentacles. In fact, the wriggling tendrils from its mouth look more like starfish limbs. Closer to a spiny Zoidberg.

"So here's what I'm thinking," Lilly says. "You two keep it busy, I'll get up on its ugly head and break its neck. And before you doubt I can do it, remember, these suits made me stronger, too. I can get it done."

"It's not a question of whether you're capable," I say. "It's that I'm not sure you—"

"Remember where I grew up?" she asks. "I've taken lives before. I won't lose any sleep killing this asshat, will you?"

She's got me there. "No."

"Then, FC-P Action Team go!" She gives a wink, moves in slow motion while making a "Dun-nuh-nuh-nuh-nuh," sound effect, and then leaps away, rising into the sky and disappearing over the roof of a nearby building.

"She's having too much fun with this," Collins says.

"What? You're not?"

The Aeros leans toward us and roars, its tendrils warbling over its open mouth. Then it's stomping toward us.

"Scary," I say, holding my ground.

"I've seen worse," Collins says. "Also, put your mask back on.

Just after we both pull on our masks, the Aeros attacks, swinging both hands down like a sledgehammer. The strike shakes the ground and shatters pavement with enough force to make me question how much Aeros punishment the combat suits can absorb. *Time to find out,* I think, as I roll to my feet, spinning around and diving for the Aeros's leg.

The limb is solid and takes the impact of my body with just the slightest flinch, but then I start punching. I see the flesh bend under each blow. By the time I've landed my third punch, the first has left a growing purple welt. Then I feel pressure wrap around my body. The pressure goes from tightening to steady when the suit's fibers start resisting, but I'm still having a hard time breathing. I'm lifted up, at the mercy of the Aeros who appears ready to consume the top half of my body.

But then Collins strikes, throwing herself at the creature's exposed midsection and boosting with her repulse discs. She hits like a cannonball, and as the Aeros pitches forward and stumbles back, I get the bright idea to trigger my own repulse discs. I'm launched forward, but still held by the Aeros. The big fist spins on the elbow and smacks into the creature's jaw. I feel the impact on my head, but the suit goes rigid and keeps my neck from snapping. The blow keeps the alien off-balance, so I do it again, forcing the Aeros to repeatedly punch its own face.

"Stop hitting yourself," I say, and I give it another boost, slapping against its face again. "Stop hitting yourself." Then I realize my comms still aren't working, and my perfectly timed gag is lost. *I can tell the story later,* I decide, and I trigger the repulse discs again. This time, the alien lets go. I catapult into the side of the building.

When I recover and crawl back to the fresh hole in the wall, I look down in time to see Collins launch an attack. But with the creature's attention focused solely on her, it easily backhands her away. She tumbles across the pavement and stops against a fire hydrant. I cringe at the way her back strikes the hydrant. Without the suit, she'd be dead for sure. With it...I'm not sure.

Like an angry shot, I leap out of the window, intent on pummeling the thing's face in, but this must be how the Ferox attacked. The Aeros swats me down like Serena Williams against a tennis ball. I hit the ground hard and roll to a stop at the giant's feet. I get a good look at the Aeros's sole, as one of the feet rises up, about to squash my head.

Then Lilly arrives, dropping down from above with enough force to stumble the Aeros down and forward. I roll out from under the foot, as it makes a crater in the pavement. Then I get to my feet. Lilly has one hand buried in the alien's back, riding it like she's at a rodeo, and she's slapping its head. *What is she doing?* I thought she was going to break its neck, but it looks like she's trying to go Gallagher on its melon. She hasn't anticipated its long reach though, and it has no trouble reaching up over its head, grasping hold of her and pitching her across the street. She crashes through a building, and at the speed she's going, I'm pretty sure she's gone through the far side as well.

A savage roar announces a new attack, but not from the Aeros. Three Ferox leap through the building behind the Aeros and attack in unison. Each lands a few fast swipes with their claws, but one is swatted away, another is caught in its massive hand and crushed and the third, after being shaken free, is stepped on. The Ferox might have savagery on their side, but they need to dial it back. *It's no wonder they need our help,* I think. The evolution of their species over the millennia has been closer to a devolution.

The Aeros charges toward the fallen Ferox and Collins, both of whom are slowly recovering, but nowhere fast enough. And as fast as

I now am, there's no way I'm going to reach them in time. But I don't have to. Chased by a streak of dust, Lilly flies—literally—through the building she'd been thrown into and crashes into the Aeros, lifting it off the ground and slamming it into the building on the far side of the street.

I join her in the middle of the street, as the Aeros leans back up. I lift my mask.

"You want to try that again?" I ask.

She lifts her mask, smiling, yellow eyes burning with excitement. "Why bother?"

The Aeros climbs out of the rubble and stands. I motion to it with both hands.

She mirrors my gesture, but adds a dramatic openmouthed smile. As though in response to her action, a sizzling sound fills the air. It's followed by a high pitched wail from the Aeros. It arches its back and grips its head for a moment. But then the hands snap away, and I see the thick fingers dissolving to mush and falling away. The alien collapses back into a sitting position. Its head lolls to the side and then folds inward. Liquefied brains ooze out of its eyes, and then its mouth. Then the whole head implodes on itself. We're seeing the devastating effects of a bacteria bomb designed to take out a Kaiju, never mind something a fraction of the size.

As the body sizzles and is consumed, Lilly smiles and says, "Plop, plop, fizz, fizz, oh what a relief it is."

And with that, the sky opens up and drops down softball sized balls of ice.

"Get Woodstock down here!" I shout to Lilly. When the girl pulls her mask back down, I run for Collins. She's groaning and sitting up when I reach her. "You okay?"

"Well, I can wiggle my fingers and toes," she says, "but everything hurts."

When a ball of ice whacks my shoulder, I say, "We're getting out of here," and I lift her up.

"Is it dead?" she asks, but then she sees the still dissolving body behind me. "Gross."

"He's on his way!" Lilly shouts from under her lifted mask, and then she runs to help up the lone Ferox.

I pull down my mask in time to save myself from being knocked unconscious. I hear Future Betty's approach as ice balls strike her hull and bounce off. Then her cargo bay door opens, revealing the craft as it settles down thirty feet away.

I get two steps toward the aircraft, when I hear Nemesis roar in pain. It sends chills through my body, but there isn't time to reflect. The Kaiju topples toward us, crushing buildings with her body, which I quickly note is cracked and bleeding, showing several patches of her more fragile white skin.

We dive inside the X-35, and I rip off my mask. "Go! Go! Go!"

The X-35 accelerates so fast that we nearly tumble out the back, but the hatch closes fast enough to catch us. I look back through the hatch, which shows a projection of what's happening behind us, and watch Nemesis crash to the ground. She's definitely hurting.

But she's not done yet.

Quick to her feet, Nemesis sides steps toward the Luminox, putting herself between the Gestorumque and the building. Hyperion isn't too far away, but the big robot is still unmoving, trapped beneath half a building.

I climb into the cockpit with Woodstock. Hail beats a chaotic rhythm over the hull. "Are we in any danger from this hail?"

He shakes his head. "Future Betty is tougher than my meemaw on Bingo night." He grins at my quizzical look. "The woman took two things in life seriously, bingo and drinking whisky. Usually at the same time. They used to let her win, just to keep people out of the hospital."

Beyond Hyperion, the writhing Giger, still fighting the effects of the bacteria bombs, rises up to its feet, shrieks at the sky and flexes its body. The creature's bony exoskeleton cracks and then falls away in big chunks, revealing a new form, which is similar to the first, but far less intimidating. Its armor has been replaced by shriveled up flesh, and the three remaining arms now resemble something closer to T-Rex limbs, small and useless. But it's still large, and no doubt powerful, and it has a mouth full of sharp teeth.

And then there is Lovecraft, storming in toward Nemesis.

The white Gestorumque shimmers with excited flashes of blue and green light. It senses the kill, and victory, and it shifts from a defensive tactic to an offensive one, charging in and swinging its long arms. Both blows strike, peeling away Nemesis's black flesh.

I know what Nemesis can do. I understand the power of her wings, and how they can bend sunlight into a powerful beam of energy hot enough to cleave Lovecraft in two, but there is no sun. Not only is this freaking Portland, land of sunny people and cloudy skies, but the hail storm and smoke rising from the city have reduced the ambient light to something closer to night.

"What are you doing?" I wonder aloud, and then I reel back as Lovecraft lunges in and bites Nemesis's face. Tentacles wrap around her, holding on tight. Rows of teeth arranged in a circle dig into Nemesis's face. And for a moment, I think the goddess of vengeance is done for. But then she pulls back her head and shoves with her arms.

Lovecraft stumbles back with a mouth full of Nemesis flesh. In fact, the Gestorumque peels off the entire front half of Nemesis's black skin and armor, allowing the back half to fall down, revealing her stark white form. The carapace on her back cracks open and spreads, as two glittering wings rise up.

With an unholy shriek, Giger charges, moving with the same skittering speed as before.

Nemesis steps back and her wings burst open, angling around to face the charging Kaiju.

But there's no sun! I think.

And then I notice Hyperion.

The robot's eyes are red.

The three circles on its chest blink to life in rapid succession.

With the speed of a snapping finger, six laser cannons pop out of its forearms, two rise from its shoulders and a ninth cannon, that dwarfs all the others in size, rises up out of the back and snaps into place over its head. All nine cannons are aimed at Nemesis.

Bright yellow beams fire from the cannons, each striking Nemesis's wings where they are reflected and redirected to a point at the center of

Giger's head. The focused beam of energy punches through the Gestorumque's head, exits the far side and then carves a line through the city beyond.

As Hyperion continues the long laser pulse, Nemesis turns her body toward Lovecraft. The Divine Retribution supplied by Hyperion and aimed by Nemesis cleaves through Giger's body on its way to Lovecraft. Steam and heat-flung bits burst out from the wound, but most of it is cauterized on contact. The Gestorumque drops to the side, legs rigid, and very, very dead.

Caught in the beam's path, Lovecraft has nowhere to go. Quick bursts of blue and green roll through the Gestorumque's skin. Then, in a move that makes everyone on board the X-35 groan in disgust, save for the Ferox, Lovecraft's mass explodes from her backside, dumping countless tons of purple and white meat, blood and who knows what else, into the city. It flows through the streets with the force of a mudslide, toppling cars and surging into storefronts. With a beat of its wings, the still vacating Kaiju launches into the air.

Nemesis spins faster to compensate. The reflective plates that make up her wings shift and start to fall away, their deadly potential all but spent. The angle is ruined and the lasers reflect as separate beams. Some strike the fleeing Kaiju, doing minimal damage. Some miss. One of the beams strikes Nemesis herself, knocking her back and putting a hole in her softer, white flesh.

Wounded and oozing, Lovecraft rises up over Nemesis. But will it attack? Nemesis glares back at the creature, both of them winged, both of them a little more frail. It would be a fight to the death, for one of them, if not both of them. And then with a strong beat of its wings, Lovecraft moves away, dodging back as the world's largest ball of ice falls from the sky, just missing the airborne, Kaiju. But it's not going to hit Nemesis either.

"No!" shouts Cole, once again in human form. "The Luminox!"

The hail ball strikes the arch in the center, folding it inward and tearing all the way through. The men on top are thrown away. The two separated halves lean inward and collapse.

With a victorious roar, Lovecraft soars higher into the air and then beats a hasty retreat west, chased by a small, black orb, no doubt heading for the deep waters where the Kaiju can rest.

Nemesis roars defiantly after Lovecraft, claiming the battle as a victory.

The rest of us know better, and Cole sums up our loss in one succinct statement. "The human race is on its own."

EPILOGUE

I'm back where it all began, like all good horror stories, at a cabin in the woods. The Watson family cabin is exactly how I remember it. The mess of beer cans and dirt I created were cleaned up years ago, but the slight musty smell mixed with pine needles brings me back to that pivotal morning: to the bear, to shooting Truck Betty and to Collins. Without that chance encounter, everything the FC-P has become would have been different. I wouldn't have actually looked into the Bigfoot sighting that drew me here. Wouldn't have stumbled across the secret lab where Nemesis and Maigo were created. Wouldn't have learned how to stop the monster in Boston. And I would have died scores of times. Collins's presence in my life has radically altered my fate.

But is it real?

Learning that a good portion of my team's lives, including the good, bad and the fugly, has been manipulated by the Ferox with the purpose of turning us into Earth's best hope, has really screwed with my head. I feel like Neo in *The Matrix*, waking up to discover that the world is not what I believed it to be. Except I don't have the option to retreat back into the program and live out a long, happy life. I never really saw the downside of living out a long life inside the Matrix. Most people on the planet will probably choose to live in a virtual world soon enough. But there's no retreating from our reality. Monsters are real, and they want to kill, torture and enslave us.

I actually miss the days when all we had to fear was being judged by an ancient goddess of vengeance.

The rest of the team is nearby, behind the tall fence and security measures, recuperating from the Battle for Portland, or more accurately, the battle for the Luminox, which we lost. Hyperion is taking a nap inside a massive hanger built at the small Beverly Airport, but I have a Zoomb team—some of whom are undoubtedly Ferox—working on a better place to keep the robot. It suffered grave damage in Portland, but it's busy repairing itself. Thanks to its connection to Maigo, and its full charge, Hyperion can be here the moment we need him.

Lovecraft was tracked back to the mid-Pacific. The Air Force hit the beast with everything they had, because why not? But it took the punishment and eventually dove down deep, lost in the vast depths and headed who-knows-where. But I suspect that the monster will remain out of sight until its brethren arrive from the stars.

Nemesis did her usual disappearing act, leaving a trail of reflective panels in her wake and charging back to the coast under military supervision. She made no effort to avoid obstacles in her path, but left us knowing that she was on the side of humanity. When she first arrived, I couldn't stop the military from taking pot shots at her, but after defeating the Tsuchis, and an obvious effort to defend Portland, no one even asked. Without a doubt, she is a force of vast destruction, and dangerous. She might turn on us some day, but for now, she is *our* force of vast destruction.

And we're going to need her.

With the destruction of the Luminox, the huge fleet of Ferox and other alien species in their vastly manipulated network, will have to travel to Earth the old-fashioned way—meaning they will most likely arrive far too late to do any good.

Cole, who disappeared shortly after the battle, and who I was happy to see go, told us that there were two hundred thousand Ferox on Earth, living among us, working with us and preparing for the coming war. They would stand with humanity, and work to form a coalition of nations, but he also believes they will die with humanity. He's not exactly a motivational speaker, but I don't believe a word he says. All of his claims might be carefully constructed words designed to forge a sharper blade. Or whatever.

So now I give everyone I meet and work with a good long look to see if I can tell the difference. Two days after the Battle for Portland, back at the Crow's Nest, everyone agreed to prick their fingers. I was relieved to see red blood from everyone. I considered performing the same test at Zoomb, but then decided it would get too much attention. The last thing we need is for the general public to find out that some of them are nasty looking aliens here to protect us from an invasion, which is probably going to wipe us out. The kind of panic *that* would cause could do the Aeros's work for them.

"Refill?" Collins asks, pushing open the cabin's creaky screen door. She's holding a pitcher of homemade hard iced tea.

"Are you trying to get me drunk so you can take advantage of me?" I hold up my glass and shake it around.

She refills the glass and says, "Pretty sure I've already done that. Like three times."

"Well, you are hard to satisfy."

She pours herself a glass and sits down in the rocking chair beside mine. The view isn't spectacular. It's just woods, a carpet of pine needles and a dirt road. But this is Maine, and when you want to relax, sitting on the front stoop and watching the cars go by—or not go by in our case—seems to be the state-sponsored activity in these parts.

"Did you talk to Maigo?" she asks.

"She's okay," I say. "And I hate to say it like this, but I think she's come to terms with what she is."

"A monster," Collins says. "You know I don't agree with that."

"Neither do I, but I think it's empowering her to not hold back."

"You think she was holding back before?" Collins's surprise is justified. We've seen her perform some pretty amazing feats of strength, speed and occasional violence.

"I think every time she let her true self out a little, she feared she might change—"

"Into Nemesis," Collins says.

"—and so she pulled back from what she's really capable of." I down half of the tea and feel it hit me. "Holy crap. A little heavy on the Vodka."

She shrugs. "It's our day off."

"Pretty sure we don't get days off," I say, and I put the glass down on the small antique side table that's starting to rot from exposure. "Wouldn't do anyone any good if we were five shades to the cosmic wind when aliens invade."

That sobers her up fast, and she puts her glass of tea down. "Thank you, Mr. Buzzkill."

"Hey, I'm just—"

She puts her hand on mine and smiles. "I'm kidding. It makes sense. But we also have to keep in mind that we don't really know when they're coming. It could be tomorrow. It could be in five years."

"Either way, we need to do everything we can to prepare." I give my wife a wink and reach for my tea. "Starting tomorrow."

My hand returns to the spot I had placed the glass of tea, but I find only empty space. I turn slowly toward the end table, believing the Vodka is already messing with my muscle memory. But the glass is no longer on the table. It's in the hand of a man I didn't hear approach, let alone sit down in the chair beside me and snatch up my glass.

The man is dressed like a cowboy, from the Stetson on his head to the boots on his feet—and the wicked looking revolvers strapped to his belt. He tilts his head back, pounding down my tea.

I hear Collins shifting beside me, no doubt reaching for her weapon. But if I've learned anything, it's that weird shit happens for a reason. If this man wanted us dead, he could have killed us. Instead, he looks content with my tea. I hold a calming hand out to Collins and turn toward the stranger.

"Enjoying my drink?" I ask.

"Is good," he says, the accent not quite Russian, but definitely Eastern European. Czech maybe. Is he here because of what happened on Big Dio-mede? Some Russian Special Ops guy? He could also be a Ferox.

He sets the empty glass on the table and smiles at me.

"Planet is in danger," he says, and I see no reason not to nod. He clearly knows things. He's here, with us, for a reason. "But not just here."

He waits for a moment, but I give him nothing.

"There are other Earths. Other...*dimensions*."

"Why not?" I say.

"I have seen what you face."

What *you* face. The way he says this implies he's not one of us. *Us* as in human. "Are you one of *them?*"

"An alien?" He chuckles. "That would be fun, no? Except that they are ugly."

"Very," I agree. "How do you know all this?"

He puts his hands on his knees and stands. "Come for walk?"

I look at Collins. She shrugs. We get up together and follow the man around to the back of the cabin. A hundred feet into the woods, I spot an aberration. It's a smooth metal surface that doesn't belong out here.

We enter a small clearing and I stagger to a stop. Collins bumps into my back and then gasps. We both know what this is. We've both seen it, recently, housed in the chest of a giant robot.

"Die Gloke," I say.

The man gives a tip of his hat.

"Did you take this from—"

"Is from *my* Earth. Is the second I have found. Was taking to a secure location when I noticed your..."

"Shit storm?" I suggest.

"Situation," he says. "The monsters. The invaders."

"Do you know when they're coming?" I ask.

The lighthearted nature I sense from the man melts away. "They are already here, destroying an Earth parallel to this one. In that place, you are already dead. And without help, this world will be next. And then mine. And countless others, until humanity is wiped out, in *all* dimensions."

"Who *are* you?" I ask.

He stands by the big metal bell-shaped object that we know as a Rift Engine. It's covered in what I assume is Atlantean script. Its dirty bronze surface looks ancient, but still full of horrible potential. He pats his revolvers and smiles. "Am gunslinger," he says. "I am Cowboy."

He puts his hand on the Rift Engine and motions for us to do the same. "Bell is alien power source. But can be used for travel. In air, or between dimensions."

It's not much of a stretch from what we've already seen Hyperion do. But do I buy his story about there being multiple versions of Earth, including one that has already been destroyed? I'm not sure. My tolerance for weird shit is at an all time high.

"Physical contact with bell is required. I can direct us." He gives a winning smile. "Is safe."

When I step forward, Collins catches my arm. "What are you doing?"

"'Is safe,'" I say, imitating the man's accent. "And if the Cosmic Cowboy here is legit, I need to follow this through. Take the risk. It's what we do, right?"

She kisses me gently on the lips, and that, more than her words, makes me second guess what I'm about to do. I look at the man.

"If he gets hurt," Collins says to the man, "I'll hunt you down, no matter what dimension you think you can hide in."

The man just smiles like it's all good fun. "Back in jiffy."

I put my hand on the smooth surface of the Rift Engine. It's cool and vibrating ever so slightly. And then we're gone, lost between worlds, and somehow able to see them all. It's like viewing reality—all of it, or all of them—through the eyes of an all-seeing creator. We're floating through imagination itself, conjured worlds separated by thin membranes of reality. Like pages in a book, separate, but conjoined. Realities flash past, heroes and monsters, familiar and fantastical, and then I see them.

The Aeros.

And an Earth that's already been destroyed.

"Is the first of many," Cowboy says, his voice echoing strangely in this surreal place. Somehow he shows me dimensions in proximity to each other, and I see Collins, looking afraid, backing away from the spot where the bell had been resting just a moment ago. The Aeros are just a world away, wiping out a version of our planet woefully unprepared for their scourge. I see massive space vessels, Gestorumque, the Aeros themselves and a weapon of vast destructive power.

"Your Earth is next," Cowboy says.

I watch the dimensions slipping in and out of view, watching people and events, some of which rival the threats faced by the FC-P. I see potential.

"Screw the Ferox," I tell him. "We have work to do, and not a lot of time to do it in."

I pick a world where a man stands boldly against a horde of monsters, point to it, and say, "In the immortal words of Jean Luc Picard: 'Engage.'"

A NOTE FROM THE AUTHOR

Dear Reader,

Four years ago, when I started working on Nemesis and the FC-P, my lofty goal was to create America's first real iconic kaiju. Sure, we have *King Kong,* but he's just a big ape and a snack for *Godzilla,* who Americans have adopted as their own. But the big green G will always be, at heart, Japan's kaiju. And now we have the kaiju in *Pacific Rim,* but they're hardly the main focus of the movie. There is *Cloverfield,* but can anyone even remember what that monster looks like?

Since her birth, Nemesis has steadily grown, both in the books and in the real world. She started as the bestselling original (not Godzilla) kaiju novel ever. After the second novel, *Project Maigo,* came along, she landed a video game deal—*Fall of Nemesis: Colossal Kaiju Combat.* The third novel, *Project 731,* expanded the audience again and shortly after that, the series was granted its own comic book series, adapting *Project Nemesis,* with issue one being released just weeks after the book in your hands. Now, with the fourth Nemesis novel, *Project Hyperion,* published, I'm looking forward to her next growth spurt. The fifth book in the series, *Project Legion,* will be released in 2016 and will make the Nemesis Saga the longest running kaiju novel series ever published, beating out the 1990s Godzilla run. I don't know if Nemesis qualifies as a franchise yet, but she is on the cusp for sure. And for that, I have YOU to thank.

Your support over the years, spreading the word, creating fan art and being passionate about the books affects the Nemesis brand in the same way people do when Nemesis eats them! With each review, blog post, video, podcast mention, etc, Nemesis grows, and who doesn't want the Goddess of Vengeance to grow?! So show your support for the Queen of the Monsters, and post reviews, at online retailers (like Amazon, Barnes & Noble and Kobo) and on Goodreads. Tell your friends about the book. Post fan art. Spread the word however you can, and maybe the next deal for Nemesis will be a TV series or movie!

Thanks again for all of your amazing support, and for reading this fourth installment in the Nemesis Saga.

—Jeremy Robinson

ART GALLERIES

The following art galleries include original creature concept designs by the amazing Matt Frank, along with step-by-step art revealing how the *Project Hyperion* cover was created by the artist known as "Shark." As always, there are several pages of amazing fan art. And if all of that wasn't enough, there are also several preview pages from issue #1 of the *Project Nemesis* comic book, also drawn by Matt Frank.

MATT FRANK CREATURE DESIGNS

This first gallery includes the original creature concept designs for Nemesis and the new Kaiju: Lovecraft and Giger, as well as the series' first giant mech: Hyperion. The designs are by the always amazing Matt Frank, who has provided art for all four Nemesis books, and is now illustrating the *Project Nemesis* comic book. You might also recognize his work from many Godzilla comic books.

Check him out at: www.mattfrankart.com.

NEMESIS

LOVECRAFT

HYPERION

GIGER

STEP BY STEP COVER CREATION BY "SHARK"

Six months ago I received a package, from Sci-Fi World, the largest Chinese publisher of Science Fiction. The package wasn't the right size or shape for a book, so I wasn't sure what they'd sent me. When I tore it open, I had no idea what to expect, but never in my wildest dreams could I have guessed that it was the Chinese edition of *Project Nemesis*, formatted like a magazine and featuring one of the most mind-blowing illustrations of Nemesis I have ever seen. I tracked down the artist, who goes by "Shark," to thank him for his work. We struck up a conversation, and when I realized that he was a true fan of the series as well, I asked him about doing the cover for *Project Hyperion*. The result of that conversation now graces the cover of this book! To check out more of Shark's amazing work, visit him at: sharksden.deviantart.com.

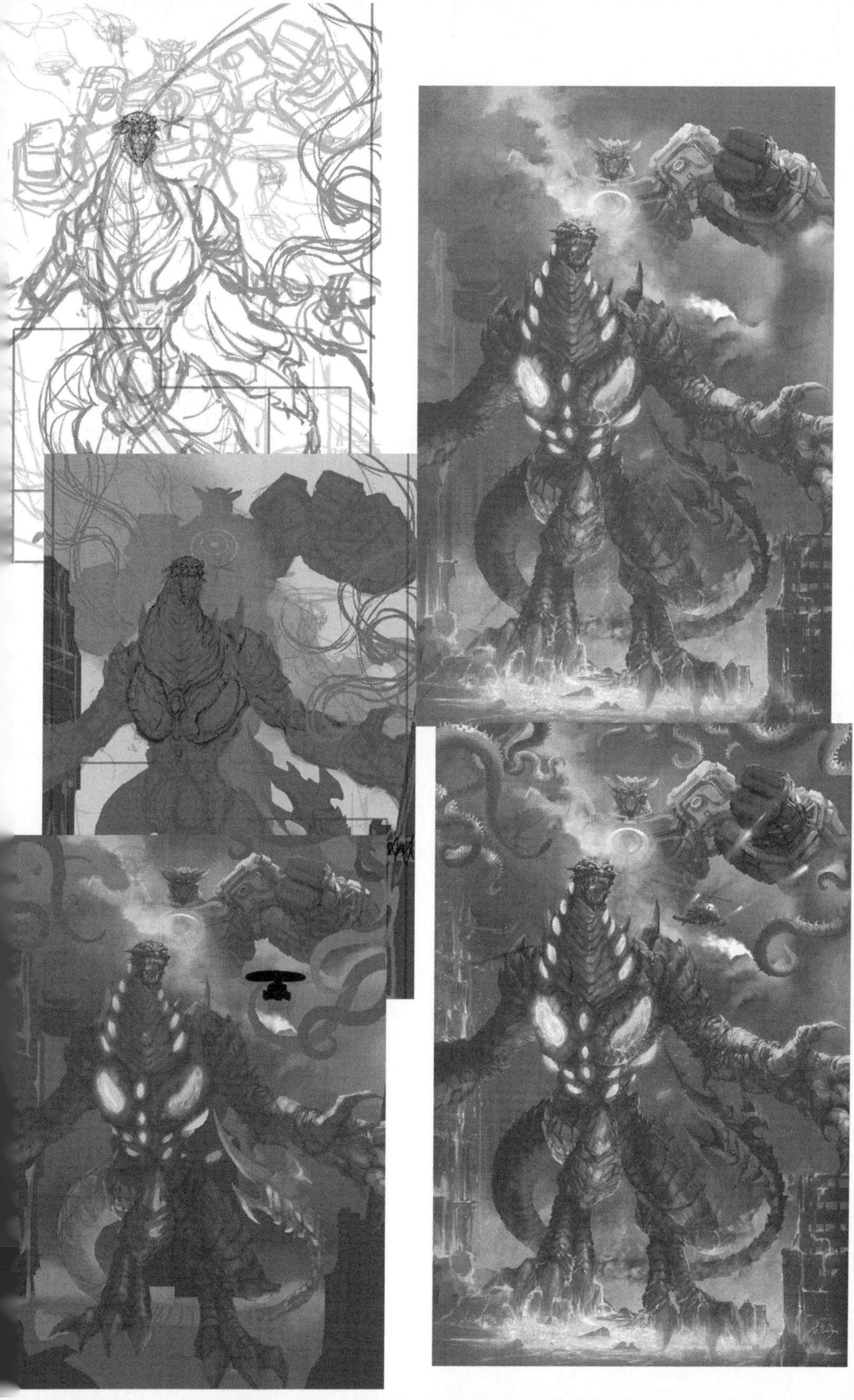

FAN ART GALLERY

Soon after the release of *Project Nemesis,* I started receiving fan art inspired by the book. After the release of *Project Maigo,* which included the first fan art gallery in any of my books, I wasn't sure if the trend would continue, but over the past few years I've been continually surprised by the amount of Nemesis art being produced, and by the quality. But more than anything else, I'm humbled by the passion people display for this monstrous creation. Nemesis might be a 350-foot-tall goddess of vengeance, but she wouldn't be anything without you all.

If you would like your fan art to be featured in any future Nemesis books, send it to info@jeremyrobinsononline.com at a 300dpi image quality. The only real rule is that the images have to feature Nemesis (or any of the characters and new Kaiju from *Project Maigo, Project 731* and *Project Hyperion*) and they cannot feature any trademarked or copyrighted Kaiju, such as Godzilla, Gamera, etc... Thank you very much to all the amazing artists who submitted their work for publication in *Project Hyperion,* and I look forward to seeing more!

—Jeremy Robinson

NEMESIS X SLUGERA
BY RANDY SHILLING

GUIRON.DEVIANTART.COM - WWW.FACEBOOK.COM-SLUGERA

NEMESIS VS BUBBLES
BY IAN HERRMANN AND CHRISTOPHER CONDE

NEMESIS VS ASURA
BY ASURA

FC-P POSTER
BY ZACH COLE
CRITTERZACH.DEVIANTART.COM

TO HUNT A GODDESS
BY RODNEY RODGERS

LILLY AND BUDDY
BY RODNEY RODGERS

BATTLE FOR WASHINGTON D.C.
BY ZACH COLE CRITTERZACH.DEVIANTART.COM

NEMESIS AND MEGATSUCHI
BY JOHN SCOTT

NEMESIS
BY GABE PAQUETTE

PROJECT 731
BY JAIME GLINOGA
KAIJUKING25.DEVIANTART.COM

THE END OF NEMESIS PRIME
BY ZACH COLE
CRITTERZACH.DEVIANTART.COM

NEMESIS SPRITE
BY MICHAEL HAWKINS

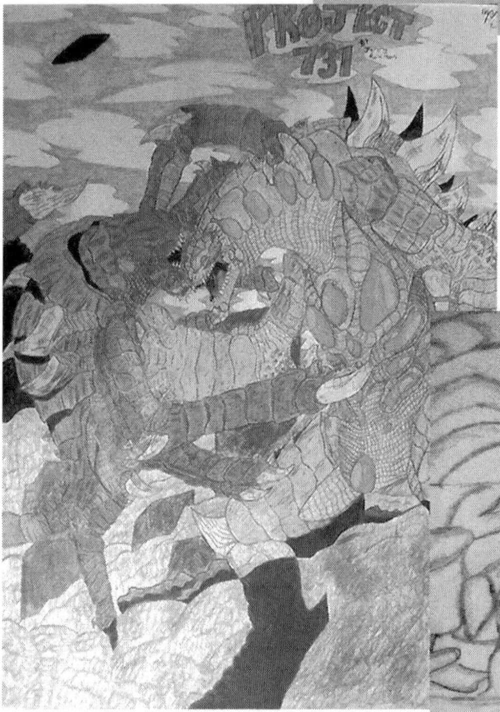

PROJECT 731 POSTER
BY ZACH COLE
CRITTERZACH.DEVIANTART.COM

RISE OF THE MEGATSUCHI
JAKE DOLAND

POOR BUBBLES
BY AARON REBAZA
AARONREBAZA.DEVIANTART.COM

NEMESIS! QUEEN OF THE MONSTERS!
BY IAN ANDRYSIAK

HYPERION
BY OSCAR ALONSO

NEMESIS VS. BUBBLES VS. BIO-SAPIEN
BY WOODZILLA

NEMESIS

BY BENNIE MARTINALI

BOCMA.DEVIANTART.COM - SPACEPOTATOPRODUCTIONS.WORDPRESS.COM

NEMESIS VS. HYPERION

The double-page spread piece of fan art on the following pages is from professional cover artist, Shark.

Visit him at: sharksden.deviantart.com.

2015.8.

HYPERION VS. GIGER

The double-page spread piece of fan art on the following pages is from professional artist, Frankie B. Washington.

Visit him at: www.frankiebwashington.com.

F8W2015

NEMESIS RAMPAGE

The double-page spread piece of fan art on the following pages is from professional artist, Tony Luke.

Visit him at: tonyluke.deviantart.com.

Tony Luke
2015

PROJECT NEMESIS ISSUE #1 PREVIEW

The following pages contain a preview of the upcoming *Project Nemesis* comic book from American Gothic Press in association with *Famous Monsters of Filmland* magazine. The facing image is the standard cover by Matt Frank. The next image is the alternate cover by Bob Eggleton. The next four images are the first four sequential art pages from the first Issue of the comic.

Interior Art by Matt Frank and written by Jeremy Robinson.

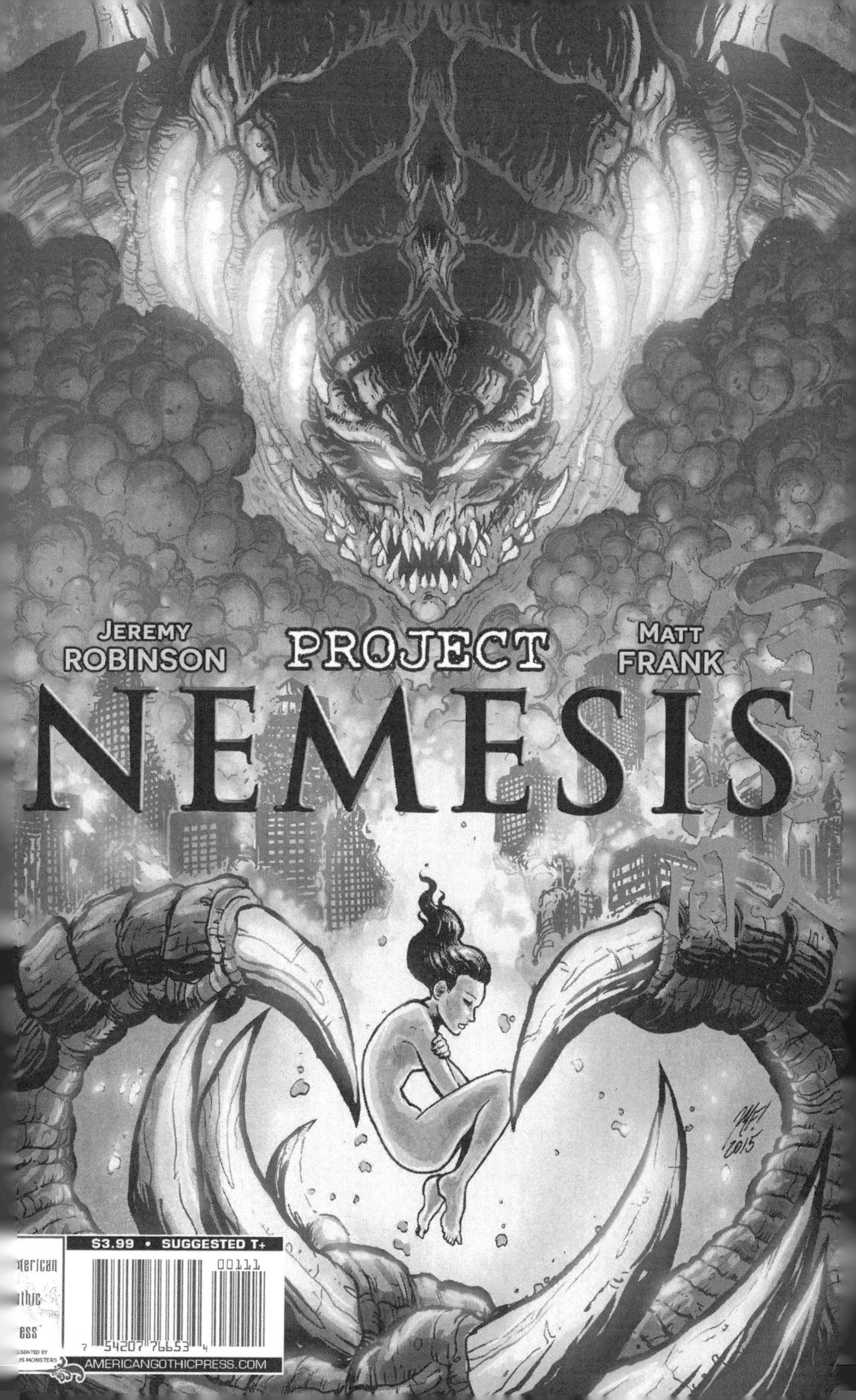
JEREMY ROBINSON
PROJECT
MATT FRANK
NEMESIS
$3.99 • SUGGESTED T+
AMERICANGOTHICPRESS.COM

JEREMY ROBINSON
PROJECT
MATT FRANK
NEMESIS
敵
$3.99 • SUGGESTED T-
American Gothic Press
PRESENTED BY FAMOUS MONSTERS
AMERICANGOTHICPRESS.CO

ONE WEEK AGO.
WINGED TILTER OF SCALES AND LIVES.
JUSTICE-BORN GODDESS WITH DISCERNING EYES.
MAIG
THOU BRIDLEST EVIL MEN WHO ROIL IN VAIN.
AGAINST THY HARSH ADAMANTINE REIN.
IMMORTAL JUDGE, I SING THY SONG NEMESIS, VENGEFUL RIGHTER OF WRONGS.

FIVE YEARS AGO.
ALASKA
MARINE CORPS COLD WEATHER TRAINING GROUNDS
GET DOWN, STAY QUIET, AND DON'T MOVE A MUSCLE, OR WE'RE STAINS.
NOT BAD, KETCHUP.
MY NAME IS CORPORAL KATSU ENDO OF THE JAPANESE DEFENSE FORCE.
OKAY CORPORAL KETCHUP. OR DUCK SAUCE?
DUCK SAUCE IS FOR CHINESE FOOD.
SNAP
RUN!
THEY'RE HERE!
HUFF! HUFF!
HERE!

CAN'T SEE SQUAT DOWN HERE.
HO LEE...
SHIT.
CORPORAL KATSU ENDO DREAMED OF A MOMENT LIKE THIS, BUT NEVER DARED TO BELIEVE IT WOULD HAPPEN.
AFTER A LIFETIME OF WATCHING MONSTERS DESTROY CITIES--OR PROTECT THEM, CHEERING AT EVERY FOOT STOMP AND TAIL SWIPE, HE KNEW EXACTLY WHAT HE WAS LOOKING AT...
KAIJU.
PROJECT NEMESIS
STAGE 1

TWENTY-FOUR HOURS LATER.
HOW MANY PEOPLE ARE IN THE KNOW ON THIS?
JUST YOU, GENERAL GORDON.
I'D LIKE TO KEEP IT THAT WAY. YOU BOTH WORK FOR ME NOW. YOU'LL NEED TO STAY HERE FOR THE NEXT FEW YEARS. EITHER OF YOU HAVE A PROBLEM WITH THAT?
UH, SIR. I'M SUPPOSED TO GO HOME IN A FEW WEEKS. SEE MY FAMILY. I HAVE TWO BOYS.
FAMILY...
HOW ABOUT YOU, ENDO? YOU HAVE FAMILY?
KETCHUP'S AN ORPHAN. HE DOESN'T HAVE--
ENDO UNDERSTOOD THE OFFER BEING MADE: END A MAN'S LIFE AND BE A PART OF SOMETHING TRULY GREAT.
MY NAME IS KATSU ENDO.
BANG
THE KIND OF CREATURES HE DREAMED ABOUT AS A CHILD EXISTED. THEY WERE THE INSTRUCTORS OF HIS CHILDHOOD MORALITY, FROM WHICH HE LEARNED THAT SOMETIMES, THE ON THING CAPABLE OF MAKING THE WORLD RIGHT WAS DESTRUCTI

ABOUT THE AUTHOR

Jeremy Robinson is the international bestselling author of fifty novels and novellas including *MirrorWorld, Uprising, Island 731, SecondWorld,* the Jack Sigler thriller series, and *Project Nemesis,* the highest selling, original (non-licensed) kaiju novel of all time. He's known for mixing elements of science, history and mythology, which has earned him the #1 spot in Science Fiction and Action-Adventure, and secured him as the top creature feature author.

Robinson is also known as the bestselling horror writer, Jeremy Bishop, author of *The Sentinel* and the controversial novel, *Torment.* In 2015, he launched yet another pseudonym, Jeremiah Knight, for two post-apocalyptic Science Fiction series of novels. Robinson's works have been translated into thirteen languages.

His series of Jack Sigler / Chess Team thrillers, starting with *Pulse,* is in development as a film series, helmed by Jabbar Raisani, who earned an Emmy Award for his design work on HBO's *Game of Thrones*. Robinson's original kaiju character, Nemesis, is also being adapted into a comic book through publisher *Famous Monsters of Filmland,* with artwork and covers by renowned Godzilla artists Matt Frank and Bob Eggleton.

Born in Beverly, MA, Robinson now lives in New Hampshire with his wife and three children.

Visit Jeremy Robinson online at www.bewareofmonsters.com.

ABOUT THE ARTIST

Matt Frank is a comic book illustrator and cover artist who has worked on well known titles such as *Transformers* and *Ray Harryhausen Presents*, but he is perhaps most well known for his contributions to multiple *Godzilla* comic books. He is also the artist of the upcoming *Project Nemesis* comic book from American Gothic Press (in association with *Famous Monsters of Filmland* magazine). He lives in Texas and enjoys pineapple juice.

Visit him online at: www.mattfrankart.com

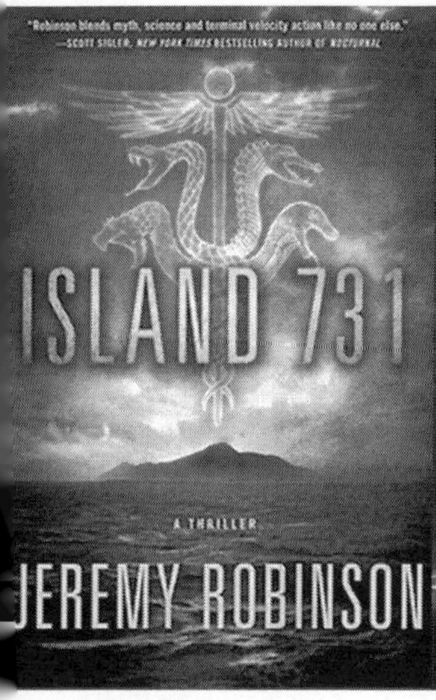

THE INTRODUCTION OF
HAWKINS, LILLY,
AND THE DEADLY TSUCHIS

THE INTRODUCTION OF
HUDSON, COLLINS,
AND THE BIRTH OF NEMESIS

THE INTRODUCTION OF
NEMESIS PRIME'S
DEADLY KAIJU BROOD

AVAILABLE NOW

HE G.O.D, ZACH COLE,
HE MEGATSUCHI, AND MAIGO

BACKGROUND ON THE
AEROS/FEROX WAR

ADVENTURE WITH
COWBOY AND DIE GLOCKE

ARE YOU A GAMER?
WANT TO DESTROY CITIES AND KAIJU...
AS NEMESIS?
THE FALL OF
NEMESIS
CLASH OF THE KAIJUJIN
RATING PENDING
RP
CONTENT RATED BY ESRB
SUNSTONE GAMES
KCS KAIJU COMBAT STUDIOS
HERE'S
YOUR
CHANCE!
THE FALL OF NEMESIS
CLASH OF THE KAIJUJIN
COMING IN 2016
COLOSSAL KAIJU COMBAT!
PRE-ORDER AT SUNSTONE.CO/STORE

17251797R00190

Printed in Great Britain
by Amazon